Words of praise for Mills & Boon® from *New York Times* and *USA TODAY* bestselling authors

"When I started writing for Mills & Boon, I was delighted by the length of the books, which allowed the freedom to create, and develop more within each character and their romance. I have always been a fan of Mills & Boon! I hope to write for it for many years to come. Long live Mills & Boon!"
—Diana Palmer

"My career began in Mills & Boon. I remember my excitement when they were introduced, because the stories were so rich and different, and every month when the books came out I beat a path to the bookstore to get every one of them. Here's to you, Mills & Boon; live long, and prosper!"
—Linda Howard

"I owe a great deal to Mills & Boon for allowing me to grow as a writer. Mills & Boon did that, not only for me but for countless other authors. It continues to offer compelling stories, with heroes and heroines readers love—and authors they've come to trust."
—Debbie Macomber

"Mills & Boon books always touch my heart. They are wonderful stories with the perfect happy ending."
—Susan Mallery

"How could I not love a series devoted to my favorite things—complex families and deep friendships? I'm so proud to have been a part of this wonderful tradition at Mills & Boon."
—Sherryl Woods

THE PRINCE'S SECRET BABY

BY
CHRISTINE RIMMER

First published in Great Britain 2012
by Mills & Boon, an imprint of Harlequin (UK) Limited,
Eton House, 18-24 Paradise Road, Richmond, Surrey TW9 1SR

© Christine Rimmer 2012

ISBN: 978 0 263 89447 9
ebook ISBN: 978 1 408 97122 2

23-0712

Harlequin (UK) policy is to use papers that are natural, renewable and recyclable products and made from wood grown in sustainable forests. The logging and manufacturing processes conform to the legal environmental regulations of the country of origin.

Printed and bound in Spain
by Blackprint CPI, Barcelona

Christine Rimmer came to her profession the long way around. Before settling down to write about the magic of romance, she'd been everything from an actress to a salesclerk to a waitress. Now that she's finally found work that suits her perfectly, she insists she never had a problem keeping a job—she was merely gaining "life experience" for her future as a novelist. Christine is grateful not only for the joy she finds in writing, but for what waits when the day's work is through: a man she loves who loves her right back and the privilege of watching their children grow and change day to day. She lives with her family in Oregon. Visit Christine at www.christinerimmer.com.

THE PRINCE'S SECRET BABY

Chapter One

"Stop here," Rule Bravo-Calabretti said to the driver.

The limousine rolled to a silent stop at the head of the row of parking spaces in the shadowed parking garage. The Mercedes-Benz sedan Rule had been following turned into the single empty space at the other end of the row, not far from the elevators and the stairs that led into the mall. From where he sat behind tinted windows, Rule could also see the breezeway outside the parking structure. It led directly into Macy's department store.

The brake lights of the Mercedes went dark. A woman emerged from the sedan, her head and shoulders appearing above the tops of the row of cars. She had thick brown hair that fell in well-behaved waves. Settling the strap of her bag on her shoulder, she shut the car door and emerged into the open aisle, where she turned back and aimed her key at the car. The Benz gave an obedient beep.

She put the key away in her bag. She looked, Rule decided, just as she'd looked in the pictures his investigators had taken of her—only more attractive, somehow. She wasn't a pretty woman. But there was something about her that he found much more interesting than mere prettiness. She was tall and slim and wore a blue silk jacket, which was perfectly and conservatively tailored. Her matching blue skirt kissed the tops of her slender knees. Her shoes were darker than her suit, with medium heels and closed toes.

He watched as she settled her bag in place again, straightened her jacket and turned for the door to the breezeway. He thought she looked very determined and somehow he found that determination utterly charming.

She hadn't glanced in the limousine's direction. He was almost certain she had no idea that he'd been following her.

And his mind was made up, just like that, in the sixty seconds it took to watch her emerge from her car, put her key in her purse and turn to go. He had to meet her.

Yes, he'd always told himself he never would. That as long as she was running her life successfully, taking good care of the child, it would be wrong of him to interfere. He'd relinquished all rights by law. And he had to live with the choices he had made.

But this wasn't about rights. This wasn't about challenging her for what was hers.

He had no intention of interfering. He simply had to... speak with her, had to know if his first reaction to seeing her in the flesh was just a fluke, a moment of starry-eyed idiocy brought on by the fact that she had what mattered most to him.

All right, it was playing with fire. And he shouldn't even be here. He should be finishing his business in Dallas and rushing back to Montedoro. He should be spending time with Lili, learning to accept that they could be a good match, have a good life.

And he *would* return to Montedoro. Soon.

But right now, today, he was going to do the thing he'd wanted to do for far too long now. He was going meet Sydney O'Shea face-to-face.

Sydney could not believe it.

The totally hunky—and oddly familiar—guy down the aisle from her in Macy's housewares department was actually making eyes at her. Men like that did not make eyes at Sydney. Men like that made eyes at women as gorgeous as they were.

And no, it wasn't that Sydney was ugly. She wasn't. But she wasn't beautiful, either. And there was something much too…practical and self-sufficient about her. Something a little too focused, as well. She also happened to be very smart. Men tended to find her intimidating, even at first glance.

So. Really. It was probably only her imagination that the drop-dead gorgeous guy by the waffle irons and electric griddles was looking at her. She pretended to read the tag on a stainless-steel sauté pan—and slid another glance in Mr. Eye Candy's direction.

He was pretending to read a price tag, too. She knew he was pretending because, at the exact moment she glanced his way, he sent a sideways look in her direction and one corner of that sinfully sexy mouth of his quirked up in a teasing smile.

Maybe he was flirting with someone behind her.

She turned her head enough that she could see over her shoulder.

Nope. Nobody there. Just more cookware racks brimming with All-Clad stainless-steel pots and pans, Le

Creuset enameled cast-iron casseroles and complete sets of Calphalon nonstick cookware—which, she firmly reminded herself, were what she *should* be looking at. She put all her attention on the business at hand and banished the implausibly flirty, impossibly smooth-looking man from her mind.

Yet another coworker was getting married, a paralegal, Calista Dwyer. Calista hadn't bothered to set up a bridal registry anywhere. The wedding was something of an impromptu affair. Tomorrow, Calista was running off with her boyfriend to some tropical island for a quickie wedding and a two-week honeymoon in paradise.

Sydney had left the office before lunch to choose a wedding gift. It was a task she had come to dislike. It happened so often and always reminded her that other people were getting married all the time. She really should do what a man in her situation would do, just have her assistant buy the wedding gifts—especially in a case like this, where she had no clue what Calista might be wanting or needing.

But no. She was still her grandmother's granddaughter at heart. Ellen O'Shea had always taken pride in personally selecting any gift she gave. Sydney continued the family tradition, even if she sometimes found the job annoying and a little bit depressing.

"Cookware. Necessary. But not especially interesting," a voice as warm and tempting as melted caramel teased in her ear. "Unless you love to cook?"

Good gravy. Mr. Hot and Hunky was right behind her. And there could be no doubt about it now. He was talking to her—and he *had* been giving her the eye.

Slowly, as if in a dream, Sydney turned to him.

Breathtaking. Seriously. There was no other word for this guy. Jet-black eyes, sculpted cheekbones, a perfect, square jaw, a nose like a blade. Broad, broad shoulders. And the way he was dressed…casual, but expensive. In light-colored trousers and a beautifully made navy jacket over a checked shirt.

He arched an ebony brow. "Do you?"

She forced herself to suck in a breath and then asked warily, "Excuse me?"

"Do you love to cook?" He gazed at her as though he couldn't tear his eyes away.

This could not be happening.

But wait. A gigolo? Maybe she looked like gigolo bait. Well-dressed and driven. Maybe it was the new black, to go trolling for a sugar mama in housewares.

And then again, well, he did look somehow familiar. She probably knew him from somewhere. "Have we met before?"

He gave her a slow once-over, followed by another speaking glance from those black-velvet eyes. That glance seemed to say that he wouldn't mind gobbling her up on the spot. And then he laughed, a low, sexy laugh as smooth and exciting as that wonderful voice of his. "I prefer to think that if we'd met in the past, you wouldn't have forgotten me so easily."

Excellent point. "I, um…" Good Lord. Speechless. She was totally speechless. And that wasn't like her at all. Enough with the stumbling all over herself. She stuck out her hand. "Sydney O'Shea."

"Rule Bravo-Calabretti." He wrapped his elegant, warm fingers around hers. She stifled a gasp as heat flowed up her arm.

The heat didn't stop at her shoulder. Arrows of what she could only categorize as burning excitement zipped downward into her midsection. She eased her hand from his grip and fell back a step, coming up short against the steel display shelves behind her. "Rule, you said?"

"Yes."

"Let me guess, Rule. You're not from Dallas."

He put those long, graceful fingers to his heart. "How did you know?"

"Well, the designer clothes, the two last names. You speak English fluently, but with a certain formality and no regional accent that I can detect. I'm thinking that not only are you not from Dallas, you're not from Texas. You're not even from the good old U.S. of A."

He laughed again. "You're an expert on accents?"

"No. I'm smart, that's all. And observant."

"Smart and observant. I like that."

She wished she could stand there by the cast-iron casserole display, just looking at him, listening to him talk and hearing his melted-caramel laugh for the next, oh, say, half century or so.

But there was still Calista's wedding gift to buy. And a quick lunch to grab before rushing back to the office for that strategy meeting on the Binnelab case at one.

Before she could start making gotta-go noises, he spoke again. "You didn't answer my question."

"Ahem. Your question?"

"Sydney, do you love to cook?"

The way he said her name, with such impossible passionate intent, well, she liked it. She liked it way, way too much. She fell back a step. "Cook? Me? Only when I have no other choice."

"Then why have I found you here in the cookware department?"

"*Found* me?" Her suspicions rose again. Really, what was this guy up to? "Were you *looking* for me?"

He gave an elegant shrug of those fine wide shoulders.

"I confess. I saw you enter the store from the parking garage at the south breezeway entrance. You were so... determined."

"You followed me because I looked determined?"

"I followed you because you intrigued me."

"You're intrigued by determination?"

He chuckled again. "Yes. I suppose I am. My mother is a very determined woman."

"And you love your mother." She put a definite edge in her tone. Was she calling him a mama's boy? Maybe. A little. She tended toward sarcasm when she was nervous or unsure—and he did make her nervous. There was just something about him. Something much too good to be true.

Mr. Bravo-Calabretti either didn't get her sarcasm— or ignored it. "I do love my mother, yes. Very much. And I admire her, as well." He studied Sydney for a moment, a direct, assessing kind of glance. "You're a prickly one, aren't you?" He seemed amused.

So he *had* picked up on her sarcasm. She felt petty and a little bit mean. And that made her speak frankly. "Yes, I am a prickly one. Some men don't find that terribly attractive."

"Some men are fools." He said it softly. And then he asked again, "Why are you shopping for pots and pans, Sydney?"

She confessed, "I need a wedding gift for someone at the office."

His dark eyes twinkled at her, stars in a midnight sky. "A wedding gift."

"That's right."

"Allow me to suggest..." He reached around her with his left hand. She turned to follow the movement and watched as he tapped a red Le Creuset casserole shaped like a heart. "This." She couldn't help noticing that he wore no wedding ring. And the casserole? Not bad, really.

"Very romantic," she said dryly. "Every bride needs a heart-shaped casserole dish."

"Buy it," he commanded. "And we can get out of here."

"Excuse me. We?"

He still had his arm out, almost touching her, his hand resting lightly on the red casserole. She caught a faint, tempting hint of his aftershave. It smelled fabulous—so subtle, so very expensive. He held her eyes, his dark gaze intent. "Yes. We. The two of us."

"But I'm not going anywhere with you. I don't even know you."

"That's true. And I find that very sad." He put on a teasingly mournful expression. "Because I want to know you, Sydney. Come to lunch with me. We can begin to remedy this problem." She opened her mouth to tell him that as far as she was concerned there was no problem and lunch was out of the question. But before she got the words out, he scooped up the heart-shaped dish. "This way." He gestured with his free hand in the direction of the nearest cashier stand.

She went where he directed her. Why not? The casserole was a good choice. And he was so charming. As soon as the clerk had rung her up, she could tell him goodbye and make him see that she meant it.

The clerk was young and blonde and very pretty. "Oh! Here. Let me help you!" She took the casserole from Rule and then kept sliding him blushing glances as she rung up the sale. Sydney sympathized with the dazzled girl. He was like something straight out of a fabulous romantic novel—the impossible, wonderful, hot and handsome, smooth and sophisticated lover who appears out of nowhere to sweep the good-hearted but otherwise perfectly ordinary heroine off her feet.

And did she actually think the word *lover?*

Really, she needed to get a grip on her suddenly too-vivid imagination.

"This casserole is the cutest thing. Is it a gift?" the clerk asked.

"Yes, it is," Sydney replied. "A wedding gift."

The girl slid another glance at Rule. "I'm sorry. We don't offer gift wrapping in the store anymore." She spoke in a breathy little voice. Rule said nothing. He gave the girl a quick, neutral nod and a barely detectable smile.

"It's fine," Sydney said. Like her grandmother, she not only bought gifts personally, she wrapped them, too. But she didn't have time to wrap this one if she wanted to give it to Calista before her wedding trip. So she would need to grab a gift bag and tissue somewhere. She swiped her card and signed in the little box and tried not to be overly conscious of the too-attractive man standing beside her.

The clerk gave Sydney the receipt—but she gave Rule the Macy's bag with the casserole in it. "Here you go now. Come back and shop with us. Anytime." Her tone said she would love to help Rule with a lot more than his shopping.

Sydney thanked her and turned to him. "I'll take that."

"No need. I'll carry it for you."

"I said I'll take it."

Reluctantly, he handed it over. But he showed no inclination to say goodbye and move on.

She told him, "Nice chatting with you. And I really have to—"

"It's only lunch, you know." He said it gently and quietly, for her ears alone. "Not a lifetime commitment."

She gazed up into those melting dark eyes and all at once she was hearing her best friend Lani's chiding voice in her head. *Seriously, Syd. If you really want a special guy in your life, you have to give one a chance now and then*....

"All right," she heard herself say. "Lunch." It wasn't a big deal. She would enjoy his exciting, flattering attention over a quick sandwich and then say goodbye. No harm done.

"A smile," he said, his warm gaze on her mouth. "At last."

She smiled wider. Because she did like him. He was not only killer-handsome and very smooth, he seemed like a great guy. Certainly there could be no harm in giving herself permission to spend a little more time with him. "So. First I need a store that sells gift bags."

He held her eyes for a moment. And it felt glorious. Just standing there in Macy's, lost in an endless glance with a gorgeous man. Finally, he said, "There's a mall directory, I think. This way." And then he shepherded her ahead of him, as he had when he ushered her to the cashier stand.

They found a stationery store. She chose a pretty bag and some sparkly tissue and a gift card. The clerk rang up the sale and they were on their way.

"Where to?" she asked, as they emerged into the mall again.

"This is Texas," he said, his elegant face suddenly open and almost boyish. "We should have steak."

He had a limo waiting for him outside, which didn't surprise her. The man was very much the limo type. He urged her to ride with him to the restaurant, but she said she would follow him. They went to the Stockyards District in nearby Fort Worth, to a casual place with lots of Texas atmosphere and an excellent reputation.

An antler chandelier hung from the pressed-tin ceiling

above their corner table. The walls were of pine planks and exposed brick, hung with oil paintings of cowboy boots, hats and bandannas. The floor was painted red.

They got a table in a corner and he ordered a beautiful bottle of Cabernet. She refused the wine when their waiter tried to fill her glass. But then, after he left them, she gave in and poured herself a small amount. The taste was amazing, smooth and delicately spicy on her tongue.

"You like it?" Rule asked hopefully.

"It's wonderful."

He offered a toast. "To smart, observant, determined women."

"Don't forget prickly," she reminded him.

"How could I? It's such a charming trait."

"Nice recovery." She gave him an approving nod.

He raised his glass higher. "To smart, observant, determined and decidedly prickly women."

She laughed as she touched her glass to his.

"Tell me about your high-powered job," he said, after the waiter delivered their salads of butter lettuce and applewood smoked bacon.

She sipped more of the wine she shouldn't really be drinking, given she had that big meeting ahead of her. "And you know I have a high-powered job, how?"

"You said the wedding gift was for 'someone at the office.'"

"I could be in data entry. Or maybe a top executive's very capable assistant."

"No," he said, with confidence. "Your clothing is both conservative and expensive." He eyed her white silk shell, her lightweight, fitted jacket, the single strand of pearls she wore. "And your attitude…"

She leaned toward him, feeling deliciously giddy. Feeling free and bold and ready for anything. "What about my attitude?"

"You are no one's assistant."

She sat back in her chair and rested her hands in her lap. "I'm an attorney. With a firm that represents a number of corporate clients."

"An attorney. Of course. *That,* I believe."

She picked up her fork, ate some of her salad. For a moment or two they shared a surprisingly easy silence. And then she asked, "And what about you? What do you do for a living?"

"I like variety in my work. At the moment, I'm in trade. International trade."

"At the moment? What? You change jobs a lot, is that what you're telling me?"

"I take on projects that interest me. And when I'm satisfied that any given project is complete, I move on."

"What do you trade?"

"At the moment, oranges. Montedoron oranges."

"Montedoran. That sounds exotic."

"It is. The Montedoran is a blood orange, very sweet, hinting of raspberry, with the characteristic red flesh of all blood oranges. The skin is smooth, not pitted like many other varieties."

"So soon I'll be buying Montedorans at my local Wal-Mart Supercenter?"

"Hardly. The Montedoran is never going to be for sale in supermarkets. We won't be trading in that kind of volume. But for certain gourmet and specialty stores, I think it could do very well."

"Montedoran…" She tested the word on her tongue. "There's a small country in Europe, right, on the Côte d'Azur? Montedoro?"

"Yes. Montedoro is my country." He poured her more

wine. And she didn't stop him. "It's one of the eight small-est states in Europe, a principality on the Mediterranean. My mother was born there. My father was American but moved to Montedoro and accepted Montedoran citizen-ship when they married. His name is Evan Bravo. He was a Texan by birth."

She really did love listening to him talk. He made every word into a poem. "So...you have relatives in Texas?"

"I have an aunt and uncle and a number of first cousins who live in and around San Antonio. And I have other, more distant cousins in a small town near Abilene. And in your Hill Country, I have a second cousin who married a veterinarian. And there are more Bravos, many more, in California and Wyoming and Nevada. All over the States, as a matter of fact."

"I take it that Calabretti is your mother's surname?"

"Yes."

"Is that what they do in your country, combine the hus-band's and wife's last name when they marry?"

He nodded. "In...certain families, anyway. It's similar to the way it's done in Spain. We are much like the Span-ish. We want to keep all our last names, on both sides of our families. So we string them together proudly."

"Bravo-Calabretti sounds familiar, somehow. I keep wondering where I've heard it before..."

He waited for her to finish. When she didn't, he shrugged. "Perhaps it will come to you later."

"Maybe so." She lowered her voice to a more confiden-tial level. "And I have to tell you, I keep thinking that *you* are familiar, that I've met you before."

He shrugged in a way that seemed to her so sophisti-cated, so very European. "They say everyone has a double. Maybe that's it. You've met my double."

It wasn't what she'd meant. But it didn't really matter.

"Maybe." She let it go and asked, "Do you have brothers and sisters?"

"I do." He gave her a regal nod. "Three brothers, five sisters. I'm second-born. I have an older brother, Maximilian. And after me, there are the twins, Alexander and Damien. And then my sisters—Bella, Rhiannon, Alice, Genevra and Rory."

"Big family." Feeling suddenly wistful, she set down her fork. "I envy you. I was an only child." Her hand rested on the tabletop.

He covered it with his. The touch warmed her to her toes—and thrilled her, as well. Her whole body seemed, all at once, completely, vividly alive. He leaned into her and studied her face, his gaze as warm as his lean hand over hers. "And you are sad, then? To have no siblings?"

"I am, yes." She wished he might hold her hand indefinitely. And yet she had to remember that this wasn't going anywhere and it wouldn't be right to let him think that it might. She eased her hand free. He took her cue without comment, retreating to his side of the table. She asked, "How old are you, Rule?"

He laughed his slow, smooth laugh. "Somehow, I begin to feel as though I'm being interviewed."

She turned her wineglass by the stem. "I only wondered. Is your age a sensitive subject for you?"

"In a sense, I suppose it is." His tone was more serious. "I'm thirty-two. That's a dangerous age for an unmarried man in my family."

"How so? Thirty-two isn't all that old." Especially not for a man. For a woman, things were a little different—at least, they were if she wanted to have children.

"It's time that I married." He said it so somberly, his eyes darker than ever as he regarded her steadily.

"I don't get it. In your family, they put you on a schedule for marriage?"

Now a smile haunted his handsome mouth. "It sounds absurd when you say it that way."

"It *is* absurd."

"You are a woman of definite opinions." He said it in an admiring way. Still, defiance rose within her and she tipped her chin high. He added, "And yes, in my family both the men and the women are expected to marry before they reach the age of thirty-three."

"And if you don't?"

He lowered his head and looked at her from under his dark brows. "Consequences will be dire." He said it in a low tone, an intimate tone, a tone that did a number on every one of her nerve endings and sent a fine, heated shiver dancing along the surface of her skin.

"You're teasing me."

"Yes, I am. I like you, Sydney. I knew that I would, the moment I first saw you."

"And when was that?"

"You've already forgotten?" He looked gorgeously forlorn. "I see I'm not so memorable, after all. Macy's? I saw you going in?" The waiter scooped up their empty salad plates and served them rib eye steaks with Serrano lime butter. When he left them, Rule slid her a knowing glance as he picked up his steak knife. "Sydney, I think you're testing me."

Why deny it? "I think you're right."

"I hope I'm passing this test of yours—and do your parents live here in Dallas?"

She trotted out the old, sad story. "They lived in San Francisco, where I was born. My mother was thrown off a runaway cable car. I was just three months old, in her arms when she fell. She suffered a blow to the head and died instantly, but I was unharmed. They called it a miracle at the time. My father was fatally injured when he jumped off to try and save us. He died the next day in the hospital."

His dark eyes were so soft. They spoke of real sympathy. Of understanding. "How terrible for you."

"I don't even remember it. My grandmother—my father's mother—came for me and took me back to Austin, where she lived. She raised me on her own. My grandfather had died several years before my parents. She was amazing, my grandmother. She taught me that I can do anything. She taught me that power brings responsibility. That the truth is sacred. That being faithful and trustworthy are rewards in themselves."

Now his eyes had a teasing light in them. "And yet, you're an attorney."

Sydney laughed. "So they have lawyer jokes even in Montedoro?"

"I'm afraid so—and a *corporate* attorney at that."

"I'm not responding to that comment on the grounds that it might tend to incriminate me." She said it lightly.

But he saw right through her. "Have I hit a nerve?"

She totally shocked herself by answering frankly. "My job is high-powered. And high-paying. And it's been… important to me, to know that I'm on top of a very tough game, that I'll never have to worry about where the next paycheck is coming from, that I can definitely take care of my own and do it well."

"And yet?"

She revealed even more. "And yet lately, I often find myself thinking how much more fulfilling it might be to spend my workdays helping people who really need me, rather than protecting the overflowing coffers of multibillion-dollar companies."

He started to speak. But then her BlackBerry, which she'd set on the table to the right of her water goblet the way she always did at restaurants, vibrated. She checked the display: Magda, her assistant. Probably wondering why she wasn't back at the office yet.

She glanced at Rule again. He had picked up his knife and fork and was concentrating on his meal, giving her the chance to deal with the call if she needed to.

Well, she didn't need to.

Sydney scooped up the phone and dropped it in her bag where she wouldn't even notice if it vibrated again.

With the smooth ease of a born diplomat, Rule continued their conversation as though it had never been interrupted. "You speak of your grandmother in the past tense...."

"She died five years ago. I miss her very much."

"So much loss." He shook his head. "Life can be cruel."

"Yes." She ate a bite of her steak, taking her time about it, savoring the taste and tenderness of the meat, unaccountably happy that he hadn't remarked on her vibrating BlackBerry, that he hadn't said he was "sorry," the way people always did when she told them she'd grown up without her parents, when she confessed how much she missed her grandmother.

He watched her some more, his dark head tipped to the side in way that had her thinking again how he reminded her of someone. "Have you ever been married?"

"No. I'm Catholic—somewhat lapsed, yes, but nonetheless, I do believe that marriage is forever. I've never found the man I want forever with. But I've had a couple of serious relationships. They...didn't work out." Understatement of the year. But he didn't need to hear it and she didn't need to say it. She'd done enough over-sharing for now, thank you very much. She added, "And I'm thirty-three. Does that seem...dire to you?"

"Absolutely." He put on a stern expression. On him, sternness was sexy. But then, on him, everything was sexy. "You should be married immediately. And then have nine children. At the very least. You should marry a wealthy man, Sydney. One who adores you."

"Hmm. A rich man who adores me. I wouldn't mind that. But the nine children? More than I planned on. Significantly more."

"You don't want children?" He looked honestly surprised.

She almost told him about Trevor right then. But no. This was a fantasy lunch with a fantasy man. Trevor was her real life. The most beautiful, perfect, meaningful, joyful part of her real life. "I didn't say I didn't want children. I do. But I'm not sure I'm ready for nine of them. Nine seems like a lot."

"Well. Perhaps we would have to settle for fewer than nine. I can be reasonable."

"We?"

"A man and a woman have to work together. Decisions should be jointly made."

"Rule." She put a hand to her breast, widened her eyes and asked him dramatically, "Could this be...oh, I can't believe it. Is it possible that you're proposing to me?"

He answered matter-of-factly, "As it happens, I'm wealthy. And it would be very easy for me to adore you." His dark eyes shone.

What was this feeling? Magical, this feeling. Magical and foolish. And that was the beauty of it. It was one of those things that happen when you least expect it. Something to remind her that life could still be surprising.

That it wasn't all about winning and staying on top—and coming home too late to tuck her own sweet boy into bed.

Sometimes even the most driven woman might just take a long lunch. A long lunch with a stranger who made her feel not only brilliant and clever, but beautiful and desired, as well.

She put on a tragic face. "I'm sorry. It could never work."

He played it stricken. "But why not?"

"You live in Montedoro." Grave. Melancholy. "My career—my whole life—is here."

"You might change careers. You might even decide to try a different kind of life."

Hah. Exactly what men always said. She wasn't letting him get away with it. "Or *you* might move to Texas."

"For you, Sydney, I might do anything."

"Perfect answer."

A moment ensued. Golden. Fine. A moment with only the two of them in it. A moment of complete accord.

Sydney let herself enjoy that moment. She refused to be guarded or dubious. It was only lunch, after all. Lunch with an attractive man. She was giving herself full permission to enjoy every minute of it.

Chapter Two

The meeting on the Binnelab case was half over when Sydney slipped in at two-fifteen.

"Excuse me," she said as she eased through the conference room doors and they all turned to stare at her. "So sorry. I had…something of an emergency."

Her colleagues made sympathetic noises and went back to arguing strategy. No one was the least angry that she was late.

Because she was never late—which meant that of course there had to be a good reason for her tardiness. She was Sydney O'Shea, who graduated college at twenty, passed the bar at twenty-four and had been made partner at thirty—exactly one year before her son was born. Sydney O'Shea, who knew how to make demands and how to return a favor, who had a talent for forging strong professional relationships and who never slacked. She racked up the billable hours with the best of them.

If she'd told them all that she'd been sidetracked in Macy's housewares by a handsome orange salesman from Montedoro and allowed him to talk her into blowing off half of the Binnelab meeting, they'd have had zero doubt that she was joking.

She knew the case backward and forward. She only had to listen to the discussion for a few minutes to get up to speed on the direction her colleagues were taking.

By the end of the meeting, she'd nudged them in a slightly different direction and everyone seemed pleased with the result. She returned to her corner office to find her so-capable assistant, the usually unflappable Magda, standing in the middle of the room holding an orchid in a gorgeous purple pot. Magda stared in dismay at the credenza along the side wall where no less than twelve spectacular flower arrangements sprouted from a variety of crystal vases.

The credenza was not the only surface in the room overflowing with flowers. There were two vases on the coffee table and one each on the end tables in the sitting area.

Her desk had six of them. And the windowsill was likewise overrun with exotic blooms. Each arrangement had a small white card attached. The room smelled like a greenhouse.

Rule. She knew instantly. Who else could it be? And a quick glance at one of the cards confirmed it.

Please share dinner with me tonight. The Mansion at Turtle Creek. Eight o'clock. Yours, Rule

She'd never told him the name of her firm. But then again, it wouldn't have been that hard to find out. Just her name typed into a search engine would have done it.

"Smothered in flowers. Literally," she said to her nonplussed assistant. She felt that delicious glow again, that sense of wonder and limitless possibility. She was crushing on him, big-time. He made her feel innocent and free.

And beautiful. And desired…

Was there anything wrong with that? If there was, she was having trouble remembering what.

"They started arriving about half an hour ago," said Magda. "I think this orchid is the last of them. But I have nowhere left to put it."

"It would look great on your desk," Sydney suggested. "In fact, take the cards off and leave them with me. And then let's share the wealth."

Magda arched a brow. "Give them away, you mean?"

"Start with the data entry crew. Just leave me the two vases of yellow roses."

"You're sure?"

"Positive." She didn't think Rule would mind at all if she shared. And she wanted to share. This feeling of hope and wonder and beauty, well, it was too fabulous to keep to herself. "Tell everyone to enjoy them. And to take them home, if they want to—and hurry. We have Calista's party at four."

"I really like this orchid," said Magda, holding out the pot, admiring the deep purple lips suspended from the velvety pale pink petals. "It looks rare."

"Good. Enjoy. A nice start to the weekend, don't you think? Flowers for everyone. And then we send Calista happily off to her tropical honeymoon."

"Someone special must be wild for you," Magda said with a grin.

Sydney couldn't resist grinning right back at her. "Deliver the flowers and let's break out the champagne."

Calista loved the heart-shaped casserole. She laughed when she pulled it from the gift bag. "I guess now I'll just have to learn how to cook."

"Wait until after the honeymoon," Sydney suggested and then proposed a toast. "To you, Calista. And to a long and happy marriage."

After the two glasses of wine at lunch, Sydney allowed herself only a half glass of champagne during the shower. But the shortage of bubbly didn't matter in the least. It was still the most fun Sydney had ever had at a bridal shower. Funny how meeting a wonderful man can put a whole different light on the day.

After the party, she returned to her office just long enough to grab her briefcase, her bag and one of the vases full of yellow roses. Yes, as a rule she would have stayed to bill a couple more hours, at least.

But hey. It was Friday. She wanted to see her little boy before he went to bed. And she really needed to talk to Lani, who was not only her dearest friend, but also Trevor's live-in nanny. She needed Lani's excellent advice as to whether she should go for it and take Rule up on his invitation to dinner.

At home in Highland Park, she found Trevor in the kitchen, sitting up at the breakfast nook table in his booster chair, eating his dinner of spaghetti and meatballs. "Mama home! Hug, hug!" he crowed, and held out his chubby arms.

She dropped her briefcase and bag, set the flowers on the counter and went to him. He wrapped those strong little arms around her neck, smearing spaghetti sauce on her cheek when he gave her a big smacker of a kiss. "How's my boy?"

"I fine, thank you."

"Me, too." She hugged him harder. "Now that I'm home with you." He smelled of tomatoes and meatballs and baby shampoo—of everything that mattered.

At two, he was quite the talker. As he picked up his

spoon again, he launched into a description of his day. "We swim. We play trucks. I shout *loud* when we crash."

"Sounds like fun." She whipped a tissue from the box on the counter and wiped the red sauce off her cheek.

"Oh, yes! Fun, Mama. I happy." He shoved a meatball in his mouth with one hand and waved his spoon with the other.

"Use your spoon for eating," Lani said from over by the sink.

"Yes, Lani. I do!" He switched the spoon to the other hand and scooped up a mound of pasta. Most of it fell off before he got it to his mouth, but he only gamely scooped up some more.

"You're early," said Lani, turning to glance at her over the tops of her black-rimmed glasses. "And those roses are gorgeous."

"They are, aren't they? And as to being early, hey, it's almost the weekend."

"That never stopped you from working late before." Lani grabbed a towel and turned to lean against the sink as she dried her hands.

Her full name was Yolanda Ynez Vasquez and she was small and curvy with acres of thick almost-black hair. She'd been working for Sydney for five years, starting as Sydney's housekeeper. The plan was that Lani would cook and clean house and live in, thus saving money while she finished college. But then, even after she got her degree, she'd stayed on, and become Trevor's nanny, as well. Sydney had no idea how she would have managed without her. Not only for her grace and ease at keeping house and being a second mom to Trevor, but also for her friendship. After Ellen O'Shea, Yolanda Vasquez was the best friend Sydney had ever had.

Lani said, "You're glowing, Syd."

Sydney put her hands to her cheeks. "I do feel slightly warm. Maybe I have a fever...."

"Or maybe someone handsome sent you yellow roses."

Laughing, Sydney shook her head. "You are always one step ahead of me."

"What's his name?"

"Rule."

"Hmm. Very...commanding."

"And he is. But in such a smooth kind of way. I went to lunch with him. I really like him. He asked me to dinner."

"Tonight?" Lani asked.

She nodded. "He invited me to meet him at the Mansion at Turtle Creek. Eight o'clock."

"And you're going." It wasn't a question.

"If you'll hold down the fort?"

"No problem."

"What about Michael?" Michael Cort was a software architect. Lani had been seeing him on a steady basis for the past year.

Lani shrugged. "You know Michael. He likes to hang out. I'll invite him over. We'll get a pizza—tell me more about Rule."

"I just met him today. Am I crazy?"

"A date with a guy who makes you glow? Nothing crazy about that."

"Mama, sketti?" Trev held up a handful of crushed meatball and pasta.

"No, thank you, my darling." Sydney bent and kissed his plump, gooey cheek again. "You can have that big wad of sketti all for yourself."

"Yum!" He beamed up at her and her heart felt like it was overflowing. She had it all. A healthy, happy child, a terrific best friend, a very comfortable lifestyle, a job most high-powered types would kill for. And a date with the best-looking man on the planet.

Sydney spent the next hour being the mother she didn't get to be as often as she would have liked. She played trucks with Trev. And then she gave him his bath and tucked him into bed herself, smoothing his dark hair off his handsome forehead, thinking that he was the most beautiful child she had ever seen. He was already asleep when she tiptoed from the room.

Yolanda looked up when she entered the family room. "It's after seven. You better get a move on if you want to be on time for your dream man."

"I know—keep me company while I get ready?"

Lani followed her into the master suite, where Sydney grabbed a quick shower and redid her makeup. In the walk-in closet, she stared at the possible choices and didn't know which one to pick.

"This." Lani took a simple cap-sleeved red satin sheath from the row of mostly conservative party dresses. "You are killer in red."

"Red. Hmm," Sydney waffled. "You think?"

"I *know*. Put it on. You only need your diamond studs with it. And that garnet-and-diamond bracelet your grandmother left you. And those red Jimmy Choos."

Sydney took the dress. "You're right."

Lani dimpled. "I'm always right."

Sydney put on the dress and the shoes and the diamond studs and garnet bracelet. Then she stood at the full-length mirror in her dressing area and scowled at herself. "I don't know…" She touched her brown hair, which she'd swept up into a twist. "Should I take my hair down?"

"No. It's great like that." Lani tugged a few curls loose at her temples and her nape. Then she eased the wide neckline of the dress off her shoulders. "There. Perfect. You look so hot."

"I am not the hot type."

"Yeah, you are. You just don't see yourself that way. You're tall and slim and striking."

"Striking. Right. Still, it would be nice if I had breasts, don't you think? I had breasts once, remember? When I was pregnant with Trevor?"

"Stop. You have breasts."

"Hah."

"And you have green eyes to die for."

"To die for. Who came up with that expression, anyway?"

Lani took her by the shoulders and turned her around so they faced each other. "You look gorgeous. Go. Have a fabulous time."

"Now I'm getting nervous."

"*Getting?* Syd. You look wonderful and you are going."

"What if he doesn't show up?"

"Stop it." Lani squeezed her shoulders. "Go."

Rosewood Mansion at Turtle Creek was a Dallas landmark. Once a spectacular private residence, the Mansion was now a five-star hotel and restaurant, a place of meticulous elegance, of marble floors and stained-glass windows and hand-carved fireplaces.

Her heart racing in mingled excitement and trepidation, Sydney entered the restaurant foyer, with its curving iron-railed staircases and black-and-white marble floor. She marched right up to the reservation desk and told the smiling host waiting there, "I'm meeting someone. Rule Bravo-Calabretti?"

The host nodded smartly. "Right this way."

And off she went to a curtained private corner on the

terrace. The curtains were pulled back and she saw that Rule was waiting, wearing a gorgeous dark suit, his black eyes lighting up when their gazes locked. He rose as she approached.

"Sydney." He said her name with honest pleasure, his expression as open and happy as her little boy's had been when she'd tucked him into bed that night. "You came." He sounded so pleased. And maybe a little relieved.

How surprising was that? He didn't look like a person who would ever worry that a woman might not show up for a date.

She liked him even more then—if that was possible. Because he had allowed her to see he was vulnerable.

"Wouldn't have missed it for the world," she said softly, her gaze locked with his.

Champagne was waiting in a silver bucket. The host served them.

Rule said, "I took the liberty of conferring with the chef ahead of time, choosing a menu I thought you might enjoy. But if you would prefer making your own choices…"

She loved that he'd planned ahead, that he'd taken that kind of care over the meal. *And* that he'd asked for her preference in the matter. "The food is always good here. Whatever you've planned will be perfect."

"No…dietary rules or foods you hate?" His midnight gaze scanned her face as though committing it to memory.

"None. I trust you."

Something flared in his eyes. "Fair enough, then." His voice wrapped around her, warm and deep and so sweet. He nodded at the host. "Thank you, Neil."

"Very good, then, your—" Neil paused almost imperceptibly, and then continued "—waiter will be with you shortly." With a slight bow, he turned to go.

"Neil seems a little nervous," she whispered, when the host had left them.

"I have no idea why," Rule said lightly. And then his tone acquired a certain huskiness. "You should wear red all the time."

"That might become boring."

"You could never be boring. And what is that old song, the one about the lady in red?"

"That's it. 'Lady in Red.'"

"You bring that song to mind. You make me want to dance with you."

How did he do it? He poured on the flattery—and yet, somehow, coming from him, the sweet talk sounded sincere. "Thank you for the flowers."

He waved a lean hand. "I know I went overboard."

"It was a beautiful gesture. And I hope you don't mind, but I shared them—with the data entry girls and the paralegals and the crew down in Human Resources."

"Why would I mind? They were yours, to do with as you wished. And sharing is good. You're not only the most compelling woman I've ever met, you are kind. And generous, too."

She shook her head. "You amaze me, Rule."

He arched a raven-black eyebrow. "In a good way, I hope?"

"Oh, yeah. In a good way. You make me want to believe all the beautiful things that you say to me."

He took her hand. Enchantment settled over her, at the warmth of his touch, at the lovely, lazy pulse of pleasure that seemed to move through her with every beat of her heart, just to be with him, to have her hand in his, flesh to flesh. "Would you prefer if I were cruel?"

The question shocked her a little. "No. Never. Why would you ask that?"

He turned her hand over, raised it to his lips, pressed a kiss in the heart of her palm. The pulse of pleasure within her went lower, grew hotter. "You fascinate me." His breath fanned her palm. And then, tenderly, he lowered their hands to the snowy tablecloth and wove his fingers with hers. "I want to know all about you. And truthfully, some women like a little more spice from a man. They want to be kept guessing. 'Does he care or not, will he call or not?' They might say they're looking for a good man who appreciates them. But they like…the dance of love, they revel in the uncertainty of it all."

She leaned closer to him, because she wanted to. Because she could. "I like you as you are. Don't pretend to be someone else. Please."

"I wouldn't. But I *can* be cruel." He said it so casually, so easily. And she realized she believed him. She saw the shining blade of his intention beneath the velvet sheath that was his considerable charm.

"Please don't. I've had enough of mean men. I…" She let the words trail off. The waiter was approaching their table. Perfect timing. The subject was one that desperately needed dropping.

But a flick of a glance from Rule and the waiter turned around and walked away. "Continue, please," Rule prompted softly. "What men have been cruel to you?"

Way to ruin a beautiful evening, Syd. "Seriously. You don't need to hear it."

"But I *want* to hear it. I meant what I said. I want to know about you, Sydney. I want to know everything." His eyes were so dark. She could get lost in them, lost forever, never to be found. And the really scary thing was that she almost felt okay with being lost forever—as long as he was lost right along with her.

"What can I say? There's just something about me…"

Lord. She did not want to go there. She tried to wrap it up with a generalized explanation. "I seem to attract men who say they like me because I'm strong and intelligent and capable. And then they get to work trying to tear me down."

Something flared in his eyes. Something...dangerous. "*Who* has tried to tear you down?"

"Do we have to get into this?"

"No. We don't. But sometimes it's better, I think, to go ahead and speak frankly of the past." Now his eyes were tender again. Tender and somehow completely accepting.

She let out a slow, surrendering sigh. "I lived with a guy when I was in law school. His name was Ryan. He was fun and a little bit wild. On the day we moved in together, he quit his job. He would lie on the sofa drinking those great big cans of malt liquor, watching ESPN. When I tried to talk to him about showing a little motivation, things got ugly fast. He said that I had enough ambition and drive for both of us and next to me he felt like a failure, that I had as good as emasculated him—and would I get out of the damn way, I was blocking his view of the TV?"

Rule gave one of those so-European shrugs of his. "So you got rid of him."

"Yes, I did. When I kicked him out, he told me he'd been screwing around on me. He'd had to, he said. In order to try and feel at least a little like a man again. So he was a cheater and a liar, too. After Ryan, I took a break from men. I stayed away from serious entanglements for the next five years. Then I met Peter. He was an attorney, like me. Worked for a different firm, a smaller one. We started going out. I thought he was nothing like Ryan, not a user or runaround or a slacker in any way. He never formally moved in with me. But he was...with me, at my house, most nights. And then he started pressuring me to get him in at Teale, Gayle and Prosser." She said the name of her firm with another long sigh.

"You weren't comfortable with that?"

"No, I wasn't. And I told him so. I believe in networking, in helping the other guy out. But I didn't want my boyfriend working at the same firm with me, especially not if he was hired on my say-so. There are just too many ways that could spell trouble. He said he understood."

Rule still had his fingers laced with hers. He gave her a reassuring squeeze. "But he didn't understand."

"Not in the least. He was angry that I wouldn't give him 'a hand up,' as he put it. Things kind of devolved from there. He said a lot of brutal things to me. I was still an associate at the firm then. At a party, Peter got drunk and complained about me to one of the partners. By the time he and I were over, I…" She sought the right way to say it.

He said it for her. "You decided you were through with men." She glanced away. He caught her chin, lightly, gently, and guided it back around so that she met his eyes again. "Are you all right?" He sounded honestly concerned. She realized that her answer really mattered to him.

She swallowed, nodded. "I'm okay. It's just…when I talk about all that, I feel like such a loser, you know?"

"Those men. Ryan and Peter. *They* are the losers." He held her gaze. "I notice you haven't told me their last names."

"And I'm not going to. As I said, it's long over for me, with both of them."

He gave her his beautiful smile. "There. That's what I was waiting to hear." He let go of her hand—but only to touch her in another way. With his index finger, he traced the line of her jaw, stirring shivers as he went. He caught one of the loose curls of hair that Lani had pulled free of her French twist, and rubbed it between his fingers. "Soft," he whispered. "Like your skin. Like your tender heart…"

"Don't be too sure about that. I'm not only prickly, I can be a raving bitch," she whispered back. "Just ask Ryan and Peter."

"Give me their last names. Ryan and Peter and I will have a long talk."

"Hah. I don't think so."

He touched her cheek then, a brushing caress of such clear erotic intent that her toes curled inside her Jimmy Choos. "As long as you're willing to give men another chance."

"I could be. If the *right* man ever came along."

He took her untouched champagne flute and handed it to her. Then he picked up his own. "To the right man."

She touched her glass to his, echoed, "The right man." It was excellent champagne, each tiny bubble like a burst of magic on her tongue. And when she set the glass down again, she said, "I always wanted to have children."

He answered teasingly, "However, not nine of them."

Suddenly, it came to her. She realized where she'd been going with her grim little tale of disappointed love. It hadn't really been a case of total over-sharing, after all.

"Actually," she said. "This is serious."

"All right."

"There's something I really do need to tell you."

His expression changed, became…so still. Waiting. Listening. He tipped his head to the side in that strangely familiar way he had. "Tell me."

She wanted—needed—for him to know about Trevor. If learning about Trev turned him off, well, she absolutely *had* to know that now, tonight. Before she got in any deeper with him. Before she let herself drown in those beautiful black eyes. "I…" Her mouth had gone desert-dry. She swallowed, hard.

This shouldn't be so difficult, shouldn't matter so very much. She hardly knew this man. Holding his interest and his high regard shouldn't be this important to her.

Yet it *was* important. Already. She cared. A lot. Way, way too much.

He seemed too perfect. He *was* too perfect. He was her dream man come to vivid, vibrant, tempting life. The first minute she saw him, she'd felt as though she already knew him.

Yes, she should be more wary. It wasn't like her to be so easily drawn in.

And yet she was. She couldn't stop herself.

She thought of her grandmother, who had been a true believer in love at first sight. Grandma Ellen claimed she had fallen for Sydney's grandfather the first time she met him. She'd also insisted that Sydney's father had fallen in love with her mother at first sight.

Could falling in love at first sight be a genetic trait? Sydney almost smiled at the thought. She'd believed herself to be in love before—and been wrong, wrong, wrong.

But with Ryan, it hadn't been like this. Or with Peter. Nothing like this, with either of them.

Both of those relationships had developed in the logical, sensible way. She'd come to believe that she loved those men over a reasonable period of time, after getting to know them well—or so she had thought.

And look what had happened. She learned in the end that she hadn't really known either Ryan or Peter. Not well enough, she hadn't. With both men, it had ended in heartbreak. Those failures should have made her more wary. Those failures *had* made her more wary.

Until today. Until she met Rule.

With Rule, her heart seemed to have a will of its own. With him, she wanted to just go for it. To take the leap, take a chance. She didn't want to be wary with him. With him, she could almost become a believer in love at first sight.

If only he wasn't put off by learning that she already had a child....

"It's all right," he said so gently. "Go on."

And she did. "I was almost thirty, when it ended with Peter. I wanted to make partner in my firm and I wanted a family. I knew I could do both."

He gave a slow nod. "But the men were not cooperating."

"Exactly. So I decided...to have a family anyway. A family without a man. I went to a top cryobank—a sperm bank, at a fertility clinic?"

"Yes," he said in a way that could only be called cautious. "I know what a cryobank is."

"Well, all right." Her hands were shaking. She lowered them to her lap so he wouldn't see. "I went to a sperm bank. I had artificial insemination. The procedure was successful. I got pregnant. And now I have a beautiful, healthy two-year-old son."

"You have a child," he repeated, carefully. "A boy."

She folded her hands good and tight in her lap to still the shaking. And her heart seemed to have stopped dead in her chest—and then commenced beating way too hard and too fast. It hurt, her own heart, the way it pounded away in there. Because she *knew,* absolutely, that it was over, between her and Rule, over before it had even really begun. And it didn't matter *how* perfect he was for her. It didn't matter if he just happened to be her dream-come-true. It didn't matter that he made her want to believe in love at first sight. She was absolutely certain at that moment that he wouldn't accept Trevor. And if he didn't accept her son, she wanted nothing to do with him.

In a moment, she would be rising, saying good-night. Walking away from him and refusing to look back.

She drew her shoulders tall. Her hands weren't shaking anymore. "Yes, Rule. I have a son, a son who's everything to me."

Chapter Three

And then, just as she was dead certain that it was finished between them, Rule smiled.

A *real* smile. He laid his warm, lean hand along the side of her face. "How wonderful. I love children, Sydney— but I already said that, didn't I? When can I meet him? Tomorrow, I hope."

She blinked, swallowed. Almost sick with emotion, she put her hand against her churning stomach. "I... You what?"

He laughed, a beautiful, low, sexy sound. "You thought I wouldn't want to meet your son?" And then he frowned. "You don't know me very well."

"I... You're right. I don't know you." She took slow, deep breaths, ordering her stomach to settle down, stunned at how much it mattered, that he wasn't rejecting Trevor. That it wasn't over after all, that she didn't have to rise and walk away and not look back. She could stay right here, in this beautiful restaurant, at this private table, with this incredible man. She chided, "I have to keep reminding myself that I don't know you well, that we only met this afternoon."

"Unbelievable." His frown had faded. "I had forgotten. Somehow, it seems that I've known you forever."

She confessed, "I have that feeling, too." And then she laughed, a laugh that felt as light and bubbly as the excellent champagne. "I had it the first moment I saw you."

"You did?" He wore that boyish look, the one that made her think of Trev.

"Yes. I thought how you couldn't be looking at me. And then I thought how familiar you looked, that I must have met you before...."

"Of course I was looking at you," he said it with a definite note of reproach. "But you were very busy reminding yourself that you were through with men."

"I was. I admit it. How dumb was that?"

"It's all right. Now that you've told me why you gave up men, I thoroughly understand. And I'm not complaining. If you hadn't decided to stay away from the male sex, you might have found someone else by now and I wouldn't have a chance with you."

"And that would have been a tragedy," she teased.

"Yes, it would. A true catastrophe. But you did give up men. Now all I have to do is convince you to give one more man a chance." He raised his glass again. She clinked hers against it. "Are you ready for the first course?"

Suddenly, she was starving. "I am, yes."

He cast a glance beyond the open curtain. That was all. Just a glance. The waiter appeared again and made straight for their table.

Two hours later, Rule walked her out to the valet stand and had her car brought around. He tipped the valet generously and then took her hand and led her away from her waiting Mercedes. "Just for a moment…"

She went with him, down the sloping front entrance, to a shadowed area next to a large brick planter thick with greenery, beneath a beautiful old oak. The spring night felt warm and close around them.

He turned to face her. His eyes gleamed like polished stones through the darkness and his fingers trailed up her bare arm, a long, slow, dancing caress that left her strangely weak and slightly breathless. "Sydney…" He clasped her shoulders, and then framed her face between both wonderful hands. "Sydney O'Shea. I was becoming frightened."

His words confused her. She scanned his shadowed features. "But why?"

"That I would never find you. Never meet you…"

"Oh. That." She felt a glad smile curve her lips.

"Yes. That." His sweet breath stirred the loose curls at her temples as he bent his head closer to her.

A kiss. *His* kiss. Their first kiss. She tipped her face up to him, offering her mouth.

He held her eyes as he lowered his lips to hers.

Warm. Soft. Easy…

Her eyes drifted shut as his mouth touched hers, lightly, cherishingly. And she trembled, the moment was so exactly as she'd imagined it might be during their lunch that afternoon, during the long, glorious meal just past.

"Sydney…" He whispered her name against her mouth and she opened for him.

Instantly, she wanted more, wanted to be closer. *Had* to be closer.

Surging up, she wrapped her arms around him. A tiny, hungry cry escaped her at the sheer glory of such a perfect moment.

He took her cue and deepened the kiss, gathering her into him, cradling her against his body, so that she felt his warmth and solidness all along the length of her. He tasted of coffee and the heavenly pistachio mascarpone cake they'd shared for dessert. And the way he kissed her, the way his warm, rough-tender tongue caressed her…oh, there was nothing, ever, in her experience, to compare to it.

Nothing to compare.

To his kiss…

She wished it would never end.

But of course, it had to end. He took her shoulders again and reluctantly lifted his mouth from hers.

"Tomorrow," he said, gazing down at her, his eyes heavy-lidded, holding her a willing captive with his light touch at her shoulders, with his tender glance.

"Yes," she vowed, though she didn't even know yet what he planned for tomorrow.

He brushed the backs of his fingers against her cheek, and then up to her temple, causing those lovely shivers to course across her skin. "In the morning? I could come and collect you and your little boy. We could…visit a park, maybe. A park with swings and slides, so he'll have a chance to play. My little niece and nephew love nothing so much as a few hours in the sunshine, with a sandbox and a slide."

"You didn't tell me you had a niece and a nephew."

He nodded. "My older brother, Max, has two children— say yes to tomorrow."

"But I already did, didn't I?"

"Say it again."

"Yes—and why don't you come for breakfast first? You can meet my best friend, Lani, who has a degree in English literature, is a fabulous cook and takes care of Trevor while I'm at work."

"I would love breakfast. And to meet your friend, Lani."

"I have to warn you. Breakfast comes early at my house."

"Early it is."

"Seven-thirty, then." She took his hand, automatically threading her fingers with his, feeling the thrill of touching him—and also a certain rightness. Her hand fit perfectly in his. "Come on." She pulled him back toward her car. "I'll give you my address and phone number."

"Where's Michael?" Sydney asked, when she let herself in the house at quarter of eleven and found Lani sitting on the sofa alone, wearing Tweety Bird flannel pajama bottoms and a yellow cami top.

"How was the big date?" Lani asked, with a too-bright smile.

Sydney slipped off her red shoes and dropped to the sofa beside her friend. "It was better than…anything. Wonderful. I'm crazy about him. He's coming for breakfast at seven-thirty."

"Good. I can check him out. See if he's good enough for you."

"He's good enough. You'll see. I thought maybe one of your fabulous frittatas…"

"You got it." Lani took off her glasses and set them on the side table.

"Hey." Sydney waited until her friend looked at her again. Then she guided a thick swatch of Lani's dark, curly hair behind her ear. "You didn't answer my question about Michael."

Lani's big eyes were a little sad, and her full mouth curved slightly down. "Tonight, when I watched you getting ready to meet this new guy, putting on your makeup, fixing your hair, waffling over that perfect red dress…"

"Yeah? Tonight, what?"

"I thought, '*That.* What Syd's feeling. I want *that.*'"

"Oh, sweetheart…"

Lani's shoulders drooped. "And then you left and Michael came over and I thought what a nice guy he is…but I couldn't go on with him. Because he's not *the* guy." She laughed a little, shaking her head. "Do you know what I mean?"

Sydney reached out. Lani sagged against her and they held each other. "Yeah," Sydney whispered into her friend's thick, fragrant hair. "Yeah, I know exactly what you mean."

The next morning, the doorbell rang at seven-thirty on the nose.

"I get it!" Trevor fisted his plump hand and tapped the table twice. "Knock, knock!" he shouted. "Who's there?"

Sydney kissed his milk-smeared cheek. "Eat your cereal, Bosco."

"Banana!" Trev giggled. "Banana who?"

Lani said, "The coffee's ready and the frittata's in the oven. Answer the door, Syd."

"Orange. Banana." Trevor was totally entranced with his never-quite-right knock-knock joke. He banged his spoon gleefully against the tabletop. "Orange your… banana…"

Lani took his spoon from him. "Well, I guess I'll have to feed you, since you're not doing it."

"Lani, no! I eat. I do it myself."

"You sure?"

"Yes!"

She handed him back the spoon. "Go," she said to

Sydney, canting her head in the general direction of the front door.

Her heart doing somersaults inside her chest, Sydney went to let Rule in.

"Hi." She said it in the most ridiculous, breathy little voice.

"Sydney," he replied in wonderful melted-caramel tones. Could a man get more handsome every time a woman saw him? Rule did. The bright April sunshine made his hair gleam black as a crow's wing, and his smile had her heart performing a forward roll. He had a big yellow Tonka dump truck in one hand and a red ball in the other.

"I see you've come armed for battle," she said.

He shrugged. "In my experience, little boys like trucks. And balls."

"They do. Both. A lot." She stared at him. And he stared back at her. Time stopped. The walls of her foyer seemed to disappear. There was only the man on the other side of the open door. He filled up the world.

Then, from back in the kitchen, she heard her son calling out gleefully, "Orange. Banana. Banana. Orange..."

Lani said something. Probably, "Eat your cereal."

"It's the never-ending knock-knock joke," she said, and then wondered if they even had knock-knock jokes in his country. "Come in, come in..."

He did. She shut the door behind him. "This way..."

He caught her elbow. Somehow he had managed to shift the toy truck to the arm with the ball in it. "Wait." He said it softly.

She turned back to him and he looked down at her and...

Was there anything like this feeling she had with him?

So fine and shining and full of possibility. He pulled her to him.

She went willingly, eagerly. Close to him was where she wanted to be. She moved right up, snug and cozy against his broad chest, sharing his strong arms with the red ball and the yellow truck. "What?"

"This." And he kissed her. A brushing kiss, tender and teasing. Just right for early on a sunny Saturday morning. She felt his smile against her own.

When he lifted his mouth from hers, his eyes were soft as black velvet and full of promise. "May I meet your son now?"

"Right this way."

Trevor was shy with Rule at first.

Her little boy stared with big, solemn dark eyes as Sydney introduced Rule to Lani.

"And this is Trevor," Sydney said.

"Hello, Trevor. My name is Rule."

Trevor only stared some more and stuck a big spoonful of cereal in his mouth.

"Say hello," Sydney instructed him.

But Trevor turned his head away.

Rule sent her an oblique glance and a slight smile that said he knew about kids, and also knew how to be patient. He put the ball and the truck under the side table against the wall and accepted coffee, taking the empty chair between Lani and Sydney.

Lani served the frittata and they ate. Rule praised the food and said how much he liked the coffee, which Lani prepared to her own exacting tastes, grinding the beans with a top-quality grinder and brewing only with a French press.

He asked Lani about her degree in literature. The two

of them seemed to hit it off, Sydney thought. Lani was easy with him, and friendly, from the first. She told him her favorite Shakespeare play was *The Tempest*. He confessed to a fondness for *King Lear,* which had Lani groaning that she might love *Lear,* too. But she had no patience for thickheaded, foolish kings. Sydney didn't know a lot about Shakespeare, but it did kind of please her, that Rule seemed well-read, that he could carry on a conversation about something other than the Mavericks and the Cowboys.

He turned to her. "And what about you, Sydney? Do you have a favorite Shakespeare play?"

She shrugged. "I saw *A Midsummer Night's Dream* once. And I enjoyed it. Everybody falling in love with the wrong person, but then it all worked out in the end."

"You prefer a happy ending?"

"Absolutely," she told him. "I like it when it all works out. That doesn't happen often enough in real life."

"I like trucks!" Suddenly, Trev was over his shyness and back in the game.

Rule turned to him. "And do you like balls?"

"Red balls! Yes!"

"Good. Because that truck and that ball over there beneath the table? They're for you."

Trevor looked away again—too much attention, apparently, from this intriguing stranger.

Sydney said, "Tell Rule 'thank you.'"

"Thank you, Roo," Trev parroted obediently, still looking away, the soft curve of his round cheek turned down.

But Rule wasn't looking away. He seemed honestly taken with her little boy. Her heart did more wild and lovely acrobatics, just to look at the two of them, Rule watching Trev, Trev not quite able to meet this new guy's eyes.

Then Rule said, "Knock, knock."

Trev didn't look, but he did say, "Who's there?"

"Wanda."

Trev peeked, looked away, peeked again. "Wanda who?"

"Wanda cookie?"

Slowly, Trev turned and looked straight at Rule. "Cookie! Yes! Please!"

Rule actually produced an animal cracker from the pocket of his beautifully made lightweight jacket. He slid a questioning glance at Sydney. At her nod, he handed the cookie over.

"Grrr. Lion!" announced Trev and popped the lion-shaped cookie in his mouth. "Yum." He chewed and swallowed. "Thank you very much—Orange! Banana! Knock, knock."

Rule gamely went through the whole joke with him twice. Trev never got the punch line right, but that didn't have any effect on his delight in the process.

"It never ends," Lani said with a sigh. But then she grinned. "And you know we wouldn't have it any other way."

"All done," Trev told them. "Get down, Mama. Play trucks!"

So Sydney wiped his hands and face with a damp cloth and swung him down from his booster seat. He went straight for Rule. "Roo. Come. We play trucks!"

"It appears you have been summoned," Sydney said.

"Nothing could please me more—or *almost* nothing." The teasing heat in his glance hinted that whatever it was that pleased him more had something to do with her. Very likely with kissing her, an activity that pleased her a bunch, too.

He tossed his jacket across the family room sofa and went over and got down on the floor with Trev, who gathered all his trucks together so they could roll them around making *vrooming* noises and crash them into each other. Sydney and Lani cleared the table and loaded the dishwasher. And soon enough, it was time to head for the neighborhood park. Lani begged off, so it was just the three of them. Since the small park was only a couple of blocks away, they walked, Trev between Sydney and Rule, holding both their hands.

Trev was an outgoing child, although he was usually pretty reserved around new people. It took him a while to get comfortable with someone. But apparently, with Rule, he was over his shyness after those first few moments at the breakfast table.

Trev chattered away at him as they strolled past the pretty, gracious homes and the wide, inviting lawns. "I walk fast, Roo. I strong! I happy!"

Rule agreed that he was very fast, and so strong—and wasn't it great that he was happy? "I'm happy, too," Rule said, and shared a speaking glance with Sydney.

Trev looked up at them, at Rule, then at Sydney, then back at Rule again. "Mama's happy, too!" he crowed. "Knock, knock!"

"Who's there?" asked Rule. And then he went through the endless loop of the joke two more times.

They stayed at the park for three hours. Sydney watched for a sign that Rule might be getting tired of pushing Trev on the swings, of sitting with him on the spinner, of playing seesaw—Trev and Sydney on one end, Rule on the other.

But Rule seemed to love every minute of it. He got down and crawled through the concrete tunnels with Trev, heedless of his designer trousers, laughing as Trev scuttled ahead of him calling out, "You can't catch me, I too fast!" Trev popped out of the tunnel.

Rule was right behind him. Rule growled, playing it scary. Trev let out a shriek of fear and delight.

Finally, at a little after eleven, Trev announced, "Okay. All done." And he was. All the fun had worn him out.

The walk back to the house took a little longer than the stroll over there. When Trevor was tired, he dragged his feet and kept trying to sit down instead of moving forward.

But they got him there, eventually. Lani took over, hustling him to the bathroom to change him out of the diaper she'd put on him for the park and back into the lighter-weight training pants he wore most of the time now.

Alone with Rule for the first time since their kiss at the front door, Sydney said, "You were wonderful with him."

His gaze held hers. She did love the way he looked at her—as though he couldn't get enough of just staring into her eyes. He said, "It wasn't difficult, not in the least. I enjoyed every minute of it." And then he added in that charming, formal way of his, "Thank you for inviting me, Sydney."

"It was my pleasure—and clearly, Trev's, too. Had enough?"

He frowned. "Are you saying you would like for me to go now?"

She laughed. "No way. I'm just giving you an out, in case you've had enough of crashing trucks and knock-knock jokes for one day."

"I want to stay, if you don't mind."

"Of course I don't mind." Now her heart was doing cartwheels. "Not in the least."

Yes, all right. Maybe she should be more cautious. Put the brakes on a little. But she didn't *want* to put the brakes on. She was having a great time and if he didn't want to go, well, why should she feel she should send him away?

He could stay for lunch if he wanted, stay for dinner.

Stay…indefinitely. That would be just fine with her. Every moment she was with him only convinced her that she wanted the *next* moment with him. And the one after that. Something about him had her throwing all her usual caution to the winds.

Was she in for a rude awakening? She just didn't think so. Every moment she was with Rule only made her more certain that he was the real deal: a great guy who liked her—a lot. A great guy who liked children, too, a guy who actually enjoyed spending the morning playing in the park with her and her little boy.

As long as he gave her no reason to doubt her confidence in him, well, she *wouldn't* doubt him. It was as simple as that.

He said, "Perhaps we could take Trevor and Lani to lunch?"

"I wish. But no. Trev's going to need to eat right away, and since he's been on the go since early this morning, he's probably going to be fussy. So we'll get some food down him and then put him to bed. His nap will last at least a couple of hours. You sure you won't mind just hanging around here for the afternoon?"

"There's nothing I would rather do than hang around here with you and your son." He said it so matter-of-factly, and she knew he was sincere.

"I'm glad." They shared a nod of perfect understanding.

As Sydney had predicted, Trev was cranky during lunch, but he did pack away a big bowl of chicken and rice. He went right to sleep when Sydney put him in bed.

Then she and Rule raided the refrigerator and carried their lunch of cheese, crackers and grapes out to the backyard. They sat under an oak not far from the pool and he told her more about his family, about how his older brother

Max's wife had tragically drowned in a water-skiing accident two years before, leaving Max with a broken heart and two little children to raise on his own.

"They were so happy together, Max and Sophia," Rule said, his eyes full of shadows right then. "They found each other very young, and knew they would marry when they were both hardly more than children. It's been terrible for him, learning to live without her."

"I can't even imagine how that must be for him. I've always envied people who find true love early and only want a chance to have a family, to grow old side by side. It's just completely wrong that your brother and his wife didn't get a whole lifetime of happiness together."

They were sitting in a pair of cushioned chaises, the platter of cheese and fruit on the low teak table between them. He held out his hand to her. She took it without hesitation and let him pull her over to his chaise.

He wrapped an arm around her, using his other hand to tip her chin up. They shared a slow, sweet kiss. And then he spoke against her softly parted lips. "I love the taste of your lips, the feel of your body pressed close to mine...."

She reached up, touched the silky black hair at his temple. A miracle, to be here with him, like this. To be free to touch him at will, to be the one *he* wanted to touch. "Oh, Rule. What's happening with us?"

He kissed her again, a possessive kiss, hard and quick. "You don't know?"

"I...think I do. But I've waited so long to meet someone like you. It almost seems too good to be true."

"You're trembling." He held her closer.

She laughed, a torn little sound. "Not so prickly now, huh?"

"Come here, relax..." He stretched out in the chaise and pulled her with him, so she lay facing him, tucked against his side, his big arms around her, his cheek touching her hair. A lovely breeze came up, stirring the warm afternoon air, making it feel cool and comfortable beneath the oak tree. "Don't be afraid. I would never hurt you. I'm only grateful that I've found you, at last."

"So, then," she teased, "you lied yesterday when you said you weren't looking for me."

"Can you forgive me?"

She took a moment, pretended to think it over and finally whispered, "I'll try."

"Good. Because I've been looking for you all my life. And now that I have you in my arms, I never want to let you go."

"I want to be with you, too." She laid her hand against his chest, felt the steady, strong beating of his heart. "And I'm not afraid," she added. And then she sighed. "Well, okay. That's not so. I *am* afraid—at least a little."

"Because of those fools Ryan and Peter?"

She nodded. "I haven't had good luck with men."

He kissed her hair. "Maybe not."

"Definitely not."

"Until now," he corrected her.

She tipped her head back and met those shining dark eyes and…well, she believed him. She honestly did. "Until now," she repeated, softly, but firmly, too.

"Come out with me tonight. Let me come for you. We'll have dinner, go dancing."

It was Lani's night out. But Sydney had more than one sitter she could call. "I would love to."

Trev woke at a little before three, completely refreshed and ready to play some more.

Rule was only too happy to oblige him. Together, they built a wobbly Duplo castle—which Trev took great delight in toppling to the floor the moment it was finished.

Then the three of them took the red ball outside to Trev's fenced play area and rolled the ball around. Finally, inside again, Rule and Trev played more trucks until Lani announced it was time for Trev's dinner.

The man amazed Sydney. He seemed completely content to spend hours entertaining her toddler. He honestly did seem to love children and Sydney couldn't help thinking that he would make a wonderful father.

Rule called his driver at five-twenty-five.

"Bye, Roo. Come back. See me soon!" Trev called, pausing to wave as Lani herded him toward the stairs for his bath.

"Goodbye Trevor."

"We play trucks!" Trev started up the stairs in his usual way, using both hands and feet.

"Yes." Rule nodded, watching his progress upward. "Trucks. Absolutely."

Trev turned to Lani and started his knock-knock joke as he and Lani disappeared on the upper landing. The moment they were out of sight, Sydney moved into Rule's open arms.

They shared a kiss and then he took her hand and brushed his lips across the back of it. "Your son is amazing. So smart. Just like his mom."

She answered playfully, "And don't forget strong. Trev is very strong. Just ask him."

"Yes, I remember. Very strong and very loud when he wants to be—and I'm honored that you shared the story of his birth so honestly with me. And that you've trusted me enough to tell me about those idiots Ryan and Peter."

"I think it's better," she said, "to be honest and forthright."

"So do I." Something happened in his eyes—a shadow of something. Uneasiness? Concern?

Her pulse beat faster. "Rule. What is it? What's the matter?"

"I'm afraid I have a confession to make."

Now her pulse was racing dizzyingly fast. And she felt sick, her stomach churning. So, then. He really *was* too good to be true. "Tell me," she said softly, but not gently. She couldn't hide the thread of steel that connected the two simple words.

"Remember how I told you I admired my mother?"

She wasn't getting it. "This confession is about your mother?"

He touched her cheek, a light touch that made her heart ache. She really liked him. So very much. And now she just knew it was all going wrong. He said, "No, it's not about my mother. Not essentially."

"What do you mean? It is, or it isn't."

"Sydney, I admire my mother for any number of reasons. And I revere her as the ruler of my country."

She was sure she must have misunderstood him. "Excuse me? Your mother rules your country?"

"My mother is Adrienne II, Sovereign Princess of Montedoro. And my father is His Serene Highness Evan, Prince Consort of Montedoro."

"Okay. You'll have to say that again. I'm sure I misunderstood. Sovereign Princess, you said?"

"Yes. My mother holds the throne. My father is Prince Consort and my brother Maximilian is the heir apparent. Before Max had his son and daughter, I was second in line to the throne."

Chapter Four

Sydney gaped up at him. "A prince. You're telling me that you're a prince? And not just as in, 'a prince of a guy,' but a *real* prince? A…royal prince?"

He chuckled. "My darling, yes. That is, more or less, what I'm telling you."

"Um. More or less?"

"The truth is that Montedoro is ruled by a prince, not a king. And, in terms of his or her title, a ruling prince is said to have a throne, but not a crown. And only those who are the children or grandchildren of ruling kings or queens, or are the spouses of royalty, are given the honorific of royal. However, in the sense that 'royal' means 'ruling,' yes. I am of the royal family of Montedoro, or more correctly, the princely family. And even though we are not addressed as royal, both our family coat of arms and our individual monograms contain the image of a crown."

She was still gaping. "I don't think I understood a word you just said."

He frowned. "I see your point. Perhaps that was more information than you require at the moment."

A prince. A prince of Montedoro. Should she have known this? "Wait. Evan Bravo. I remember now. Your dad was in the movies, right?"

He nodded. "It was a big story in all the newspapers and tabloids of the day. My mother married a film actor and he returned with her to Montedoro, where they had many children and lived happily ever after." He gave a wry smile. "Sydney, you look pale. Would you like to sit down?"

"No. No, really. I'm fine. Just fine."

"Perhaps you would like to see my diplomatic passport…."

"Ohmigod. No. Really. I believe you. I do." Still, she couldn't help looking around nervously, half expecting Ashton Kutcher and the *Punk'd* camera crew to be making their appearance any second now. She turned her gaze up to him again and tried to look stern. "You should have told me."

"I know." He did seem honestly contrite. "But the moment never seemed right. I wanted you to know me, at least a little, before we got into all of that."

"Last night. At the Mansion. The nervous host…"

"Yes. I'm staying there. He knows who I am." He took her chin, tipped it up to him. "But none of that matters."

"Rule. Of course it matters."

"Only if you let it. To me, what matters most of all, more than anything, is this…" And he lowered his dark head and claimed her lips.

And by the time that kiss was through, she was inclined

to agree with him. "Oh, Rule…" She clung to him, feeling light-headed and slightly weak in the knees.

"I'll leave you now," he said ruefully, stroking her hair, his eyes full of tenderness and understanding. She thought how crazy she was for him—and how she would look him up on Google the minute he was out the door. One side of his mouth curled up in the gorgeous half smile that totally enchanted her. He said, "You'll have time to look me up on the internet before I come to collect you for the evening."

She shook her head. "You know me too well. How is that possible? We only met yesterday."

"Forgive me. For taking so long to tell you…"

"I'll consider forgiving you as soon as my head stops spinning."

"One last kiss…"

She gave it. She simply could not resist him—and beyond that, she didn't *want* to resist him.

When he lifted his head that time, he released her. She opened the door and watched him jog down the front walk to his waiting limousine.

As soon as the long, black car disappeared from sight, she shut the front door and went upstairs to get with Lani about her plans for the evening.

She found her friend on her knees filling the tub. Trev sat on the bathroom floor in his training pants, putting a new face on his Mr. Potato Head.

"Lani…"

"Hmm?" Lani tested the water, turned the hot water tap up a little.

"Just wondering if you were going out tonight?"

"Nope, I'm staying in. And yes, I'd be happy to watch Trev."

"Wonderful." So that was settled.

"Mama, see?" Trev held up Mr. Potato Head, whose

big, red lips were now above his moustache and who had only one eye in the middle of his forehead. She bent down and kissed him. He asked, "Mama read a story?"

"After your bath, I promise."

"O-*kay!*" He removed Mr. Potato Head's red hat and reached for a blue plastic ear.

Sydney kissed him again and then ran back downstairs to her office off the foyer. She kept a PC in there and she figured she had maybe twenty minutes before Trev finished his bath and would come looking for her.

Sydney was good at research, and she knew how to get a lot of information quickly. By the time Trev came bouncing down the stairs and demanded her attention again, she intended to know a whole lot more about Rule.

She found pages and pages of references to the courtship and marriage of Rule's father and mother.

Evan Bravo was born in San Antonio, second of seven sons, to James and Elizabeth Bravo. Several sources cited early estrangement from his overbearing father. Determined to make his mark in Hollywood, Evan Bravo moved West at the age of eighteen. Talent and luck were on his side. He was never a big star, but at twenty-five, he won a Golden Globe and a Best Supporting Actor Oscar for his portrayal of a charming but crooked L.A. detective in a big-budget box office hit called *L.A. Undercover.* Then he met Princess Adrienne of Montedoro. There ensued a whirlwind courtship, a fabulous palace wedding—and celebrating in the streets of the whole of Montedoro when their first child, Maximilian, was born. Princess Adrienne, as the last of her line, was expected to provide her country with an heir and a spare and then some. She did exactly that, bearing eight more children in the succeeding eleven years.

Sydney read the story of the tragic death of Maximilian's wife, Sophia—drowning while water-skiing, just as Rule had already told her. Also, she learned that third-born Alexander had been captured by terrorists in Afghanistan and held prisoner for four years, until somehow engineering a miraculous and daring escape only a few months ago.

Prince Rule, she learned, had obtained his degree in America, from Princeton. He was the businessman of the family, the glamorous bachelor, big in international trade, and was known to champion and generously contribute to several worthy causes. Over the years, his name had been linked with any number of gorgeous models and actresses, but those relationships had never seemed to last very long. Some sources claimed that he was "expected" to marry his longtime friend from childhood, HRH Liliana, aka Princess Lili, heir presumptive to the throne of the island state of Alagonia. However, no actual announcement of an engagement had so far been made.

Sydney went looking for images of the princess in question and found several. Liliana of Alagonia was blonde, blue-eyed and as beautiful as a princess in a fairy tale.

Sudden apprehension had Sydney catching her lower lip between her teeth and shifting in her swivel chair. Princess Lili, huh? Rule had never mentioned this supposed "childhood friend." Tonight, she would definitely have a few questions for him.

"Mama, read me books!"

Sydney looked up from the computer to find her little boy and Lani standing in the open doorway to the front hall.

Lani said, "Sorry to interrupt, but he hasn't forgotten that you said you would read to him."

"And I will, absolutely."

Trev, all pink and sweet from his bath, wearing his Captain America pajamas, marched over and tugged on her arm. "Come *on,* Mama."

Further research on Princess Liliana would have to wait. Sydney swung him into her arms and carried him upstairs where he'd already picked out the books he wanted her to read to him.

Later, after he was in bed, as she hurried to get ready for the evening, she told Lani that Rule was a Montedoran prince.

"Whoa. And I didn't even curtsy when you introduced me to him."

"It's a little late to worry about protocol." Sydney leaned close to the mirror as she put on her makeup. "Which is fine with me."

"What would it be like to marry a prince?" Lani wondered out loud.

"Did I mention marriage? We've only just met."

"But it's already serious between you two, I can tell. Isn't it?"

Sydney set down her powder brush and turned to her friend. "Yeah. I think it is—and I may be late coming home tonight." Unless Rule confessed that he intended to marry the lovely Princess Lili. In that case, she would be coming home early, crying on Lani's shoulder and swearing off men for the next decade, at least.

"Oh, Syd…" Lani grabbed her and gave her a hug. And then she took Sydney by the shoulders and held her away. "You look wonderful. I love that dress. It brings out the color of your eyes." Lani sighed. "Enjoy every moment."

"I will." Sydney smoothed her hair and tried to banish any thought of pretty Princess Lili from her mind.

Rule arrived in his limousine at eight.

Once on the inside of the tinted-glass windows, Sidney

saw there were two men in the front seat: the driver in his dark livery and chauffeur's cap and also a thick-necked military-looking guy with a crew cut, who had a Bluetooth device in his ear and wore sunglasses even though it was nearly dark.

Sydney leaned close to Rule, drawn to his strength and his warmth and the fine, subtle scent of the aftershave he wore. She whispered, "Don't tell me. You keep the Secret Service on retainer."

He gave a shrug. "Effective security is something of a necessity. It's a sad fact of life in this modern age."

They went to another really wonderful restaurant, where they were once again ushered into a private room.

She waited until they were served the main course before she brought up the subject that had been bothering her. "So tell me about Princess Liliana of Alagonia."

He sent her a wry sort of smile. "I see you've been checking up on me."

"Did you think I wouldn't?"

"I absolutely knew that you would."

She told him exactly what she'd learned. "Rumor has it that you and the princess are 'expected' to marry."

He held her gaze. "You should know better than to put your faith in rumors."

"You're hedging, Rule." She sat back in her chair and took a drink from her water goblet.

"Lili's eight years younger than I am. She's like one of my little sisters."

"But she's *not* your sister—little or otherwise."

"All right, enough." He said it flatly. "I am not going to marry Liliana, Sydney. We are not affianced. I have never proposed marriage to her."

She took a wild guess. "But *she* wants to marry *you*. It's *assumed* that you will marry her."

He didn't look away. But his eyes were definitely guarded now. "She…looks up to me."

Did he imagine she would wimp out and leave it at that? Hah. "Just say it. She *does* want to marry you."

He sat back in his chair, too. And he looked at her so strangely, so distantly. When he spoke, his voice was cold. "I would not presume to speak for Liliana. She's a sweet and lovely person. And yes, if I married Lili, it would be considered a brilliant match, one that would strengthen the bonds between our two countries."

She said sharply, "So, then you *should* marry her."

"Not only that." His eyes were so dark right then, dark and full of secrets, it seemed to her. Suddenly, she was thinking that she didn't know him at all, that this brief, magical time she'd shared with him had truly been just that: magic, not reality. Nothing more than a beautiful, impossible fantasy. That the truth was coming out now and the fantasy was over.

So soon. Way too soon…

He spoke again. "Do you recall how I told you I had to marry by my thirty-third birthday?"

"Yes."

"Did you think I was only teasing you?"

"Well, I thought you meant that there was pressure in your family, as there is in a lot of families, for you to settle down, start providing your parents with grandchildren, all that."

"It's considerably more than just pressure. It's the law."

She looked at him sideways. "Now you really are kidding."

"On the contrary, I'm completely serious. My country was once a French protectorate. And France…casts a long shadow, as they say. We have signed any number of treaties with France, treaties wherein the French promise to guarantee Montedoro's sovereignty."

As a lawyer, she knew what he was getting at. "And the simple fact that another country is in a position to guarantee your sovereignty is…problematic?"

"Precisely. Although my family is officially in charge of succession, the French government must approve the next ruling prince or princess. There is even a stipulation that, should the throne go vacant, Montedoro will revert to a French protectorate. That is why we have a law designed to ensure that no prince will shirk his—or her—obligation to produce potential heirs to the throne. Montedoran princes and princesses are required to marry before their thirty-third birthday or be stripped of all titles and income. I will be thirty-three on June twenty-fourth."

"Two and a half months from now."

"Yes," he said softly.

Sydney was certain of it then. No matter what he'd said a few moments ago, he did intend to marry the lovely Lili. This thing between the two of them was only…what? A last fling before his ingrained sense of duty finally kicked in, before he went back to Montedoro and tied the knot with the pretty blonde princess he'd known since childhood—and then got to work having a bunch of little princes with her.

And why, oh, why, if he just *had* to have a final fling, couldn't he have chosen someone else? Sydney was a hard-driving, overworked single mom and the last thing she needed was a whirlwind romance with a man who was planning to marry someone else. Plus, she'd already suffered through more than her share of disappointments when it came to the male gender, thank you very much.

Bottom line? She really did not have time for this crap.

And she wanted desperately to be furious with him.

But she wasn't. The whole situation only made her miserable. She longed to put her face in her hands and burst into tears.

But no—in fact, *hell* no. She was an O'Shea and an O'Shea was tougher than that. No way was she letting him see her break down and cry. Instead, coolly, she advised, "Don't you think you're cutting it a little close?"

"More than a little. And the truth is I *have* considered asking Liliana to be my wife."

Surprise, surprise. "So what's stopped you?"

"No man wants to marry a woman he thinks of as a sister. Not even if she is a fine person, not even to keep his inheritance, not even for the good of his country. And so I've hesitated. I've put off making my move."

"Rule. I have to say it. You need to stop dithering and get with the program."

That slow smile curved his beautiful mouth. "A prince does not *dither*."

"Call it what you want. Looks like dithering to me."

"If I *was* dithering, Sydney—and I'm not admitting that I was—I'm not dithering anymore."

She cast a pained glance toward the ceiling. "Okay. You lost me there."

"I'm absolutely certain now that Liliana will never be my bride. In one split second, everything changed for me."

She didn't get where this was going. She really didn't. And she told herself firmly that she didn't care. What mattered was that it was over between them. It had to be, she saw that now. Over and done before it even really got started. "In one split second," she parroted with a heavy dose of sarcasm. "So…the realization that you're definitely not marrying dear Princess Lili hit you like a lightning bolt, huh?"

"No."

"I'm not following you."

"It's quite simple. While everything changed for me in an instant, it took a little longer than that for me to accept that marriage to Lili had become impossible."

"I have no idea what you're telling me."

"*That* happened after lunch yesterday."

"*What* happened?"

"You said goodbye and got into your car and drove away. I stood and watched you leave and tried to consider the concept of never seeing you again. And I couldn't do that. Right then, marrying Lili became impossible."

"So there was no lightning bolt, after all."

"Of course there was a lightning bolt. It struck the moment I saw you, striding into Macy's, indomitable. Unyielding. Ready to take on the world. At that moment, Liliana was the last thing on my mind. Right then, all I could think of was you."

Sydney reached for her untouched glass of wine and took an extra-large gulp of it. She set the glass down with care. "Well, I…" Her voice had a definite wobble to it. She drew in a slow, steadying breath. "You're not marrying the princess. You're sure about that?"

"Yes. Absolutely certain."

"You mean that? You really mean that?"

"I do, Sydney. With all my heart."

"Don't mess with me, Rule."

"I promise you, I'm not."

Her throat felt tight, so tight it ached. She gulped to relax it a little. "Okay," she said softly, at last. "You're not marrying the princess, after all."

"I'm so glad we're finally clear on that." His voice was gentle, indulgent. "You've hardly touched your food. Is it unsatisfactory?"

"Oh, no. It's fine. Really. Delicious." She picked up her fork again.

They ate in silence for a while.

Finally, he spoke. "I like you in that emerald-green satin. Almost as much as I like you in red."

"Thank you."

"I still want to take you dancing."

She sipped her wine again, suddenly as certain as he seemed to be. About the two of them. About…everything. Whatever happened in the end, she wanted this night with him. She wanted it so much. She wanted *him.* "I have a suggestion."

"And I am always open to suggestion. Especially if the suggestion is coming from you."

"Take me back to the Mansion, Rule. Take me to your room. We can dance there."

Chapter Five

His room was one of the two Terrace Suites on the Mansion's top floor. It was over thirteen hundred square feet of pure luxury.

There was champagne waiting for them in the sitting room—champagne and a crystal bowl full of Montedoran oranges. He took off his jacket and tie and they sat on the sofa, sipping the champagne. She slipped off her shoes as he peeled an orange for her.

"Oh, this so good," she said, savoring the ruby-red sections, one by one. They tasted like no orange she'd ever had before.

He bent close and kissed her then, a slow kiss that started out light and so tender and deepened until she was slightly breathless—scratch that. More than slightly. A lot more than slightly. "Very sweet," he said when he lifted his mouth from hers. He wasn't talking about the orange.

She only gazed at him, her heart beating in a slow, deep,

exciting way, her body warm and lazy, her eyelids suddenly heavy.

The sofa was nice and fat and comfortable. She considered stretching out on the cushions, reaching for him as she went down, pulling him with her, so they were stretched out together.

But he set his half-full flute aside and picked up the remote on the coffee table. The large flat screen above a bow-fronted cabinet flared to life. Before she could ask him why he suddenly wanted to watch *Lockup,* he changed the channel to a music station. A slow romantic song was playing.

"Come." He offered his hand and they rose together. They went out to the terrace, where the lights of downtown Dallas glittered in the balmy darkness of the April night.

They danced. It was like a dream, a dream come to life, just the two of them, holding each other, swaying to the music, not saying anything.

Not needing to speak.

Then he put a finger under her chin and she looked up into his eyes, into the light shining within that velvet darkness. She tried to remind herself that she still wasn't sure about the whole love at first sight thing, didn't really believe that you could meet someone and know instantly that here was the person you wanted to spend the rest of your life with. It took time to know another person, time to learn his ways, time to discover if there really was any chance for the relationship in the long-term.

But when Rule looked at her, well, she believed that *he* believed. And his belief was powerful. His belief made her want to believe, too.

"I see you," he whispered, and she couldn't help smiling. He reminded her of Trev again, Trev playing peekaboo: *I see you, Mama. I see you, I do.* "I know," he said. "It sounds silly when I say it. It sounds self-evident. And not important in the least."

"I didn't say that. It was only, for a moment, you reminded me of Trev."

"Ah." He searched her eyes some more. "Well, good, then. I'm pleased if I make you think of him. And it *is* important that I see you. I see in you all that I've been looking for, though I didn't even realize I *was* looking until yesterday. I see in you the best things, Sydney. The things that matter. I see that with you I can be a better man, and a happier man. I see that you will always interest me. That you will challenge me. I want to…give you everything. I want to spend my life making sure you have it all, whatever makes you happy, whatever your heart desires."

She searched his astonishingly gorgeous face. "You are tempting me, you know that?"

"I hope so." He brushed one soft, warm kiss against her lips, a kiss that lingered like a tender brand on her skin even after he had lifted his head to gaze down at her once more. "I want to tempt you, Sydney. Because I've never met anyone like you. You amaze me. I want to be with you. I never want to let you go." He kissed her again, an endless kiss, as they danced. His mouth was so soft, not like the rest of him at all. His mouth was hot and supple and his tongue eased past the trembling barrier of her lips, sliding hot and knowing, over the edges of her teeth, across the top of her tongue, and then beneath it.

She felt…lost. Lost in a lovely, delicious kind of way. She didn't know where she was going. And Sydney Gabrielle O'Shea *always* knew where she was going. She'd always kept her focus, because she had to. Who would keep her on track if she didn't? Her parents were gone without her even knowing them. And then, too soon, so was her strong, steady grandmother. The men to whom she gave her trust were not dependable.

There was only Lani, her true, forever friend. And then there was Trevor to light up her days.

And now this. Now Rule.

At last. Long after she'd been sure there would never be a man for her. Her doubts, her hesitations were falling away. *He* was peeling them away. With his tenderness and his understanding, with his honesty and his frank desire for her.

Who had she been kidding? She *could* believe in love at first sight. Like her beloved grandmother before her, she *did* believe in love at first sight.

As long as it was love at first sight with a certain man. With the *right* man. The one she could trust. The one she could count on to be there when she needed someone to lean on. The one who honestly seemed to like everything about her, even her prickly nature and her sometimes sharp tongue.

Maybe that wasn't so surprising, that he had no issues with her strength and determination, with her ambition and her drive. After all, she had no issues with him— or whenever she did have issues, he would patiently and calmly put them to rest.

And she certainly liked the feelings he roused in her. The excitement, the desire. And the unaccustomed trust. Every time she felt her doubts rising—about him, about the impossibility of this thing between them—he stepped right up and banished them. He kept proving to her that he was exactly the man he seemed to be, exactly the man she'd never dared to dream she might someday find.

They danced some more, still kissing. She wrapped her arms around his neck, threaded her fingers up into the warm silk of his dark, dark hair. He lifted his head, but only to slant his mouth the other way and continue to kiss her, endlessly, perfectly. She sighed and lifted closer to him, loving the feel of her breasts against his hard chest, of her body and his body, touching so lightly, striking off sparks.

Sparks of promise, sparks of building desire.

He broke the kiss. She sighed at the loss. But then he only lowered his mouth again and kissed her cheek and then her temple. He caught her earlobe between his teeth, worried it so gently.

She made a soft, pleasured sound and pressed her body even closer to him, wanting to melt right into him, wanting to become a part of him, somehow—his body, her body, one and the same. He went on kissing her—his wonderful lips gliding over the curve of her jaw, down the side of her neck.

Her green dress had spaghetti straps. With a lazy finger, he pushed the left strap out of his way and kissed her shoulder, a long, lingering kiss. She felt his tongue, licking her, sending hot shards of pleasure radiating out along her skin. And then his teeth…oh, those teeth. He nipped her, but carefully, tenderly.

They had stopped dancing. They stood in the shadow of a potted palm, in a corner of the terrace. He eased the side of her dress down. She felt the sultry night air touch her breast.

And then he kissed her there. He took her nipple into his mouth and sucked it, rhythmically. He whispered her name against her skin.

She cradled his head, close—closer, her fingers buried in his hair. The heat of him was all around her, and down low, she was already liquid, weak, yearning. A silver thread of pure delight drew down through the core of her, into the womanly heart of her, from her breast, where he kissed her endlessly. He drew on her eager flesh in a slow, tempting rhythm, making her bare toes curl on the terrace flagstones. She moaned, held him closer, murmured his name on a slow, surrendering sigh.

And then he lifted his head. She blinked, dazed, and gazed up at him, feeling like a sleepwalker, wakened from the sweetest dream.

"Inside." He bent close again, caught her lower lip between his teeth, licked it, let it go. "Let's go in…"

She trembled, yearning. Her nipple was drawn so tight and hard, it ached. It ached in such a lovely, thrilling way. "Yes. Oh, yes…" And she tried to pull her strap back up, to cover herself.

"Don't." He caught her hand, stilled it, then brought her fingers to his lips and kissed them. "Leave it." His voice was rough and infinitely tender, both at once. "Leave it bare…" He bent, kissed her breast again, but only briefly that time. "So beautiful…"

And then he swept her up as though she weighed nothing and carried her through the open door into the sitting room, pausing only to turn and slide the door shut. A new song began.

He stopped in midstride. Their gazes locked. "'Lady in Red,'" he whispered.

"Not tonight," she whispered.

"It doesn't matter, whether you happen to be wearing red or not. To me, this song is you. This song is *yours*. You're my lady in red…"

"Oh, Rule." She touched his cheek with the back of her hand. His fine tanned skin was slightly rough with the beginnings of his dark beard, slightly rough and so very warm.

He took her mouth again, in a hard, hot kiss. She surrendered to that kiss. She let him sweep her away with the heat of it. She was seduced by the carnal need in it.

And he was moving again, carrying her through the door that led to his bedroom. The bed was turned back. He bent to put her down on the soft white sheets, so carefully, as though she might break, as though she was infinitely precious to him.

He laid her down and he rose to his height again. Swiftly, without ceremony, he took off his shirt, undid his belt, took down his trousers and his briefs. He sat and removed his shoes and socks. And then he rose once more to toss everything carelessly onto the bedside chair. The view of his magnificent body from behind stole every last wisp of breath from her body.

And then he turned to face her again. His eyes were molten.

Naked. He was naked and he was as beautiful—*more* so—than she had even imagined, the muscles of his chest and arms and belly so sharply defined. His legs were strong and straight and powerful, dusted with black hair, black hair that grew dense and curly where his big thighs joined.

The proof that he wanted her jutted out hard and proud. She dragged in a ragged breath and let it out with care.

And then he came down to her.

More kisses. Long, deep kisses, until she was pliant and more eager than ever. Until she whimpered with need. He took down the other strap of her dress and he kissed her right breast so slowly and deliciously, with the same erotic care he had lavished on the left.

By the time he eased her to her side facing away from him and took the zipper of her dress down, she was ready. For him. For the two of them. For whatever he might do to her, do *with* her. Ready for tonight. And tomorrow night. And all the nights to come.

With him. Beside him. Always.

Was this a dream? If it was, she prayed she might never wake up.

Tucked close behind her, his front to her back, he eased the dress down, gently, carefully, making the simple act of peeling the fabric away from her body into a caress. A long, perfect thrilling caress.

She lifted enough that he could take the dress down over her thighs and off. She wore no bra. She didn't need one.

He cupped her breasts, one and then the other, his hand engulfing them. He whispered that they were beautiful. "Delicate," he said. "Perfect."

She believed him. Seduced by the magic of his knowing touch, she had relinquished everything, even the wisdom of a little healthy skepticism. She believed all the things he whispered to her. She believed every last rough-tender, arousing word. Every knowing, skilled caress. He touched her face and she smelled the tart sweetness of blood oranges on his fingers. And it seemed to her that the scent was his scent—sweet, tempting, ruby-red.

His hand moved downward, over her breasts again and lower, along her belly. She gasped as his fingers eased under the elastic of her panties.

He found the feminine heart of her. He whispered that she felt like heaven there, so wet and hot and slick for him. He stroked her, a touch that quickly set every last nerve she possessed ablaze. Her whole body seemed to be humming with excitement, with electricity, with heat. She was liquid and burning and close to the brink.

She wanted it to last, wanted the climb to the top to go on forever, wanted to hold off on completion until she had him within her. But in no time, she was shuddering, going over the edge, moaning his name, working her hips against his fingers—oh, those fingers of his: magic, just…magic. She cried out.

He whispered, "Yes, like that. Just like that."

And then she was sailing out from the peak, into the wide open, drifting slowly, slowly down into her body again, her body that had his body wrapped around it.

"You feel…so good," she murmured, lazy. And she took his hand and tucked it tenderly close to her heart.

But he wasn't through yet.

Which was totally fine with her. She could go on like this, touching him, *being* touched by him, forever.

He was moving, shifting her onto her back, resettling himself close against her side. She sighed and let him do as he wished with her. She was drifting, satisfied, deeply content, on the borderline of sleep.

"Sydney…"

Reluctantly, still lost in the echoes of so many beautiful sensations, she opened her eyes. He was up an elbow, gazing down at her, his eyes liquid, black as the middle of a very dark night.

She reached up, touched his mouth. "So soft. You're such a good kisser…"

He bent near again, kissed her with that mouth of his, her fingers still on his lips, so he kissed them, too. "Sydney…" He kissed her name against her mouth, against her fingers.

"Mmm." She eased her hand away, parted her lips, took his tongue inside. "Mmm…" Maybe she wasn't so sleepy after all. She clasped his hard shoulder, loving the rock-like contour of it, and then she let her hand glide around to his strong nape. She caressed the amazing musculature of his broad back. "I just want to touch you…"

He didn't object. He went on kissing her, as she indulged herself. She wanted to touch every inch of him—his back, his powerful arms, his fine, strong chest. He had a perfect little happy trail and she did what a woman tends to do—she followed it downward.

And when her fingers closed around him, she took great satisfaction in the low groan he let out. She drank in that groan like wine.

Was there ever a guy like this? She doubted it. Every part of him was beautiful, her fairy-tale prince made flesh.

She closed her eyes again and reveled in the feel of him. She wanted…everything from him. All of him. Now.

She whispered in a shattered sort of wonder, against his beautiful lips. "Oh, Rule. Now. Please, now…" And she urged him to come even closer, all the way closer, opening her thighs for him, pulling him onto her, so eager, so hungry.

More than ready.

"Wait…" He breathed the word against her parted lips.

"What?" She moaned in frustration. "No. I don't want to wait."

"Sydney…" He took his mouth from hers.

And again, she lifted her heavy eyelids and gazed up at him, impatient. Questioning. "What?"

He gave her one of those beautiful, wry, perfect smiles of his. And he tipped his dark head toward his raised hand. She tore her gaze away from all that manly beauty to see what he held.

A condom.

"Oops." She felt her cheeks flush even redder than they already were. She let out a ragged sigh. "I can't believe it. I didn't even think about that. How could I not think of that? I'm never that foolish, that irresponsible."

His shining midnight gaze adored her—and indulged

her. "It's all right. There are two of us, after all. Only one of us had to remember. And I haven't minded at all seeing you so carried away that you didn't even think about using protection."

"I *should* have thought of it."

He shook his head, slowly, lazily, that tempting smile of his a seduction in itself. "You are so beautiful when you're carried away." His smile, his tender words, the hot-candy sound of his voice. She was seduced by every aspect of him.

Seduced and loving it.

Still, she tried to hold out against him. "I'm not beautiful, Rule. We both know that."

"You *are* beautiful. And please give me your hand and stop arguing with me."

Really, the guy was irresistible. She held out her hand.

He put the little pouch in the center of her palm. "Do the honors?"

She laughed, a soft, husky laugh, a laugh that spoke so clearly of her desire. "Now you're talkin'."

He lay back on the pillows and watched her, his eyes so hot now, molten, as she removed the wrapper and set it aside.

She bent over him, kissed him, in the center of his chest, on that silky trail of hair, not far from his heart. His skin was hot. He smelled so good. She rained a flood of kisses on him, to each side of his big chest, over his rib cage, on his ridged, amazing belly, all the way to her goal.

When she got there, she kissed him once more, a light, feathery breath of a kiss. He moaned. The sound pleased her. She stuck out her tongue and she licked him, concentrating first on the flare, then centering on the sensitive tip. And then, at last, taking him inside—then slowly, by agonizing degrees, lifting once more to release him.

A strangled sound escaped him. And he touched her hair, threading his fingers through it, lifting himself toward her, begging wordlessly, on another groan, for more.

She gave him what he asked for. She took him in again slowly, all the way, relaxing her throat to accommodate him, and then, just as slowly, let him out. She used her tongue on him, licking, stroking, swirling, teasing.

His moans and his rough, ragged breathing told her that he couldn't take much more. Good. She wanted to lead him all the way to the brink. She wanted to make him go over, into a perfect satisfaction, as he'd done to her.

But then he caught her face between his hands and he guided her up his body again, until she was looking right into those beautiful eyes.

"Put it on," he commanded in a rough, hungry growl. "Put it on now."

And she realized she was fine with that. More than fine. She rolled on the condom carefully. Once it was on, she rose onto her knees, intending to take the top position.

But then he reached for her, and he lifted up from the pillows and she happily surrendered as he guided her so gently down onto her back again. He eased her thighs wide and settled between them, his arms against the mattress to either side of her head, his fingers in her hair.

"Sydney…" His mouth swooped down to claim another kiss. Deep and hot and perfect, that kiss.

And she felt him, nudging against her, so slick and hard and wonderfully insistent. He pressed in slowly, filling her. She opened for him eagerly, her mouth fused to his as he came into her.

Oh, it was glorious, thrilling, nothing like it.

Not ever.

Not ever in her life before.

He began to move, rocking into her, his hips meeting hers, retreating—and returning. Always, returning.

She lifted herself up to him, wrapped her legs around his waist, her arms around his shoulders, clasping his strong neck, her fingers clutching his hair.

She was lost, flying, burning, free. There was nothing, just this. This beauty. This magic. The two of them: her body, his body—together. One.

Retreating. Returning. Over and over. Wet and hot and exactly as she'd never realized she'd always wished it might be.

Nothing like it.

Not ever.

Not ever in her life before.

"Sydney…" His voice in her ear. His breath against her skin. "Sydney…"

She sighed, turned her head away, so luxuriously comfortable, only wanting to sleep a little more.

"Sydney…" He nuzzled her temple, caught the curling strands of hair there between his lips, gave them a light, teasing tug.

She kept her eyes stubbornly shut, grumbled, "I was sleeping…"

His mouth on her cheek. Warm. Tempting. His words against her skin. "But you have to wake up now."

Wake up. Of course. She knew he was right. She turned her head to him, opened her eyes, asked him groggily, "What time is it?"

"After three." He was on his side, braced up on an elbow, the sheet down around his lean waist, clinging like an adoring lover to the hard curve of his left hip.

With a low groan, she sat up, raked her hair back off her forehead, stretched and yawned. Then she let her arms drop to the sheets. "Ugh. You're right. I do have to get home." She started to push back the covers.

He caught her hand. "Wait."

She smiled at him, searched his wonderful face. "What?"

"Sydney..." His mouth was softer than ever and his eyes gleamed and he looked so young right then. Young and hopeful and...nervous.

He did. He actually looked nervous. Prince Rule of Montedoro. Nervous. How could that be? He really wasn't the nervous type.

"Rule?" She laid her palm against his beard-roughened cheek. "Are you okay?"

He took her wrist, turned his head until her hand covered those soft lips of his. And he kissed her, the most tender, sweetest kiss, right in the heart of her palm, the way he had done the night before when he asked her if she would prefer him to be cruel.

A shiver went through her, a premonition of...

What? She had no idea. And already the strange, anxious feeling had passed.

There was only his mouth, so soft against her palm. Only the beauty of the night they had shared, only the wonder that he was here with her and he was looking at her like she hung the moon, as though she ruled the stars.

He lowered her hand so it no longer covered his lips. And then, raising his other hand, he put something in her palm, after which he closed her fingers tenderly over it.

And then he said the impossible, incredible, this-must-be-a-dream-and-can't-really-be-happening words, "Marry me, Sydney. Be my bride."

Chapter Six

Still trying to believe what she thought he'd just said, Sydney uncurled her fingers and stared down in what could only be called shock and awe at the ring waiting there.

The brilliant emerald-cut diamond was huge. And so icily, perfectly beautiful. Flanking it to either side on the platinum band were two large, equally perfect baguettes.

She looked up from the amazing ring and into his dark eyes. "Just tell me…"

"Anything."

"Is this really happening?"

He laughed, low, and he brushed the hair at her temple with a tender hand. "Yes, my darling. It's really happening. I know it's crazy. I know it's fast. But I don't care about any of that. In my heart, I knew the moment I saw you. And every moment since then has only made me more certain. Until there is nothing left. Nothing but absolute certainty that you are the woman for me."

"But you... I... We can't just—"

"Yes. We can. Today. We can fly to Las Vegas and be married today. I don't want to wait. I want you for my wife now. I have to return to Montedoro on Tuesday. I want you and Trevor with me."

"I don't... I can't... Oh, Rule. Wait."

He shook his head. "My darling, I don't want to wait. Don't make me wait."

"But, I mean, I have a c-career," she sputtered. "I have a house. I live in Texas. Can you even marry someone from Texas?"

"Of course I can. As long as that someone will have me."

"But you can't possibly... I mean, now that I think about it, well, don't you have to marry someone with at least a title? A duchess. A countess. A Lady Someone-or-Other?"

"My mother married an American actor and it's worked out quite well, I think. Times change. And I'm glad. I can marry whomever I choose, Sydney. I choose you—and I hope with all my heart that you choose *me*."

"I can't... I don't..."

"My love, slow down."

"Slow down? You're telling *me* to slow down? You just asked me to marry you and you meant today!"

He laughed then. "You're right. I'm no position to talk about slowing down. But I do think it wouldn't hurt if you took a breath. A nice, deep one." It was pretty good advice, actually. She drew in a slow breath and let it out with care. "Better?" he asked so tenderly.

She looked down at the ring again. "I think I might faint."

"No." He chuckled. "You are not a woman who faints." Still, he pulled her against him. She went, leaning her head on the hard bulge of his shoulder, loving the warmth and solidity of him, the scent of him that was so fine, yet at the same time so undeniably male. Loving everything about him.

Love. Was it possible? She knew that *he* thought it was.

And yet, still. Even given the possibility that it really was love at first sight between the two of them, well, she'd thought she would have a little more time than this before he asked her to commit to forever…

She pulled away, enough that she could meet his eyes. "It's so fast, Rule. I mean, so soon to jump into marriage. It's just…really, really fast."

"I know. I don't care." His gaze was steady on hers. He spoke with absolute certainty. "I know what I want now. At last. I told you, I've waited my whole life for this, for *you*."

"Yes. I know. We've…spoken of that. But still. Marriage. That's a lot more than talk as far as I'm concerned. For me, marriage would be a lifetime thing."

"Yes. I know. We agree on that, on what it is to be married, that it's forever."

She searched his face. "It's the marriage law, right? You have to choose a wife and you have to do it soon."

"I do, yes."

"But not until June. You have until then. We could… have more time together, a few weeks, anyway. We could get to know each other better."

"I don't need more time, Sydney. You're the one. I know it. More time isn't going to change that—except to make me even more certain that you are the woman for me. I don't need to be more certain. I need…you. With me. I need at last to begin the life I've always wanted. The life my parents have. The life Max had with Sophia before he lost her. I want you to be mine. I want to be yours. I want every moment that God will grant us, together. Because fate can be cruel. Look what happened to Max. He thought he had a whole life ahead of him with Sophia. And now he's alone. Every day they did have is precious to him. I don't want to waste a day, an hour, a moment now, Sydney. I want us to begin our lives together today."

"Oh, Rule…"

"Say yes. Just say yes."

She wanted to. So much. But her inner skeptic just had to ask, "But…for a lifetime? I mean, come on. I looked you up on Google. You're the sexy bachelor prince. I'm pretty certain you've never dated a woman like me before. A really smart, really capable, average-looking, success-driven career woman."

His eyes flashed fire. "You are not average-looking."

"Oh, fine. I'm not average. I'm attractive enough. But I'm no international beauty."

"You are to me. And that's all that matters. Plus, you're brilliant. You're charming. People notice you, they want to…follow you. I don't think you realize your own power. I don't think you truly see yourself as you appear to others. I don't think you understand that strength and determination and focus in a woman—in the right woman—can be everything to a man. You're not the only one who knows how to use a search engine, Sydney. I looked you up. I read of how you graduated college at twenty. I read about the cases you've won for your law firm. And with all that ambition and drive, you have a good heart. And a deep, honest, ingrained sensuality. And last but in no way least, you're a wonderful mother—and you *chose* motherhood. Even with all your accomplishments, you also wanted a family. And when the men around you refused to be worthy of you, you found a way to be a mother, to make your own family. Of course I want you for my wife. You're everything I've been looking for." He brushed a hand, so lightly, along the curve of her cheek and he whispered, "Marry me, Sydney."

"I…" Her throat felt tight. She had to gulp to relax it. "You make me sound so amazing."

"Because you *are* amazing." He pulled her into his arms again.

She went without resisting. "Oh, Rule…"

"Say yes."

She tried to order her thoughts. "Can you move here, to Texas?"

His lips touched her hair. "That, I can't do. I have obligations to my country, obligations I couldn't bring myself to set aside."

She puffed out her cheeks with another big breath. "Just like a man. I knew you were going to say that."

"We can return often. My business dealings bring me to the States several times a year. Would it be so terrible, to live in Montedoro?"

"No. Not terrible. Just…huge. I would have to leave Teale, Gayle and Prosser…"

He rubbed her arm, a soothing, gentle caress. "I seem to recall that you said you were ready for a change in your work, that you would like a chance to help people who really needed your help."

"Yes. I said that. And I meant it."

"As my wife, there would be any number of important causes you might tackle. You would have many opportunities to make a difference."

"But what causes? What opportunities?"

He tipped up her chin, kissed the tip of her nose. "My darling, I think that would be for you to discover." She knew he was right on that score. And she was strong and smart and she learned fast. There wasn't a lot she couldn't do, once she set her mind and heart to doing it.

What about Trevor? He was young enough that the move probably wouldn't be as big a deal for him as it might have been—if he were already in school, if he had to leave close friends behind.

She thought of Lani then. "My God. Lani…"

"What about your friend?"

"I would lose Lani."

"You wouldn't *lose* her. A friend is a friend, no matter the miles between you—and who knows? If you asked her to come with us, she might say yes."

"So, Lani could come, too? If that worked for her. You wouldn't mind?"

"Of course not. What I know of her, I like very much. And I want you to be happy. I want you to have your dear friend with you."

"She might find it interesting. She writes, did I tell you?"

"No, I don't believe you did."

"She does. Right now she's working on a novel. She might find lots to write about in Montedoro. She might enjoy the experience of living somewhere she's never been before. Maybe she *will* want to come.…"

"So, then. You will ask her." He kissed her again, on the cheek.

And she wanted more than that. So she turned her head enough that their lips met.

Heaven. Just heaven, kissing Rule. He guided her back onto the pillows and kissed her some more. She could have gone on like that indefinitely. But it was after three in the morning—on what she was actually starting to let herself think of as her wedding day.

She had a thousand things to do before they left for Las Vegas. She pushed at his chest.

He leaned back then, enough to capture her gaze. "What is it?"

"You really want to fly to Vegas today?"

"Yes. That's exactly what I want. Be my wife, Sydney. Make me the happiest man in the world. Bring your beautiful child and your excellent friend and we'll be married today. And after that, come live with me in Montedoro."

She reached up, touched that soft mouth of his. Oh, she did love touching him. Lightly, she smoothed the dark hair at his temples. She loved everything about him. And she was ready, to make a change.

To take a chance on love.

He spoke again, those black eyes shining. "I think Trevor would thrive if we married. I know you already have so much to offer him, that you're giving him an excellent start in life. But if we're together, he can have even more. For one thing, you would be able to spend more time with him. You could plan the work you choose to do specifically around him, during these years when he needs his mother most of all. And I would hope that, in time, we can speak of my adopting him."

Was there a more fabulous man in the whole world? She doubted it. "You would want to adopt him?"

"I would. So much. And I would hope that we also might have more children—I know, I know. I promise not to expect *eight* more. But maybe one or two…?"

"Oh, Rule…"

"Say yes."

She still had her hand on his chest, where she could feel the sure, steady beat of his heart. "I would need more time, here, in Dallas, before I could move to Montedoro. I have to give my partners reasonable notice. I can't leave them scrambling when I go. *I* may be ready to move on, but it would be wrong to leave *them* high and dry."

"Is it possible that you could be ready to go in two weeks?"

She gasped. "No way. Cases have to be shuffled, clients reassigned. I was thinking three months, if I really pushed it."

"What if you brought them more clients, big clients, as a…compensation for making a quick exit?" He named a couple of big oil companies, a major health food and vitamin distributor and a European bank that had branches in the U.S.

Sydney realized her mouth was hanging open. She shut it—and then she asked, "You're serious? You can deliver those?"

"Yes. I have a number of excellent connections worldwide. And if it doesn't work out with one or two of those particular companies, I'm sure I can offer others just as good."

"Well, I could possibly get away in a month or so, if my partners were grateful enough for what I brought them before I left."

"I'll get to work on that potential client list in the next few days. And I'll arrange the introductions, of course. I think you might be surprised at how quickly you can wrap things up with Teale, Gayle and Prosser, once they know exactly how much business you'll be bringing in before you go."

He was right. It would make all the difference, if she brought in some big clients. "I can't do it in two weeks. But if you bring the right clients, I'll give it my best shot. I could manage it in a month. Maybe."

His whole fabulous face seemed to light up from within. "I believe that you just said yes."

"Yes." She said the beautiful word out loud. "I did. Yes, Rule. Yes." And she threw her arms around his neck and let her kisses say the rest.

"Wow, Syd. When you finally go for it with a guy, you *really* go for it." Lani, in her pj's, still groggy from sleep, was shaking her head as she reached for her glasses. But at least she was smiling.

It was ten of five on Sunday morning. Sydney had headed for Lani's room the moment she walked in the front door and they were sitting on Lani's bed. Rule had said he would return at eight and Sydney had promised to be ready to go. He'd told her that he would have a private jet waiting at the airport. It helped to be a rich prince when you wanted to elope to Vegas at a moment's notice.

"So...you don't think I'm crazy?" Sydney asked, apprehensions rising.

"No way. I knew he was the one for you the moment I saw him."

"Uh, you did?"

"Oh, yeah. I mean seriously, Syd. The guy is your type."

"Well, yeah. In my wildest fantasies."

"Which have now become reality. He's intelligent, smooth and sophisticated. He's tall, dark, killer handsome—and I really think he's a good man. It's quite the major bonus that he happens to be a prince. And seeing him with Trevor, well, he's terrific with Trev. And have you noticed they look enough alike to be father and son?"

Sydney chuckled. "I have, actually."

"I go a lot on instinct," Lani said. "You know that. And my instinct with Rule is you've made the right choice."

Sydney beamed. "You are the best friend any woman ever had."

"Likewise."

"Say you'll come to Vegas with us." Sydney put on her most pitiful, pleading expression.

"Are you kidding? Like I would miss that? No way. I'm going."

"Oh, I'm so glad!" Sydney grabbed her friend and hugged her hard.

"How long am I packing for?" Lani asked when Sydney released her.

"Just overnight. I'll take tomorrow off. But Tuesday, I've got to get back to the office and start wrapping things up for the move to Montedoro."

"Oh. My. God. You're marrying a prince and moving to Europe. I don't believe it—or, I *do* believe it. But still. It's beyond wild."

"Yep. I think I need to pinch myself." Sydney let out a joyous laugh. "Is this really real?"

"Oh, yes, it is!" Lani replied. "Let me see the ring again." She grabbed Sydney's hand. "Just gorgeous. Absolutely gorgeous." And then she stuck out her lower lip and made out a small, sad puppy-dog sound. "But you know I will be sulking. I'll miss you way too much. And Trev, oh, how will I get along without him?" She put her hand on her chest and pantomimed a heartbeat.

Sydney had the answer to that one ready. "You don't have to miss us, not if you come with us."

"Come with you? You mean, permanently?"

"Oh, yeah. I would love that."

Lani blinked. "You're serious."

"You bet I am. I've already discussed it with Rule. He's good with it. More than good. And I would love it if you were there—I mean, if that could work for you."

"Me. Living in Montedoro with my best friend, the prince's bride. Interesting."

"I was hoping you might think that. But don't decide now. Take your time. No pressure. I mean that."

Lani bumped her shoulder affectionately. "I'll give it serious consideration—and thank you."

"Hey. Don't thank me. I'll miss you like crazy if you decide you don't want to do it. If you come, *I'll* be the grateful one."

"I'll think about it," Lani promised. "And we'd better get cracking if we're going to be ready to head for Vegas at eight."

As it turned out, Rule had Bravo relatives in Las Vegas. Aaron and Fletcher Bravo ran a pair of Las Vegas casino/hotels. Rule was a second cousin to both men. His grandfather James and their grandfather Jonas had been brothers.

"Fletcher and Aaron are half brothers," Rule told Sydney during the flight to Nevada. "They have different mothers, but both are sons of Blake Bravo."

"I have to ask. You don't mean *the* Blake Bravo?"

"Ah. You've heard of the infamous Blake?"

She nodded. "He died in Oklahoma about a decade ago, and at the time, the story made the front page of every paper in Texas. He *was* pretty notorious."

Rule nodded. "Yes, he was. Kidnapping his own brother's son for a fortune in diamonds, marrying all those women…" Beyond the whole kidnapping thing, Blake Bravo had been a world-class polygamist. He'd married any number of women all over the country and he'd never divorced a single one of them. Each woman had believed she was the only one.

Sydney said, "A very busy man, that Blake."

"*Busy* is not the word I would have chosen," Rule said dryly. "But yes, both Aaron and Fletcher are his sons."

The flight took a little under three hours, but they

gained two hours because of changing time zones, so they touched down at McCarran International Airport at ten after ten in the morning.

There was a limo waiting. The driver loaded the trunk with their luggage, the security guy who had flown from Dallas with them got in front on the passenger side and off they went to High Sierra Resort and Casino.

Aaron Bravo was CEO of High Sierra. The resort was directly across Las Vegas Boulevard from Impresario Resort and Casino, which Fletcher ran. The two giant complexes were joined by a glass breezeway five stories up, above the Strip.

Aaron greeted them at the entrance to his resort. Tall and lean with brown hair, Aaron wasn't classically handsome. But he was attractive, very much so, with a strong nose, sharp cheekbones and a square jaw. He said how pleased he was to meet Sydney and Lani—and Trevor, too. Then he introduced them to his wife, Celia, who was cute and friendly, a redhead with big hazel eyes.

Celia led the way to their suite, which had its own kitchen, a large living area and four bedrooms branching off of it. The security guy, whose name was Joseph, had the room next door.

The first order of business was to get the marriage license. Lani stayed behind with Trevor. Sydney, Rule and Joseph headed for the Las Vegas Marriage Bureau. An hour later, they were back in the suite, where Trev was playing with his trucks and Lani was stretched out on the sofa with her laptop.

"Ready for pampering?" she asked. "Celia says the spa is called Touch of Gold and it's full service...."

"Go," said Rule. "Both of you. The wedding's not until four." The short ceremony would be held in the wedding chapel right there at High Sierra. "I'll watch Trevor."

Sydney hesitated to let him do that. How strange. Here she was about to marry this wonderful man, and she felt reluctant to leave him alone with her son.

But no. Her reaction was only natural. It was one thing to trust her own heart. Another to leave her child alone with someone for the first time—even someone like Rule, who was so good with Trevor.

Lani spoke up. "Uh-uh. I'm onto something with this chapter and I'm not giving it up now. You go, Syd. I'm staying."

"Roo!" called Trev from under the table. "Come. We play trucks!"

So Rule and Lani both stayed in the suite with Trevor. Sydney went by herself to the spa. On the way, she stopped in at the resort's florist and ordered a bouquet of yellow roses, which she told them she would pick up personally in a few hours. She also asked to have a yellow rose boutonniere sent up to the suite for Rule.

At Touch of Gold, she decided to start with a hot rock massage. After the massage, she had it all, mani-pedi, haircut and blow dry and the expert attention of the spa's cosmetician, too.

And then, when she was perfectly manicured, with her hair smooth and shiny and softly curling to her shoulders and her makeup just right, Celia appeared with a tall, stunning brunette, Cleo, who was Fletcher's wife. The two women took Sydney to the bridal boutique not far from the spa.

Sydney chose a simple sleeveless fitted sheath dress of white silk and a short veil. Her shoes were ivory satin platform high heels, with side bows and peep toes. Celia had Sydney's street clothes sent back to the suite and Sidney left the boutique dressed for her wedding. After that, they stopped off at the florist to pick up her bouquet.

And then the two women led her straight to the High Sierra wedding chapel. Sydney waited in the chapel's vestibule for the "Wedding March" to begin. Staying to the side, out of sight, she peeked around the open door.

The rest of the small wedding party was already there: Lani, holding Trev, and Aaron and another dark-haired man who was obviously Cleo's husband, Fletcher Bravo. She saw him in profile and noted the family resemblance between him and Aaron—and Rule, too, she realized.

Her groom was waiting for her, standing down in front with the justice of the peace, looking fabulous as always in a black silk suit with a lustrous cobalt-blue tie and a shirt the color of a summer sky. In his lapel, he wore the yellow rose she'd sent him.

Sydney's pulse beat faster, just at the sight of him. And she smiled to herself, thinking of all the years she'd been so sure she would never find him—the right man, a good man, solid, smart and funny and true. The fact that he'd turned out to be a real-life prince who was total eye candy and had a voice that turned her insides to jelly, well, that was just the icing on the cake.

He was exactly the man for her. He made her feel beautiful and bold and exciting—or maybe he simply saw her beauty and made her see it, too. It didn't matter. With him, she could have it all. She could not wait to start their life together.

The only thing that could have made this day more perfect was if her Grandma Ellen could have been here, too.

Cleo helped Sydney pin the short veil in place.

And then the "Wedding March" began.

With a smile of pure happiness curving her lips and the glow of new love in her heart, Sydney walked down the aisle toward her waiting groom. She was absolutely certain she was making the right choice, marrying a man who saw beyond the walls she had erected to protect her injured heart. A man who had loved her the first moment he saw her, a man who wanted to be a real father to her son. A man who had been charmingly reluctant to reveal his princely heritage. A man of honor, who spoke the truth.

A man who did not have a deceptive bone in his body.

Chapter Seven

The justice of the peace said, "I now pronounce you husband and wife. You may kiss the bride."

His eyes only for her, Rule raised the short veil and guided it back over her head.

And then he drew her closer to him and he kissed her, a tender, perfect kiss. A kiss that promised everything: his love and his devotion, the bright future they would share. Sydney closed her eyes and wished the special moment might last forever.

After the ceremony, they all went to dinner in a private dining room in High Sierra's nicest restaurant. More children joined them there, six of them. Celia and Aaron had three, as did Fletcher and Cleo. The food was great and the company even better.

Aaron and Fletcher proposed a series of excellent toasts and when the kids were done eating, they were all allowed to get down and play together. There was much childish laughter. Trev loved every minute of it. He seemed quite taken with Fletcher and Cleo's oldest child, Ashlyn. He followed her around the private dining room, offering her dazzling smiles whenever she glanced his way. Ashlyn didn't seem to mind. And she knew several knock-knock jokes. She patiently tried to teach them to Trev, who inevitably got carried away and started playing both parts.

"Knock, knock," Ashlyn would say gamely.

And Trev would crow, "Who's there? Bill! Orange! Wanda!"

There was a cake, three tiers tall, a yellow cake with white fondant icing and edible pearls, crowned with a circle of yellow rosebuds. Celia took pictures as Sydney and Rule fed each other too-big bites of the sweet confection.

Trev tore himself away from his adoration of Ashlyn to join them at the cake table. "Roo, Mama, cake! Now!" He reached up his chubby arms.

So Rule swept him up against his chest and Trev laughed in delight. "Roo!" he cried. "Kiss," and puckered up his little mouth.

Rule puckered up as well and kissed him with a loud, smacking sound, which made Trev laugh even harder. A second later, he demanded, "Cake, Mama!"

"Cake, *please?*" she suggested.

And he shouted, "Cake! Please!"

So Sydney fed him a few bites of cake while Celia snapped more pictures. Then they served everyone else. The kids were silent—for a few minutes anyway—as they devoured their dessert.

After that, everyone lingered, reluctant to call an end to an enjoyable event. The adults chatted, the children went back to running in and out under the table, laughing, playing tag.

Eventually though, the little ones started getting fussy. Lani said she would take Trev up to the suite. Sydney offered to go, but Lani said she wanted to get back to her writing anyway. She could handle Trevor and work on her book at the same time, and often did. She would keep her laptop handy and sneak in a sentence or two whenever Trevor gave her a moment to herself.

So Lani took him up. Soon after, Celia and Cleo gathered their respective broods and left for the onsite apartments each family kept in the resort complex.

That left Fletcher and Aaron playing dual hosts to the newlyweds. The men talked a little business. The Bravo CEOs agreed that Montedoran oranges would be a perfect addition to the complimentary fruit baskets they offered in their luxury suites.

Rule invited his two second cousins and their families to Montedoro. Both said they would love to come. They would stay at the Prince's Palace and visit the fabulous casino in Montedoro's resort ward of Colline d'Ambre.

Finally, after more good wishes for a long and happy life together, the half brothers went to join their families. Rule and Sydney were left alone in the private dining room.

He drew her close to him, tipped up her chin and kissed her slowly and so sweetly. "My wife…" he whispered against her lips. "My own princess."

She chuckled. "Just like that? I only have to marry you and I get to be a princess?"

He took her hand, laid it against his chest. "And you will always rule my heart."

She laughed then. "Oh, you are so smooth." And then she frowned.

He kissed her furrowed brow. "What?"

"Your mother, the princess. Your family. This will be quite a surprise to them."

"A happy surprise," he said.

"So…you haven't told them anything about me yet?"

"Only my father. He knows…everything. And by now he will have told my mother that I've married the only woman for me."

She searched his face. "The way you say that. *Everything.* It sounds mysterious somehow."

He touched her cheek, smoothed a few strands of hair behind her ear. "Not mysterious at all. I spoke with my father this morning, before I came to take you to the airport. He wished us much happiness and he looks forward to meeting his new daughter-in-law and grandson."

"So he's not overly disappointed that you're not marrying Princess Lili?"

He traced the neckline of her wedding dress, striking sparks of excitement. "My father is a great believer in marrying for love. So he wants me to be happy. And he understands that I *will* be happy—with you."

"And your mother?"

"I know that she will be happy for me, as well." He kissed her again, slowly. A kiss that deepened, went from tender to scorching-hot. Her mind went hazy and her body went loose.

When he lifted his mouth from hers that time and the small dining room swam into focus again, a busman stood at the door. "Excuse me. I'll come back…."

Rule shook his head. "No. We're just leaving." He stood and pulled back her chair for her. "Shall we try our luck in the casino?"

"I'm terrible at games of chance."

"Never admit that. Lady Luck will hear you."

Her bouquet and her short veil, which she'd removed a while ago, lay on the table. Rule signaled the busman over, tipped him hugely and asked him to have both items delivered to their suite.

The busman promised it would be done.

Sydney took the rose from Rule's lapel, feeling wonderfully wifely and possessive of him as she did it. "This, too," she told the busman. "And the cake. I want the rest of the cake."

The busman promised he'd have the cake boxed and sent to their suite with the veil, the bouquet and the boutonniere.

They took the wide glass breezeway across the Strip to Impresario, which was all in blacks and reds and golds, a Moulin Rouge theme. They played roulette for over two hours. Sydney surprised herself by winning steadily. When they left the roulette table she was up more than a thousand dollars.

She caught sight of Joseph a few feet away and leaned close to her new husband to whisper, "Joseph is following us."

He brushed a kiss against her hair. "Joseph is always following us. That's his job."

"You're kidding. You mean every time I've been out with you…?"

"That's right. Joseph has been somewhere nearby."

"I swear I never noticed before."

"You're not supposed to notice. He's paid to be invisible until he's needed."

"Well, he's very good at it."

"He'll be pleased to hear that. Joseph takes great pride in his work—and what would you like to play next?"

"I was kind of thinking it would be fun to try my luck at blackjack."

"Blackjack it is, then." They found a table and played for another hour. Sydney won some more.

When they left the blackjack table it was after ten.

He leaned close. "I think you're lucky, after all."

"I think it's you," she whispered back. "You bring me luck."

He had his arm around her and pulled her closer, right there in the aisle, on their way toward the elevators that led up to the fifth floor and the breezeway back to High Sierra. Their lips met.

And a flash went off.

She laughed. "I think I'm seeing stars."

But he wasn't smiling. "The jackals are onto us."

"Ahem. Excuse me....?"

"Paparazzi. We have to go." He already had her hand and was moving fast toward the elevators. She hurried to keep up. More flashes went off.

A balding guy in tight pants and a black shirt with a big gold chain around his neck stepped in front of them. He stuck a microphone in Rule's face and started firing questions at him, racing backward to keep up with them. "Enjoying your visit to America, Your Highness? Who is the woman in white? Is that a wedding ring I see on the lady's finger?"

Rule only said, "Excuse me, no comment," and kept walking fast.

That was when Joseph appeared. He must have grabbed the guy with the microphone, because the man stumbled and fell back, out of their path.

Rule forged on. They reached the elevators and one rolled open as if on cue. He pulled her in there, pushed the button for the fifth floor and the doors slid shut.

"Whew," she said, laughing a little. "Looks like we're safe."

He just looked grim. "I should have known they would spot us." A moment later, the doors slid open wide. They got off and a group of men in business suits got on. Rule had her hand again. They were headed for the breezeway. Halfway across it, Joseph caught up with them. "Is it handled?" Rule asked low.

"Too many cameras." Joseph spoke softly, but his face looked carved in stone. "And they refused to deal, anyway. They got away with the shots they took."

Rule swore under his breath and pulled her onward.

On the High Sierra side, they took an elevator up to their floor. When the elevator stopped and the door opened, Joseph stuck his head out first. "We're clear," he said and signaled them out.

They walked at a brisk clip down the hallway to their suite. Rule had the key ready. He swiped it through the slot and they were in as Joseph entered the room next door.

The suite was silent. Trev had been put to bed hours ago and Lani must have retreated to her room. She'd left the light in the suite's granite-tiled foyer on for them.

Sydney sagged against the door. "Wow. That was exciting."

Rule braced a hand by her head and bent to kiss her—a hard, passionate kiss that slowly turned tender. When he pulled away, he whispered, "I'm sorry..."

"Whatever for? I had a great time."

"I knew it was unwise, to take you out on the casino floor and then stay there for hours. We were bound to be spotted."

She touched the side of his face, brushed the backs of her fingers along the silky, beautifully trimmed hair at his temples. "It's not the end of the world, is it, if our pictures end up in some tabloid somewhere?"

"In my family, we prefer to control the message."

"Meaning?"

"I was hoping we could keep our marriage private for the next few weeks, until I had you with me in Montedoro. From there, a discreet and carefully worded announcement could be made. And pictures could be taken by the palace photographer to send to the press, pictures of our choosing."

"What? A candid shot of you and me racing down a hallway with our mouths hanging open in surprise isn't discreet enough for you?"

He laughed then. But his eyes were troubled. "No, it's not."

She smoothed his lapel, straightened his collar. "Well, no matter how bad it is, just remember how much fun we had. As far as I'm concerned, I had so much fun, it's worth a few ugly pictures in some scandal sheet. Plus, I won almost two thousand dollars, about which I am beyond thrilled. I never win anything. But all I have to do is marry you, and suddenly it's like I've got a four-leaf clover tattooed on my forehead."

He was looking at her in *that* way again. The lovely, sexy way. The way that set small fluttery creatures loose in her stomach and had her feeling distinctly sultry lower down. "There is no four-leaf clover on your forehead." He kissed the spot where it might have been.

"Oh, it's there," she said softly, breathlessly. "You just can't see it. I was clever that way. I insisted on an invisible tattoo."

"Wait. I think I see it, after all." He breathed the words against her skin. And then he kissed his way down between her brows, trailing that wonderful mouth along the top of her nose. He nipped her lips once and then kissed her chin. "And I'm glad you enjoyed yourself."

"Oh, I did." Her voice was now more breath than sound. "I really did...."

He covered her mouth with his again. Luckily, she had the door at her back to lean against. She stayed upright even though her knees had gone deliciously wobbly. And as it turned out, she didn't need to hold herself upright much longer anyway. Still kissing her, he scooped her up in his arms carried her through the open archway to the central room of the suite.

The busman had kept his promise. On the dining table, she saw the large cake box, her veil and bouquet and also Rule's boutonniere. She smiled against his lips as he turned and carried her through the open door to their room, where the lamp by the bed had been left on low. Also, on a long table against the wall, a pair of crystal flutes flanked an ice bucket holding a bottle of champagne. The covers on the king-size bed were turned invitingly down.

She stretched out an arm to push the door shut behind them. Rule carried her to the side of the wide bed and set her down on her feet. They shared another kiss, one that went on for a lovely, endless space of time.

When he lifted his head, he guided her around so her back was to him. She read his intention and smoothed her hair to the side. He lowered the zipper at the back of her dress.

She took it from there, easing her arms free, pushing the dress down. Stepping out of it, she bent and picked it up and carried it to the bedside chair, where she took time to lay it down gently, to smooth the white folds.

"Come back here," he said, his voice rough with wanting.

"In a moment..." She sent him a teasing glance over her shoulder as she returned to the door long enough to engage the privacy lock. From there, she went to the dressing table on the far side of the room. She took off her shoes, her bra, her white lace panties and pearl earrings. And after that, she removed the single strand of pearls her grandmother had given her and the blue lace garter provided by the bridal boutique. Finally, wearing nothing but a tender smile, she faced him again. "Your turn."

He made a low sound in his throat, his gaze moving over her, hot and possessive. "Don't move. I'll be right back."

The room had a walk-in closet. He entered it and came back out a moment later. Returning to the side of the bed, he laid two wrapped condoms on the nightstand.

She told him softly, "We won't need those."

Something flared in his eyes—triumph? Joy? But then he stood very still. "Are you sure?"

She nodded. "We both want more children. I'm thinking there's no time like the present to get going on that."

"Sydney O'Shea Bravo-Calabretti," he said. "You amaze me."

She did like the sound of her name, her new name, on his lips. And she had no doubts. None whatsoever. She told him so. "I know what I want now, Rule. I want you. I want a family, with you and Trev. And I'm greedy. I want more babies. I honestly do."

He took a step toward her.

She put up a hand. "Your clothes. All of them. Please."

He didn't argue. He undressed. He did it swiftly, with no wasted motion, tossing the beautifully tailored articles of clothing carelessly aside as he removed them. His body was so fine and strong. Just looking at him stole her breath.

When he had everything off, she went to him. She lifted her arms to him and he drew her close. Nothing so fine as that, to be held in his powerful arms, to feel the heat and hardness of him all around her.

He smoothed her hair, caressed her back with a long stroke of his tender hand. "I think I'm the happiest man in the world tonight."

She tipped her head up to him. "I'm glad. So glad…"

He kissed her and she thought how she would never, ever get enough of his kisses. That with him, she'd finally found everything she'd almost let herself forget that she'd been looking for.

She pulled him down onto the bed with her and gave herself up to his touch, to the magic of his lips on her skin.

He kissed her everywhere, each secret hollow, each curve, even the backs of her knees and the crooks of her elbows. He kissed her breasts, slowly and thoroughly, and then he moved lower. He kissed all her secret places, until she cried out and went over the edge, clutching his dark head, moaning his name.

She was still sighing in sweet satisfaction when he slid up her body again. All at once, he was there, right where she wanted him most. She wrapped her arms around him, so tightly. And he came into her, gliding smoothly home. Her body was as open to him as her mind and her heart. She accepted him eagerly, the aftershocks of her climax still pulsing through her. And when he filled her, she let out a soft cry of joyous abandon.

Did it get any better than this?

She didn't see how it could. Somehow, she'd finally found the man she wanted for a lifetime—or rather, *he* had found *her*.

There was nothing, ever, that could tear them apart.

Rule wasn't sure what woke him.

A general sense of unease, he supposed. He turned to

look at the woman sleeping beside him. The lamp was off and the room in darkness. Still, he could hear her shallow, even breathing. So peaceful. Content. He could make out her shadowed features, just barely. A soft smile curved her mouth.

She pleased him. Greatly. In so many ways.

No, she wasn't going to be happy with him when she found out the truth. But she was a very intelligent woman. And there was real chemistry between them. Surely, when the time came, she would forgive him for his deception. He would rationally explain why he'd done what he had done. She would see that, even if he hadn't been strictly honest with her, it had all worked out perfectly anyway. She wanted to be with him and he wanted her *and* the boy. They could work through it and move on.

He wanted to touch her. To kiss her. To make love to her again. When he was touching her, he could forget that he'd married her without telling her everything.

But no. He wouldn't disturb her. Let her have a few hours of uninterrupted sleep.

Settling onto his back, he stared into the darkness, not happy with himself, wondering why he had become so obsessive over this problem. His obsession served no one. It was going to be a long time before he told her the truth, anyway. Maybe he never would.

In the past twenty-four hours or so, he'd found himself thinking that there was no real reason she ever had to know....

Except that he'd always considered himself an honest man. And it gnawed at his idea of his own character and his firm belief in fair play, to have this lie between them.

Which was thoroughly ironic, the more he considered it. He'd chosen the lie when he realized he wanted her for his wife. He'd seen it as the only sure way to his goal. So he supposed that meant his idea of himself as an honest man was only another lie.

And damned if he wasn't giving himself a headache, going around and around about this in his mind, when he was set on his course and there was no going back now.

He heard a faint buzzing sound: the cell phone in his trouser pocket, flung across that nearby chair.

Slowly, carefully, so as not to wake her, he eased back the covers and brought his feet to the floor. By then, the phone had stopped buzzing. He collected it from the trousers and tiptoed to the room's bath, where he checked to see who had called.

His father.

The voice mail signal beeped. He called to pick up the message.

His father's voice said "Rule. Call me on this line as soon as you get this. We need to touch base on the subject of Liliana."

Lili. What now?

With the nine-hour time difference, it would be around noon in Montedoro, which made it as good a time to call as any.

But not from the bathroom, where Sydney might wake up and walk in on him.

So he returned to the dark bedroom, where his bride was still sleeping the untroubled slumber of the blameless. He found his briefs and his trousers and put them back on. He tiptoed to the door and pulled it slowly open. The hinges played along and didn't squeak. He slipped through and closed it soundlessly behind him.

The suite had a balcony. He went out there, into the warm desert night, and closed the slider behind him.

His father answered on the first ring. "I understand congratulations are in order?"

The balcony had a café table and a couple of chairs. He dropped into one of them. "Thank you. I'm a very happy man."

"How is the boy?"

"Trevor is…a revelation to me. More than I ever might have wished for. Wait till you see him."

"I'm looking forward to that. When will you bring them home to us?"

"Sydney needs a month, she says. I'll come home ahead for a week or so and take care of my commitments there, and then return to help her through the transition."

"I heard that you had a little run-in with the press."

Rule didn't ask how his father knew. Joseph could have turned in a report—or the information could have come from any number of other sources. "Yes. They got away with pictures. And they put it together—Sydney's white dress, her engagement diamond and wedding band."

"So I understand. It won't take the story long to end up in the tabloids."

"I know." Rule felt infinitely weary thinking of that.

"Liliana is still here, still our guest at the palace. She has no idea that you've already married someone else."

"I know," Rule said again. He got up, stood at the iron railing, stared down at the resort pool, at the eerie glow the pool lights made, shining up through the water, at the rows of empty lounge chairs.

"Your mother is waiting to hear from you. She's always thought of you as the most considerate and dependable of her children."

"I've disappointed her."

"She'll get over it." His father's voice was gentler now.

"I'm trusting you to keep my secret," he reminded his father.

"I haven't told anyone, not even your mother." His father sighed.

"I should have spoken to Lili first, I know, for the sake of our long friendship—and in consideration of Montedoro's sometimes strained relationship with Leo." King Leo was Lili's hot-tempered, doting father. "But it was awkward, since I had made no proposal to her. How exactly was I to go about telling her that I *wouldn't* be proposing? Also there was the timing of it. As soon as I finally met Sydney and made my decision, I felt it was imperative to move forward, to attain my goal before leaving the States."

"You are so certain about this woman you have married, this woman you have only just met?"

"Yes," Rule said firmly. "I am."

"You *wanted* to marry her, for herself? Not simply for the child. You feel she is…right for you?"

"Yes. I did. I do."

"Yet you don't feel confident enough of her trust in you to tell her the basic truth of the situation?"

Rule winced. His father had cut a little too close to the bone with that one. He said, "I made a choice. I'm willing to live with the consequences."

His father was silent. Rule braced himself for criticism, for a very much deserved lecture on the price a man pays for tempting fate, for doing foolish, thoughtless, irresponsible things and telling himself he's breaking free, that he's trying to help others.

More than three years ago, Rule had let his hunger for something he didn't even understand win out over his good sense. And now, when he'd finally found what he was looking for, he'd lied to secure the prize he sought. And he was continuing to lie.…

But then his father only said, "Fair enough, then. I see

your dilemma. And I sympathize. But still, it's only right that you explain yourself to Liliana, face-to-face, as soon as possible. She should hear it from you first. She's an innocent in all this."

"I agree. I was planning to return on Tuesday, but I'll try to get away Monday…I mean, today."

"Do your best."

Rule promised he would and they said goodbye.

He turned to go inside and saw Sydney, her hair tangled from sleep, her green eyes shadowed, full of questions. Wearing one of the white terrycloth robes provided by the resort, she stood watching him through the sliding glass door.

Chapter Eight

He'd been facing away from the suite, he reminded himself. And speaking in low tones. She couldn't have heard the conversation through the thick glass of the door.

Tamping down his anxiety that she might have overheard something incriminating after all, he pulled the door open and murmured regretfully, "I woke you…."

"No. The *absence* of you. That's what woke me." She took his hand, pulled him into the suite and slid the door shut. After that, she stood gazing up at him, and he had that feeling he so often had with her, the feeling he'd just described to his father. The feeling of rightness, that he was with her, that he had finally dared to approach her, to claim her. Too bad the sense of rightness was liberally mixed with dread at the way-too-possible negative outcome of the dangerous game he played. "Is there something wrong?" She searched his face.

He still had her hand in his, so he pulled her back to

their room. Once he had her inside, he shut and locked the door.

"Rule, what?"

He framed her sweet, proud face between his hands. He loved her wide mouth, her nose that was perhaps a little too large for her face. A nose that made her look interesting and commanding, a nose that demanded a man take her seriously. One lie, he had already told her. A huge lie of omission. All else must be the absolute truth. "You're going to be angry with me…."

"You're scaring me. Just tell me what's going on. Please."

He caught her hand again, took her to the bed, sat her down and then sat beside her. "That was my father, on the phone. He asked me to come back to Montedoro today. He thinks I should talk to Liliana, that I owe her an explanation, that I should be the one to tell her that any proposal she might have been expecting is not forthcoming, that I'm already married."

She pulled her hand from his and drove right to the point. "And what do *you* think, Rule?"

"I think my father is right."

She speared her fingers through her night-mussed hair, scraping it back off her forehead. He wanted to reach for her, but he didn't dare. "Princess Lili is still waiting, I take it, for you to ask her to marry you?"

"That's the general assumption. She's a guest at the palace. It would be pretty unforgivable of me to let her find out in the tabloids that I'm already married."

"*Pretty* unforgivable?"

"All right. Simply unforgivable. As I said before, she's like a sister to me. While a man doesn't want to marry his sister—he doesn't want to see her hurt, either."

"I understand that."

"Sydney…" He tried to wrap his arm around her.

She dodged away from his touch. "Why, exactly, is she expecting you to marry her?" She looked at him then. Those green eyes that could be so soft and full of desire for him, were cool now, emerald-bright.

"I told you, she's always believed herself to be in love with me, ever since we were children. She's looked up to me, she's…waited for me. And as the years have gone by and I never married, it has been spoken of, between our two families, that I would need to marry soon due to the laws that control my inheritance. That Lili would be a fine choice in any number of ways."

"What ways?"

He suppressed an impatient sigh. "Ways of state, you might say. Over the years, there has been conflict, off and on, between Montedoro and Alagonia."

"Wars, you mean?"

"No. Small states such as ours rarely engage in wars. In Montedoro, we don't even have a standing army. But there has been discord—bad feelings, you could say—between our two countries. The most recent rift occurred because King Leo, Lili's father, wanted to marry my mother. My mother didn't want to marry him. She wanted to rule Montedoro and she wanted, as much as possible, to protect our sovereignty. If she'd married a king, he could so easily have encroached on her control of the throne. Plus, while she's always been fond of King Leo, she didn't feel she could love him as a husband. And she wanted that, wanted love in her marriage. She managed to avoid a situation where Leo might have had a chance to propose to her. And then she met my father."

"Don't tell me." At least there was some humor in her voice now. "It was love at first sight."

"So my mother claims. And my father, as well. They

married. King Leo is known for his hot temper. He was angry and even went so far as to put in place certain trade sanctions as something of a revenge against my mother and Montedoro for the injury to his pride. But then he met and married Lili's mother, an Englishwoman, Lady Evelyn DunLyle. The king loved his new wife and found happiness with her. He gave up his vendetta against my mother and Montedoro. Leo's queen and my mother became fast friends. Though Queen Evelyn died a few years ago, relations between our countries have been cordial for nearly three decades and we all think of Lili as one of our family."

"You're saying that if you'd married the princess, it would have bolstered relations between your countries. But now that you've essentially dumped her, if she goes crying to her father, your country and her country could end up on the outs again."

"I have not dumped her." He felt his temper rising, and quickly restrained it. "A man cannot dump a woman he's never been with in any way. I swear to you, Sydney, I have never so much as kissed Liliana, except as a brother would, chastely, on the cheek."

"But she thinks you're *going* to kiss her for real. She thinks you're going to *be* with her. She thinks that she'll be married to you before the twenty-fourth of June."

"Yes." He said it resignedly. "I believe she does."

"You realize that's kind of pitiful, don't you? I mean, if you've never given her any sort of encouragement, why would she think that you'll end up proposing marriage— unless she's a total idiot?"

"Lili is not an idiot. She's a romantic. She's more than a little…fanciful."

"You're saying she's weak-minded?"

"Of course not. She's a good person. She's…kind at heart."

Sydney shook her head. "You strung her along, didn't you?"

"No. I did no such thing. I simply…failed to disabuse her."

"Come on, Rule. She was your ace in the hole." Those green eyes were on him. He had the rather startling intuition that she could see inside his head, see the cogs turning as he tried to make excuses for what he had to admit was less than admirable behavior. "You never encouraged her. But you didn't *need* to encourage her. Because she'd decided you were her true love and she's a romantic person. You figured if you never met anyone who…worked for you, as a partner in life, you could always marry Lili when your thirty-third birthday got too close for comfort."

"All right." He threw up both hands. "Yes. That's what I did. That is exactly what I did."

She gave him a look that seared him where he sat. "And it was crappy what you did, Rule. It was really crappy."

"Yes, Sydney. It was…crappy. And I feel accountable and I want to apologize to her in person."

"I should hope so." She huffed out a disgusted breath.

And then there was silence. He stared straight ahead and hated that she was angry with him.

And by God, if she was angry over Lili, what was he in for when she found out about Trevor?

He couldn't stop himself from pondering his own dishonesty. About Trevor. About Lili. He was beginning to see that he wasn't the man he'd believed himself to be. That he was only an honest man when it suited him.

Such thoughts did not make him proud.

Plus, he found himself almost wishing he'd told her another lie just now, given her some other excuse as to why he had to go back right away to Montedoro. He hated this—the two of them, so late on their wedding night it was already the next morning, sitting side by side on the edge of their marriage bed, not looking at each other.

"We'll leave right after breakfast," she said. "You can go straight to Montedoro. I'll get a commercial flight for Lani and Trevor and me."

"I will take you to Dallas," he said.

"Really. It's fine. I'll—"

"No." He cut her off in a voice that brooked no argument. "I will take you to Texas. And then I'll go straight on from there."

A half an hour later, they lay in bed in the darkness together, but not touching, facing away from each other. Sydney knew it was the right thing, for him to go, to make his peace with the woman he'd kept on a string.

She knew it was the right thing...

But she didn't like it one bit. She was disappointed in Rule. And more than a little angry that because of him, their wedding night had ended in such a rotten, awful way.

Here she'd married her prince, literally. She'd been so sure he was the perfect man for her—and the day after their wedding, he had to leave her to fly back to his country and apologize to the woman everyone had *thought* he would marry. A woman Rule said was like a sister to him, a woman who was pretty and delicate and romantic at heart. Sydney was none of those things. Not pretty. Not the least delicate.

Okay, maybe she *was* a bit of a romantic. But she'd never had the luxury of indulging her romantic streak—not until her own personal prince came along.

Maybe her prince wasn't such a fine man, after all. Maybe she should have slowed things down between them, at least a little, given herself more time to make sure that marrying him was really right for her. She'd been hurt before, and badly. She should have kept those past heartaches more firmly in mind. Ryan and Peter had proved that she didn't have the best judgment when it came to giving her heart. And yet, after knowing Rule for—*oh, dear God,* under forty-eight hours—she'd run off to Vegas and married him.

Sydney closed her eyes tightly. Was she a total fool, after all? She'd followed her heart yet again. And look at her now, hugging the edge of the bed on her wedding night, curled into a tight ball of pure misery.

And then the truth came to her, cool and sweet as clean water poured on a wound. Rule wasn't Ryan or Peter. He hadn't lied to her or manipulated her.

He'd told her the truth about Princess Lili on Saturday night *before* he'd asked her to marry him. And when his father had called him home to make peace with Lili, Rule hadn't lied to her about what was going on. Even though he so easily could have, he hadn't taken the easy way, hadn't made up some story for why he needed to get back. After all, she knew he had responsibilities in Montedoro and she would have most likely accepted any credible story he'd told her about the sudden necessity for him to go.

But he *hadn't* lied. He'd taken the hard way, the way that proved his basic integrity. He'd told her what was really going on, and told her honestly. Told the truth, even when the truth didn't show him in the greatest light.

All at once, her stomach didn't feel quite so tight anymore. And her heart didn't ache quite so much.

Carefully, slowly, she relaxed from the tight little ball she'd curled herself into. She stretched out her legs and then, with a sigh, she eased over onto her back.

She could feel him beside her, feel his stillness. A concentrated sort of stillness. She couldn't hear his breathing. He must be awake, too. Lying there in misery, hating this situation as much as she did.

No, she didn't forgive him, exactly. Not yet, anyway. She couldn't just melt into his arms, just send him off to Princess Lili with a big, brave smile and a tender kiss goodbye.

But she could…understand the position he was in. She could sympathize.

The sheet between them was cool. She flattened her hand on it, and then moved her fingers, ever so slowly, toward his unmoving form.

He moved, too. Only his hand. His fingers touched hers and she didn't pull back.

She lay very still. No way was she going to let him wrap those big, warm arms around her.

But when his fingers eased between hers, she let them. And when he clasped her hand, she held on.

She didn't let go and neither did he. In time, sleep claimed her.

Rule had a car waiting for them in Dallas. He exited the jet to say goodbye to them as their bags were loaded into the trunk and airport personnel bustled about, preparing the jet for the flight to Montedoro.

Trev went eagerly into his arms. "Bye, Roo! Kiss!" And he kissed Rule's cheek, making a loud, happy smacking sound.

Rule kissed him back. "I will see you very soon."

"Soon. Good. Come see me soon."

"You be good for your Mama and Lani."

"I good, yes!"

Rule handed Trev over to Lani and turned to Sydney. "A moment?" he asked carefully. Lani left them, carrying Trev to the open backseat door where the driver had already hooked in his car seat. Rule brushed a hand down Sydney's arm—and then instantly withdrew it. She felt his touch like a bittersweet echo on her skin, even through the fabric of her sleeve. He said, "You haven't forgiven me." It wasn't a question.

"Have a safe trip." She met his eyes, made her lips turn up in a fair approximation of a smile.

He muttered, low, "Damn it, Sydney." And then he reached for her.

She stiffened, put her hands to his chest, started to push him away. But then he was kissing her. And he tasted so good and he smelled like heaven and…

Well, somehow, she was letting her hands slide up to link around his neck. She melted into him and kissed him back. A little moan of frustrated confusion escaped her, a moan distinctly flavored with unwilling desire.

And when he finally lifted his head, she couldn't make up her mind whether to slap him or grab him around the neck, pull him down and kiss him again.

"Kisses don't solve anything," she told him tightly, her hands against his chest again, keeping him at a safer distance. She should have jerked free of his hold completely. But he would be gone in a minute or two. And she'd already kissed him. She might as well go all the way, remain in the warm circle of his arms until he left her.

"I know they don't. But damned if I can leave you without a goodbye kiss."

Okay, he was right. She was glad he had kissed her. Sometimes a kiss said more than words could. She lifted a hand and laid it cherishingly against his lean cheek. "Tell the princess I…look forward to meeting her."

He turned his lips into her palm, kissed her there, the way he had that first night, in their private alcove at the

Mansion restaurant, his breath so warm and lovely across her skin. "I'll return for you. Within the week."

A week wasn't going to cut it. He should know that. She reminded him, "I told you I would need a month, at least, to tie up loose ends at the firm—and that's with you giving my partners a few rich clients as a going-away present."

"I will do what I said I would. And I'm still hoping you can be finished faster."

"Well, that's not going to happen. Get used to it."

"I'll try. And when I return, you're going to have to make room for me at your house." He added, so tenderly, "Because I can't live without you."

His words softened her heart and she wasn't sure she wanted that. She was all turned around inside, wanting him so very much, *not* wanting to be vulnerable to him. She rolled her eyes. "Can't live without me. Oh, right. Kissing up much?"

He took her by the arms. "Correction. I don't *want* to live without you. I'm wild for you. And you know that I am."

Well, yeah. She did, actually. She relented a little. "Of course you'll be staying at my house. I don't want to live without you, either, no matter how angry I happen to be with you."

"Good."

"After all, we're only just married—we only just *met,* if you want to get right down to it."

"Don't." He said it softly. But his eyes weren't soft. His eyes were as black and stormy as a turbulent sea. "Please." He took her hand and kissed the back of it and the simple touch of his mouth on her skin worked its way down inside her, into the deepest part of her. It warmed her and thrilled her—and reassured her, too. "One week," he said fervently. "At the most. I will miss you every day

I'm away from you. I will call you, constantly. You'll be sick and tired of hearing the phone ring."

"I won't mind running to answer the phone. I'll answer and answer gladly," she confessed in a near-whisper. "As long as it's you on the other end of the line."

"Sydney…" He kissed her again, a quick, hard press of his lips against hers. "A week."

And he let her go. She watched him mount the steps to the plane. And she waited to wave to him, when he paused to glance back at her one more time before going in.

Finally, too soon, he was gone.

Rule arrived at Nice Airport at five in the morning. From there, it was only a short drive to Montedoro. He was in his private apartments at the Prince's Palace before six.

At eight, Caroline deStahl, his private secretary, brought him the five newspapers he read daily—*and* the three tabloids that contained stories about him and Sydney. All three tabloids ran the same pictures, one of the two of them kissing, and another of them fleeing down an Impresario hallway. And all three had similar headlines: The Prince Takes a Bride and Wedding Bells for Calabretti Royal and Prince Rule Elopes with Dallas Legal Eagle.

It was a little after 1:00 a.m. in Dallas. Sydney would be in bed. He hated to wake her.

But he did it anyway.

She answered his call on the second ring. "It's after one in the morning, in case you didn't notice," she grumbled sleepily.

"I miss you. I wish I was there with you."

"Is this an obscene phone call?"

He laughed. "It could become one so easily."

"Are you there yet?"

"In my palace apartment, yes. My secretary just delivered the tabloids. We are the main story."

"Which tabloids?"

He named them. "I'm sure we're all over the internet, as well. You are referred to by name. And also as my bride, the 'Dallas Legal Eagle.'"

"Ugh. I was hoping to explain things to my partners at the firm before the word got out. Have you spoken with Princess Liliana yet?"

"No. But I will right away, this morning."

"What can I say? Good luck—and call me the minute it's over."

He pictured her, eyes puffy, hair wild from sleep. It made an ache within him, a sensation that some large part of himself was missing. He said ruefully, "I'll only wake you again if I call…."

"Yeah, well. It's not like I'll be able to go back to sleep now. At least, not without knowing how it went."

He felt thoroughly reprehensible. On any number of levels. "I shouldn't have called."

"Oh, yeah. You should have. And call me right away when it's over. I mean it."

"Fair enough. Sydney, I…" He sought the words. He didn't find them.

She whispered, "Call me."

"I will," he vowed. And then he heard the faint click on the line, leaving him alone, half a world away from her, with just his guilty conscience to keep him company.

Two hours later, he sat in the small drawing room of the suite Liliana always took whenever she visited the palace. He'd been waiting for half an hour for her to appear and he didn't know yet whether she had heard about his marriage or not. Her attendant, one of Lili's Alagonian cousins,

Lady Solange Moltano, had seemed welcoming enough, so he had hopes that he'd arrived in time to be the first to tell her what she didn't want to know.

The door to the private area of the suite opened. He stood.

Lili emerged wearing all white, a pair of wide-legged trousers and a tunic-length jacket, her long blond hair loose, her Delft-blue eyes shining, her cheeks pink with excitement. She was absolutely beautiful, as always. And he really was so fond of her. He didn't want to see her hurt.

He'd never wanted to see Lili hurt.

"Rule." She came toward him, arms outstretched.

They shared an embrace. He looked down at the golden crown of her head and wished he were anywhere but there, in her sitting room, about to tell her that a brilliant, opinionated and fascinating brunette from Texas had laid claim to his heart.

She caught his hands in her slender ones, stepped back and beamed up at him. "You're here. At last…"

So. She didn't know.

"Lili, I came to see you right away, as soon as I got in. I have something important to tell you."

She became even more radiant than a moment before— if that was possible. "Oh." She sounded breathless. "Do you? Really? At last…"

What if she fainted? She'd always been so delicate. "Let's…sit down, shall we?"

"Oh, absolutely. Let's." She pulled him over to a blue velvet sofa. They sat. "Now. What is it you'd like to say to me?"

He had no idea where to begin. His tongue felt like a useless slab of leather in his mouth. "I… Lili. I'm so sorry about this."

Her radiance dimmed, marginally. "Ahem. You're...
sorry?"

"I know you've always had an expectation that you and
I would eventually marry. I realize I've been wrong, very
wrong, to have let things go on like this, to have—"

She cut him off. "Rule."

He coughed into his hand. "Yes?"

Her perfect face was now scarily composed. "All right.
So, then. You're not here to propose marriage to me."

"No, Lili. I'm not. I'm here to tell you that I'm already
married."

Lili gasped. Her face went dead-white.

He got ready to catch her as she collapsed.

Chapter Nine

But Lili remained upright on the sofa. She asked in a voice barely louder than a whisper, "Would you mind telling me her name, please?"

"Sydney. Sydney O'Shea."

"Not Montedoran?"

"No. I met her in America. In Texas."

Lili swallowed, her smooth white throat working convulsively. "Sydney O'Shea. From Texas."

"Yes. Lili, I—"

She waved a hand at him. "No. Please. I… Fair enough, then. You've told me. And I hope you'll be very happy together, you and this Sydney O'Shea." Her huge blue eyes regarded him, stricken. Yet she remained so calmseeming. She even forced a tight smile. "I hope you will have a lovely, perfect life." She shot to her feet. "And now, if you don't mind, I think I would like you to go."

"Lili…" He rose. He wanted to reach out to her. But that

would be wrong. He would only be adding insult to injury. What good could he do for her now? None. There was no way he could help her through this, nothing he could do to make things better.

He *was* the problem. And he really needed to leave, now, before she broke down in front of him and despised him even more for bearing witness to her misery.

"Go," she said again. "Please just go."

So he did go. With a quick dip of his head, he turned on his heel and he left her alone.

He called Sydney again the moment he reached his own rooms.

"How did it go?" she asked.

"Not well. She sent me away as soon as I told her."

"Is there someone with her? Someone she can talk to?"

"She has a cousin with her. But I don't think that they're close."

"Who *is* she close to?"

"My God, Sydney. What does it matter? What business is it of mine or yours?"

"Men are so thickheaded. She needs someone to talk to, someone to comfort her, someone who understands what she's going through."

He needed a stiff drink. But then again, it was barely eleven in the morning. "You don't know her, Sydney. How can you possibly know what she needs?"

"Rule. She's a woman. I *know* what she needs. She needs a true friend with a shoulder she can cry on. She needs that friend now."

"Sydney. I adore you," he said in his coolest, most dangerous tones. "You know that. And I'm very sorry to have made such a balls-up of all this. But you don't know Liliana and you have no idea what she needs. And I'll thank you to stop imagining that you do."

"I'm getting seriously pissed off at you. You know that, right?"

"Yes. I realize that. And we're even. Because I am becoming pretty damn brassed off at *you*."

Dead silence on the line. And then, very flatly, "I think I should hang up before I say something I'm bound to regret."

"Yes. I agree. Go back to sleep, Sydney."

"Hah. Fat chance of that." *Click*. And silence.

"Goodbye," he said furiously, though it wasn't in any way necessary, as she had already hung up.

He put down the phone and then he just stood there, staring blindly at an oil painting of a pastoral scene that hung over the sofa, wanting to strangle someone. Preferably his bride.

A tap on the outer door interrupted his fuming. "Enter."

His secretary, Caroline, appeared to inform him that Her Sovereign Highness and Prince Evan wished to speak with him in the Blue Sitting Room of their private apartment.

In his parents' private rooms, they didn't stand on ceremony.

His mother embraced him and told him she forgave him for running off and marrying his Texas bride without a word to the family beforehand. His father congratulated him as well and said he was looking forward to meeting Sydney and her son. Prince Evan said nothing about the secret Rule had finally shared with him a few weeks before. Rule was grateful to see that his father, at least at this point, was keeping his word and telling Her Sovereign Highness nothing about how Rule had come to meet his bride in the first place.

And when his mother asked him about that, about how he and Sydney had met, he told her the truth, as far as it went. "I saw her going into a shopping mall. One look, and I knew I wanted to know her. So I followed her. I convinced her that she should have lunch with me and after that, I pursued her relentlessly until she gave in and married me. I knew from that first sight of her, getting out of her car, settling her bag on her shoulder so resolutely, that she was one of a kind."

His mother approved. She'd more or less chosen his father that way, after seeing him across a room at a Hollywood party during a visit to the States. "You did have us worried," she chided. "We feared you would fail to make your choice before your birthday. Or that you would marry our darling Lili and the marriage would not suit in the end."

Rule had to keep from gaping. "If you thought that Liliana and I were a bad match, you might have mentioned that to me."

His mother gave a supremely elegant shrug. "And what possible good would that have done? Until you met the *right* woman, you were hardly likely to listen to your mother telling you that the perfectly lovely Lili, of whom you've always been so fond, was all wrong for you."

Rule had no idea how to reply to that. He wanted to say something angry and provoking. Because he felt angry and provoked. But that had more to do with his recent conversation with Sydney than anything else. So he settled for saying nothing.

And then his mother and father shared a look. And his mother nodded. And his father said, "I hope you'll be having a private word with Liliana soon."

At which point he went ahead and confessed, "As it happens, I've already spoken with her."

His mother rose abruptly. Rule and his father followed suit. She demanded, "Why ever didn't you say so?"

Yes. No doubt about it. To strangle someone or put his fist through a wall about now would be extremely satisfying. "I *did* tell you. I told you just now."

"When did you speak with her?" his mother asked.

He glanced at his wristwatch. "Forty-five minutes ago."

"You told her of your marriage?"

"Yes." His parents shared a speaking glance. "What? I *shouldn't* have told her?"

"Well, of course you needed to tell her."

"Then I don't understand what—"

"Is she alone now?"

"I have no idea. Solange Moltano answered the door to me. I'm assuming she's still there, in Lili's apartment."

"The Moltano woman will never do. Lili will need someone to *talk* with, someone to comfort her."

It was exactly what Sydney had said. And that made him angrier than ever. He gritted his teeth and apologized, though he was sick to death of saying how sorry he was. "It's all my fault. I can see now I've handled everything wrong."

His mother put her cool hand against his cheek. "No, darling. You did what you had to do—except for not telling me the moment you left her. Lili will need me now. I'll go to her right away." And with that, she swept from the room.

Into the echoing silence after her departure, Rule said, "I think I would like to hit someone."

His father nodded. "I know the feeling."

"I've broken Lili's heart. And my wife is furious at me."

"Lili will get over this, Rule. Leave it to your mother.

She loves Lili like one of our own and she will know just what to say to comfort her—and why is your bride angry with you?" His father frowned. "You've *told* her already, about the boy?"

Rule swore. "No. Not yet. And I won't. Not…for a while, in any case. Sydney's upset about Lili. She sympathizes with Lili. She says I used Lili as my 'ace in the hole,' as a way to hedge my bet in case I didn't find someone I really wanted to marry before Montedoran law took my title and my fortune."

"She sounds like a rare person, your new wife. Not many brides have sympathy for the 'other' woman."

"Sydney is like no one I've ever known," he said miserably.

"That's good, don't you think?"

"I don't know what to think. She has me spinning in circles. I don't know which end is up."

"A good woman will do that, turn your world upside down."

"I've mucked everything up." Rule sank to the sofa again, shaking his head. "Sydney believes absolutely in honesty and truth and integrity. She's disappointed in me because I wasn't honest with Lili, because I didn't make my true feelings—or lack of them—clear to Lili long ago. I keep thinking, if Sydney can hardly forgive me for not being totally honest with Lili, how can I ever tell her the truth about Trevor?"

His father sat down beside him. He said gently, "You have a real problem."

"I used to see myself as a good man, a man who did what was right…."

"Do you want my advice?"

"You'll only tell me to tell her, and to tell her now."

His father's lips curved in a wry smile. "So that would be a no, then. You don't want my advice?"

"I can't tell her. Honesty is everything for her. If I was going to tell her, I should have done it at the beginning, that first day I met her, before I pushed for marriage…"

"Why didn't you?"

"She confided in me concerning her past romantic relationships. I knew she had very good reasons not to put her trust in men. If I'd told her before I married her, she might never have allowed me to get close to her. Certainly she wouldn't have let me near her in the time allotted before the twenty-fourth of June. It's as I said to you on the phone. There was no good choice. I made the choice that gave me a fighting chance. Or at least, so I thought at the time."

"What do you have on your calendar?"

Rule arched a brow. "And what has my schedule got to do with my complete failure to behave as a decent human being?"

"I think you should clear it."

"My calendar?"

"Yes. Fulfill whatever obligations you can't put off here and do it as quickly as possible. Reschedule everything else. And then return to Texas. Make it up with Sydney, get through this rough patch, spend time with Trevor, strengthen your bonds with both of them. And return to Montedoro when your wife is ready to come with you."

That morning, Sydney actually had two reporters lurking on her front lawn. When she backed out of her garage on the way to the office, she stopped in the driveway, rolled her window down and let them snap away with their cameras for a good sixty seconds.

They fired questions at her while they took the pictures.

She told them that yes, she had married her prince and she was very happy, thank you. No, she wasn't willing to share any of their plans with the press.

One asked snidely if she'd met the Alagonian princess yet. She said no, but she was looking forward to making Princess Liliana's acquaintance—and in case they hadn't noticed, hers was a gated community. She would be calling neighborhood security the next time she found them on her property. That said, she drove away.

At the firm, she met with three of her partners. They already knew about her marriage.

And they weren't surprised when she told them she would be leaving Teale, Gayle and Prosser. They weren't happy with her, either. She was a valued and very much counted-on member of the team, after all. And they were going to be scrambling to fill the void that would be created by her absence.

When she told them she hoped to leave for her new home within the month, an icy silence descended. After which there was talk of her obligations, of the contract she had with the firm.

Then she told them about the potential clients she would be bringing in before she left. She named the ones Rule had mentioned the night before their wedding. And she explained that His Highness, her husband, had excellent business connections worldwide—connections he was willing to share with Teale, Gayle and Prosser.

By the time the meeting was over, her partners were smiling again. Of course, they would be waiting to see if she delivered on her promises. But at least she had a chance of getting out quickly with her reputation intact and zero bridges burned.

She went to work with a vengeance, getting her office and workload in order.

Rule hadn't called since the second time she'd talked to him the night before, when she'd gotten all up in his face. Had she been too hard on him?

Oh, maybe. A little.

But she couldn't believe he'd just dropped the bomb of his elopement on the poor, lovesick princess and then left her all on her own because she'd *asked* him to. Sydney hoped her harsh words had put a serious bug up his butt—as her Grandma Ellen might have said—and that he'd found a way to make sure Liliana had the confidant she needed at a time like this.

At five that afternoon, Sydney was called into the main conference room, which was packed with her partners, the associates, the paralegals, the secretarial staff and even the HR people. There was champagne and a pile of wedding gifts and a cake.

Sydney couldn't believe it. It was really happening. She was getting the office wedding shower she'd been so certain she'd never have.

She thanked them and made a little speech about how much they all meant to her and how she would miss them. And then she ate two pieces of cake, sipped one glass of champagne and did the rounds of the room, her spirits lifted that her colleagues had made a party just for her.

It was nine at night when she left the office. She was seriously dragging by then. Sleep had been in short supply for five days now—since last Friday, when her whole life had changed in an instant, because she'd gone into Macy's to buy a wedding gift for Calista Dwyer.

At home, Lani helped her carry in the gifts from the party. "You look exhausted," Lani said. "Just leave everything on the table. I'll deal with it tomorrow."

Sydney dropped the last box on the stack and sank into a chair. "How was your day?"

"Fabulous. Trevor took a three-hour nap and I got ten pages done. And then later, we went to the park. He seems to have slacked off on the endless knock-knock jokes."

"That's a relief."

"I so agree—he asked twice about 'Roo.' He wanted to know when Rule was coming to see him again so they could play trucks."

Sydney was happy that her son was so taken with his stepfather. She only wished she didn't feel edgy and unsure about everything. But it had all happened so fast between them, and now he was gone. A sense of unreality had set in.

She told Lani, "He said he'd be back in a week."

"Well, all right. Good to know—and is everything okay with you two?"

Sydney let her shoulders slump. "There are some issues."

Lani knew her so well. "And you're too wiped out to talk about them now." At Sydney's weary nod, she asked, "Hungry?"

"Naw. I had takeout at the office—and two pieces of cake at the party. I think I'll go upstairs and kiss my sleeping son and then take a long, hot bath."

Forty-five minutes later, Sydney climbed into bed. She set the alarm for six-thirty, turned off the light and was sound asleep almost as soon as her head hit the pillow.

Rule didn't call that night. Or the next morning.

Apparently, he really was "brassed off" at her. She thought it was rather childish of him, to cut off communication because she'd pissed him off. Then again, nothing was stopping her from picking up the phone and calling *him*.

She felt reluctant to do that, which probably proved that she was being every bit as childish as he was. And she did wonder how things had worked out with Liliana, if he'd done what she'd asked him to do and found someone for the poor woman to talk to.

And okay, she hadn't *asked*. She'd more like *commanded*. And he hadn't appreciated her ordering him around.

Maybe she shouldn't have been so hard on him. Maybe she should have...

Who knew what she should have done? She was totally out of her depth with him. She'd only known him since Friday and now they were married and already he was halfway around the world from her. No wonder they were having "issues."

She hardly knew him. And how would she *get* to know him, with him there and her here?

All she knew for certain was that she ached with missing him. The lack of him was like a hole in her heart, a vacancy. She needed him with her, to fill that lack. She wanted him there, with her, touching her. She wanted it so bad. She wanted to grab him in her arms and curl herself into him, to hold on so tight, to press herself so close. She wanted to...somehow be inside his skin.

She wanted the scent of him, the sound of his voice, the sweet, slow laugh, the feel of his hands on her, the touch of his mouth...

She was totally gone on him. And he'd better return to her in a week, as he'd promised, or she would do something totally unconstructive. Track him down and shoot him, maybe. Not fatally, of course. Just wing him.

At the office the next day, she got calls from a couple of oil company executives, representatives of two of the companies Rule had said he could deliver to her firm. The calls eased her mind a little.

Okay, he hadn't been in touch the way he'd promised

that he would. But he was moving ahead with his plans to help her get away from Texas gracefully. That was something. A good sign.

Before the end of the day, she'd set up the first getting-to-know-you meetings between her partners and the reps from the oil companies.

Thursday morning at six-thirty, at the exact moment that her alarm went off, the phone rang. Jarred awake, she groped for the alarm first and hit the switch to shut it off.

Then she grabbed the phone. "Hello, what?" she grumbled.

"I woke you."

Even half-asleep, gladness filled her. "Hello."

"Are you still angry with me?"

She rolled over onto her back, and raked her sleep-scrambled hair back off her face. "I could ask you the same question."

"I know I said I'd call every day…" God. His voice. How could it be better, smoother, deeper, just plain sexier than she remembered?

She corrected him. "You said you would call *constantly.* That's *more* than every day."

"Will you ever forgive me?"

She chuckled, a low, husky sound. She just couldn't help it. All he had to do was call and her world was rosy again. "I would say forgiveness is a distinct possibility."

"I'm so glad to hear that." He said it tenderly. And as if he really, really meant it.

"I miss you, Rule. I miss you so much."

"I miss you, too."

"How can I feel this way? I've only known you for, what, five days?"

"Four days, nineteen hours and…three minutes—and

you'd better miss me. You're my wife. It's your job to miss me when we're apart."

"Well, I'm doing my job, then."

"Good."

"And I'm sorry," she said, "that we argued."

"I am, too."

"Those two oil men called yesterday. I set them up with my partners."

"Excellent."

She hesitated to ruin the conciliatory mood by bringing up a certain princess. But she really did want to know what had happened. "Did everything work out then, with Liliana?"

"You were right," he said quietly. "I should have sent someone to be with her."

"Oh, no. What *happened?*"

"When I told my mother that Lili hadn't seemed to take the news of our marriage well, she rushed off to comfort her. Lili wasn't in her rooms. Lili's attendant said that she'd fled in tears."

"Omigod. She's missing, then?"

"No. They found her shortly thereafter. She simply turned up, looking somewhat disheveled, or so I was told, and insisting she was perfectly fine."

"Turned up?"

"One of the servants found her in the hallway between Maximilian's apartments and Alexander's. She claimed she'd simply gone for a stroll."

"A *stroll?*"

"That's what she said."

"Is she friends with your brothers? Did she talk it out with one of them?"

"Not possible."

"Why not?"

"Max is with his children, at his villa. And Alex and Lili have never gotten on, not since childhood."

"That doesn't mean he might not have been kind to her, if he saw that she was upset."

"Sydney, he's hardly come out of his rooms since he returned from Afghanistan. But you're right, of course. Anything is possible. Perhaps she talked to him, though no one told me that she did."

"But…she's all right, then?"

"Yes. She did end up confiding in my mother. And in the end, Lili promised my mother that she is perfectly all right and that no one is to worry that her father's famous temper will be roused. Lili said she had finally realized that she and I were not right for each other, after all. She told my mother to wish me and my bride a lifetime of happiness. My mother believes that Lili was sincere in what she said."

"Okay. Well. Good news, huh?"

"I believe so, yes. Lili departed yesterday morning for Alagonia. King Leo has not appeared brandishing a sword or insisting on pistols at dawn, so I'm going to venture a guess that renewed animosity between our two countries has been safely averted."

"I'm so glad. I have to admit, I was worrying—that Liliana might have done something crazy, that her father might have taken offense. And then, when you never called, I only worried more."

"I'm a complete ass."

"Do you hear me arguing? Just tell me you're coming back here to me by Tuesday or Wednesday, as promised."

"Sorry. I can't do that." He said it teasingly.

Still, her heart sank. She tried to think of what to say, how to frame her disappointment in words that wouldn't get them started fighting all over again.

And then he said, "I'll be there tomorrow."

She felt deliciously breathless. "Oh, Rule. Say that again."

"You *do* miss me." The way he said that made her heart beat faster.

"Oh, yes, I do," she fervently agreed. "I want to have *time* with you. I want you near me. Here we are, married. We're going to spend our lives together, yet in many ways we hardly know each other."

"Tomorrow," he said. "It'll be late, around ten at night, by the time I reach your house."

"Tomorrow. Oh, I can't believe it—and late is fine. I'm lucky to get home by nine-thirty, anyway. I'll be here. Waiting."

"I have work to do there, too, you know. I have to introduce your partners to any number of excellent potential clients, so they'll realize they owe it to you to let you go right away."

She beamed, even though he wasn't there to see it. "I can't tell you how glad I am that you're coming back now. It will be so good, to be with you every day—even if I do spend way too much of every day at work. But I'm going to change that. When I'm through at the firm, I'm going to make sure I never again take a job where I hardly see my son, where I'm rarely with my husband."

"I do like the sound of that."

"Good— Oh, and I forgot to tell you. Trevor will be so pleased to see you. He's been asking for you."

"Tell him I'm on my way."

Chapter Ten

Sydney was waiting at the picture window in the living room Friday night when the long, black limo pulled in at the curb. The sight of his car had her heart racing and her pulse pounding so hard, it made a roaring sound in her ears.

With a glad cry, she spun on her heel and took off for the door. Flinging it wide, she ran down the front steps and along the walk. He emerged from the car and she threw herself into his arms.

He kissed her, right there beneath the streetlight. A hard, hot kiss, one that started out desperate and ended so sweet and lazy and slow.

When he lifted his head, he said, "I thought I'd never get here."

She laughed, held so close and safe in his arms. "But you *are* here. And I may never let you go away from me again." She took his hand. "Come inside…"

The driver was already unloading Rule's bags. He followed them up the front walk. Joseph followed, too.

In the house, the driver carried the bags up to the master suite and then, with a tip of his cap, took his leave.

Joseph remained. For once, he wasn't wearing those dark glasses. But he still had the Bluetooth device in his ear. And he carried a black duffel bag.

Rule looked slightly embarrassed. "I'm afraid Joseph goes where I go."

Sydney spoke to the bodyguard. "I hope you don't mind sleeping in a separate room from His Highness."

The severe-looking Joseph almost cracked a smile. "Ma'am, if you have a spare room, that would be appreciated. If not, the sofa will do well enough."

"I have a guest room." She indicated the doorway at the end of the hall. "The kitchen is through there. While you're here, make yourself at home. You're welcome to anything you find in the pantry or the fridge."

"Thank you, ma'am."

She turned to Rule. "Are you hungry?"

His dark eyes said, *Not for food,* and she felt the loveliest warmth low in her belly, and a definite wobbliness in her knees. He told her, "I ate on the plane."

So she led the way up the stairs and showed Joseph to his room, indicating Trevor's bathroom across the hall. "I'm afraid you'll have to share the bathroom with my son."

"Thank you. This will suit me very well."

Before joining Rule in her room, she tapped on Lani's door and told her friend that Rule's bodyguard was staying in the guest room.

Lani, reading in bed, looked up from her eReader, over the top rims of her glasses. "Thanks for the warning—and don't stay up all night."

"Yes, Mother."

"Say hi to Rule."

"Will do."

She went to her own room and found Rule standing in the bow window, staring out at the quiet street. "Lani says hi."

He turned to her. "I like your house. It's comfortable, and the rooms are large. Lots of windows…"

She hovered in the open doorway, her stomach suddenly all fluttery. "We've been happy here. It will be strange, to live in a palace."

"I have other properties. Villas. Town houses. You might prefer one of them."

All at once, the life that lay before her seemed alien, not her own. "We'll see." The two words came out on a breath.

He held out his hand to her. "Are you shy of me now, Sydney?"

Her throat clutched. She spoke through the tightness. "A little, I guess." A nervous laugh escaped her. "That's silly, isn't it?"

He shook his dark head. "Come here. Let me ease your fears."

Pausing only to shut the door and engage the lock, she went to him and took the hand he offered. His touch burned her and soothed her at once.

He reached out with the hand not holding hers and shut the blinds. "I put my suitcases in your closet…."

She moved in closer. He framed her face. She said, "It seems like forever, since you left…."

"I'm here now."

"I'm so glad about that."

He kissed her. And the throat-tight nervousness faded. There was only his mouth on her mouth, his hands against her cheeks, brushing down the sides of her throat, tracing the collar of her cotton shirt, and then going to work on the buttons down the front of it.

She was breathless and sighing, pulling him closer. He took away her shirt and her bra. He pushed down the leggings she had pulled on after work. She kicked away her little black flats and wiggled the rest of the way out of the leggings.

And then he went to work on his own clothes, kissing her senseless as he ripped off his jacket, his shirt, his trousers…everything. She had only her panties on and he was completely naked when he started walking her backward toward the bed.

"Wait," she breathed against his lips.

He only went on kissing her—until she gave a gentle shove against his chest. With an impatient growl, he lifted his mouth from hers. "You know you're killing me…."

She put her finger to those amazing lips of his. "Only a moment…"

"A moment is too long." But he did let her go.

She turned around and pulled the covers down, smoothing them. "There."

"Sydney…" He clasped her by the hips and drew her back against him.

"I'm here. Right here…" She lifted her arms and reached for him, clasping his neck, turning her head to him so their mouths could fuse once again.

His tongue plundered her mouth and his hands covered her breasts. And she could feel him, all along her body, feel the power of him, the heat. Feel the proof of how much he wanted her, silky and hard, pressing into her back.

And then he was turning her and guiding her down onto the sheets and right then, at that moment on that night, she was the happiest woman in Texas. There was only the feel of his big body settling against hers, only his kiss, only his skilled touch, on her breasts, her belly and lower.

He took away her panties and those wonderful fingers of his found the womanly core of her and she moaned into his mouth. He kissed her some more as he caressed her, bringing her higher, making her clutch his hard shoulders and press herself closer.

Closer…

And then she couldn't wait. Not one second longer. She eased her hand between them and she wrapped her fingers around him and she guided him into place.

When he came into her, she let out a soft cry at the sheer beauty of it, at the feel of him filling her. So perfectly. So right.

He kissed her throat, and then scraped the willing flesh there with his teeth. And then he licked her. And then he blew on her wet skin and she moaned and pulled him closer again, lifting her legs to wrap around his waist, pushing herself harder against him, demanding everything of him, wanting it all.

When he held her like this, when he worked his special magic on her skin, she had no doubts at all. She would follow him anywhere, and she would be happy.

Just the two of them and Trevor. And maybe, if they were lucky, more children. Three or four. Nine or ten…

She'd forgotten how many she wanted, how many they had finally agreed on. And what did it matter how many? She would love them all, every one.

And by then, she'd forgotten everything—everything but this, but the man who held her, the man who filled her. The pleasure was building, spinning fast, and then gathering tight.

Only to open outward, a sudden blooming, so hot and

perfect. She cried out again, loud enough that he had to cover her mouth with his hand.

She laughed against his fingers, a wild sound. And then he was laughing with her. And still the pleasure bloomed and grew. And all at once, they were silent, serious, concentrated, eyes wide open, falling into each other.

Falling and spinning, set gloriously free: the two of them, locked together. She was lost in his eyes. And more than happy to be so.

She whispered his name.

With a low groan, he gave hers back to her.

She must have slept for a time.

When she woke, he was braced up on an elbow, looking down at her, his eyes black velvet, his mouth an invitation to sin.

She reached up, curved her fingers around the back of his head, pulled him closer. They shared a quick, gentle kiss. "It's so good, to wake up and find you here. I want to do that for the rest of my life."

"And my darling, you shall. Now go back to sleep."

"Soon. Tell me about your parents. Are they angry, that you married me?"

"No. They're pleased. Very pleased."

She wasn't buying that. "They don't even know me. You met me and married me in like, ten minutes or less. How can they be pleased with that? I mean, I could understand if you said they were…accepting. But *pleased?*"

"They know me. They know that I'm happy, that I've found the woman I want to be with for a lifetime. They're relieved and they're grateful."

"Well, okay." She traced the shape of his ear. It was such a good-looking ear. "I get that. I mean, they were probably getting pretty concerned, right, that you wouldn't marry in time?"

"They were, yes." He caught her hand, kissed the tips of her fingers.

"But if you'd married the Princess of Alagonia, wouldn't that have made them a lot happier?"

"No. Evidently not. They told me they didn't think Lili and I would have been a good match."

"You'd think they might have said that earlier."

"My response exactly."

"Someone should change that ridiculous law."

"My mother's great-grandfather, who ruled Montedoro for fifty years, *did* change it. He abolished the law. And then my mother's father put the law in place once again."

"But why?"

"My mother's *grand*father didn't marry until late in life. He had eight children, but only one was legitimate, my mother's father, *my* grandfather. Then my grandfather had just one child, a daughter, legitimate, my mother. The family was dying out. My grandfather took action. He put the law back in place."

She laughed. "And then your mother obeyed it. She married young, brought in fresh blood and took her reproductive duties to heart."

"Yes, she did. And look at us now."

"Heirs and spares all over the place."

"That's right. So you see, the law has its uses."

She frowned, considering. "There must be any number of ways around it. You could marry someone in time to keep your inheritance, and then divorce her as soon as your thirty-third birthday has passed."

He nuzzled her neck. "Already planning how you'll get rid of me, eh?"

She laughed, and caught his face and kissed him, hard,

on the mouth. "Never. But you know what I'm saying, right?"

"We are Catholic. The heir to the throne always marries in the church. Divorce is not an option in the church. There is annulment, but there are specific grounds for that, none of them pretty. And you have to understand. In my family, we are raised to respect the Prince's Marriage Law. We believe it is a good law, good for Montedoro—especially after we saw what happened when my great-great-grandfather abolished it. And we grow up committed to the spirit of that law, to finding a proper marriage partner by the required date. My parents were good parents, parents who spent time with their children, what you would call in America 'hands-on' parents. My mother considers each of her nine children to be every bit as important as her throne."

"Well, all right," she said. "I guess I can't argue with success. But I do have a couple more questions."

"Ask."

"Do *we* have to marry in the church in order for you to keep your inheritance?"

"No. The heir must marry in the church. The rest of us are only required to be legally wed before the age of thirty-three. But, should I become the heir—which is most unlikely at this point—you and I would have to take steps for a church-sanctioned marriage. That would not be complicated, as neither of us has been married before."

"Do you want us to be married in the church?"

He kissed the tip of her nose. "I do, yes."

"Good answer." She slid her hands up his chest and wrapped them around his neck. "I want that, too."

"Then we shall take the necessary steps to make it happen as soon as we're settled in Montedoro."

"Agreed. I think we should seal it with a kiss."

"Beyond a doubt, we should."

So they kissed. A long, slow one. The kiss led to more kisses and then to the usual stimulating conclusion.

Rule told her again to go sleep.

She said, "Soon."

And then they talked for another hour about everything from the success of his plan to sell Montedoran oranges to a number of exclusive outlets in the U.S., to why his brother Alex and Princess Lili had never gotten along. Alex, Rule said, had always thought Lili was silly and shallow; Lili considered Alex to be overly brooding and grim, with a definite tendency toward overbearing self-importance.

Sydney learned that his brother Max's son was named Nicholas and Max's little girl was Constance. And Rule told her that in his great-grandfather's day, the economy of Montedoro was almost solely dependent on gambling revenues. His grandfather and his mother had made a point to expand the principality's economic interests beyond its traditional gambling base.

"Now," he said, "gambling accounts for only four percent of our nation's annual revenues."

She reminded him that he knew all about Ryan and Peter. But other than Liliana, she knew nothing of the women who had mattered in his life.

"You already know that I admire my mother," he said with a gleam in his eye.

"Your mother and your sisters don't count. I'm talking love affairs, Rule. You know that I am."

So he told her about the Greek heiress he'd loved when he was fourteen. "She had an absolutely adorable space between her two front teeth and she spoke with a slight lisp and she intended to run away to America and become a musical theater star."

"Did she?"

"Unfortunately, she was tone deaf. I heard her sing once. Once was enough."

"Destroyed your undying love for her, did it?"

"I was young and easily distracted. Especially when it came to love." He spoke of the girl he'd met in a Paris café when he was eighteen. And of an Irish girl he'd met in London. "Black hair, blue eyes. And a temper. A hot one. At first, I found her temper exciting. But in time it grew tiresome."

"Luckily there were any number of actresses and models just waiting for their chance with you."

"You make me sound like a Casanova."

"Weren't you?"

"No. I was not. Yes, I've spent time with a number of women, but seduction for its own sake has never interested me. I was…looking for someone. The *right* someone." He lowered his head until their noses touched. "You."

Her heart did that melty thing. "Oh, Rule…"

He kissed her forehead, her cheeks, and finally her lips—sweet, brushing kisses. "Will you please go to sleep now?" He tucked the covers closer around her. "Close your eyes…"

And she did.

The next day was Saturday. Sydney left Rule having breakfast with Trevor and Lani and spent the morning at the office, where things were pretty quiet and she got a lot done.

She returned home at lunchtime and spent the rest of the day with Rule and her son and her best friend. She and Rule went out to dinner that night and then, at home, made slow, wonderful love. They fell asleep with their arms wrapped around each other. Her last thought before she drifted off was that she had it all now. Her life was exactly as she'd once dreamed it might be.

Sunday she stayed home, too. She and Rule took Trevor to the park in the morning. She watched Rule pushing Trev on the swings and thought how already they seemed like father and son. Trev adored him. It was "Roo" this and "Roo" that. The feeling was clearly mutual. Rule seemed to dote on Trev. He never tired of listening to Trev babble on about the things that mattered to a curious two-year-old.

And an older lady, a woman there with her grandson, leaned close to Sydney when they sat on the bench together. "Your boy looks just like his daddy."

Sydney smiled at the woman. "He does, doesn't he?"

Later, at lunch, Trev was back into his knock-knock jokes. He and Rule played a never-ending game of them until Sydney put her hands over her ears and begged them to stop.

Trev laughed. "Mama says, 'No more knock-knock!'"

Rule piped up with, "Mama says, 'Touch your nose.'" He touched his nose and then Trev, delighted, touched his. And Rule said, "Mama says, 'Rub your tummy.'" They both rubbed their tummies.

Trev caught on about then and they were off on the "Mama" version of Simon Says. Sydney laughed along with them.

The woman at the park had been right. And Lani had noticed the resemblance, too. They were so much alike, really. They even had mannerisms in common—the way they each tipped their head, a little to the left, when thoughtful. Even the way they smiled was similar—slow and dazzling.

Sydney supposed it wasn't all that surprising, how much Trev resembled his new stepdad. The sperm donor she'd chosen had a lot of characteristics in common with Rule—hair and eye color, height and build. And the similarities weren't only physical. The donor had an advanced degree in business and enjoyed travel and sports. And the description of him compiled by the staff at the cryobank? All about how charming and handsome and bright and dynamic he was. How well-spoken and articulate, a born leader *and* a good listener. His profile also said that family was important to him and he believed in marriage, that he felt it could and should last a lifetime.

She'd selected that particular donor mostly because he sounded like the kind of man she'd given up on finding. After all, a woman hopes her child might inherit traits that she admires.

A little shiver skittered up her spine as she watched her son and Rule together and compared her husband with the man who had supplied half of her child's DNA. Life could be so strange and amazing. Really, she'd chosen her own personal fantasy man as her sperm donor, not even realizing that he was destined to materialize in the flesh and promptly sweep her off her feet into their very own happy-ever-after—let alone that he would so quickly become a doting father to her son.

That Sunday was sunny and clear, with a high in the mid-eighties, a little warm for mid-April. It was a great day for splashing around in the pool—which they did as soon as Trevor woke up from his nap. Later, Lani made dinner, a fabulous Greek-style shrimp scampi.

Monday it was off to work again. Rule showed up at a little after eleven. Sydney introduced him around the office and two of the partners were only too happy to join them for lunch at the Mansion.

It was a working lunch, and a very productive one. By the end of it, Rule had set up three dinner dates where he would introduce her colleagues to more potential clients. After lunch, he returned to the house and she went back to work.

Their days fell into a certain rhythm. The office owned her during the long weekdays, but she spent her nights with her new husband and managed to get most of the weekend free to be with Trevor, too. Rule spent a lot of time with her son and the growing bond between the man and the boy was something special to see. Rule would play with him for hours during the day and read him his bedtime stories most nights.

Sydney worked and worked some more. Rule often appeared to take her to lunch—and he moved forward on the goal he'd set for himself of giving her partners enough new business that they wouldn't consider themselves cheated when she moved on.

There were more tabloid stories. Sydney didn't read them, but evidently a few of her coworkers did. She found more than one discarded scandal rag on the lunch table in the break room. Somehow, they'd gotten her high school and college graduation pictures, and there were pictures of Rule, bare-chested on a sailboat with a blonde, and also wearing a tux at some gala event, a gorgeous redhead on his arm. Sydney hardly glanced at them. Rule said that when they got to Montedoro, a press conference would be arranged. They would answer questions for a roomful of reporters and let them take a lot of pictures. That should satisfy them if they hadn't already moved on to the next big story by then.

Twice during the weeks it took her to finish up at the firm, Rule had to travel. He had business in New York and spent four days in Manhattan. And he also returned briefly to Montedoro to meet with a certain luxury car manufacturer who was considering giving one of his new designs, a sleek high-end sports car, the name "Montedoro."

Sydney missed him when he was gone. Her bed seemed so empty without him there to keep her warm in the middle of the night. Trev missed him, too. "I sad, Mama. I want Roo," he would say. And she would remind him that Rule would return soon.

On the last Friday in April, Sydney came home late as usual. Rule was back from Montedoro. He and Lani had waited to have dinner with her. They'd even invited the ever-present but usually silent Joseph to join them. Lani had outdone herself with a crown roast of lamb. Rule opened a lovely bottle of Syrah. And Lani announced that she'd decided to take them up on their offer and come with them to Montedoro.

Sydney jumped from her chair and ran around the table and hugged her friend good and hard. "Whew. I didn't want to pressure you, but I really was hoping you would come with us."

Lani laughed. "Are you kidding? Miss the chance to live on the Mediterranean in the Prince's Palace? I couldn't pass it up."

Even Joseph was smiling. "Good news," he said and raised the glass of wine he'd hardly touched.

Lani said, "Life experience is everything for a novelist. Plus, well, what would I do without you?"

"Exactly." Sydney hugged her again. "And how could we possibly get along without *you?*"

Deep in the night, Sydney woke suddenly from a sound sleep. It was after three and she had no idea what had wakened her.

And then she heard Trev crying. "Mama...Mama..."

Beside her, Rule woke, too. He sat up. "I'll go..."

She kissed his beard-scratchy cheek and pushed him back down to the pillow. "No. I'll do it." She threw on a robe and went to see what was wrong.

Trev was fussy and feverish, his dark hair wet with sweat. He kept putting his hands to his cheeks and crying, "Hurt, Mama. Hurt..."

Lani came in, her hair every which way, a sleep mark on her cheek, belting her robe. "Can I do something?"

"It's all right. I think he's teething. Go back to bed. I've got him."

"Come get me if you need me."

"Will do."

Yawning, Lani returned to her room.

Sydney took Trev's temperature. It was marginally elevated. She gave him some children's acetaminophen and took him downstairs to get one of the teething rings she kept in the freezer. She was back in his room, sitting in the rocker with him as he fussed and chewed on the teething ring when Rule appeared in the doorway to the upstairs hall, bare-chested in a pair of blue pajama bottoms.

"He's not a happy camper," she said. "I think it's his teeth. I gave him a painkiller. It should take effect soon."

Trev pushed away from Sydney. "Roo! Hurt. I have hurt..." He held out his chubby little arms.

Rule came for him, scooping him up out of Sydney's lap without a word or a second's hesitation. Trev wrapped his arms around his stepfather's neck and held on, sticking the ring back in his mouth and burrowing his dark head against Rule's chest. Rule began walking him, back and forth across the bedroom floor.

Sydney, still in the rocker, stared up at the man and the little boy, at their two dark heads so close together, and tried to get a grip on exactly what she was feeling.

Jealousy?

Maybe a little. Rule had become nothing short of proprietary about Trev—and Trev about him. In recent weeks, with Rule around day in and day out, Trev had grown to count on him, to expect him to be there, to demand his attention. Since Rule was only too happy to spend lots of time with Trev, and did, it was natural that a powerful bond had swiftly developed between them.

And wasn't that bond a *good* thing? As a father figure, Rule had so far proved himself to be pretty much the ideal. So what was bothering her?

Did she want Rule to defer to her when it came to Trev, was that it? When he'd grabbed her son from her arms without so much as a do-you-mind, had that somehow threatened her, made her feel that her status as Trev's parent was in jeopardy? Lani and Trev had a close relationship, but Lani always remembered that Sydney was the mom, that her claim on him came first.

Rule, though...

He didn't defer to her anymore, if he ever had. He seemed to consider himself as much Trev's dad as Sydney was his mom.

And what was wrong with that?

Wasn't that what she'd been hoping for all along?

Ugh. Maybe it was guilt—scratch the "maybe." *Probably* it was guilt. *Her* guilt, because she knew she'd never been around enough. She worked killer hours and a lot of days she didn't see her son awake except early in the morning, when she kissed him goodbye on her way out the door.

No wonder he chose Rule over her when he needed comforting. Rule was more a consistent presence in his life than she was.

But that was going to change. Very soon. And it would change *because* of Rule, because of what he offered her and Trev, because of the kind of husband and father he was. Not only deeply committed to his family, but also an excellent provider.

As soon as she was finished at the firm, *she* would be available to Trev more consistently—constantly, in fact, at least at first. And even when she found interesting work in Montedoro, it was going to be work with reasonable hours for a change. She would truly have it all. Time to be a mom, time to be a wife, time to do good work that mattered.

It was all going to be fine and she needed to get over her guilt and her jealousy. Trev had a dad now, that was all that was happening here. Sometimes a child wanted his dad over his mom. And there was nothing at all wrong with that.

She leaned her head back in the rocker and closed her eyes.

The next moment—or so it seemed to her—Rule was whispering in her ear. "Come back to bed, sleepyhead."

She forced her heavy eyes to open, asked, "Trev?"

He put a finger to his lips, tipped his head toward the toddler bed across the room, where Trev was curled up under the blankets, his arm around his favorite stuffed dinosaur.

She gave Rule her hand and he pulled her out of the chair. He drew her close and she leaned against him as they returned to the master bedroom.

In bed, he gathered her close to him. "You work too hard." He stroked her hair.

"Not for long. Another week or so, the way I figure it, and I'm so outta there."

"I can't wait to take you home with me—you and Trevor both."

She traced his dark brows, one and then the other, by

feel more than sight. They had turned off the lamp. "I have a secret to tell you."

"I love secrets." He bent closer, kissed her temple. "Especially *your* secrets."

"Don't laugh."

"I promise, I won't." He stroked her hair.

"You and Trev look a lot alike."

He kissed her lips, a brushing kiss, his breath so warm across her cheek. "We do, a little, don't we—and is that your secret?"

"No. I'm getting to it, though. And it starts with the resemblance between you and Trev, which is pretty striking, really. Beyond the dark hair and eyes, you both tip your heads at the same angle when you're thinking. And when you smile…you make me think of him. In fact, that first day we met, remember how I've said I kept thinking how you looked familiar? Remember, I even asked you if we'd met before?"

"Yes. I remember."

"I've been thinking about that a lot lately, kind of marveling over it. And then I realized it's not surprising in the least."

"Why not?"

"Simple. The sperm donor I chose was a lot like you—and yes, that would be my big secret." She traced the so-manly strong line of his jaw. "I chose him because he was just like you—I mean, the you I didn't even know then. He had your same height and build, dark eyes and dark hair. I chose him because he seemed like the man I always hoped to meet someday. The man I had by then decided I would *never* meet."

He withdrew from her then, turning over onto his back beside her.

She wondered at that. "Rule? Are you okay? Did I say something that upset you?"

"Of course you didn't." He sounded...distant. And a little strange. "I'm perfectly all right."

"You don't *seem* all right."

He found her hand under the covers, twined his fingers with hers. "I'm fine."

"Good." She smiled into the darkness. "You sure you were never a sperm donor?"

"You're joking."

"Well, yeah. I guess I am. But sometimes, it's almost eerie, the resemblance between you and Trev."

He didn't say anything.

She went on, "I always kind of hoped to meet him. But he was a confidential donor. I left permission that he could contact me if he ever changed his mind. He didn't. Not so far, anyway—and that reminds me. I need to change my contact information with Secure Choice—that's the clinic I used, Secure Choice Cryobank." She waited for his response, thinking of his possessiveness concerning Trev—and also a little worried about the dreamy way she'd spoken of a man she'd never met.

Was he jealous? Would he try to talk her out of keeping her information current, want her to make it more difficult for the donor to get in touch should he ever decide he wanted to?

But then Rule only reached for her again. He eased his arm under her nape and drew her into him, bringing her to rest against his warm, hard chest. "Go to sleep."

She closed her eyes and let the steady, even sound of his heartbeat lull her.

Of course he'd never been a sperm donor. She knew what a donor went through. She'd researched the whole process when she decided on artificial insemination. It wasn't just a matter of doing the happy hand in a cup.

A man went through all kinds of testing before he could become a donor. Only a small percentage of applicants were accepted. A man had to donate weekly, at least, and he couldn't have sex for two days before each donation. He also couldn't go more than five days *without* ejaculating, because not often enough was as bad for sperm production as too often. Most sperm donors signed contracts for six months to a year of donations—six months to a year of having sex in a cup on a strict schedule. The money wasn't even all that much, averaging under a hundred dollars per viable donation.

To have been her donor, Rule would have had to sign on for all of the above with the fertility clinic she had used, or an affiliate. What were the odds of that?

He was a hardworking man who traveled the world doing business for his country. Not only would being a donor be unprofitable, time-consuming and a logistical nightmare for Rule, it just…wasn't like him. He felt so strongly about family and fatherhood. He wasn't a man who could help to give a child life and not want to be there while that child was growing up.

Still, she didn't get the way he'd pulled away from her when she talked about how much alike he and Trevor were, when she'd confessed that he, Rule, was pretty much her dream man come to life. He'd turned onto his back before she said anything about how she'd given permission to be contacted, so his original withdrawal really couldn't be chalked up to apprehension that the donor might show up someday.

She didn't like the way he'd said, *You're joking,* when she'd asked him if he'd ever been a donor. He could so easily have given her a simple, direct denial.

It wasn't that she actually suspected he might be Trevor's biological father. She only wondered why he'd seemed so defensive and why he'd pulled away from her when she'd only been trying to tell him that he was everything she'd ever wanted in a man.

Chapter Eleven

But by the next morning, in the bright light of day, as Sydney hurried to get ready to head to the office, her vague suspicions about Rule…

Well, they seemed downright ridiculous.

He hadn't really pulled away from her last night, had he? He'd only rolled over to his back. And when she'd asked if anything was wrong, he'd told her there was nothing.

And his seeming evasiveness when she teased him about being a sperm donor? It just didn't strike her as all that odd now that she'd had a little time to think it over. He was very attached to Trevor. He didn't want to dwell on the stranger who had fathered her child. She could understand that.

She decided that she would put the whole issue from her mind. She had so much work to do and not all that much time to do it in. The last thing she needed was to waste her energy stewing about stuff she'd made up in her head.

Plus, if she wanted to dwell on something, why not choose something real? Something important. Something potentially quite wonderful.

As of that morning, her period was one week late. It was beginning to look as though she and her new husband were already getting their start on that larger family they both hoped for.

But she shouldn't get ahead of herself. She *had* been under a lot of stress lately—meeting and marrying Rule in the space of forty-eight hours, and then having to send him away to make his apologies to the "other woman" in his life. And then there was the way she was working like crazy to finish up at the firm, planning a move halfway around the world.

Yes. Her life was especially stressful right now. And stress could really mess up a woman's cycle.

She decided she would wait a few weeks before she said anything to Rule. No reason to get his expectations up unnecessarily—or her own, for that matter. She would let that question rest for a while, not allow herself to get too excited about it until more time had passed.

Trev was much better that morning. He seemed to be over the bout of teething pain. His temperature was normal and he was eating his breakfast cereal, chattering away, when she left for work.

He gave her a big kiss. "Come back soon, Mama!"

"Don't you worry, I will."

And that evening, she managed to get away from the officer earlier than usual. She was even in time to give Trev his bath before bed. Once he was in bed, Rule said he wanted to take her out to dinner.

They went to the Mansion. Sydney loved the food and

service there and Rule liked it, too. The staff knew him and protected his privacy.

He made a toast. "To us. To our family. To our whole lives together."

She clinked her wineglass with his, aglow with happiness, knowing that she had to be the most fortunate woman in all of Texas. After a couple of sips, she set her glass down and didn't pick it up again. Might as well be cautious. Just in case she really was pregnant.

Not that she thought she was. Uh-uh. She wasn't going there. Not yet.

Four days later, on the first Friday in May, Sydney said goodbye to Teale, Gayle and Prosser.

She left her desk clean and neat and her clients effectively shifted to other attorneys in the firm. She also departed on good terms with her former partners, all thanks to her strict dedication to doing things right—and her new husband's willingness to share his connections.

The next week was all about packing for the move. Lani, one of the most organized human beings on the planet, had already gotten a good head start on that. But there was more to do. Sydney got to work on the rest of the job with her usual enthusiasm. They were leaving the house furnished and in the hands of an excellent Realtor.

Their passports were current. Even Trevor's. Sydney had gotten his for him months before, when she'd been thinking of taking a vacation in Ireland.

On the second Friday in May, they boarded the private jet for Montedoro. Lani's brother, Carlos, and her parents, Iris and Jorge, came to the airport to see them off. There were also reporters. They snapped lots of pictures and asked an endless number of way-too-personal questions.

Rule told them he had no comment at this time and Joseph herded them up the ramp and into the plane.

The flight was a long one and there was a seven-hour time difference between Dallas and their destination. They took off from Love Field at two in the afternoon and arrived at the airport in Nice at eight the next morning. A limo was waiting to whisk them to Montedoro and the Prince's Palace. So were more paparazzi. Again, they hurried to get into the car and away from the questions and cameras.

The first sight of the palace stole Sydney's breath. White as a dove's wing against the clear blue sky, it was a sprawling edifice of crenellated towers and paladin windows and balconies and arches. It stood on a rocky promontory overlooking the sapphire-colored sea.

The driver took them around to a private entrance. By a little after nine, they were filing into Rule's apartment.

After the grandeur of the arched, marble-floored hallways decorated in gorgeous mosaics, Sydney was relieved that Rule's private space was more low-key. The furniture was simple, plush and inviting, the walls were of stucco or something similar, with tall, curving ceilings and dark wood floors covered with beautiful old rugs woven in intricate patterns, most of them deep reds and vivid blues. Balconies in the large sitting room and in the master suite opened onto stunning views of the main courtyard and the crowns of the palms and mimosas, the olive and oak trees that covered the hillside below. Farther out, the Mediterranean, dotted here and there with pretty sailboats and giant cruise ships, shone in the afternoon sun.

The palace staff set right to work unpacking and putting everything away. In no time, that job was done and the soft-spoken, efficient maids had vanished. Lani retreated to her room at one end of the apartment, probably to work on her novel or jot down her first impressions of Montedoro in her journal. Trev sat on a glorious red rug in the sitting room playing with his plastic blocks, and Rule was off somewhere conferring with his private secretary, Caroline.

For a while, Sydney leaned on the carved stone balcony railing, the doors to the sitting room wide open behind her, and stared out at the boats floating on the impossibly blue sea. There was a soft breeze, like the lightest brush of silk against her skin. She felt tempted to pinch herself. It almost seemed like a dream that they were actually here, in Montedoro, at last.

And it got even better. Her period was now almost three weeks late. She had no morning sickness, but she'd had none with Trev, either. What she did have were breasts.

They weren't huge or anything, but they were definitely fuller, and more sensitive than usual. That was the same as with Trev, too.

Another baby. She put her hand against her flat stomach, the way mothers had been doing since the beginning of time. *Another baby.* When she'd had Trevor, she'd told herself to be grateful for one. And she had been. So very grateful.

But now, well, she was pretty much positive she would be having her second. Incredible. Talk about impossible dreams coming true.

She'd bought a home test the week before. And today, as she leaned on the stone railing and admired the sea, she was thinking it was about time to take the test.

And about time to tell Rule that their family was growing.

"Mama! Come. Play…"

She turned to smile at her son, who had stacked several brightly colored blocks into a rickety tower and waved two more at her, one in each chubby hand. "All right, sweetheart. Let's play." She went and sat on the rug with him.

"Here, Mama." He handed her a drool-covered block. Lately, as his back teeth came in, anything he got his little hands on ended up with drool on it.

"Thank you." She wiped the drool off on her jeans and hooked the block at the base of his tower. As long as she was helping, she might as well improve the stability a tad.

A few moments later, Rule appeared. Trev cried his name in sheer delight, "Roo!" And he came right over and scooped him high into his big arms. "Roo, we play blocks!"

"I can see that. Quite a fine tower you have there."

"Mama helps."

"Oh, yes, she does." Rule gave her a smile. Her heart did a couple of somersaults. "My parents are impatient to meet you."

"I'm eager to meet *them*." She gazed up at him from her cross-legged seat on the red rug and wondered if there was a woman alive as fortunate as she. At the same time, she was just a little nervous to be meeting his mom and dad, aka Their Highnesses, for the first time. "But maybe I need a few tips on palace protocol first...."

He shook his head as he kissed the fingers that Trev was trying to stick into his mouth. "We're invited to their private apartment at six. We'll visit, you'll get to know them a little. Then we'll have an early meal. There will be no ceremony, no protocol to observe. Just the family. Just us. Together."

"Perfect," she said.

"I knew you would think so." He asked Trev, "How about you, young man? Ready to meet your new grandpa and grandma?"

Trev beamed. "Yes!"

* * *

The sovereign's apartments were larger than Rule's, but even the private foyer had a welcoming quality about it. She got the sense that real people lived there. The floor was marble, inlaid with ebony and jade, and the chandelier was a fabulous creation of ironwork and crystal. But the hall table had a bowl filled with shells on it and a family photo taken outside, beneath the wide-spreading branches of a gnarled oak tree. Sydney barely had time to pick out a much-younger Rule from the nine children arrayed at the feet of the two handsome dark-haired parents, before the thin, severe-looking woman who had opened the door to them was leading them on, down a hallway lined with oil portraits of princely relatives, the men wearing uniforms loaded down with ribbons and medals and the women resplendent in fancy ball gowns and glittering tiaras.

Rule had hold of Sydney's hand. He carried Trev high against his chest on his other arm. As they approached the end of the hall, he squeezed her fingers. She sent him a smile and squeezed back, all too aware of the fluttery, anxious sensation in her stomach.

The hallway ended at a sitting room. The tall woman nodded and left them. The same dark-haired man and woman as in the picture in the foyer rose from a matched pair of gold-trimmed velvet chairs to greet them.

"At last," said the woman, who was tall, full-figured and quite beautiful. She seemed ageless to Sydney. She could have been anywhere from forty to sixty. She had the eyes of an Egyptian goddess and a wide, radiantly smiling mouth. "Come. Come to me." She held out slender arms.

Sydney might have stood there, gaping in admiration at Rule's mom forever. Luckily, he still had her hand. He started forward and she went with him.

Then, all at once, they were there.

Rule said, "Mother. Father. This is Sydney, my wife."

And then Rule's mom was reaching for her, gathering her into those slender arms. "Sydney," she said, with such warmth and fondness. "I'm so pleased you're here with us."

"Uh. Hello." *Smooth, Sydney. Very smooth.* Really, she should have insisted that Rule at least tell her what to call this amazing creature. Your Highness? Your Sovereign Highness? Your Total Magnificence? What?

And then Rule's mom took her by the shoulders. She gave her a conspirator's grin. "You shall call me Adrienne, of course—except during certain state functions, before which, I promise you will be thoroughly briefed."

"Adrienne," Sydney breathed in relief. "Rule speaks of you often, and with deep affection."

Those Egyptian eyes gleamed. "I am so pleased he has found what he was seeking—and just in time, too."

And then Rule was saying, "And this is Trevor."

Rule's mom turned to bestow that glowing smile on Trev. "Yes. Trevor, I…" HSH Adrienne's sentence died unfinished. She blinked and shot a speaking glance at Prince Evan. It only lasted a split second, and then she recovered and continued, "Lovely to meet you." Trevor, suddenly shy, buried his head against Rule's neck. Adrienne laughed. She had an alto laugh, a little husky, and compelling. "How are you, Trevor?"

"I fine," Trevor muttered, his head still pressed tight to Rule.

Rule rubbed his back. "Say, 'Hello, Grandmother. So nice to meet you.'"

It was a lot of words for a suddenly shy little boy. But he said them, "'Lo, Gamma. Nice to meet you," with his face still smashed into Rule's neck.

"And it's a delight to meet you, as well." Adrienne loosed that husky musical laugh again.

And then Trevor's dad was taking Sydney's hand. "A Texas girl," he said in a voice as smooth and rich and deep as his son's. "Always a good choice."

Sydney thanked him and thought that he was almost as good-looking as his wife. No wonder Rule was drop-dead gorgeous. How could he be otherwise with a mom and dad like these two?

They all sat down. The severe-looking woman reappeared and offered cocktails. They sipped their drinks and Evan wanted to know about her parents. So she told them that she had lost them very young and been raised by her grandmother. They were sympathetic and admiring, of her Grandma Ellen and of the successes Sydney had achieved in her life. They knew she was an attorney and asked about her work. She explained a little about her experiences at Teale, Gayle and Prosser.

The talk shifted to Rule and the progress on his various projects. It was a bit formal, Sydney thought. But in a nice, getting-to-know-you sort of way.

She was so proud of Trev. He sat quietly on Rule's lap for a while, watching the adults, big dark eyes tracking from one face to another. Both Adrienne and Evan seemed taken with him. They kept sending him warm looks and smiles.

Slowly, Trev was drawn in. After twenty minutes or so, during a slight lull in the conversation, he held out his arms to Adrienne. "Gamma. Hug, please."

Adrienne reached for him and Rule passed him over. She wore a gorgeous designer jacket and a silk dress underneath. Sydney worried a little that Trev would drool on Her Highness's lovely outfit.

But Adrienne didn't seem concerned. She hugged him and kissed his cheek and he allowed it, all shyness fled.

Lani appeared about half an hour into the visit, ushered in by the thin woman. After a brief introduction, she took Trevor with her back to their rooms.

The rest of them went in to dinner, where they were joined by two of Rule's brothers—Maximilian, the heir apparent, who'd come up from his villa to meet Rule's bride, and Alexander, the one who'd been a prisoner in Afghanistan.

Sydney liked Maximilian from the first. He was almost as handsome as Rule and he seemed to her to be a kind man, and very charismatic. He had sad eyes, though. She remembered what Rule had told her, about Max losing his wife in a water-skiing accident, and wondered if he was still grieving the loss.

It was difficult to like Alex. He was darkly handsome like the rest of the family, but more powerfully built and very quiet. He seemed…angry. Or perhaps sunk in some deep depression. Sydney supposed his attitude wasn't all that surprising. She imagined that being kept prisoner by terrorists would give anyone a bad attitude. But she could easily see why he and Princess Lili didn't get along. Sydney doubted that Alex got along with anyone.

Rule's other brother, Alex's twin, Damien, was something of a jet-setter. He was off on a friend's yacht. Two of his sisters, the youngest and second-youngest, Rory and Genevra, were away at school. Alice and Rhiannon were at an event in Luxembourg. And the oldest sister, Arabella, had gone to Paris. When they were home from school, Rory and Genevra still lived at the palace. The three older sisters had their own villas.

Dinner was several courses. The food was delicious. There was wine. Excellent French wine. As she'd done since she first suspected she might be pregnant, Sydney took care to drink very little of it.

Later, back in their own apartment, she and Rule celebrated her move to Montedoro by making love—twice. Once, while standing up against the tall, beautifully carved bedroom doors. Very well hung, those doors, she'd teased, as he was moving so deliciously inside her. Those doors didn't rattle once no matter how enthusiastic they became.

Eventually, they got into bed, where they made love the second time. It was after that second time, when she lay tucked close against him, that she told him, "Your mother says there's a large library here at the palace. A lot of books on Montedoran history. She also says the palace librarian can answer just about any question I might have about your country."

He stroked her arm in an idle, thoroughly distracting way. "Going to become a Montedoran scholar, are you?"

"I need to catch up, to understand how things work here, so I can begin to consider the kind of work I want to do, to discover where and how I can be most useful to my new country."

"So ambitious." He said it admiringly as he caressed her breast.

"You know I lose IQ points when you do that…"

He covered her breast with his warm hand. "I love your breasts."

"Good. You'll be seeing a lot of them as the years go by."

He caught her nipple between his fingers and squeezed. She sighed. He said, in a gentle, careful voice, "I believe they are fuller than they used to be."

It was the perfect opportunity to tell him that there was

a reason her breasts were bigger: she was having his baby. But instead, she elbowed him in the ribs. "Oh. You like them because they're *bigger*."

He nuzzled her hair. "*Are* they bigger?"

She got up on one elbow, where she could see his eyes. "Yes." She knew then. She could see it in his face, in the breathless way he looked at her. *He* knew already. She gave him a teasing smile. "My breasts are bigger. It's a miracle."

He asked, almost shyly, "Sydney...is it possible that you...?"

She smiled even wider. "That I *what,* Rule?"

"Don't tease me. Please." His eyes had gone dark as the middle of the night. It was a soft, yearning sort of darkness. He really, really wanted to know.

And her heart just...expanded. It felt suddenly twice as big as a moment before, as if it were pushing at her ribs, trying to make more room inside her chest. "I think so," she whispered. "I think we're going to have a baby."

He held her gaze, steadily, surely. "You *think?*"

"All the signs are there. The same ones I had with Trev. And my period is almost three weeks late. I haven't taken the home test I bought yet, though."

He touched her chin, brushed his thumb across her lips. "When will you take it?"

She smiled against his touch. "How about tomorrow morning?"

"Sydney..."

"What?"

"That's all. Just Sydney. Sydney, Sydney, Sydney..." He took her shoulders and pulled her close so he could kiss her. A long kiss, so tender. So thorough. So right.

She settled back onto his chest again, her chin on her arms. "So. You're happy?"

He stroked her hair. "I am. I can't tell you how happy."

"You're a good father. Trev is crazy about you."

He smoothed her hair, guided it behind her ear. "Trevor is everything I ever wanted in a son. And you are everything I ever dreamed of in a wife."

She remembered his mother's reaction at her first sight of Trev and smiled to herself. "Did you see how surprised your mother was when she met Trev? I'm guessing she noticed the uncanny resemblance between you two."

His hand stilled on her hair. "What makes you think that?"

Had something changed in his eyes?

She asked herself the question—and then decided it was nothing. He was stroking her hair again, regarding her so tenderly. She said, "I thought she looked pretty stunned when she saw him—you didn't notice the look on her face?"

"Hmm. Yes, I suppose…"

She asked, "Did you see it, or didn't you?" At his shrug, she frowned. "It was only there for a second and then gone. I guess I might have imagined it…."

He framed her face between his hands. "Come here. Kiss me."

She pretended to consider. "Well, now. That's a pretty tempting offer."

"Come here. Let me show you *how* tempting…."

She lifted up over him and then, with a happy sigh, settled her mouth on his. He was right. The kiss tempted her to kiss him some more.

Kisses led to more caresses and they made love again. Slowly. Beautifully.

She gazed up at his unforgettable face above her and thought how it just kept getting better between them. How there was nothing, ever, that could tear them apart.

* * *

An hour later, Rule lay in the dark staring up at the ceiling, listening to his wife's even, relaxed breathing beside him.

His pregnant wife...

He was sure of it. And so was she. The test in the morning was only a formality. She was having his baby.

His *second* baby.

And yes. He'd seen that look on his mother's face, too.

His mother had known that Trevor was his. One look at the boy and she'd had no doubt.

Very soon now, Her Sovereign Highness would be summoning him for a private talk. She was going to want to discuss the startling resemblance between him and his supposed stepson.

She would also be going after his father, working on the poor man. She would be insisting that her Prince Consort tell her the truth if he knew *anything* about what was really going on with Rule and his new wife and the child who was the mirror image of Rule at that age. One way or another, Adrienne would get to the bottom of it.

And as soon as she knew the truth, she was going to be after Rule to come clean with his wife. His mother was as much about integrity and truth in life and marriage as his wife was.

Rule felt the day of reckoning approaching. He had everything now: the woman he'd almost given up on finding; a healthy, happy, perfect son—and a second child on the way.

The only real question was how much he was going to lose when Sydney finally learned the truth.

Sydney's hands were shaking.

She turned her back to the test wand she'd left on the

corner of the serpentine marble counter and held both hands out in front of her. Yep. Her fingers trembled like leaves in the wind.

"Silly," she whispered. "So silly…" With a low moan, she lifted her hands and covered her face with them.

Really, there was no reason she should be such a bundle of nerves over this. She was either pregnant or not—and she just knew that she *was.* In a moment, the timer would go off and she would have proof.

No reason to be freaked out over it. No reason at all.

Rule tapped on the bathroom door. "Sydney? Are you all right in there?" As if in response to his question, the timer she'd set on the marble enclosure around the ginormous sunken tub started beeping. "Sydney! Are you all right?"

She went over and flipped the switch on the timer. It fell blessedly silent.

Rule didn't. "Sydney, my God!" He pounded on the door.

She whirled, stalked to the door, twisted the lock and flung it wide. He stood there looking fabulous, wearing nothing but a worried expression. Through clenched teeth she informed him, "I am *fine.* Get it? Fine."

He held out his arms.

With a cry, she threw herself into them, wrapped her arms around his lean bare waist and held on tight. She buried her face against his beautiful hard chest. "It's time," she said into that wonderful trail of hair that started between his perfect pectoral muscles and went on down, all the way to heaven. "I can't look."

"Sydney…" He said her name in that special way that only he could, so tenderly, so reassuringly. He stroked her back and then he took her chin and tipped it up. His dark eyes were waiting. "We both know what the test will say." He brushed a kiss across her lips.

Her mouth trembled. Sheesh. She was a trembling fool. She bit her lower lip to make it stop and then she said, "I *know* we both know. But what if we're wrong?"

He drew in a slow breath and dared to suggest, "Only one way to find out."

She shoved her face into his chest again, feeling like Trevor, the day before, clinging to his precious *Roo* upon meeting his new grandparents. "*You* look. I can't do it."

He chuckled. Oh, wasn't that just like a man? To chuckle at a time like this. He chuckled, and then he kissed the top of her head and then he gently took hold of her arms. "You will have to release me if you want me to be the one to look."

Reluctantly, with another soft cry, she let go of him and stepped out of his way. "Do it. Now."

He indicated the wand on the edge of the marble sink counter and slanted her a questioning glance.

She nodded.

He went to it, picked it up, frowned at it.

What? Suddenly, he couldn't read? She said, "The little window, it either says 'pregnant' or 'not pregnant.'"

He made a big show of squinting at the wand. "Well, now, let's see here…"

"I am going to grab that thing and hit you on the head with it. Just see if I don't."

He waved his free hand in a shushing kind of gesture. "All right, all right. It says… Well, what do you know? It says…"

"Rule. Stop it. I mean it. You stop it right now."

And then he dropped the wand in the sink, turned and grabbed her, lifting her high, spinning her around. She squealed and then she laughed. And then he was letting her down, slowly, the short silk nightie she wore catching, riding up, leaving her bare from the waist down. Her feet touched the floor toes-first.

Finally, he leaned close and whispered in her ear, "Pregnant."

Pregnant. The magic word.

She threw her arms around him. "Oh, I can't believe it. It's true. It's really true. We're having a baby. We really, really are. How amazing is that?"

"Extremely amazing," he agreed.

And then he scooped her high in his arms and carried her back to the bed where they celebrated the positive test result in their favorite way.

Later, Sydney asked Rule if he would mind keeping the news about the baby to themselves for a while. She was only a few weeks along, after all. No one else needed to know for another month or so, did they? She wanted a little time to have it be just between the two of them.

He kissed her. "However you want it."

"You're so easy."

"For you, anything," he told her. And he meant it.

He was feeling so good—about their life together, about the new baby, about everything—that he almost succeeded in forgetting his dread of the eventual moment of truth concerning Trevor.

And as that day went by and the one after that and his mother failed to invite him to a private audience, his dread diminished even further. For whatever reason, it appeared that his mother was not going to call him to task on the subject of his look-alike "stepson." Perhaps she'd decided that the similarity was merely a coincidence. Or perhaps she simply didn't wish to interfere.

Or possibly, she had come to the conclusion that when

Rule was ready to talk about it with her, he would. Whatever her rationale on the subject, she was staying out of it.

Rule was grateful. And relieved.

That first Tuesday, they got through the press conference where they formally announced their marriage to the press, though by then, their marriage was old news in the fast-moving world of the scandal sheets. Wednesday, they visited with the archbishop of Montedoro to request a wedding in the church. The archbishop was only too happy to help speed up the process. They took their expedited marriage classes on Thursday and Friday and then, quickly and quietly, on the Saturday after Rule moved his new family to Montedoro, he and Sydney were married in the church.

Rule had three days of meetings in Paris that next week. Sydney, Lani and Trevor stayed in Montedoro, where Sydney and his mother spent some time alone, getting to know each other a little. In bed the night of his return from France, Sydney said that his mother had asked her about Trevor's father.

Rule kept his voice light and easy. "And what did you tell her?"

"The truth, of course. That I wanted a family and I didn't have a man and so I went to a sperm bank. She took it well, I think. She smiled and said what a determined woman I am."

"And you are." He kissed her. She kissed him back. Nature took its course from there.

The next day, Liliana returned to Montedoro for a brief visit at HSH Adrienne's invitation. Sydney got to meet her. The two hit it off—the delicate Alagonian princess and Rule's tall, brilliant and determined American bride. Rule wasn't really all that surprised that they got along. They were both good women with tender hearts.

It was the same with his sisters. Sydney liked them all and the sentiment was mutual.

Rule and Sydney began to talk of a more private life. Sydney said she would prefer to live in their own house by the time the new baby came. So they engaged an architect to renovate Rule's nearby villa, modernizing and enlarging it to make it more comfortable for their growing family.

He and Sydney were so happy. He never wanted to do anything to hurt her, or to damage what they had together. In fact, sometimes he found himself wondering why, realistically, she even needed to know that he was actually Trevor's father.

Why *should* she know? What good could the truth possibly do her—or anyone—now? He had found her and his son and he had made things right for all of them. To tell her now would only upset her and drive a wedge between the two of them. It would threaten, and might even destroy, what they had as a family.

Rule's father would keep his secret, especially if his mother wasn't pushing to know more. And sometimes the wisest course was to do nothing, to leave a perfectly wonderful situation alone. He decided he would do just that.

And then he would realize how despicable that was. He should have told her at the first. It was information she had every right to know.

He should tell her now. Today.

But then, somehow, the moment was never right. Another day would go by.

Soon, he would promise himself.

He would tell her soon.

But he didn't tell her. And every day he said nothing, it only got harder to imagine being truthful. Every moment that went by in which he kept his silence, he was more and more deeply mired in the lie, more and more convinced that his silence was the best thing for everyone.

And then, on the last Wednesday in May, the truth finally caught up with him.

Chapter Twelve

It happened in the morning two weeks and five days after Rule brought his new family to Montedoro.

Caroline was waiting for him when he entered his office at the palace. She held a tabloid newspaper in her hand.

"Sir," said his secretary, her expression carefully neutral, "a particularly annoying article has appeared in *The International Sun*." *The Sun* was a London-based paper. A weekly, it claimed to deliver news. And it did. News on such burning issues of the day as which celebrity was heading for rehab again and which film star was having a torrid affair with His Grace, the very married Duke of So-and-So. "I thought I should bring it to your attention right away." It was one of Caroline's duties to keep up with both the legitimate news of the day and the scandal sheets. She made certain Rule knew of any and all information that appeared in print about him, his country, his business dealings and/or the people who mattered to him.

Usually, she simply left the various publications on the credenza, having red-flagged articles that she thought required particular attention. Her choosing to hand this one to him personally did not bode well.

"Thank you, Caroline."

With a nod and a murmured, "Sir," she left him, quietly closing the door behind her.

Circling around behind his desk, he dropped into his chair. Aware of a terrible, crushing sensation of dread, he spread the paper on the leather desk pad before him. For a time, he stared furiously down at it, as if by glaring at it long enough, he could somehow make the words and the pictures rearrange themselves into something else, something that had nothing to do with him or his family.

But no matter how long and hard he stared, what was printed on the front page didn't change.

The headline read, Stepchild—Or Love Child?

There were several pictures of him—by himself and holding Trevor, pictures of him holding Trevor with Sydney beside him, pictures of him at the same age as Trevor. Since the resemblance between Rule and Trevor really was so strong, the pictures themselves told a very clear story. Anyone glancing at them would say that Rule must be Trevor's biological father—or at the very least, a close relation.

The article itself was a total fabrication. It proposed that he and Sydney had earlier enjoyed a "torrid secret affair." When it ended, she was pregnant with his child. And he had walked out on her, left her to "have his baby alone," because he felt duty bound to marry in "the aristocracy of Europe."

But then, "as fate would have it," he'd been unable to forget the one woman who "held his heart." After more than two years had gone by, the "handsome prince" had at last realized that his child and his true love "mattered more than royal blood." He'd returned to claim the woman he'd "always loved" and the child he'd "left behind."

There was even a long explanation of how Sydney had "put it out" that her child was the result of artificial insemination. But *The International Sun* wasn't fooled and neither should its readership be.

"A picture is worth a thousand words." And the pictures showed clearly that the child in question was Prince Rule's. At least the prince had "done the right thing" in the end and married the mother of his child. Since "all was well that ended well," *The Sun* wished the prince and his newfound family a lifetime of happiness.

It was ugly, stupid, insulting and riddled with clichés. Not to mention mostly fiction. However, within the general ridiculousness lurked the all-important twin kernels of truth: that Trevor was in fact Rule's child. And that Sydney really had used a sperm bank.

And that was why deciding what to do in response to this absurd flight of pseudo-literary fantasy was of the utmost importance. Really, anything he did—from making no statement, to issuing an outraged denial, to suing the paper for slander—could make things worse. And no matter what he did next, some ambitious and resourceful reporter might decide to dig deeper. It was possible that someone, somehow, could unearth the fact that he'd been a donor at Secure Choice. If that happened, and he still hadn't told Sydney his secret…

No. He couldn't allow even the possibility that it might go that far.

He was going to have to tell her. Now. Today. And when he did, she was going to be angry with him. More than angry. She might never forgive him. But if she found out in the tabloids, the likelihood was exponentially greater that he would lose her forever.

Rule shoved the tabloid aside, braced his elbows on the desk pad and put his head in his hands. He should have told her by now, should have told her weeks ago. Should have told her at the first....

Should have told her...

How many times had he reminded himself of that? A hundred? Five hundred?

And any one of those times, he *could* have told her.

Yes, it would have been bad.

But not as bad as it was going to be now.

He'd made his choice—the wrong choice—a hundred, five hundred, a thousand times. He'd wagered their happiness on that choice. He should have known better than that. Wagers were not a good idea—not when it came to the things that mattered most.

Half an hour later, Rule and his father met in Evan's private office. Also in the meeting were Donahue Villiers, a family advocate, or legal advisor, and Leticia Sprague, Palace Press Secretary. Leticia had been a trusted member of the palace staff for over twenty years.

They discussed what their next move should be and decided that Donahue would be in contact with the paper's legal department to discuss the lawsuit the family intended to file. He would also demand that the paper print a full retraction which, he would assure them, would go a long way toward mollifying Prince Rule once a settlement for damages was under discussion. Leticia suggested that Rule release a statement wherein he refuted the story and made his outrage at such ridiculous allegations crystal clear.

Rule's father said, "Before we proceed with any of this,

there must be a *family* conference. Her Sovereign Highness must be brought up to speed and given the opportunity to make her wishes in the matter known. So, of course, must Sydney."

And that was it. The meeting ended. Leticia and Donahue left Rule and his father alone.

Rule and Evan exchanged a long, bleak glance.

And then Evan said, "It's not the end of the world, son."

Rule started to speak.

Evan put up a hand. "You will get through this—with your family intact. And you *could* look on the bright side."

Rule made a scoffing sound. "So unfortunate that there isn't one."

"Of course there is. The article is absurd. *The International Sun* is going to end up looking very bad."

"It's a tabloid. It's not as though they care if they look bad."

His father regarded him solemnly for a moment. "What you did, becoming a donor, you did in a good cause. With an honest heart."

"I was an idiot. It was an act of rebellion against everything I am, everything we stand for as Bravo-Calabrettis."

Patiently, his father continued, "You would never have found the wife you wanted if not for your 'act of rebellion.' There would be no Trevor. And that you finally arranged to meet Sydney, that you pursued her and convinced her to make a family with you, that you became a real father to your son…I find that not only admirable, but truly honorable."

Rule wanted to grab the crystal paperweight from the corner of his father's desk and smash it against the far wall. "You don't understand. Sydney still doesn't know. I still haven't told her."

"Then you *will* tell her. Right away."

"I could lose her over this."

"I don't think you will. She loves you. She will stick by you."

Rule said nothing to that. What was there to say? Evan had been for honesty with Sydney from the first. His father wouldn't rub it in. That wasn't Evan's way. But the knowledge that his father had been right all along made this unpleasant discussion doubly difficult.

Evan said, "I think it's time that you told your mother the truth."

Rule gave him a scowl. "Wonderful."

His father said gently, "You can't put it off any longer. One look at that child and your mother was certain he had to be yours. She asked me what *I* knew. I told her that you had taken me into your confidence and gotten my agreement that I would keep your secret. I said that if she demanded it, I would tell her everything, I would break my word to you."

Rule affected an American accent. "Gee, thanks, Dad."

His father's chuckle had little humor in it. "Once she saw Trevor, I couldn't have kept her in the dark if she needed to know. She rules my heart as she rules this land. Maybe that's beyond your understanding."

Rule thought of Sydney. "No. I understand. I do."

"As it turned out, I didn't have to break my word to you. Your mother said that I should keep your secret for you, that she preferred to respect your wishes in the matter."

"So she only knows that Trevor is mine."

"As I said, I never told her the truth outright. She has drawn her own conclusions and kept them to herself. It's time that you were honest with her."

"I have to tell Sydney first."

"Of course you do."

* * *

Sydney wasn't in their apartment when Rule entered a few minutes later, the offending tabloid rolled in his hand. Lani told him that she'd gone to the palace library and would return by eleven.

It was ten forty-five.

Trevor tugged on his trouser leg. "Roo. Come. Play…"

His heart like a large ball of lead in his chest, he got down on the floor with his son, set the rolled paper to the side and helped him build a fanciful machine with a set of connectable plastic wheels and gears.

Trevor glanced up, a plastic propeller in his hand. "See, Roo. 'Peller." He stuck the propeller on a bright-colored stick and blew on it. Then he chortled in delight as it spun. Rule tried to laugh with him, but didn't succeed. Trevor bent to fiddle with the wheels and cogs some more, leaving Rule to stare down longingly at his dark head. Rule wanted to grab him and hold him close and never, ever let him go, as if by clutching his son tight, he might somehow escape the impending moment of truth.

But there was no escape. He was done with this lie.

It wasn't long before he heard brisk footsteps approaching from the foyer. And then Sydney was there, laughing, asking Lani how many pages she'd written.

"Three paragraphs," Lani grumbled, pushing her glasses higher on her nose. "It's just not coming together."

"It will," Sydney reassured her friend. "It always does."

"Yeah, well. I hope you're right."

"Persistence is the key."

Lani grumbled something else. Rule didn't make out the words over the rushing of his own blood in his ears as Sydney's footsteps came closer.

She stood above them. "What kind of fantastical machine is this?"

For a moment, Rule stared at her pretty open-toed shoes, her trim ankles. Then, forcing his mouth to form a smile, he lifted his head to meet her eyes. "You'll have to ask your son."

Trev glanced up. "Hi, Mama. I make a machine, a machine with a 'peller."

"I see that and I…" Her glance had shifted. Rule followed her gaze. The paper beside him had opened halfway, revealing the outrageous headline and half of the pictures. "What in the…?"

He grabbed the paper and swiftly rolled it up again. "We need a few moments in private, I think."

Both of her eyebrows lifted. And then she nodded. "Well, I guess we do."

Trev sat looking from Rule to Sydney and back again, puzzled by whatever was going on between the grown-ups. "Mama? Roo?"

Rule laid a hand against his son's cheek. "Trevor," he said, with all the calm and gentleness he could muster. "Mama and I have to talk now."

Trev blinked. "Talk?" He frowned. And then he announced, "Okay. I build machine!"

Lani put her laptop aside. "C'mon, Trev." She jumped up from the sofa and came to stand over them. "How 'bout a snack?" She reached down and lifted him into her arms.

Trevor perked up. "I want graham crackers and milk. In the *big* kitchen." He loved going down to the palace kitchens where the chefs and prep staff doted on him.

"Graham crackers and milk in the big kitchen it shall be."

"Thank you." Rule forced a smile for Lani as he rose from the floor.

With a quick nod, Lani carried Trevor to the door. He heard it close behind her.

He and Sydney were alone in the apartment.

She said, "Well?"

He handed her the tabloid.

She opened it and let out a throaty sound of disbelief. "Please. They have got to be kidding."

"Sydney, I—"

She put up a hand. "Give me a minute. Let me read this garbage."

So they stood there, on either side of Trevor's pile of bright plastic wheels and cogs, as she read the damned thing through. She was a quick study. It didn't take her long.

Finally, in disgust, she tossed the paper to the floor again. "That is the most outrageous bunch of crap I've ever read. Do you believe it? The nerve of those people. We're suing, right?"

"I believe that is the plan."

"You *believe?* It's a pack of lies. Not a single shred of truth in the whole disgusting thing."

"Well, and that's the problem, actually. There *is* some truth in it. More than a shred."

"What are you talking about?" She regarded him sideways. "Rule, what's wrong?"

He gulped—like a guilty child caught stealing chocolates. "There's something I really must tell you."

"What?" She was starting to look frightened. "Rule. *What?*"

"You should...sit down, I think." He tried to take her arm.

She eased free of his grip. "Okay. You're scaring me. Whatever it is, you need to just go ahead and say it."

"I will, of course. It's important and I should have told you long ago, right at the first."

"Rule." Now she was the one reaching for him. She took

hold of both of his arms and she looked him squarely in the eye. "Tell me. Whatever it is, tell me right now."

Was there any way to do this gently? He couldn't think of one. So he went ahead and just said it outright. "I was a donor for Secure Choice Cryobank. It was my profile you chose. Trevor is my son."

Chapter Thirteen

She still clutched his arms, her fingers digging in. Her face had gone chalk-white. "No," she whispered.

"Sydney, I—"

She let go of him, jumped away as though she couldn't bear to touch him. "No." She put her hands to her mouth, shook her head slowly. "No, no, no. You never said. Ever. I asked you, I asked you directly…" She whispered the words. But to him, that whisper was as loud as a shout. As a scream.

"I know. I lied. Sydney, if we could just—"

"No." She shook her head some more. "No." And then she whirled on her heel and she marched over to the sofa where Lani had been sitting. Carefully, she picked up the laptop and set it on the low table in front of her. Then she sat down. "Here." She pointed at one of the wing chairs across from her. "Sit."

What else could he do? He went over there. He sat.

There was a silence.

They regarded each other across the low table, across a short distance that seemed to him endless. And absolutely uncrossable. He only had to look at her—the pale, locked-away face, the lightless eyes—to know the worst had happened.

He had lost her.

She asked in a carefully controlled voice, "So you did take my information from Secure Choice, after all?"

"I did, yes."

"Um. When?"

"Almost three years ago."

"When I was pregnant? You've known since then?"

"Yes. I knew from the first."

With another gasp, she put the back of her hand to her mouth. And then she seemed to catch herself. She let her hand drop to her lap. "All that time. You did nothing. And then, suddenly, out of nowhere, you were there. Lying to me, pretending it was all just a happy little accident, that you had happened to see me going into Macy's. That you were so very *intrigued* by my *determination*. But it wasn't an accident. Not an accident at all."

His throat clutched. He gulped to clear it. "No. It was no accident. I was following you that day." She pressed her fist to her stomach. *The baby.* He started to rise. "Sydney. Are you—?"

She stuck out her hand at him, palm flat. "No. Stay there. Don't you dare get up. Don't you come near me."

"But you—"

"I am not ill. I am…there are no words, Rule. You know that, don't you? No words. None."

He sank back to the chair, said the only thing he *could* say. "I know."

"Why now? I don't get it. After all the times you might

have said it, might have come clean about it, why now?" And then she blinked. He watched comprehension dawn in her eyes. "That stupid article. The pictures. You and Trevor, so much alike. It even mentions that I 'claim' to have used a sperm donor. You're afraid someone might do more digging, and reach the truth. You couldn't *afford* to keep me in the dark any longer."

What could he give her but shamefaced confirmation? "Yes. That's right."

"Oh, Rule. I thought it was bad, when you had to rush back here to Montedoro to explain yourself to Lili the morning after our wedding. I was…disappointed in you then. But I told myself that you had never lied to me. That you were a truly honest man, that you didn't have a lying bone in your body…" Though her eyes were dry, a sob escaped her. She covered her mouth again for a moment, hard, with her palm that time, as though she could stuff that sob back inside. When she had control of herself, she lowered her hand and said, "What a fool I was. How could I have *been* such a fool? All the signs were there. I saw them, *knew* them. And still you convinced me not to believe the evidence of my own eyes."

"I wanted to tell you," he heard himself say, and then cursed the words for their weakness.

Her sweet, wide mouth curved in a sneer. "Then why *didn't* you tell me?"

He said it right out. "At the first? Because I knew I wouldn't have a chance with you if I did."

"You couldn't know that."

"Of course I knew. After your wonderful grandmother who taught you that honesty was everything. After those bastards, Ryan and Peter…"

She waved her hand that time, dismissing his excuses.

"If not at the beginning, why not that night I asked you directly if you'd ever been a donor?"

"We've been so happy. I didn't want to lose that, our happiness. I didn't want to lose *you*."

"Were you *ever* going to tell me?" Her voice was furious and hopeful, both at the same time.

He longed to reassure her. To give her more lies. But he couldn't. Some…line had been crossed. All that was left to him now was the brutal truth. "I don't think so. I kept telling myself I would, but there was always an excuse, to wait a little longer, to put it off. I kept choosing the excuses over telling you what you had a right to know."

"So, then." The hope was gone. Only her cool fury remained. "You were never going to tell me."

He refused to look away. "No. I wasn't willing to risk losing you."

"And how's that worked out for you, Rule?" Her sarcasm cut a ragged hole in his heart.

He answered without inflection. "As of now, I would have to say not very well."

She sat very still. She…watched him. For the longest, most terrible stretch of time. And then she said, "I don't get it. It makes no sense to me, that you would become a donor. Why did you? It's…not like you. Not like you at all."

"Does it matter now?"

"It matters to me. I am trying very hard to understand."

"Sydney, I—"

"Tell me." It was a command.

He obeyed. "My reasons were… They seemed real to me, seemed valid, at the time." How could he make her see when he still didn't completely understand it himself? He gave it his best shot. "I wanted…something. I wanted my life to be more than the sum of its parts. I wanted what my parents have together. What Max and Sophia had. It seemed I went through the motions of living but it wasn't a rich life. Not a full life. I enjoyed my work, but when I came home I wanted someone to come home to." He shook his head. "It makes no sense, does it?"

She was implacable. "Go on."

He tried again. "There were women. They were… strangers to me. I enjoyed having sex with them, but I didn't want them beyond the brief moments of pleasure they gave me in bed. I looked into their eyes and I didn't feel I would ever truly know them. Or they, me. I was alone. I had business, in Dallas. I spent over a year there."

"When?"

"Starting a little more than four years ago. I would go down to San Antonio on occasion, to visit with my family there. But it was empty, my life. I had only casual friends at that time. Looking back, I can't remember a single connection I made that mattered to me other than in terms of my business. Except for one man. He turned up at a party I went to. We'd been at Princeton together. We…touched base. Talked about old times. He'd been a donor. He'd come from an American public school, was at Princeton on full scholarship. He became a donor partly for the money—which, he told me, laughing, wasn't really much at all. But also because he said it did his heart good. It felt right, he said. To help a couple who had everything but the child they wanted most. That struck a chord with me. It seemed that being a donor would be…something good, that I could do, something I could give—but you're right. It wasn't like me. I'm a Bravo-Calabretti all the way to the core. I just refused to see that until it was too late and my profile was available to clients. Until two women had chosen me as their donor."

Those lightless eyes widened. "*Two* women?"

"The other didn't become pregnant. By the time she ordered again, I'd had my profile taken down."

"Just two of us? But...I can't believe more women wouldn't have chosen you."

Under other circumstances, he might have laughed. "My profile was only available for a short period of time. I withdrew my samples when I realized what an idiot I'd been to become a donor in the first place. Secure Choice was not the least happy with me. Our agreement was for ten pregnancies resulting in births or nine months of availability. I made arrangements to reimburse them for the money they would have made if I'd fulfilled my commitment with them. In the end, I simply couldn't...let it go. And that's the basic job of a donor. To *donate* and let it go."

She continued for him. "But that was never going to work for you, was it? You realized that you *had* to know—if there were children, if they were all right..." She understood him so well.

He said softly, "Yes. And that was my plan, after I found out that you had become pregnant. That was all I ever intended to do, make certain that you and the child were provided for. I swear it to you. As long as you and Trevor were all right, I was never going to contact you or interfere in your life in any way. I had assured myself that you were a fine mother *and* an excellent provider. I knew Trevor was healthy. I knew you would do all in your considerable power to make certain he had a good start in life."

"Yes. I could give him everything—except a father."

It was her first misreading of his motives. He corrected her. "I didn't think of it that way. I swear that I didn't."

She crossed her long, slim legs, folded her hands tightly

in her lap and accused, "Oh, please. You are all about being a father. We both know that."

Her words hit him like blows.

They were much too true.

And they proved all over again what a hopeless idiot he'd been to become a donor in the first place, how little he'd understood his own mind and heart.

"All right," he said. "I'm guilty. Guilty in a hundred ways. It *is* important to me. That my child have a father."

"So you set out to see that he did."

He felt, somehow, like a bug on a pin under the cool regard of those watchful eyes of hers. And in the back of his mind a cruel voice would not stop whispering, *You have lost her. She will leave you. She will leave you now.* Somehow, no matter what happened, he had to make her see the most basic motivation for his actions concerning her. "No. I swear to you, Sydney. It wasn't…that way. It was *you.*"

"Oh, please."

He repeated, insisted, "*You.* It was you. Yes, Trevor mattered. He mattered more than I can say. But *you* were the starting point. I pursued *you,* not my son. I lied, yes, by omission. I never told you why I happened to be in that parking lot outside of Macy's that first day we met. That it was because of you that I was there, in the first place. Because you fascinated me. So bright and capable. So successful. And apparently, so determined to have a family, with or without a man at your side. I told myself I only wanted to see you in the flesh, just one time. That once I'd done that, I could let you go, let Trevor go. Return here to Montedoro, make my proposal to Lili…"

"You were lying to *yourself.*"

"Yes. The sight of you that first time, getting out of your car in the parking garage…the sight of you only made me realize I had to get closer, to see you face-to-face, to look in your eyes. To hear your voice, your laugh. I followed you into the store. And as soon as you granted me that adorable, disbelieving sideways glance while you pretended to read a price tag on a frying pan, I knew that there had to be more. Every word you spoke, every moment in your presence, it only got worse. Stronger. I swear to you, I didn't set out to seduce and marry you."

She made another of those low, scoffing sounds.

And he was the one putting up a hand. "Yes," he confessed, "it's what I did in the end. But it started with *you*. It was always about you. And by that first evening we spent together, when we had dinner at the Mansion, I knew I wanted you for my wife."

Her eyes were emerald-bright now. With tears.

The tears gave him new hope.

Hope she dashed by turning away and stealing a slow breath. When she faced him again, the tear-sheen was gone.

She said in the cold, logical voice of an accuser, "You had so many options. *Better* options than the ones you chose."

He didn't deny it. "I know. In hindsight, that's all so painfully clear."

"You could have asked to see me as soon as you managed to find out you'd been my donor. I *would* have seen you. I was as fascinated by the idea of you—of the man I had chosen as my donor—as you claim you were by me."

"As I *am* by you," he corrected. "And I had no reason to believe you would have been happy to see me. It seemed to me that the last thing a single mother really wants is a visit from a stranger who might try to lay a claim on her child."

"I had given permission for you to contact me. That should have been enough for you to have taken a chance."

"Yes. I see that, now that I know you. But I didn't know you then. I didn't know how you would react. And it seemed wrong for me to…interfere in your life."

"If you had sought me out at the beginning, you would have had more than two years until the marriage law went into effect. We would have had the time to get through all this garbage. *You* would have had time for the truth."

"Sydney, I know that. I see that now. But it's not what I did. Yes, I should have been braver. I should have been… truer. I should have taken a chance, arranged to meet with you early on. But I hesitated. I hesitated much too long. I see that. And by the time I acted, I was down to the wire."

"Wire or not," she said, refusing to give him an inch, as he'd known that she would, "you owed it to me to tell me the truth before you asked me to marry you. You owed that to me then, at the very least."

"I know that. We've already been through that. But by then there was all you had told me about how you valued honesty."

"So you should have been honest."

"And what about Ryan and Peter? What about your distrust of men? You would have assumed right away that I was only after Trevor."

She looked at him unwavering. "Telling me the truth was the right thing to do."

"Yes. And then I would have lost you. You were not about to give a third man the benefit of the doubt. It was too big a risk. We were getting along so beautifully. I couldn't stand to lose you when I'd only just found you. Are you going to deny that I *would* have lost you?"

"No. You're right. At that time, I…didn't know you well enough. I would have broken it off for a while, slowed things down between us. I would have needed more time to learn to trust you."

"You would have needed longer than I could afford."

She made a low sound. "Because of the Prince's Marriage Law."

"Yes."

"You're telling me you were trapped." She spoke with disdain.

"No. I'm telling you that I knew what I wanted, at last. After all the years of being so sure I would never find it, find *you*. I wanted you. I wanted our child. And I wanted my inheritance, too. I made choices to give myself— and us—the best chance that we could both get what we wanted."

"And you kept making choices. Kept making the *same* choice. To lie to me. Over and over and over again. Since our marriage, I can't even count the times when you could have made a different choice."

"I know it. And we're back to the beginning again. Back to where I remind you that we have been so happy, and that telling you the truth would have destroyed our happiness, back to where I say I did what I did because I couldn't bear to lose you."

She stood up. And then, looking down at him, she said, "In making the choice to lie to me, you stole *my* choices. You treated me like a child, someone not fully responsible, someone unable to deal with the facts and make reasonable decisions based on all the available information. For generations, men did that to women, treated them as incompetent, as unable to face reality and make rational choices. Treated them as possessions rather than thinking human beings. I will not be treated as your possession, Rule, no matter how prized. Do you understand?"

He did understand. And at that point, there was nothing left for him but to admit the wrong he'd done her—done them both—and pay the price for it. "Yes. I understand."

"It matters. That you believe in me. That you trust me. That you treat me as your equal."

"And I see that," he said. "I do."

"But given the same set of circumstances, you would lie to me all over again—don't you tell me that you wouldn't."

He wanted to deny it. But somehow, he couldn't. And his denial wouldn't matter anyway. He couldn't undo what he'd done. What mattered now was that, no matter what the circumstances, he wouldn't lie to her again. "I simply didn't want to lose you. That's all. I lied because I was certain the truth would cost me what we have together. And now, you can be assured I see that I made the wrong choice. I swear I'll never lie to you again." Her face was set against him. He shook his head. "But then, I look at you and I see that it doesn't matter what I promise you. I see in your eyes that I'm going to lose you anyway."

Her cold expression changed. She looked…puzzled. And also disbelieving. And then she actually rolled her eyes. "Of course you're not going to lose me, Rule."

He gaped at her, convinced he couldn't have heard her right. "What did you just say?"

"I said you're not going to lose me. I would never leave you. I'm your wife and I love you more than my life. But I am not the least happy with you. And I'm not going to hide how I feel about this, or pretend to get past it when I'm *not* past it. You may end up wishing that I *would* go."

"My God," he said, hope rekindled, catching fire. "I would never wish for you to go. You have to know that."

"We'll see."

He rose. His arms ached to reach for her. But her expression signaled all too clearly the reception he would get if he tried. "I want our marriage," he said, and longed to give her words back to her. *I love you more than my life.* But it seemed wrong to speak of his love now, wrong and cheap. So instead, he said, "I want only you, always. That isn't going to change, no matter what you do, no matter how angry you are at me."

"We'll see," she said again. And for a moment, he saw the sadness in her eyes. Men had disappointed her before. And now he was just like the others.

Except he wasn't. He refused to be.

Whatever it took, he would be more, better, than he had been until now. Whatever the cost, he would win back her trust again and reclaim his right to stand at her side.

She was watching him, assessing him. "How much do your parents know?"

"My father knows everything. I confided in him. But my mother knows nothing—beyond being certain that Trevor is my son as well as yours."

"You told her?"

"No. She guessed that he was mine the moment she saw him. She asked my father what he knew. He offered to betray my confidence and tell her everything. She didn't think that would be right, so she declined his offer to break his word to me."

"I do like your mother."

"Yes," he said dryly. "Like you, she is thoroughly admirable—and you remind me I need to speak with her."

She indicated the tabloid she'd tossed to the floor and asked him wearily, "About all this?"

He nodded. "By now, she'll have had her morning look at the newspapers, including *The Sun.* I have to go to her and explain."

Sydney said, "We'll go together."

It was more than he'd hoped for. Much more. "Are you sure?"

"I'll just leave a note for Lani."

They met with his mother in the apartments she shared with his father. It was just the four of them—Adrienne, Evan, Rule and Sydney.

Rule told the whole story all over again. His mother's face remained unreadable throughout.

When he was done at last, she turned to Sydney. "I am so sorry that my son misled you."

Sydney replied with a slow nod. "Yes. I am, too."

Rule stared straight ahead. He felt like the bad child in school, sent to the corner to sit on a stool facing the wall and contemplate the terrible extent of his transgressions.

His mother said, "All right. Where are we now in terms of dealing with *The International Sun* and their absurd pack of lies?"

His father outlined the brief earlier meeting with Leticia and Donahue, concluding with, "To start, at least, Donahue will demand a retraction."

His mother looked at Rule, at Sydney, and then at Rule again. "Would a retraction satisfy you two?"

Satisfy me? Rule thought. Hardly. What would satisfy him was to have his wife once again look at him with affection and desire, to have her forgiveness. "That would be fine," he said, not caring in the least anymore about the damned tabloid story.

"It's *not* fine with me," Sydney said.

He glanced at her, took in the tightness of her mouth, the spots of hectic color high on her cheeks. She was as furious at the tabloid as she was at him. It hurt him, to look at her. It made him yearn for the feel of her skin under his hand, for the pleasure of simply holding her. Despair dragged at him. She'd said she wouldn't leave him.

But how long would it be before she allowed him to hold her again?

Sydney went on, "The retraction, yes. Absolutely. They should *start* with a retraction. And then we should sue their asses off."

"Their asses," his mother repeated, exchanging a glance with his father. "I do admire your enthusiasm, Sydney."

"It's an outrage." Sydney pressed her lips more tightly together. She blew out a hard breath through her nose.

His mother said, "I agree. And we will have a retraction."

"It's not enough," Sydney insisted. "That article is a gross misrepresentation of Rule's integrity, of his character. Rule would never simply walk away and desert a woman who was pregnant with his child. Never."

Rule realized he was gaping at her again. He couldn't help it. She astonished him. As infuriated as she was at him, she still defended him. He reminded her gently, "Sydney. It's just a silly tabloid story. It doesn't matter."

Her eyes were green fire. "Of course it matters. It's a lie. And they deserve to have their noses rubbed in it. I think we should hold a press conference and tell the world what liars they are. I think we need to tell the world the truth."

Tell the world the truth. She couldn't be serious.

He said, with slow care, "You want me to tell the world that I was your sperm donor? That it took me more than two years to get up the nerve to approach you? That when I did, I didn't tell you I was your child's father, but instead seduced you and got you to marry me under false pretenses?"

"Yes," she said hotly. "That's what I want from you, Rule. I want you to tell the truth."

For the first time on that awful day, he felt his own anger rising. It was all coming much too clear. "You want to see me humiliated. And it's not enough for you that *The Sun* should make me look like a fool. You want to see me make a fool of *myself.*"

She sucked in a sharp breath and put her hand to her throat. "No. No, that's not it. That's not what I meant."

He told her icily, "Of course it's what you meant."

"Oh, Rule," she said softly after several seconds had passed. "You don't get it. You don't get it at all."

He said nothing. He had nothing to say.

Finally, his mother spoke softly. "Whatever action the two of you decide to take, you have our complete support. I can see this is something the two of you must work out between yourselves."

Chapter Fourteen

But Rule and Sydney didn't work it out. They returned to their apartment—together, but not speaking.

That night, Rule slept in the small bedroom off the master suite. He lay alone in bed in the darkness and realized he wasn't angry anymore.

He missed his anger.

It was a lot easier to be furious than it was to be ashamed.

Now his anger had left him, he could see that for Sydney it was as it had always been; it was about honesty. She saw that insane press conference of hers as a way to clear the air once and for all, to lay the truth bare for everyone to see. She saw it as a way to beat *The International Sun* at its own game. She was an American, an egalitarian to the core.

She didn't have generations of proud, aristocratic Calabretti ancestors behind her, staring down their formidable noses, appalled at the very idea that one of their own would even consider getting up in a public forum and explaining his shameful personal shortcomings to the world at large.

Such things were not done.

A Calabretti had more pride than that.

He had more pride than that. Too much pride. He could see that now.

He was not about to tell the world the unvarnished truth about his private life. Even if he'd behaved in an exemplary fashion, that would have been extraordinarily difficult for him.

But his behavior had not been exemplary. Far from it.

He'd been an imbecile. On any number of levels. And it just wasn't in him, to stand up and confess his own idiocy to the world.

The next day was as bad as the one before it. He and Sydney were polite with each other. Excruciatingly so. But they hardly spoke.

In his office, the phone rang off the hook. Every newspaper, every magazine, every radio and TV station wanted a few brief words with Prince Rule. He declined to speak with any of them.

And he stayed another night in the extra room. And then another after that.

The weekend went by. He spent time with his son. He and Sydney continued to speak to each other only when necessary.

Monday evening they had a meeting with Jacques Fournier, the architect they'd chosen, about the renovations at the villa. Sydney sent Rule an email about that on Monday afternoon.

An email. She was one room away, but she talked to him via email.

Do you want me to contact Fournier and tell him we won't be available tonight?

He zipped her off a one-word reply. Yes.

She didn't email back to update him on her conversation with Fournier. Just as well. He didn't really care if the architect was annoyed with them for backing out on him.

What he cared about was making things right with his wife. Unfortunately, he had no idea how to do that.

Or if he *did* have an idea, he had altogether too much pride to go through with it.

That evening, she surprised him.

She came and hovered in the doorway to his little room. Hope flared in him yet again, that this might mean she was ready to forgive him. But her face gave him nothing. She seemed a little nervous, maybe. But not like a woman on the verge of offering to mend a serious breach.

"I called Fournier," she said.

He set the book he'd been trying to read aside. "Thank you," he said stiffly.

"Fournier said it was fine, to call and reschedule when we were…ready." Her sweet mouth trembled.

He wanted to kiss the trembling away. But he stayed in the room's single chair, by the window. "All right."

"I'm sure he must know about that awful article…"

He shrugged. "He might."

"Not that it matters what the architect knows." She looked tired, he thought. There were dark smudges beneath her eyes. Was she having as much trouble sleeping as he was? "I… Oh, Rule…" She looked at him sadly. And pleadingly, too.

His heart beat faster. Hope, that thing that refused to die, rose up more strongly, tightening his throat, bringing him to his feet. "Sydney…"

And then she was flying at him and he was opening his

arms. She landed against his chest with a soft cry and he gathered her into him.

He held on tight.

And she was holding him, too, burying her face against his chest, sighing, whispering, "Rule. Oh, Rule…"

He lowered his lips to her fragrant hair, breathed in the longed-for scent of her. "Sydney. I'm so sorry. I can't tell you…"

"I know." She tipped her head back, met his waiting gaze.

Crying. She was crying, tears leaking from the corners of her eyes, leaving shining trails along her flushed cheeks.

"Don't cry." He caught her face between his hands, kissed the tear trails, tasted their salty wetness. "Don't cry…"

"I want…to make it right with us. But I don't know how to make it right."

He dared to kiss her lips—a quick kiss, and chaste. It felt wrong to do more. "You can't make it right. *I* have to do that."

She searched his face. "Please believe me. I didn't suggest that press conference to shame you. I swear that I didn't."

"I know. I see that now. Don't worry on that account. I understand."

"I'm…too proud, Rule. I know that I am. Too proud and too difficult. Too demanding."

He almost laughed. "Too prickly."

"Yes, that, too. A kinder, gentler woman would be over this by now."

He kissed the tip of her nose. "I have no interest in a kinder, gentler woman. And you are not *too* anything. You are just right. I wouldn't want you to change. I wouldn't want you to be anyone other than exactly who you are, any way other than *as* you are."

"Oh, Rule…"

He took her shoulders and he set her gently away from him. "Can you forgive me?"

She shut her eyes, drew herself taller. And when she looked at him again, she wasn't smiling. "I'm working on it."

Strangely, he understood exactly what she was telling him. "But you aren't succeeding. You can't forgive me."

She pressed her lips together, shook her head—and started to speak.

He touched his thumb to her mouth. "Never mind. You don't have to answer. Let it be for now."

"I miss you so. It hurts so much."

Gruffly, he confessed, "For me, as well."

She took his hand, placed it on her still-flat belly where their unborn baby slept. The feel of that, the *promise* of that, came very close to breaking his heart. "We have to… do something," she said in a torn little whisper. "We have to…get past this. For the baby's sake, for Trev. For the sake of our family. *I* have to get past this, put aside my hurt pride that you lied, that you didn't treat me as an equal. We have to move on. But then, just when I'm sure I'm ready to let it go, I think of all the times you might have told me, might have *trusted* me…."

"Shh," he said, and lifted his hand to touch her lips again with the pads of his fingers. "It's not your fault. I am to blame and I know that I am. Somehow, I have to make you believe that I do trust you in all ways, that no matter how hard the truth is, I will never lie to you again."

She let out a ragged breath. "I *want* to believe you. So much."

He lifted her chin and brushed one last kiss against her

tender lips. "Give it time," he said again. "It will be all right." Would it? *Yes.* Somehow, he would make it so.

She stepped back and turned. And then she walked away from him.

It was the hardest thing he'd ever done, to watch her go. To *let* her go. Not to call her back. Not to grab her close again and kiss her senseless. Not to promise them both that everything was all right now.

When it wasn't all right.

When something precious was shattered between them and he knew that, as the one who had done the shattering, it was up to him to mend a thousand ragged pieces into one strong, shining whole.

The answer came to him in the middle of the night.

Or rather, in the middle of the night, he accepted fully how far he was actually willing to go to make things right.

He saw at last that he was going to have to do the one thing he'd said he would never do, the thing he'd rejected out of hand because it was going to be difficult for him. More than difficult. Almost impossible.

But whatever it took, if it gave him a chance of healing the breach between him and Sydney, he was ready to do it. To move forward with it.

And to do so willingly.

Pride, she had told him. *"I'm...too proud, Rule."*

They were alike in that. Both of them prideful, unwilling to bend.

But he would bend, finally. He would do the hardest thing. And he would do it gladly.

If it meant he would have her trust once more. If it meant she would see and believe that he knew the extent of the damage he'd done and would never do such a thing again.

He turned over on his side and closed his eyes and was sound asleep in seconds.

When he woke, it was a little after seven. He rose, showered, shaved and dressed.

Then he went to his office where he got out the stack of messages he'd tossed in the second drawer of his desk—the stack he'd known somewhere in the back of his mind he shouldn't throw away.

Not yet. Not until he was willing to make his choice from among them.

He chose quickly. It wasn't difficult: Andrea Waters. She was a household name, with her own prime-time news and talk show in America, on NBC. She was highly respected as a television journalist. And women loved her warmth and personal charm.

He glanced at his watch.

It would be two in the morning in New York City. He would have to wait several hours until he could call her producer back himself.

He made the first call to New York at two that afternoon. By seven that evening, everything was arranged.

Now, to tell his wife. He rose from his desk to go and find her.

And there was a tap at his office door.

At seven in the evening? Caroline wasn't out there to screen visitors. He'd told her she could go more than an hour before.

He called, "It's open. Come in."

The door opened—and Sydney slipped through.

He stood there behind his desk and drank in the sight of her. His lady in red—a red skirt and silk blouse, wearing those pearls her grandmother had given her, her hair smooth on her shoulders, just as it had been that first day, when he saw her in the parking garage and couldn't stop himself from following her inside. She looked tired, though. There were still shadows under her eyes.

"I've been waiting to talk to you," she said. "I...couldn't wait any longer. I came to find you."

"It's been a busy day. I'm finished here now, though." He tried on a smile. "I was just coming to find *you*...."

Hesitantly, she returned his smile. "I hardly slept at all last night."

"I know how that goes." His voice sounded strange to his own ears—a little rusty, rougher than usual. "I haven't been getting a lot of sleep, either."

"I told you yesterday that I wasn't there yet, I...hadn't really forgiven you."

"And I said I understood. I meant what I said."

"Oh, but Rule..." Her smile widened. And all at once, her whole face had a glow about it. She hardly even seemed tired anymore. She had her hands folded in front of her. He thought she looked so young right then. A girl, an innocent. Looking at her now he would never have guessed that she'd given birth to his son, that she carried his second child under her heart. "Something happened," she said. "Something wonderful."

Something wonderful. His heart beat a swift tattoo beneath his ribs. "Tell me."

"I don't know. I...I was lying there, alone in our bed. It was almost one in the morning. I was thinking of how I missed you, beside me, in the dark. Thinking that I knew, I understood, why you had kept the truth from me. Objectively I could see how it must have been for you. Waiting too long to contact me, knowing you were up against the deadline of the marriage law. Telling yourself you were only waiting for the right moment to say the words. And then hearing about Ryan, about Peter. Fearing that if you told me the truth, I would suspect that you only wanted Trevor. And then, when you *didn't* tell me, I could see how it only got harder for you, how every day the truth became more and more impossible for you to reveal."

He shook his head. "None of which is any excuse."

She put her hands to her cheeks, as if to cool the hectic color in them. "I just want you to know that I *did* understand...I *do* understand, intellectually." She let her left hand drop to her side. Her right, she laid above her breast. "But my heart...my heart wanted you to trust in me. My heart wanted you to be bigger than your very realistic fears. My heart wanted you to give me the truth no matter the cost."

"And I should have trusted you," he said. "I was wrong. Very wrong. And I want you to stop torturing yourself because you can't forgive me."

She laughed then. A happy laugh, young and so free. And her eyes had that tear-shine, the same as the day before. She sniffed, swiped the tears away. "But that's just it. I was lying there, thinking about everything, how wrong things had gotten between us, how I wanted to work it out but my heart wouldn't let me. And all of a sudden, just like that...I saw *you*. I saw you, Rule. I...felt you, as though you were there, in our dark bedroom with me. And I saw that you love me and I love you and that's what matters, that's what makes it all worthwhile. And I didn't even need to think about forgiveness anymore. It just... happened. I let my anger and my hurt and my resentment go. I realized I do believe in you. I believe in your goodness and your basic honesty. I believe that you love me as I love you. I want...our family back. I want *us* back." She was crying again, the tears dribbling down her cheeks, over her chin.

"Sydney…" He was out from behind his desk and at her side in four long strides. "Sydney…"

She fell against him, sobbing. "Rule, oh, Rule…"

He wrapped his arms around her and held on tight. "Shh. Shh. It's all right. It's going to be all right…"

Finally, pressing herself close, she tipped her chin back and he met her shining, tear-wet eyes. "Rule. I love you, Rule."

"And I love you, Sydney. With all of my heart. You *are* my heart. I looked for you for far too long. I'm so glad I finally found you. I'm so glad what we have together is stronger than my lies." He lowered his head.

And he kissed her. A real kiss. A deep kiss. A kiss of love and tears and laughter. A kiss to reaffirm their life together. Again. At last…

That kiss went on forever. And still it wasn't long enough.

But finally, he lifted his head. He took her face between his hands and brushed away the tear tracks. "I think you're right. I think we're going to make it, after all."

"I know we will. I always knew—or at least, I kept promising myself that somehow, eventually, it would all work out."

"I was coming to find you when you knocked on the door."

She held his gaze, searching. "What? What is it?"

"You wanted me to call a press conference…."

"Yes. I see now that was probably a bad idea."

"At first, I though it was a bad idea, too. Mostly because of my pride."

"It's okay, Rule. Truly."

"But I reconsidered."

"You're kidding."

"No. I did reconsider—and I still decided against it."

"It's fine. I understand."

"Instead, I'm going to give Andrea Waters an exclusive interview."

She gasped. And then she made a sputtering sound.

He laughed then. "My darling, I believe you are speechless. I don't remember that ever happening before."

She groaned. "Oh, you…" And she gave him a teasing punch on the arm.

"Ouch!" He grinned.

"Really, Rule. You're not serious."

"Oh, yes I am. I'm going to tell the truth about you and me and our son. I'm going to tell it on *Andrea Waters Tonight*."

"Um. *Everything?*"

"Well, I think it would be acceptable to *manage* the message, at least to a degree."

She reached up, laid her hand on the side of his face. That simple touch meant so much to him. It was everything. To have her in his arms again, to feel her cool palm against his cheek, to know they were together, and that they always would be. "It isn't necessary," she said in a whisper. "It was too much for me to ask of you."

"No. It wasn't."

She touched his lips with her thumb. "Shh. Hear me out." She waited for his nod before she spoke again. "Yes, when it comes to us, to you and me, I demand total honesty. But I certainly don't expect you to share all your secrets with the rest of the world."

He took her hand, opened it, kissed the soft heart of her palm the way he'd always loved to do. "I think it should be possible to do this with dignity. With integrity."

"You can cancel. I'll be completely accepting of that."

He only shook his head and kissed her palm again.

She said, "Okay. If you're determined to do this…"

SAVE UP TO 25%

Subscribe to Cherish today and get 5 stories a month delivered to your door for 3, 6 or 12 months and gain up to 25% OFF! That's a fantastic saving of over £40!

MONTHS	FULL PRICE	YOUR PRICE	SAVING
3	£43.41	£36.90	15%
6	£86.82	£69.48	20%
12	£173.64	£130.20	25%

As a welcome gift we will also send you a FREE L'Occitane gift set worth £10

PLUS, by becoming a member you will also receive these additional benefits:

- 🌹 FREE Home Delivery
- 🌹 Receive new titles TWO MONTHS AHEAD of the shops
- 🌹 Exclusive Special Offers & Monthly Newsletter
- 🌹 Special Rewards Programme

No Obligation - You can cancel your subscription at any time by writing to us at Mills & Boon Book Club, PO Box 676, Richmond. TW9 1WU.

To subscribe, visit
millsandboon.co.uk/subscriptions

MILL
BOO

"Yes?"

"I want to be there, beside you, when Andrea Waters starts asking the questions."

He turned her hand over, kissed the backs of her fingers, one by one. "I was hoping you would say that."

"Are we going to New York?"

"No. She will come here, to Montedoro. There will be a tour of the palace as part of the broadcast. And then we'll sit down, the three of us, and chat."

"Chat." Sydney shivered.

"Are you cold, my darling?"

"With your arms around me?" Her green gaze didn't waver. "Never. But I *am* a little scared."

"Don't be. It's going to go beautifully. I'm sure of it."

"Kiss me, Rule."

And he did, for a very long time.

Epilogue

Her Royal Highness Liliana, Princess of Alagonia, Duchess of Laille, Countess of Salamondo, sat alone in her bedroom in her father's palace.

She wore a very old, very large green The Little Mermaid T-shirt, bought on a trip to America years before—and nothing else. Perched cross-legged on her bed, she held a delicate black plate decorated with yellow poppies and piled high with almond cookies. Lili intended to eat every one of those cookies. It was her second plate of them. She'd finished the first plateful a few minutes before.

Also, close at hand, she had a big box of tissues. Already, she'd used several of those. The discards littered the bed around her.

She was watching the television in the armoire across the room. It was *Andrea Waters Tonight,* an American program. Andrea Waters was interviewing Rule and Sydney.

Lili thought the interview was absolutely wonderful. Such a romantic story. She'd had no idea. Rule, a sperm donor? She never would have imagined that, not in a hundred thousand years. And Sydney's little boy, Trevor—he was Rule's all along.

Of course, Lili should have guessed. The resemblance was nothing short of striking.

And didn't Sydney look adorable? She was such a handsome woman. And she sat so close to Rule, holding his hand. And the glances those two shared...

That. Yes. Exactly. Lili wanted that, what Rule and Sydney had. She wanted real love, strong love, true love, forever, with the right man.

Unfortunately, that she would ever find the right man was looking less and less likely. Especially after what had happened with Alex.

Really, how *could* she?

With Alex, of all people?

And now, just look at the mess she was in.

Lili ate another almond cookie, whipped out another tissue and blotted up tears. Unceremoniously, she blew her nose.

And then she sighed.

Rule and Sydney. They looked so happy. They *were* so happy. And Lili was happy *for* them.

Yes, it was true. She'd been something of a fool over Rule for all those years. He was so handsome and such a good man and he'd always treated her with warmth and affection. She'd let her vivid imagination carry her away. She'd dreamed of being Rule's bride.

She'd thought that she loved him. And she *did* love him. But now, at last, she understood that the love she felt for Rule wasn't the kind of love a woman feels for the man to whom she binds her life.

Again, Lili wondered if she would ever find that man.

It was beyond doubtful. Maybe even impossible, given her current condition.

Besides the cookies and the tissues, Lili also had her phone. It was on the bed beside her. She reached out and grabbed it and dialed the number she'd been putting off calling for too long now.

She waited, hardly daring to breathe, as the phone rang. And rang. Finally, an answering machine picked up.

Alex's recorded voice said, "I'm not available. Leave a message."

She waited for the beep and then she said, "Alexander. You are the most exasperating man." She wanted to blurt out the truth right then and there. But it wasn't a good idea. Not on the phone. "Read the letter I sent you," she said. "And then you'd better call me, Alex. We really do need to speak privately." She waited some more. Maybe he was there, listening. Maybe for once he'd behave like a reasonable person and pick up the phone.

But he didn't. She heard the click that meant the machine had disconnected her.

Very gently, she hung up.

And after that, she just sat there, not even crying anymore, not even wanting another almond cookie, feeling terrible about everything. Wondering what was going to happen when her father found out.

* * * * *

"In one breath, you assert that you're not propositioning me, and in the next, you say that you find me attractive."

"Actually, my comment was more objective than subjective," Michael told her. "But while I do think you're a very attractive woman, I didn't hire you in order to pursue a personal relationship with you."

"Okay," Hannah said, still sounding wary.

Not that he could blame her. Because even as he was saying one thing, he was thinking something else entirely.

"In fact, I wouldn't have invited you to spend the summer here if I thought there was any danger of an attraction leading to anything else."

"Okay," she said again.

"I just want you to understand that I didn't intend for this to happen at all," he said.

And then he kissed her.

Dear Reader,

It has been a sincere pleasure to return to the island paradise of Tesoro del Mar, to revisit some familiar characters and introduce some new ones. Hannah Castillo is one of the new characters you'll meet in *Prince Daddy & the Nanny*.

After the death of her mother when Hannah was only eight years old, her father sent her to Tesoro del Mar to live with her uncle Phillip, the royal physician. Eighteen years later, when Hannah takes a summer job looking after widowed Prince Michael's four-year-old daughter, she can't help but see parallels between the princess's lonely childhood and her own. As she works to help bridge the gap between father and daughter, Hannah finds herself falling for both of them and wishing that the summer would never end.

But of course, Hannah knows that the idea of a prince loving a commoner is nothing more than a fairy tale, and fairy tales don't come true. Except, maybe, in Tesoro del Mar…

I hope you enjoy Hannah's story.

Best,

Brenda Harlen

PRINCE DADDY
& THE NANNY

BY
BRENDA HARLEN

All rights reserved including the right of reproduction in whole or in part in any form. This edition is published by arrangement with Harlequin Enterprises II B.V./S.à.r.l. The text of this publication or any part thereof may not be reproduced or transmitted in any form or by any means, electronic or mechanical, including photocopying, recording, storage in an information retrieval system, or otherwise, without the written permission of the publisher.

This book is sold subject to the condition that it shall not, by way of trade or otherwise, be lent, resold, hired out or otherwise circulated without the prior consent of the publisher in any form of binding or cover other than that in which it is published and without a similar condition including this condition being imposed on the subsequent purchaser.

All the characters in this book have no existence outside the imagination of the author, and have no relation whatsoever to anyone bearing the same name or names. They are not even distantly inspired by any individual known or unknown to the author, and all the incidents are pure invention.

All Rights Reserved including the right of reproduction in whole or in part in any form. This edition is published by arrangement with Harlequin Books S.A.

This is a work of fiction. Names, characters, places, locations and incidents are purely fictional and bear no relationship to any real life individuals, living or dead, or to any actual places, business establishments, locations, events or incidents. Any resemblance is entirely coincidental.

® and ™ are trademarks owned and used by the trademark owner and/or its licensee. Trademarks marked with ® are registered with the United Kingdom Patent Office and/or the Office for Harmonisation in the Internal Market and in other countries.

First published in Great Britain 2012
by Mills & Boon, an imprint of Harlequin (UK) Limited,
Eton House, 18-24 Paradise Road, Richmond, Surrey, TW9 1SR

© Brenda Harlen 2011

First published in Great Britain 2012
by Mills & Boon, an imprint of Harlequin (UK) Limited,
Eton House, 18-24 Paradise Road, Richmond, Surrey TW9 1SR

© Brenda Harlen 2011

ISBN: 978 0 263 89447 9
ebook ISBN: 978 1 408 97123 9

23-0712

Harlequin (UK) policy is to use papers that are natural, renewable and recyclable products and made from wood grown in sustainable forests. The logging and manufacturing processes conform to the legal environmental regulations of the country of origin.

Printed and bound in Spain
by Blackprint CPI, Barcelona

Brenda Harlen grew up in a small town, surrounded by books and imaginary friends. Although she always dreamed of being a writer, she chose to follow a more traditional career path first. After two years of practicing as an attorney (including an appearance in front of the Supreme Court of Canada), she gave up her "real" job to be a mom and to try her hand at writing books. Three years, five manuscripts and another baby later, she sold her first book—an RWA Golden Heart winner—to Mills & Boon.

Brenda lives in southern Ontario with her real-life husband/hero, two heroes-in-training and two neurotic dogs. She is still surrounded by books (too many books, according to her children) and imaginary friends, but she also enjoys communicating with real people. Readers can contact Brenda by e-mail at brendaharlen@yahoo.com.

To Kate Weichelt—
who has helped brainstorm solutions to many story
problems over the years, including a few in this one.

Thanks for being a friend, an inspiration,
and especially for being you!

Chapter One

So this is how the other half lives.

Hannah Castillo's eyes widened as she drove through the gates into the upscale neighborhood of Verde Colinas.

Actually, she knew it was more likely how half of one percent of the population lived, and she couldn't help wondering what it would be like to grow up in a place like this. Having spent the first eight years of her life moving from village to village with her missionary parents, she hadn't realized there was anything different until her uncle Phillip had brought her to his home in Tesoro del Mar.

And even then, she wouldn't have imagined that there was anything like *this.* She hadn't known that real people lived in such luxury. Not regular people, of course, but billionaires and business tycoons, musicians and movie stars, philanthropists and princes. Well, at least one prince.

Prince Michael Leandres was the thirty-eight-year-old president of a multimedia advertising company, cousin of the prince regent, widowed father of Tesoro del Mar's youngest princess, and the first man who had ever made her heart go pitter-patter.

As she slowed to wait for another set of gates to open so that she could enter the drive that led to the prince's home, she couldn't help but smile at the memory. She'd been twelve at the time, and as flustered as she was flattered when Uncle Phillip asked her to accompany him to the by-invitation-only Gala Opening of the Port Augustine Art Gallery.

She'd been so preoccupied thinking about what she would wear (she would have to get a new dress, because a gala event surely required a gown) and whether she might be allowed to wear makeup (at least a little bit of eyeliner and a touch of lip gloss) that she hadn't given a thought to the other guests who might be in attendance at the event. And then she'd walked through the doors on her uncle's arm and spotted Prince Michael.

To a preteen girl who was just starting to take note of the male species, he was a full six feet of masculine perfection. He was also a dozen years older than she, and already there were rumors swirling about his plans to marry his longtime sweetheart, Samantha Chandelle. But Hannah's enamored heart hadn't cared. She'd been content to admire him from afar, her blood racing through her veins just because he was in the same room with her.

Since then, she'd met a lot of other men, dated some of them and even had intimate relationships with a few. But not one of them had ever made her feel the same kind of pulse-pounding, spine-tingling excitement that she'd felt simply by being in the presence of Prince Michael—not even Harrison Parker, the earl who had been her fiancé for a short time.

Now, fourteen years after her first meeting with the prince, she was going to come face-to-face with him again. She might even have a conversation with him—if she could manage to untie her tongue long enough to form any coherent words—and hopefully persuade him that she was the perfect woman to take care of his adorable daughter. Of course, it might be easier to convince him if she believed it herself, but truthfully, she wasn't sure how she'd let Uncle Phillip convince *her* that the idea of working as a nanny for the summer wasn't a completely ridiculous one.

Or maybe she did know. Maybe it was as simple as the fact that she was in desperate need of an income and a place to stay for the summer, and working as a nanny at Cielo del Norte—a royal estate on the northern coast—would provide her with both. But on top of that, her uncle claimed that he "would be most grateful" if she would at least meet with the prince—as if it would be doing him some kind of favor, which made the request impossible for Hannah to deny. That the salary the prince was offering was more than enough to finally pay off the last of her student loans was a bonus.

As for responsibilities, she would be providing primary care for the widowed prince's almost-four-year-old daughter. She didn't figure that should be too difficult for someone with a master's degree, but still her stomach was twisted in knots of both excitement and apprehension as she turned her ancient secondhand compact into the winding drive that led toward the prince's home.

Having grown up in tents and mud huts and, on very rare occasions, bedding down on an actual mattress in a cheap hotel room, she was unprepared for life in Tesoro del Mar. When she moved into her uncle's home, she had not just a bed but a whole room to herself. She had clothes in an actual closet, books on a shelf and a hot meal on the table every night. It took her a long time to get used to living in such luxurious surroundings, but pulling up in front of the prince's home now, she knew she was about to discover the real definition of luxury.

The hand-carved double front doors were opened by a uniformed butler who welcomed her into a spacious marble-tiled foyer above which an enormous crystal chandelier was suspended. As she followed him down a long hallway, their footsteps muted by the antique Aubusson carpet, she noted the paintings on the walls. She had enough knowledge of and appreciation for art to recognize that the works that hung in gilded frames were not reproductions but original pieces by various European masters.

The butler led her through an open doorway and into what was apparently the prince's office. Prince Michael himself was seated behind a wide desk. Bookcases filled with leather-bound volumes lined the wall behind him. The adjoining wall boasted floor-to-ceiling windows set off by textured velvet curtains. It even smelled rich, she thought, noting the scents of lemon polish, aged leather and fresh flowers.

"Miss Castillo, Your Highness." The butler announced her presence in a formal tone, then bowed as he retreated from the room.

The nerves continued to twist and knot in her stomach. Was she supposed to bow? Curtsy? She should have asked her uncle about the appropriate etiquette, but she'd had so many other questions and concerns about his proposition that the intricacies of royal protocol had never crossed her mind.

She debated for about ten seconds, then realized the prince hadn't looked away from his computer screen long enough to even glance in her direction. She could have bowed *and* curtsied *and* done a tap dance and he wouldn't even have noticed. Instead, she focused on her breathing and tried to relax, reminding herself that Michael Leandres might be a prince, but he was still just a man.

Then he pushed away from his desk and rose to his feet, and she realized that she was wrong.

This man wasn't "just" anything. He was taller than she'd remembered, broader across the shoulders and so much more handsome in person than he appeared in newspaper photos and on magazine covers. And her heart, already racing, leaped again.

He gestured to the chairs in front of his desk. "Please, have a seat."

His voice was deep and cultured, and with each word, little tingles danced over her skin. She couldn't be sure if her reaction to him was that of a girl so long enamored of a prince or of a woman instinctively responding to an undeniably attractive man, but she did know that it was wholly inappropriate under the circumstances. She was here to interview for a job, not ogle the man, she sternly reminded herself as she lowered herself into the Queen Anne–style chair and murmured, "Thank you."

"I understand that you're interested in working as my daughter's nanny for the summer," the prince said without further preamble.

"I am," she agreed, then felt compelled to add, "although I have to confess that I've never actually worked as a nanny before."

He nodded, seemingly unconcerned by this fact. "Your uncle told me that you're a teacher."

"That's correct."

"How long have you been teaching?"

"Six years," she told him.

"Do you enjoy it?"

"Of course," she agreed.

He frowned, and she wondered if her response was somehow the wrong one. But then she realized that his gaze had dropped to the BlackBerry on his desk. He punched a few buttons before he looked up at her again.

"And I understand that you've met Riley," he prompted.

"Only once, a few months ago. I was with a friend at the art gallery—" coincidentally, the same art gallery where she'd first seen him so many years earlier, though it was unlikely that he had any recollection of that earlier meeting "—and Princess Riley was there with her nanny."

Phillip had explained to her that the nanny—Brigitte Francoeur—had been caring for the princess since she was a baby, and that Prince Michael had been having more difficulty than he'd anticipated in his efforts to find a replacement for the woman who was leaving his employ to get married.

"The way Brigitte told it to me was that my daughter ran away from her, out of the café—and straight into you, dumping her ice cream cone into your lap."

Hannah waited, wondering about the relevance of his recounting of the event.

"I kept expecting to read about it in the paper," he explained. *"Princess Riley Accosts Museum Guest with Scoop of Strawberry."*

She couldn't help but smile. "I'm sure, even if there had been reporters in the vicinity, they would not have found the moment newsworthy, Your Highness."

"I've learned, over the years, that a public figure doesn't only need to worry about the legitimate media but anyone who feels they have a story to tell. A lot of ordinary citizens would have happily sold that little tale to *El Informador* for a tidy sum. Not only did you not run to the press to sell the story of the out-of-control princess, but you bought her a new ice cream cone to replace the one she'd lost."

"It wasn't her fault that the strawberry went splat," she said lightly.

"A gracious interpretation of the event," he noted. "And one that gives me hope you might finally be someone who could fill the hole that Brigitte's absence will leave in Riley's life."

"For the summer, you mean," Hannah sought to clarify.

"For the summer," he agreed. "Although I was originally hoping to find a permanent replacement, the situation has changed. The current nanny is leaving at the end of this week to finalize preparations for her wedding, and my daughter and I are scheduled to be at Cielo del Norte by the beginning of next. None of the applicants I've interviewed have been suitable, and your uncle has managed to convince me to settle for an interim solution to the problem."

She wasn't sure if she should be amused or insulted. "Is that why I'm here? Am I—"

"Excuse me," he interrupted, picking up the BlackBerry again. He frowned as he read the message, then typed a quick response. "You were saying?" he prompted when he was done.

"I was wondering if I'm supposed to be your 'interim solution.'"

His lips curved, just a little, in response to her dry tone. "I hope so. Although my royal duties are minimal, my responsibilities to my business are not," he explained. "I spend the summers at Cielo del Norte because it is a tradition that began when Samantha—"

His hesitation was brief, but the shadows that momentarily clouded his dark eyes confirmed her uncle's suspicion that the prince was still grieving for the wife he'd lost only hours after the birth of their daughter, and Hannah's heart couldn't help but ache for a man who would have faced such an indescribable loss so quickly on the heels of intense joy.

"—when Samantha and I first got married. A tradition that she wanted to carry on with our children." He cleared his throat, dropping his gaze to reshuffle some papers on his desk. "But the truth is that I still have a company to run. Thankfully I can do that from the beach almost as easily as I can do it from my office downtown. I just need to know that Riley is in good hands so that I can focus on what I need to do."

Be a good girl and stay out of the way so that Daddy can do his work.

The words, long forgotten, echoed in the back of Hannah's mind and sliced through her heart.

Maybe they had been born into completely different worlds, but Hannah suddenly wondered if she and Princess Riley might have a lot more in common than she ever would have suspected.

Her own father had rarely had any time for her, and then, when she was eight years old, her mother had died. She still felt the void in her heart. She still missed her. And she wanted to believe that in some small way, she might be able to fill that void for the prince's daughter. If he would give her the chance.

"Are you offering me the job, Your Highness?" she asked him now.

"Yes, I am," he affirmed with a nod.

"Then I accept."

Michael knew he should be relieved. He'd needed to hire a nanny for the summer, and now he'd done so. But there was something about Hannah Castillo that made him uneasy. Or maybe he was simply regretting the fact that his daughter would have to say goodbye to her long-term caregiver. Brigitte had been a constant in Riley's life almost from the very beginning, and he knew it would take his daughter some time to adjust to her absence.

He wished he could believe that being at Cielo del Norte with him would give Riley comfort, but the truth was, his daughter was much closer to her nanny than she was to her father. It was a truth that filled him with grief and regret, but a truth nonetheless.

He and Sam had long ago agreed that they would both play an active role in raising their child. Of course, that agreement had been made before Sam died, so soon after giving birth to their baby girl. How was one man supposed to care for an infant daughter, grieve for the wife he'd lost and continue to run the company they'd built together?

It hadn't taken him long to realize that there was no way that he could do it on his own, so he'd hired Brigitte. She'd been a child studies student at the local university who Sam had interviewed as a potential mother's helper when the expectation was that his wife would be around to raise their daughter.

For the first couple years, Brigitte had tended to Riley during the day and continued her studies at night, with Michael's sister, Marissa, taking over the baby's care afterhours. Then when Brigitte finished university and Michael's sister took on additional responsibilities elsewhere, the young woman had become Riley's full-time nanny.

I don't want our child raised by a series of nannies.

Sam's voice echoed in the back of his mind, so clearly that he almost expected to turn around and see her standing there.

He understood why she'd felt that way and he'd shared her concerns, but he convinced himself that a wonderful and energetic caregiver like Brigitte was the exception to the rule. She certainly wasn't like any of the harsh disciplinarians who had been hired to ensure that he and his siblings grew up to become proper royals.

Still, he knew his failure wasn't in hiring Brigitte—or even in hiring Hannah Castillo. His failure was in abdicating his own responsibilities as a father.

He'd wanted to do more, to be more involved in Riley's life. But the first few months after Sam's death had been a blur. He'd barely been able to focus on getting up every morning, never mind putting a diaper on a baby, so those tasks had fallen to Brigitte or Marissa.

At six months of age, Riley had broken through the veil of grief that had surrounded him. He'd been drinking his morning coffee and scanning the headlines of the newspaper when Marissa had carried her into the kitchen. He'd glanced up, and when he did, the little girl's big brown eyes widened. "Da!" she said, and clapped her hands.

. He didn't know enough about a baby's developmental milestones to know that she was speaking her first word several months ahead of schedule. All he knew was that the single word and the smile on her face completely melted his heart.

Sam had given him the precious gift of this baby girl, and somehow he had missed most of the first six months of her life. He vowed then and there to make more of an effort, to spend more time with her, to make sure she knew how much she was loved. But he was still awkward with her—she was so tiny and delicate, and he felt so big and clumsy whenever he held her. Thankfully, she was tolerant of his ineptitude, and her smiles and giggles gave him confidence and comfort.

And then, shortly after Riley's second birthday, Brigitte made a discovery. Riley had been an early talker—not just speaking a few words or occasional phrases but in complete sentences—and she often repeated the words when the nanny read her a story. But on this particular day, Brigitte opened a book that they'd never read before, and Riley began to read the words without any help or prompting.

A few months after that, Brigitte had been playing in the music room with the little girl, showing her how she could make sounds by pressing down on the piano's ivory keys, and Riley had quickly started to put the sounds together to make music.

Before she turned three, Riley had been examined by more doctors and teachers than Michael could count, and the results had been unequivocal—his daughter was intellectually gifted.

He was proud, of course, and more than a little baffled. As if he hadn't struggled enough trying to relate to the tiny little person when he'd believed that she was a normal child, learning that she was of superior intelligence made him worry all the more. Thankfully, Brigitte had known what to do. She'd met with specialists and interviewed teachers and made all of the arrangements to ensure that Riley's talents were being nurtured. And when the advertising company he and Sam had established ran into difficulties because an associate stole several key clients, Michael refocused his attention on the business, confident his daughter was in much more capable hands than his own.

It had taken a while, but the business was finally back on solid ground, Riley was happy and healthy, Brigitte was getting married and moving to Iceland, and he had a new nanny for the summer.

So why was he suddenly worried that hiring Hannah Castillo had set him upon a path that would change his life?

He didn't want anything to change. He was content with the status quo. Maybe it wasn't what he'd envisioned for his life half a dozen years earlier, and maybe there was an empty place in his heart since Samantha had died, but he knew that he could never fill that void. Because there would never be anyone he would love as he'd loved Sam. There was no way anyone else could ever take her place.

Each day that had passed in the years since Sam's death had cemented that conviction. He had no difficulty turning away from the flirtatious glances that were sent in his direction, and even the more blatant invitations did nothing to stir his interest.

Then Hannah Castillo had walked into his office and he'd felt a definite stir of…something.

The morning weather reports had warned of a storm on the horizon, and he'd tried to convince himself that the change in the weather was responsible for the crackle in the air. But he knew that there was no meteorological explanation for the jolt that went through his system when he'd taken the hand she offered, no logical reason for the rush of blood through his veins when she smiled at him.

And he'd felt an uneasiness in the pit of his belly, a tiny suspicion that maybe hiring a young, attractive woman as his daughter's temporary nanny wasn't the best idea he'd ever had.

Because as much as he'd kept the tone of the interview strictly professional, he hadn't failed to notice that the doctor's niece was quite beautiful. She wasn't very tall—probably not more than five feet four inches without the two-inch heels on her feet. And while the tailored pants and matching jacket she wore weren't provocative by any stretch of the imagination, they failed to disguise her distinctly feminine curves. Her honey-blond hair had been scraped away from her face and secured in a tight knot at the back of her head in a way that might have made her look prim, but the effect was softened by warm blue eyes and sweetly shaped lips that were quick to smile.

Even as he'd offered her the job, he'd wondered if he was making a mistake. But he'd reassured himself that it was only for two months.

Now that she was gone and he was thinking a little more clearly, he suspected that it was going to be a very long summer.

Chapter Two

Hannah went through her closet, tossing items into one of two separate piles on her bed. The first was for anything she might need at Cielo del Norte, and the other was for everything else, which would go into storage. Thankfully, she didn't have a lot of stuff, but she still had to sort and pack everything before she handed over her keys, and the task was much more time-consuming than she would have imagined.

Subletting her apartment had seemed like a good idea when she'd planned to spend the summer in China as an ESL teacher. Unfortunately the job offer had fallen through when she'd declined to share a tiny one-bedroom apartment with the coworker who'd made it clear that he wanted her in his bed. She felt like such a fool. She should have realized that Ian had ulterior motives when he first offered to take her to China, but she honestly hadn't had a clue.

Yes, they'd been dating for a few months, but only casually and certainly not exclusively. When she'd sidestepped his advances, he'd seemed to accept that she didn't want to take their relationship to the next level. So when he'd presented her with the opportunity to teach in China during the summer break, she'd trusted that he was making the offer as a colleague and a professional. Finding out that he expected them to share an apartment put a different spin on things.

Ian's ultimatum was further evidence that she had poor judgment with respect to romantic entanglements, a truth first revealed by her broken engagement three years earlier. Now she had additional confirmation in the fact that she was fighting an attraction to a man who wasn't just a prince but grieving the death of his wife. With a sigh, Hannah taped up yet another box and pushed it aside.

When she finished in the bedroom, she packed up the contents of the bathroom. By the time she got to the kitchen, her legs were protesting all the bending and her shoulders were aching from all the lifting. But she still had to empty the pantry of boxed food and canned goods, which she was in the process of doing when the downstairs buzzer sounded.

She stopped packing only long enough to press the button that released the exterior door locks. It was six o'clock on a Friday night, so she knew it was her uncle Phillip at the door. Weekly dinners had become their way of keeping in touch when Hannah moved out of his house, and she sincerely regretted that she would have to skip the ritual for the next couple of months.

"It's unlocked," she said in response to his knock.

"A woman living alone in the city should lock her doors," her uncle chided, passing through the portal with a large flat box in his hand and the sweet and spicy aroma of sausage pizza enveloping him. "Didn't I ever teach you that?"

"You tried to teach me so many things," she teased, standing up and wiping her hands on her jeans. "I thought I'd seen more than enough boxes today, but that one just changed my mind."

"Packing is hard work." He set the pizza on the counter

and gave her a quick hug. He smelled of clean soap with subtle hints of sandalwood—a scent that was as warm and dependable as everything else about him.

"I'm almost done." She moved out of his embrace to retrieve plates from the cupboard. "Finally."

"How long have you been at it?" He opened the refrigerator, pulled a couple of cans of soda from the nearly empty shelves.

"It seems like forever. Probably about seven hours. But I've already moved a lot of stuff into a storage locker downstairs, so it shouldn't take me too much longer."

Hannah took a seat on the opposite side of the table from him and helped herself to a slice of pizza. She hadn't realized how hungry she was until she took the first bite. Of course, she'd been too nervous about her interview with Prince Michael to eat lunch earlier, which reminded her that she hadn't yet told her uncle about the new job.

But he spoke before she could, saying, "I heard you're heading up to Cielo del Norte on Monday."

Phillip was a highly regarded doctor in the community and his network of contacts was legendary, but she still didn't see how he could have learned the outcome of her interview with the prince already. "How did you hear that?"

He smiled, recognizing the pique in her tone. "The prince called to thank me for the recommendation."

"Oh." She should have considered that possibility. "Well, his appreciation might be a little premature."

"I have every confidence that you're just what his daughter needs," Phillip said.

She wasn't so sure. She was a teacher, and she loved being a teacher, but that didn't mean she was qualified to work as a nanny.

And yet that wasn't her greatest worry. A far bigger concern, and one she was reluctant to admit even to herself, was that she now knew she'd never completely let go of her childhood infatuation with Prince Michael Leandres.

She should have outgrown that silly crush years ago. And she'd thought she had—until she stood in front of him with her heart beating so loudly inside of her chest she was amazed that he couldn't hear it.

So now she was trying *not* to think about the fact that she would be spending the next two months at Cielo del Norte with the sexy prince who was still grieving the loss of his wife, and attempting to focus instead on the challenges of spending her days with an almost-four-year-old princess.

"I wish I shared your faith," Hannah said to her uncle now.

"Why would you have doubts?"

"I'm just not sure that hiring a temporary replacement is the best thing for a young child who has just lost her primary caregiver." It was the only concern she felt comfortable offering her uncle, because she knew that confiding in him about her childhood crush would only worry him.

"Your compassion is only one of the reasons I know you'll be perfect for the job," Phillip said. "As for Riley, I think she'll surprise you. She is remarkably mature for her age and very well-adjusted."

"Then why does the prince even need a nanny? Why can't he just enjoy a summer at the beach with his daughter without pawning off the responsibility of her care on someone else?"

"Prince Michael is doing the best that he can," her uncle said. "He's had to make a lot of adjustments in his life, too, since losing his wife."

Hannah used to wonder why people referred to a death as a loss—as if the person was only missing. She'd been there when her mother died, so she knew that she wasn't "lost" but gone. Forever.

And after her death her husband had handed their daughter over to his brother-in-law, happy to relinquish to someone else the responsibility of raising his only child. Just as the prince was doing.

Was she judging him too harshly? Possibly. Certainly she was judging him prematurely. There were a lot of professionals who hired caregivers for their children, and although Prince Michael kept a fairly low profile in comparison to other members of his family, she knew that he had occasional royal duties to perform in addition to being president and CEO of his own company. And he was a widower trying to raise a young daughter on his own after the unexpected death of his wife from severe hypoglycemia only hours after childbirth.

Maybe her uncle was right and he was doing the best that he could. In any event, she would be at Cielo del Norte in a few days with the prince and his daughter. No doubt her questions would be answered then.

"So what are you going to do with your Friday nights while I'm gone this summer?" she asked her uncle, hoping a change in the topic of conversation would also succeed in changing the direction of her thoughts.

"I'm sure there will be occasional medical emergencies to keep me occupied," Phillip told her.

She smiled, because she knew it was true. "Will you come to visit me?"

"If I can get away. But you really shouldn't worry about me—there's enough going on with the Juno project at the hospital to keep me busy over the next several months."

"Okay, I won't worry," she promised. "But I will miss you."

"You'll be too busy rubbing elbows with royalty to think about anyone else," he teased.

She got up to clear their empty plates away, not wanting him to see the flush in her cheeks. Because the idea of rubbing anything of hers against anything of Prince

Michael's—even something as innocuous as elbows—made her feel hot and tingly inside.

Heading up to Cielo del Norte on Saturday afternoon had seemed like a good idea to Michael while he was packing up the car. And Riley had been excited to start their summer vacation. Certainly she'd given him no reason to anticipate any problems, but if there was one thing he should have learned by now about parenting, it was to always expect the unexpected.

The trip itself had been uneventful enough. Estavan Fuentes, the groundskeeper and general maintenance man, had been waiting when they arrived to unload the vehicle; and Caridad, Estavan's wife and the longtime housekeeper of the estate, had the beds all made up and dinner ready in the oven.

As Michael had enjoyed a glass of his favorite cabernet along with the hot meal, he'd felt the tensions of the city melt away. It was several hours later before he recognized that peaceful interlude as the calm before the storm.

Now it was after midnight, and as he slipped out onto the back terrace and into the blissful quiet of the night, he exhaled a long, weary sigh. It was the only sound aside from the rhythmic lap of the waves against the shore in the distance, and he took a moment to absorb—and appreciate—the silence.

With another sigh, he sank onto the end of a lounge chair and let the peacefulness of the night settle like a blanket across his shoulders. Tipping his head back, he marveled at the array of stars that sparkled like an exquisite selection of diamonds spread out on a black jeweler's cloth.

He jolted when he heard the French door slide open again.

"Relax—she's sleeping like a baby." His sister's voice was little more than a whisper, as if she was also reluctant to disturb the quiet.

He settled into his chair again. "I thought you'd be asleep, too. You said you wanted to get an early start back in the morning."

"I do," Marissa agreed. "But the stars were calling to me."

He smiled, remembering that those were the same words their father used to say whenever they found him out on this same terrace late at night. They'd spent a lot of time at Cielo del Norte when they were kids, and Michael had a lot of fond memories of their family vacations, particularly in the earlier years, before their father passed away. Their mother had continued the tradition for a while, but it was never the same afterward and they all knew it.

Gaetan Leandres had been raised with a deep appreciation for not just the earth but the seas and the skies, too. He'd been a farmer by trade and a stargazer by choice. He'd spent hours sitting out here, searching for various constellations and pointing them out to his children. He'd once told Michael that whenever he felt overwhelmed by earthly burdens, he just had to look up at the sky and remember how much bigger the world was in comparison to his problems.

Marissa sat down on the end of a lounger, her gaze on something far off in the distance. "I know they're the same stars I can see from my windows in the city, but they look so different out here. So much brighter."

"Why don't you stay for a few days?" he offered, feeling more than a little guilty that she'd driven all the way from Port Augustine in response to his distress call.

"I wish I could, but I've got three full days of meetings scheduled this week."

"Which you should have told me when I got you on the phone."

She lifted a shoulder. "I couldn't not come, not when I heard Riley sobbing in the background."

And that was why he'd called. His daughter, tired from

the journey, had fallen asleep earlier than usual. A few hours later, she'd awakened screaming like a banshee and nothing he said or did seemed to console her. She'd been in an unfamiliar bed in an unfamiliar room and Brigitte—her primary caregiver—was on a plane halfway to Iceland. Michael had tried to console Riley, he'd cuddled her, rocked her, put on music for her to listen to, tried to read stories to her, but nothing had worked.

It hadn't occurred to him to call his mother—the princess royal wouldn't know what to do any more than he did. It wasn't in her nature to offer comfort or support. In fact, the only things he'd ever been able to count on his mother to do were interfere and manipulate. So he'd picked up the phone and dialed his sister's number. During the first year and a half after Sam's death, before he'd hired Brigitte full-time, Marissa had been there, taking care of both him and his daughter. And, once again, she'd come through when he needed her.

"Do you think I should have stayed in Port Augustine with her?" he asked his sister now.

"That would have meant a much shorter trip for me," she teased, "but no. I'm glad you're maintaining the family tradition."

Except that he didn't have a family anymore—for the past four summers, it had been just him and Riley. And Brigitte, of course.

"When does the new nanny arrive?"

Marissa's question drew him back to the present—and to more immediate concerns.

"Tomorrow."

She tilted her head. "Why do you sound wary?"

"Do I?" he countered.

"Are you having second thoughts about her qualifications?"

"No," he said, then reconsidered his response. "Yes."

Her brows rose.

No, because it wasn't anything on Hannah's résumé that gave him cause for concern. Yes, because he wasn't completely convinced that a teacher would be a suitable caregiver for his daughter—even on a temporary basis.

"No," he decided. "Dr. Marotta would never have recommended her if he didn't believe she was capable of caring for Riley."

"Of course not," his sister agreed. "So what are you worried about?"

He didn't say anything. He didn't even deny that he was worried, because his sister knew him too well to believe it. Worse, she would probably see right through the lie to the true origin of his concern. And he was concerned, mostly about the fact that he'd been thinking of Hannah Castillo far too frequently since their first meeting.

He'd had no preconceptions when he'd agreed to interview her. His only concern had been to find someone suitable to oversee the care of his daughter during the summer— because after conducting more than a dozen interviews, he'd been shocked to realize how *un*suitable so many of the applicants had been.

Almost half of them he'd automatically rejected because of their advanced age. Logically, he knew that was unfair, but he had too many unhappy memories of strict, gray-haired disciplinarians from his own childhood. Another few he'd disregarded when it became apparent that they were more interested in flirting with him than caring for his daughter. Two more had been shown the door when they'd been caught snapping photos of his home with the cameras on their cell phones.

At the conclusion of those interviews, he'd almost given up hope of finding a replacement for Brigitte. Then, during a casual conversation with Riley's doctor, he'd mentioned his dilemma and Phillip had suggested that his niece might be interested in the job—but only for the summer.

So Michael had agreed to interview her and crossed his fingers that she would be suitable. Then Hannah had walked into his office, and *suitable* was the last thought on his mind.

"Oh," Marissa said, and sat back, a smile playing at the corners of her lips.

He scowled. "What is that supposed to mean?"

"She's very attractive, isn't she?"

His scowl deepened.

"I should have guessed. Nothing ever flusters you—okay, nothing except anything to do with Riley," she clarified. "But this woman has you completely flustered."

"I am not flustered," he denied.

"This is good," Marissa continued as if he hadn't spoken. "And it's time."

"Mar—"

She put her hands up in a gesture of surrender. "Okay, okay. I won't push for any details."

"There are no details," he insisted.

"Not yet," she said, and smiled.

His sister always liked to get in the last word, and this time he let her. It would serve no purpose to tell her that he wasn't interested in any kind of relationship with Riley's temporary nanny—it only mattered that it was true.

And he would repeat it to himself as many times as necessary until he actually believed it.

With every mile that Hannah got closer to Cielo del Norte, her excitement and apprehension increased. If she'd been nervous before her previous meeting with the prince—simply at the thought of meeting him—that was nothing compared to the tension that filled her now. Because now she was actually going to live with him—and his daughter, of course.

She could tell herself that it was a temporary position, that she was only committing two months of her time. But two months was a heck of a long time to maintain her objectivity with respect to a man she'd fallen head over heels for when she was only twelve years old, and a little girl who had taken hold of her heart the very first time she'd met her.

Hannah cranked up the radio in the hope that the pulsing music would push the thoughts out of her head. It didn't.

She wrapped her fingers around the steering wheel, her palms sliding over the smooth leather, and was reminded of the feel of his hand against hers. Warm. Strong. Solid.

She really was pathetic.

She really should have said no when her uncle first suggested that she could be anyone's nanny. But as she drove through the gates toward the prince's summer home, after showing her identification to the guard on duty, she knew that she'd passed the point of no return.

Cielo del Norte was even more impressive than the prince's home in Verde Colinas. Of course, it had once been the royal family's official summer residence, bequeathed to the princess royal by her father upon the occasion of her marriage to Gaetan Leandres.

Hannah had been advised that there were two full-time employees who lived in a guest cottage on the property, the groundskeeper and his wife. Hannah had been thrilled to hear that Caridad, the housekeeper, also cooked and served the meals, because she knew that if she'd been put in charge of food preparation as well as child care, they might all starve before the end of the summer.

She parked her aging little car beside a gleaming black Mercedes SUV and made her way to the door. An older woman in a neatly pressed uniform responded to the bell.

"Mrs. Fuentes?"

"Sí. Caridad Fuentes." She bowed formally. "You are Miss Castillo?"

"Hannah," she said, stepping into the foyer.

"The prince has been expecting you." There was the slightest hint of disapproval beneath the words.

"I was a little late getting away this morning," she explained. "And then traffic was heavier than I expected. Of course, taking a wrong turn at Highway Six didn't help, either, but at least I didn't travel too far out of my way."

The housekeeper didn't comment in any way except to ask, "Are your bags in the car?"

"Yes, I'll get them later."

"Estavan—my husband—will bring them in for you," Mrs. Fuentes told her.

"Okay. That would be great. Thanks." She paused, just taking a minute to absorb the scene.

She'd thought passing through the gates at Verde Colinas had been a culture shock, but now she felt even more like a country mouse set loose in the big city. The house, probably three times the size of the prince's primary residence in Port Augustine, almost seemed as big as a city—a very prosperous and exquisite one.

"There's a powder room down the hall, if you would like to freshen up before meeting with Prince Michael," the housekeeper told her.

Hannah nodded. "I would."

"First door on the right."

"And the prince's office?"

"The third door on the left down the west corridor."

Michael sensed her presence even before he saw her standing in the open doorway. When he looked up, he noticed that she'd dressed less formally today than at their first meeting, and that the jeans and T-shirt she wore made her look even younger than he'd originally guessed. He'd told her that casual attire was acceptable, and there was nothing inappropriate about what she was wearing. But he couldn't help noticing how the denim hugged her thighs and molded to her slim hips. The V-neck of her T-shirt wasn't low enough to give even a glimpse of cleavage, but the soft cotton clung to undeniably feminine curves. She wore silver hoops in her ears, and her hair was in a loose ponytail rather than a tight knot, making her look more approachable and even more beautiful, and he felt the distinct hum of sexual attraction through his veins.

Uncomfortable with the stirring of feelings so long dormant, his voice was a little harsher than he'd intended when he said, "You're late."

Still, his tone didn't seem to faze her. "I told you that I would come as soon as possible, and I did."

"I had a conference call at 8:00 a.m. this morning that I had to reschedule because you weren't here."

He expected that she would apologize or show some sign of remorse. Instead she surprised him by asking, "Why on earth would you schedule a conference call so early on the first morning of your vacation?"

"I told you that I would be conducting business from here," he reminded her. "And your job is to take care of my daughter so that I can focus on doing so."

"A job I'm looking forward to," she assured him.

"I appreciate your enthusiasm," he said. "I would expect that someone who spends ten months out of the year with kids would want a break."

"Spending the summer with a four-year-old is a welcome break from senior advanced English and history," she told him.

Senior English and history? The implications of her statement left him momentarily speechless. "You're a *high school* teacher?" he finally said.

Now it was her turn to frown. "I thought you knew that."

He shook his head. "Phillip said you would be perfect for

the job because you were a teacher—I assumed he meant elementary school."

"Well, you assumed wrong." She shrugged, the casual gesture drawing his attention to the rise and fall of her breasts beneath her T-shirt and very nearly making him forget the reason for his concern.

"So what kind of experience do you have with preschool children, Miss Castillo?" he asked, forcing his gaze back to her face.

"Other than the fact that I was one?" she asked lightly.

"Other than that," he agreed.

"None," she admitted.

"None?" Dios! How could this have happened? He was the consummate planner. He scheduled appointment reminders in his BlackBerry; he took detailed notes at every meeting; he checked and double-checked all correspondence before he signed anything. And yet he'd somehow managed to hire a nanny who knew absolutely nothing about being a nanny.

"Well, my friend Karen has a couple of kids, and I've spent a lot of time with them," Hannah continued.

He shook his head, trying to find solace in the fact that their agreement was for only two months, but he was beginning to question why he'd been in such a hurry to replace Brigitte. Had he been thinking of Riley—or had he been more concerned about maintaining the status quo in his own life? Or maybe he'd been spellbound by Miss Castillo's sparkling eyes and warm smile. Regardless of his reasons, he knew it wasn't her fault that he'd hired her on the basis of some mistaken assumptions. But if she was going to spend the summer with Riley, she had a lot to learn—and fast.

"You'll need this," he said, passing a sheaf of papers across the desk.

In the transfer of the pages, her fingers brushed against his. It was a brief and incidental contact, but he felt the jolt sizzle in his veins. Her gaze shot to meet his, and the widening of her eyes confirmed that she'd felt it, too. That undeniable tug of a distinctly sexual attraction.

As he looked into her eyes, he realized he'd made another mistake in thinking that they were blue—they were actually more gray than blue, the color of the sky before a storm, and just as mesmerizing.

Then she glanced away, down at the papers he'd given to her, and he wondered if maybe he'd imagined both her reaction and his own.

"What is this?" she asked him.

"It's Riley's schedule."

She looked back at him, then at the papers again. "You're kidding."

"A child needs consistency," he said firmly, because it was something Brigitte had always insisted upon, and he usually deferred to the nanny with respect to decisions about his daughter's care.

"If you're referring to a prescribed bedtime, I would absolutely agree," Hannah said. "But a child also needs a chance to be spontaneous and creative, and this—" she glanced at the chart again, obviously appalled "—this even schedules her bathroom breaks."

Maybe the charts Brigitte had prepared for the new nanny did provide a little too much detail, but he understood that she'd only wanted to ease the transition for both Riley and her temporary caregiver. "Brigitte found that taking Riley to the bathroom at prescribed times greatly simplified the toilet-training process."

"But she's almost four years old now," Hannah noted. "I'm sure…" Her words trailed off, her cheeks flushed. "I'm sorry—I just didn't expect that there would be so much to occupy her time."

He'd had some concerns initially, too, but Brigitte had made him see the benefits for Riley. Maybe she was young, but she was so mature for her age, so focused, and she was learning so much. She had a natural musical talent, an artistic touch and a gift for languages, and there was no way he was going to let this temporary nanny upset the status quo with questions and criticisms on her first day on the job. Even if her doubts echoed his own.

"It is now almost eleven o'clock, Miss Castillo," he pointed out to her.

She glanced at the page in her hand. "I guess that means it's almost time for the princess's piano lesson."

"The music room is at the end of the hall."

She folded the schedule and dropped a curtsy.

He deliberately refocused his attention back on the papers on his desk so that he wouldn't watch her walk away.

But he couldn't deny that she tempted him in more ways than he was ready to acknowledge.

Chapter Three

Well, that hadn't gone quite as she'd expected, Hannah thought as she exited Prince Michael's office. And she couldn't help but feel a little disappointed, not just with their meeting but in the man himself. She'd thought he might want to talk to her about Riley's favorite activities at the beach, give her some suggestions on how to keep the little girl busy and happy, but she'd gotten the impression he only wanted her to keep the child occupied and out of his way.

As she made her way down the hall in search of the princess, she realized that she'd never actually seen him with his daughter. The first time she'd met Riley—the day of the ice cream mishap at the art gallery—the little girl had been in the care of her nanny. When Hannah had arrived at the prince's house to interview for the position, Riley had been out with Brigitte. She'd gone back for a second visit, to spend some time with the child so that she wouldn't be a complete stranger to her when she showed up at Cielo del Norte, but she hadn't seen the prince at all on that occasion.

Now he was in his office, and the princess was apparently somewhere else in this labyrinth of rooms preparing for a piano lesson. Did they always lead such separate lives? Did the prince really intend to spend most of his supposed holiday at his desk?

Once she'd gotten over her wariness about taking a job for which she had no experience, she'd actually found herself looking forward to spending the summer with the young princess. She'd imagined that they would play in the water and have picnics on the beach. She hadn't anticipated that the little girl wouldn't have time for fun and frivolity. Yes, she'd been born royal and would someday have duties and obligations as a result, but she wasn't even four years old yet.

Brigitte had made a point of telling Hannah—several times—that Riley was an exceptionally bright and gifted child who was already reading at a second-grade level—in French. She'd encouraged the young princess to demonstrate her talents at the piano, and Riley had done so willingly enough. Hannah couldn't help but be impressed, but in the back of her mind, she wondered why the child didn't seem happy.

Somehow that question had Hannah thinking about what she'd been doing as a four-year-old. Her own childhood had hardly been traditional, but it had been fun. In whatever village had been their current home, she'd always had lots of local children to play with. She'd raced over the hills and played hide-and-seek in the trees. She'd gone swimming in watering holes and rivers and streams. She'd created rudimentary sculptures out of riverbank clay and built houses and castles from mud and grass.

Her parents had never worried about the lack of formal education, insisting that the life skills she was learning were far more important than reading and writing. While the teacher in her cringed at that philosophy now, she did understand the importance of balance between life and learning.

At the princess's age, she'd picked up some words and phrases in Swahili and Hausa and Manyika, enough to communicate with the other kids on a basic level; Riley was studying French, Italian and German out of textbooks. And whereas Hannah had learned music by banging on tribal drums or shaking and rattling dried seed pods, Riley had lessons from professional instructors.

She could hear the piano now, and followed the sound of the sharp, crisp notes to the music room to find the prince's daughter practicing scales on a glossy white Steinway.

She was sitting in the middle of the piano bench, her feet—clad in ruffled ankle socks and white patent Mary Janes—dangling several inches above the polished marble floor. Her long, dark hair was neatly plaited and tied with a pink bow. Her dress was the same shade of cotton candy, with ruffles at the bottoms of the sleeves and skirt. The housekeeper was in the corner, dusting some knickknacks on a shelf and surreptitiously keeping an eye on the princess.

The soaring ceiling was set off with an enormous chandelier dripping with crystals, but the light was unnecessary as the late-morning sun spilled through the tall, arched windows that faced the ocean. The other walls were hung with gorgeous woven tapestries, and while Hannah guessed that their placement was more likely for acoustics than aesthetics, the effect was no less breathtaking.

Suddenly, the fingers moving so smoothly over the ivory keys stopped abruptly. Riley swiveled on the bench, a dark scowl on her pretty face. "What are you doing in here?"

"Hello, Riley," Hannah said pleasantly.

"What are you doing in here?" the princess asked again.

"I wanted to hear you practice."

"I like to be alone when I practice," she said, demonstrating that she'd inherited her father's mood as well as his dark eyes.

Hannah just shrugged, refusing to let the little girl's attitude affect her own. "I can wait in the hall until you're finished."

"I have my French lesson after piano."

Hannah referred to the schedule she'd been given, which confirmed Riley's statement. "I'll see you at lunch, then."

The princess's nod dismissed her as definitively as the prince had done only a few minutes earlier.

On her way out, Hannah passed the piano teacher coming in.

The older woman had a leather bag over her shoulder and determination in her step. Clearly *she* had a purpose for being here. Hannah had yet to figure out her own.

The conference call that Michael had rescheduled came through at precisely eleven o'clock and concluded twenty minutes later. A long time after that, he was still struggling to accept what he'd learned about Miss Castillo—high school teacher turned temporary nanny.

Phillip Marotta had said only that she was a teacher; Michael had assumed that meant she had experience with children. Because he trusted the royal physician implicitly, he had taken the doctor's recommendation without question. Apparently he should have asked some questions, but he acknowledged that the mistake had been his own.

Still, despite the new nanny's apparent lack of experience, he knew that the doctor had stronger reasons than nepotism for suggesting his niece for the job. And from what Brigitte had told him, Riley seemed to accept her easily enough. Of course, his daughter had had so many doctors and teachers and instructors in and out of her life that she accepted most newcomers without any difficulty.

So why was he uneasy about Miss Castillo's presence at

Cielo del Norte? Was he really concerned about Riley—or himself?

When Sam died, he'd thought he would never stop grieving the loss. He was certain he would never stop missing her. But over the years, the pain had gradually started to fade, and Riley's easy affection had begun to fill the emptiness in his heart. He'd been grateful for that, and confident that the love of his little girl was enough.

He didn't need romance or companionship—or so he'd believed until Hannah walked into his life. But he couldn't deny that the new nanny affected him in a way that no woman had done in a very long time.

A brisk knock at the door gave him a reprieve from these melancholy thoughts.

"Lunch will be served on the terrace as soon as you're ready," Caridad told him.

He nodded his thanks as he checked his watch, surprised that so much time had passed. Twenty minutes on the phone followed by an hour and a half of futile introspection. Maybe he did need a vacation.

The housekeeper dropped a quick curtsy before she turned back toward the door.

"Caridad—"

"Yes, Your Highness?"

"What is your impression of Miss Castillo?"

Her eyes widened. "I'm not sure I understand why you'd be asking that, sir."

"Because I value your opinion," he told her honestly. "During the summers that I spent here as a kid, you were always a lot more of a mother to me than my own mother was—which makes you Riley's honorary grandmother and, as such, I'd expect you to have an opinion of her new nanny."

"We've only spoken briefly, sir, I'm certainly not in any position—"

"Quick first impressions," he suggested.

"Well, she's not quite what I expected," Caridad finally admitted.

"In what way?"

"She's very young and…quite attractive."

He didn't think Hannah was as young as Brigitte's twenty-four years, though he could see why the housekeeper might have thought so. Brigitte had dressed more conservatively and she hadn't been nearly as outspoken as the doctor's niece.

"Not that Brigitte wasn't attractive," she clarified. "But she was more…subtle."

She was right. There was absolutely nothing subtle about Hannah Castillo. While she certainly didn't play up her natural attributes, there was something about her—an energy or an aura—that made it impossible for her to fade into the background.

"But I'm sure that neither her age nor her appearance has any relevance to her ability to do her job," she hastened to add.

No—the most relevant factor was her employment history, which he decided not to mention to the housekeeper. No doubt Caridad would wonder how he'd ended up hiring someone with a complete lack of experience, and he was still trying to figure that one out himself.

"If I may speak freely…" Caridad ventured.

"Of course," he assured her.

"You should spend more time around young and beautiful women and less behind your desk."

"Like the young and beautiful woman you 'hired' to help in the kitchen when you sprained your wrist last summer?" he guessed.

"I wasn't sure you'd even noticed," she admitted.

"How could I not when every time I turned around she was in my way?" he grumbled good-naturedly.

"Maybe she was a little obvious, but I thought if I had to

hire someone, it wouldn't hurt to hire someone who might catch your eye."

"Caridad," he said warningly.

"Your daughter needs more than a nanny—she needs a mother."

The quick stab that went through his heart whenever anyone made reference to Samantha's passing—even a reference as veiled as Caridad's—was no longer a surprise, and no longer quite so painful.

"And in a perfect world, she would still have her mother and I would still have my wife," he stated matter-of-factly. "Unfortunately, this is not a perfect world."

"Four years is a long time to grieve," she said in a gentler tone.

"When Sam and I got married, I promised to love her forever. Is that time frame supposed to change just because she's gone?"

"Unless your vows were different than mine, they didn't require you to remain faithful forever but only 'till death do us part.'"

"Could you ever imagine loving anyone other than Estavan?" he countered.

"No," she admitted softly. "But we have been together forty-one years and I am an old woman now. You are still young—you have many years to live and much love to give."

He glanced at the calendar on his desk. "I also have another quick call to make before lunch."

"Of course, Your Highness." She curtsied again, but paused at the door. "I just have one more thing to say."

He knew it was his own fault. Once he'd opened the door, he had no right to stop her from walking through. "What is it?"

"No one questions how much you loved your wife," she told him. "Just as no one would raise an eyebrow now if you decided it was time to stop grieving and start living again."

He hadn't been with anyone since Sam had died, almost four years ago. And he hadn't been with anyone but Sam for the fourteen years before that. He'd loved his wife for most of his life. After meeting her, he'd never wanted anyone else—he'd never even looked twice at any other woman.

But Caridad was right—Hannah Castillo was beautiful, and he'd found himself looking at her and seeing not just his daughter's new nanny but a desirable woman.

Thankfully the buzz of his BlackBerry prevented him from having to respond to the housekeeper. Acknowledging the signal with a nod, she slipped out of the room, closing the door behind her.

Michael picked up the phone, forcing all thoughts of Hannah from his mind.

Lunch for the adults was pan-seared red snapper served with couscous and steamed vegetables. For Riley, it was chicken nuggets and fries with a few vegetables on the side. She eagerly ate the nuggets, alternately played with or nibbled on the fries and carefully rearranged the vegetables on her plate.

Throughout the meal, Hannah was conscious—almost painfully so—of the prince seated across the table. She'd pretty much decided that she didn't really like him, at least not what she'd seen of him so far, but for some inexplicable reason, that didn't stop her pulse from racing whenever he was near. Remnants of her childhood crush? Or the shallow desires of a long-celibate woman? Whatever the explanation, the man sure did interfere with her equilibrium.

Thankfully, he paid little attention to her, seeming content to make conversation with his daughter. Hannah found it interesting to observe their interaction, noting how alive and animated the princess was with her father. Certainly there was no evidence of the moody child who had banished her from the music room earlier.

"Is there something wrong with your fish?"

Hannah was so caught up in her introspection that it took her a moment to realize that the prince had actually deigned to speak to her. She looked down at her plate now, startled to notice that her meal had barely been touched.

"Oh. No." She picked up her fork, speared a chunk of red snapper. "It's wonderful."

"Are you not hungry?"

She *was* hungry. The muffin and coffee that had been her breakfast en route were little more than a distant memory, and the meal the housekeeper had prepared was scrumptious. But not nearly as scrumptious as the man seated across from her—

She felt her cheeks flush in response to the errant thought. "I'm a little nervous," she finally admitted.

"About seafood?"

The teasing note in his voice surprised her, and the corners of her mouth automatically tilted in response to his question. "No. About being here…with you."

"With me," he echoed, his brows drawing together. "Why?"

"Because you're a prince," she admitted. "And I'm not accustomed to dining with royalty."

"I'm a princess," Riley interjected, lest anyone forget her presence at the table.

"It's only a title," her father told both of them.

"That's easy to say when you're the one with the title," Hannah noted.

"Maybe," he agreed. "But the matter of anyone's birthright seems a strange reason to miss out on a delicious meal."

She scooped up a forkful of vegetables, dutifully slid it between her lips. "You're right—and it is delicious."

She managed to eat a few more bites before she noticed the princess was yawning. "Someone looks like she's ready for a nap," she noted.

"I don't nap," Riley informed her primly. "I have quiet time."

"Right, I saw that on the schedule," Hannah recalled, noting that Brigitte had indicated "nap" in parentheses.

And then, as if on schedule, the little girl yawned again.

"I think you're ready for that quiet time," the prince said, glancing at his watch.

His daughter shook her head. "I want ice cream."

He hesitated.

"Please, Daddy." She looked up at him with her big brown eyes.

"Actually, Caridad said something about crème caramel for dessert tonight," he said, attempting to put off her request.

"I want ice cream now," Riley insisted.

"One scoop or two?" Caridad asked, clearing the luncheon plates from the table.

"Two," the princess said enthusiastically. "With chocolate sauce and cherries."

The housekeeper brought out the little girl's dessert, but as eagerly as the child dug in to her sundae, Hannah didn't believe she would finish it. Sure enough, Riley's enthusiasm began to wane about halfway through, but she surprised Hannah by continuing to move her spoon from the bowl to her mouth until it was all gone.

"Could I please have some more?" Riley asked when Caridad came back out to the terrace, looking up at the housekeeper with the same big eyes and sweet smile that she'd used so effectively on her father.

"You can have more after dinner," the housekeeper promised.

The upward curve of Riley's lips immediately turned down. "But I'm still hungry."

"If you were really still hungry, you should have asked

for some more chicken, not more ice cream," the prince told his daughter.

"I didn't want more chicken," she said with infallible logic.

Hannah pushed away from the table. "Come on, Riley. Let's go get you washed up."

"I'm not a baby—I don't need help washing up."

It seemed to Hannah that the young princess didn't need help with much of anything—certainly not with manipulating the adults in her life, a talent which she had definitely mastered.

But she kept that thought to herself, at least for now.

She didn't want to lose her job on the first day.

"Riley," Michael chastised, embarrassed by his daughter's belligerent response. "Hannah is only trying to help."

"Actually," Hannah interjected, speaking to Riley, "maybe you could help me."

The little girl's eyes narrowed suspiciously. "With what?"

"Finding my way around this place," the new nanny said. "I've only been here a few hours and I've gotten lost three times already. Maybe you could show me where you spend your quiet time."

Riley pushed away from the table, dramatically rolling her eyes as she did so. If Hannah noticed his daughter's theatrics, she chose to ignore them.

"If you'll excuse us, Your Highness," she said.

"Of course." He rose with her, and watched as she followed Riley into the house.

He wasn't pleased by his daughter's behavior, but he didn't know what to do about it. As much as he loved Riley, he wasn't blind to her faults. But the adolescent attitude in the preschooler's body was just one more of the challenges of parenting a gifted child, or so he'd been told. Was Riley's behavior atypical—or did he just not know what was typical for a child of her age?

Surely any four-year-old going through a period of adjustment would need some time, and losing her longtime nanny was definitely an adjustment. He hoped that within a few days, after Riley had a chance to get to know Hannah and settle into new routines with her, her usual sunny disposition would return.

After all, it was a new situation for all of them, and it was only day one.

But as he made his way back to his office, he found himself thinking that he probably missed Brigitte even more than his daughter did. Everything had run smoothly when Brigitte was around.

More importantly, he'd never felt any tugs of attraction for the former nanny like the ones he was feeling now for Hannah.

Chapter Four

According to Brigitte's schedule, Riley's quiet time was from two o'clock until three-thirty. When that time came and went, Hannah didn't worry. She figured the little girl wouldn't still be sleeping if she wasn't tired, and since there wasn't anything else on her schedule until an art class at four-thirty, she opted not to disturb her before then.

Hannah was staring at her laptop screen when she heard, through the open door across the hallway, what sounded like drawers being pulled open and shut. She immediately closed the lid on her computer, wishing she could as easily shut down the shock and betrayal evoked by her father's email announcement.

He'd gotten married, without ever telling her of his plans, without even letting her meet the woman who was now his wife. But she forced herself to push those emotions aside and crossed the hall to the princess's room, a ready smile on her lips, determined to start the afternoon with Riley on a better foot.

Riley didn't smile back. Instead, she scowled again and her lower lip trembled.

"I want Brigitte," she demanded.

"You know Brigitte isn't here," Hannah said, attempting to keep her tone gentle and soothing.

"I want Brigitte," Riley said again.

"Maybe I can help with whatever you need," she suggested.

The young princess shook her head mutinously, big tears welling in her eyes. "It's your fault."

"What's my fault?"

"You made me wet the bed."

Only then did Hannah notice that the little girl wasn't wearing the same dress she'd had on when she'd settled on her bed for quiet time. She was wearing a short-sleeved white blouse with a blue chiffon skirt now, and the lovely pink dress was in a heap on the floor beside her dresser. A quick glance at the unmade bed revealed a damp circle.

"Accidents happen," Hannah said lightly, pulling back the covers to strip away the wet sheet. "It will only—"

"It wasn't an accident," Riley insisted. "It was your fault."

Hannah knew the child was probably upset and embarrassed and looking to blame anyone else, but she couldn't help asking, "How, exactly, is it my fault?"

"You're supposed to get me up at three-thirty—when the big hand is on the six and the little hand is halfway between the three and the four," Riley explained. "But now it's after four o'clock."

She probably shouldn't have been surprised that the child knew how to tell time—that basic skill was hardly on par with speaking foreign languages—and she began to suspect that the next two months with Riley would be more of a challenge than she'd imagined.

"Brigitte would have woke me up," Riley said, swiping at the tears that spilled onto her cheeks.

"Woken," Hannah corrected automatically as she dropped the sheet into the hamper beside Riley's closet. "And I know you miss Brigitte a lot, but hopefully we can be friends while I'm here."

"You're not my friend, you're the new nanny, and I hate you."

"I promise that you and I will have lots of fun together this summer. We can go—"

"I don't want to go anywhere with you. I just want *you* to go *away!*" Riley demanded with such fierce insistence that Hannah felt her own eyes fill with tears.

She knew that she shouldn't take the little girl's rejection personally. Despite her extensive vocabulary and adolescent attitude, Riley was only a child, reacting to her feelings of loss and abandonment. But Hannah understood those feelings well—maybe too well, with the news of her father's recent marriage still fresh in her mind—and she hated that she couldn't take away her pain.

"What's going on in here?" a familiar, masculine voice asked from the doorway.

Riley flew across the room and into her father's arms, sobbing as if the whole world had fallen down around her.

The prince lifted her easily. "What's with the tears?"

"I want Brigitte to come back." She wrapped her arms around his neck and buried her face against his throat, crying softly.

He frowned at Hannah over her daughter's head, as if the new nanny was somehow responsible for the child's tears.

"She's feeling abandoned," she told him.

His brows lifted. "Is she?"

She couldn't help but bristle at the obvious amusement in his tone. Maybe she didn't know his daughter very well yet, but she understood at least some of what the little girl was feeling, and she wasn't going to let him disregard the depth of those feelings.

"Yes, she is," she insisted. "She was upset when she woke up and the only person who was anywhere around was me—a virtual stranger."

The prince rubbed his daughter's back in an easy way that suggested he'd done so countless times before. "She'll get used to being here and to being with you," he insisted.

Hannah wished she could believe it was true, but she sensed that the princess would resist at every turn. "Maybe, eventually," she allowed. "But in the meantime, you're the only constant in her life and you weren't around."

"I was only downstairs," he pointed out.

"Behind closed doors."

"If I didn't have other things to deal with, Miss Castillo, I wouldn't have hired you to help take care of Riley for the summer." Now that the little girl had quieted, he set her back on her feet.

Hannah wanted to ask if his business was more important than his daughter, but she knew that it wasn't a fair question. She had to remember that the prince wasn't her own father, and she couldn't assume that his preoccupation with other matters meant he didn't care about the princess.

"You're right," she agreed, watching as Riley went over to her desk to retrieve a portfolio case. "I'm sorry. I just wish this wasn't so difficult for her."

"I get the impression she's making it difficult for you, too."

She hadn't expected he would see that, much less acknowledge it, and she conceded that she may have been a little too quick to judgment.

"I teach *Beowulf* to football players—I don't mind a challenge," she said lightly. "Although right now, the challenge seems to be finding a spare set of sheets for Riley's bed."

"I'll send Caridad up to take care of it," he told her.

"I don't mind," she said, thinking that it would at least

be something useful for her to do. "I just need you to point me in the direction of the linen closet."

Before he could respond, Riley interjected, "I need flowers for my art project."

"Why don't you go outside with Hannah to get some from the gardens?" the prince suggested. "I'm sure she would love to see the flowers."

"Can't you come with me, Daddy?" she asked imploringly.

"I'm sorry, honey, but I have a big project to finish up before dinner."

With a sigh, Riley finally glanced over at Hannah, acknowledging her for the first time since the prince had come into the room.

"I need freesias," she said. "Do you know what they are?"

Hannah smiled. "As a matter of fact, freesias happen to be some of my favorite flowers."

Michael was going to his office to pick up a file when the phone on the desk rang. He'd just tucked Riley into bed and didn't want her to wake up, so he answered quickly, without first bothering to check the display. The moment he heard his mother's voice, he realized his mistake.

"I have wonderful news for you, Michael."

"What news is that?" he asked warily, having learned long ago that her idea of wonderful didn't always jibe with his own.

"Your daughter has been accepted for admission at Charlemagne Académie."

"I didn't even know she'd applied," he said dryly.

Elena huffed out an impatient breath. "I pulled a lot of strings to make this happen, Michael. A little appreciation would not be unwarranted."

"I didn't ask you to pull any strings," he pointed out. "In fact, I'm certain I never mentioned Charlemagne at all."

"Your sister went there—it's a wonderful educational institution."

"Even so, I'm not sending Riley to boarding school."

"Of course you are," Elena insisted. "And while they don't usually accept children as young as five—"

"Riley's not yet four," he interrupted.

His mother paused, as if taken aback by this revelation, but she recovered quickly. "Well, if they could take a five-year-old, they can take a four-year-old."

"They're not taking her at all," he said firmly.

"Be reasonable, Michael. This is the perfect solution to your child-care dilemma."

"There's no dilemma, no reason for you to worry."

"I thought your nanny was leaving."

"Brigitte did leave, and I hired someone new for the summer."

"And what will you do at the end of the summer?" she challenged.

"I'm not worrying about that right now."

"The fall term starts in September."

"I'm not sending my four-year-old daughter away to boarding school in Switzerland."

"The child will benefit from the structure and discipline."

"The child has a name," he pointed out.

"A wholly inappropriate one for a princess," his mother sniffed.

"You've made your opinion on that perfectly clear," he assured her. "But it doesn't change the fact that Riley is her name."

"Getting back to my point—*Riley* will benefit from the structure and discipline at Charlemagne, and you will no longer be burdened—"

"Don't." Though softly spoken, the single word silenced her as effectively as a shout. "Don't you dare even suggest that my daughter is a burden."

"I didn't mean that the chi—that *Riley* was a burden," she hastened to explain. "But that the responsibilities of caring for a young daughter must seem overwhelming at times."

He couldn't deny that was true any more than he could expect his mother to understand that Riley was also the greatest joy in his life, so he only said, "I'll let you know if I change my mind about Charlemagne."

"I really do believe it would be best for Riley and for you," she said.

"I appreciate your concern," he lied.

Elena sighed. "I'll look forward to hearing from you."

Michael began to respond, but she'd already disconnected the call.

He dropped the receiver back in the cradle and went around his desk. Only then did he notice the figure curled up in the oversized wing chair facing the fireplace.

"I beg your pardon, Your Highness." Hannah immediately rose to her feet. "I should have made my presence known, but I didn't have a chance to say anything before the phone rang. Then I wanted to leave and to give you some privacy for your call, but you were blocking the door."

He waved off her apology. "It's okay."

"I really didn't intend to eavesdrop," she assured him. "But for what it's worth, I'm glad you're not planning to send Riley to boarding school."

He shook his head. "I can't believe she would expect me to even consider such a thing."

"She?" Hannah prompted curiously.

"My mother."

Her eyes widened. "That was your mother on the phone?"

He could only imagine how his half of the conversation had sounded to her, and shrugged. "We don't have a traditional parent-child relationship," he said.

Truthfully, there was more apathy than affection between them, especially since his wife had died. Elena had never respected boundaries and had never trusted her children to make their own decisions, and he had yet to forgive her for interfering in his marriage and convincing Sam that it was her wifely duty to provide him with an heir—a decision that had ultimately cost her life.

"Riley's grandmother wanted to send her to Switzerland?" Hannah pressed, apparently unable to get past that point.

"She even pulled strings to ensure she would be accommodated," he said.

"But she's just a child."

"My mother isn't an advocate of hands-on parenting," Michael told her.

Hannah seemed to think about this for a minute, then asked, "Did you go to boarding school?"

He nodded. "My brother and sister and I all did, but not until high school. Before that, we attended Wyldewood Collegiate."

"It would be easy to send her away," she said. "To let someone else assume the day-to-day responsibilities of her care."

"No, it wouldn't," he denied. "It would be the hardest thing in the world."

Hannah's conversation with the prince gave her some unexpected insight into his character and a lot to think about, but she was mostly preoccupied with trying to figure out his daughter. She tried to be patient and understanding, but as one day turned into two and then three, it seemed that nothing she said or did could change the princess's attitude toward her. And if there was one thing Hannah was certain of, it was that the princess's attitude very definitely needed changing.

On Saturday, after Riley had finished her lessons for the day, Hannah decided to take the little girl down to the beach. She'd made a trip into town the day before to get buckets and shovels and various other sand toys, and she was excited to watch Riley play. She should have guessed that the child would be less than enthusiastic about her plans.

"I don't like sand," the princess informed her. "And I get hot in the sun."

"That's why we wear our bathing suits—so we can cool off in the ocean after we play in the sand."

Riley folded her arms over her chest. "You can't make me go."

"Go where?" the prince asked, stepping out of his office in time to catch the tail end of their conversation.

"Hannah's trying to make me go to the beach." She made it sound as if her nanny was proposing a new kind of water torture.

"That sounds like a lot of fun."

The little girl wrinkled her nose, clearly unconvinced. "Will you come with us?"

He hesitated, and Hannah knew he was going to refuse, so she spoke quickly, responding before he did in the hope that it might lessen the sting of his refusal for Riley.

"I'm sure your daddy would love to come if he didn't have important business that needed his attention right now."

"But it's Saturday," Riley said, looking up at him pleadingly.

"Well, in that case," he said, "I could probably play hooky for a couple of hours."

His daughter's eyes lit up. "Really?"

"Sure, just give me a few minutes to change."

While the prince disappeared to don more appropriate beach attire, Hannah made sure that the princess was covered in sunscreen. Although the little girl obviously didn't like having the cream rubbed on her skin, she didn't protest. Apparently she was willing to put up with the process—and even Hannah—so long as she got to go to the beach with her daddy.

Hannah glanced up when she heard his footsteps, and exhaled a quiet sigh of purely female admiration. Over the past week, she'd come to appreciate how good the prince looked in his customary Armani trousers and Turnbull & Asser shirts, but the more formal attire had given her no indication of how muscular and toned he was beneath the clothes. Now he was wearing only board shorts slung low on his hips with a striped beach towel draped across very strong, broad shoulders, and just looking at him made Hannah's knees go weak.

She'd admired him from afar for so many years. As a teen, she'd snipped every photo of him out of newspapers and magazines and created her own personal scrapbook. Back then, she'd never expected that their paths would ever cross again. And now he was only a few feet away from her—almost close enough to touch. In fact, if she took only two steps forward, she could lay her hands on his smooth, tanned chest to feel the warmth of his skin and the beating of his heart beneath her palms. She could—

"Are we ready?" he asked.

"I'm ready, Daddy!"

It was the excitement in the little girl's response that snapped Hannah out of her fantasy and back to the present. She reached down for the bucket of toys, conscious of the warm flush in her cheeks. She should have outgrown her adolescent crush on the prince long ago, but as embarrassing as it was to accept that some of those feelings remained, it was somehow worse to realize that the man she was ogling was her boss. Obviously she had to work on maintaining appropriate boundaries.

"Let's go," she said brightly.

She'd barely taken a dozen steps out the door when she heard a familiar chime. Startled, she turned back to see the prince reaching into the pocket of his shorts.

"You weren't really planning to take your BlackBerry down to the beach, were you?" she asked incredulously.

"I've been waiting to hear back from a new client," he said without apology. And without another word, he turned away and connected the call.

Riley watched him, her big brown eyes filled with disappointment.

Hannah shook her head, acknowledging that while the prince might have a fabulous body and a face worthy of magazine covers, his priorities were completely screwed up.

Then she remembered the telephone conversation she'd overheard and the prince's adamant refusal to send his daughter away to school. Obviously he loved his little girl and wanted to keep her close—so why did he keep himself so distant from her? And why was she so determined to uncover the reason for this contradictory behavior?

Pushing the question from her mind, at least for now, she continued toward the water and the expensive private beach that had been calling to Hannah since her arrival at Cielo del Norte. "Do you want to know one of my favorite things about the beach?" she asked the princess.

The little girl shrugged but trudged along beside her.

"When the waves break against the shore, you can give them your troubles and they'll take them back out to the sea."

"No, they won't," the princess protested.

But instead of her usual confrontational tone, this time the denial was spoken softly, and the quiet resignation in her voice nearly broke Hannah's heart.

"Well, not really," she agreed. "But I'll show you what I mean."

She found a long stick and with it, she wrote in the sand, right at the water's edge: M-A-R-K-I-N-G-T-E-S-T-S.

"I'm a teacher," she explained. "And I love teaching, but I don't like marking tests."

The little girl looked neither interested nor impressed, but she did watch and within a few moments, the movement of the water over the sand had completely erased the letters.

Hannah offered the stick to Riley, to give her a turn. The princess seemed to consider for a moment, then shook her head.

So Hannah wrote again: T-O-F-U. She smiled when the letters washed away.

"What's tofu?" Riley asked.

"Bean curd," Hannah said. "It comes from China and is used in a lot of vegetarian dishes."

Thinking of China made her think of Ian, so she wrote his name in the sand.

"Who's Ian?"

"Someone I thought was a friend, but who turned out not to be. He's in China now."

"Eating tofu?"

She chuckled at Riley's question. "I don't know—maybe he is."

The little princess reached for the stick. She paused with the point of it above the sand, her teeth nibbling on her bottom lip. Finally she began to make letters, carefully focusing on the formation of each one until she spelled out: R-A-M.

"You don't like sheep?"

Riley smiled, just a little. "It's 'Riley Advertising Media.'"

"Your dad's company?"

The little girl nodded.

Hannah frowned as a strange thought suddenly occurred to her. "Did he actually name you after his business?"

Now the princess shook her head. "Riley was my mommy's middle name—because it was her mommy's name before she married my granddad."

"Oh. Well, it makes more sense that you'd be named after your mom than a corporation," Hannah said lightly.

But the little girl was writing in the sand again, this time spelling out: H-A-N-A…

She tried not to take it personally. After all, this game had been her idea, and she should feel grateful that Riley was finally communicating with her, even if she didn't like what she was communicating.

"Actually, my name is spelled like this," she said, and wrote H-A-N-N-A-H in the sand.

Riley studied the word for a moment, and when it washed away, she wrote it again, a little further from the waves this time. "Your name is the same backwards as forwards."

Hannah nodded. "It's called a palindrome."

"Are there other palindromes?"

"There are lots, not just words—" she wrote R-A-C-E-C-A-R in the sand "—but phrases and even complete sentences."

"Do you know any sentences or phrases?" Riley challenged.

N-E-V-E-R-O-D-D-O-R-E-V-E-N.

"That's pretty cool," the princess admitted. Her gaze flickered back toward the house. The prince was pacing on the terrace, his phone still attached to his ear.

She took the stick from Hannah again and wrote D-A-D.

"Good job," Hannah said, then winced when the little girl crossed the word out with so much force the stick snapped.

"Do you want to go back inside?" she asked gently.

Riley shook her head again. "I need to wash off this sand."

Michael had just ended his call when he spotted Hannah and Riley coming out of the water. Obviously he'd missed the opportunity to join them for a swim, and he was as sincerely disappointed as he knew his daughter would be. But as she made her way up the beach with Hannah toward the lounge chairs where they'd left their towels, his attention and his thoughts shifted from his little girl to the woman with her.

He hadn't expected that she would swim in the shorts and T-shirt she'd worn down to the beach. Truthfully, he hadn't even let himself think about what kind of bathing suit she had on beneath those clothes. But it wasn't the bathing suit that snared his attention so much as the delectable curves showcased by the simple one-piece suit of cerulean Lycra.

He didn't feel the phone slip from his fingers until it hit the top of his foot. With a muttered curse, he bent to retrieve the discarded instrument—and smacked his head on the rail coming up again. This time his curse wasn't at all muted.

Rather than risk further bodily injury, he remained where he was, watching through the slats of the railing as the nanny helped Riley dry off. After his daughter's cover-up had been slipped back on, Hannah picked up a second towel and began rubbing it over her own body. From the curve of her shoulders, down slender, shapely arms. From narrow hips, down endlessly long and sleekly muscled legs. Across her collarbone, dipping into the hollow between her breasts.

There was nothing improper about her actions—certainly she wasn't trying to be deliberately seductive. But like a voyeur, he couldn't tear his gaze away.

She tugged her shirt over her head, then shimmied into her shorts, and Michael blew out a long, slow breath, urging the hormones rioting in his system to settle down. But he now knew that, regardless of what she might be wearing, he would forever see the image of her rising out of the water like a goddess.

It was a good thing he would be going out of town for a few days.

Chapter Five

By the time Michael joined his daughter and her new nanny, Riley was packing sand into a long rectangular mold. She glanced up when he lowered himself onto the sand beside her, but didn't say a word. She didn't need to say anything—he could tell by the reproachful look in her big brown eyes that she was displeased with him.

He could handle her quick mood changes and even her temper tantrums, but her evident disappointment cut him to the quick. He was trying his best to be a good father, though it seemed increasingly apparent to him that he didn't know how. Every time he thought he was getting the hang of things, the rules changed.

"Sorry I missed swimming," he said, tugging gently on a lock of her wet hair. "But that was a really important client."

"They're all really important." She turned the mold over and smacked the bottom of it, perhaps a little too hard, with the back of a plastic shovel.

She was right. And she certainly wouldn't be the first person to suggest that he might be too focused on his company. But his work was at least something he understood. In his office, he was competent and capable and completely in charge. With Riley, he often felt helpless and overwhelmed and absolutely terrified that he was going to screw up—as if he hadn't done so enough already.

He glanced over at the nanny, to gauge her interpretation of the stilted exchange with his daughter, but Hannah's eyes were hidden behind dark glasses so that he couldn't tell what she was thinking. He decided he would wait to tell both of them of the meeting that would take him back to the city on Monday.

"What are you making?" he asked Riley instead.

"What does it look like?"

He wasn't pleased by her sarcastic tone, but he knew that she wasn't pleased with him at the moment, either, so he only said, "It looks like a sand castle."

She didn't respond.

"Is it Cinderella's castle or Sleeping Beauty's?" he prompted.

"Uncle Rowan's."

He should have realized that a child who had run through the halls of an authentic castle would be less fascinated by the fairy-tale versions. He should also have realized that she would be as methodical and determined in this task as with any other. Riley didn't like to do anything unless she could do it well. As a result, she quickly grew frustrated with any task she couldn't master.

Though Hannah didn't say anything, she pushed a cylindrical mold toward him with her foot. He let his gaze drift from the tips of her crimson-painted toenails to the slim ankle, along the curve of her slender calf—

She nudged the cylinder again, with a little less patience

this time. He tore his attention away from her shapely legs and picked up the vessel.

"Building a castle is a pretty big project for one person," he said to Riley. "Do you think maybe I could help?"

She just shrugged, so he picked up the small shovel and began filling the receptacle.

"You can't use that sand," she said impatiently, grabbing the mold from him and tipping it upside down to empty it out. "You need the wet stuff, so it sticks together."

She looked to Hannah for verification, confirming that this castle-building knowledge had been recently imparted by the new nanny, and was rewarded by a nod. Then she demonstrated for him—showing him how to pack the container with sand, then turn it over and tap it out again.

There were a few moments of frustration: first when one of the walls collapsed, and again when she realized the windows she'd outlined weren't even. But Michael patiently helped her rebuild the wall and assured her that sand-castle windows wouldn't fall out if they weren't perfectly level. That comment finally elicited a small smile from her, and he basked in the glow of it.

While he remained outwardly focused on the castle-building project, he was conscious of the nanny watching their interactions. He was conscious of the nicely rounded breasts beneath her T-shirt, and of the long, lean legs stretched out on the sand. He noticed that her hair had dried quickly in the sun and that the ends of her ponytail now fluttered in the breeze.

She could have passed for a teenager who'd skipped school to hang out at the beach with her friends, the way she was leaning back on her elbows, her bare feet crossed at the ankles and her face tipped up to the sun. And his immediate physical response to the sexy image was shockingly adolescent.

Dios, it was going to be a long two months. Especially if, as he suspected, he was going to spend an inordinate amount of that time fighting this unexpected attraction to her. On the other hand, the time might pass much more quickly and pleasantly if he *stopped* fighting the attraction. If he reached over right now to unfasten the band that held her hair back in order to slide his hands through the silky mass and tip her head back to taste her—

"Is it okay to dig a moat?" Riley asked, and the fantasy building in his mind dissipated.

He forced his gaze and his attention back to her construction.

"Every castle should have a moat," he assured her.

"Uncle Rowan's doesn't."

"But it should, to protect the princes and princesses inside from ogres and dragons."

She giggled. "Ogres and dragons aren't real, Daddy."

"Maybe not," he allowed. "But a moat is a good idea, just in case."

Riley tipped her head, as if considering, then nodded and began digging.

"What do you think?" he asked Hannah. "Is it worthy of the Sand Castle Hall of Fame?"

"An impressive first effort, Your Highness," she replied, and he knew she wasn't just talking about the construction.

"But I shouldn't quit my day job?" he guessed lightly.

"I don't imagine you would ever consider doing so."

He winced at the direct hit.

"But if you did, you might have a future in castle-building," she relented. "Your spire looks pretty good."

His brows rose. "My spire?"

Her cheeks colored as she gestured to the cone shape on top of the tower he'd built. She was obviously flustered by his innuendo, and he couldn't help but smile at her.

"But your flagpole is crooked," she said, and smiled back at him.

His gaze dropped automatically to her mouth, to the seductive curve of her lips. He wondered if they would feel as soft as they looked, if they would taste as sweet as he imagined. And he thought again about leaning forward to press his mouth to hers, to discover the answers to those questions.

Instead, he straightened the twig that was the castle flag and mused that it had been a long time since he'd shared this kind of light, teasing banter with a woman. A long time since he'd felt the slightest hint of attraction for a woman who wasn't his wife, and what he was feeling for Hannah was more than a hint.

He pushed himself up from the sand and picked up an empty bucket.

"Let's get some water for your moat," he said to Riley.

When the moat was filled and the finished project adequately *ooh*ed and *aah*ed over, they returned to the house. Hannah ran a bath for the princess so that Riley could wash the salt off her body and out of her hair. When she was dried and dressed, the little girl had taken a book and curled up on her bed. Hannah suspected that she would be asleep before she'd finished a single page.

After she'd showered and changed, the nanny ventured back downstairs, looking for Caridad to inquire if the housekeeper needed any help with the preparations for dinner. Hannah was embarrassingly inept in the kitchen but with so much time on her hands, she thought she might start hanging around while Caridad cooked. Even if she didn't learn anything, she enjoyed spending time with the older woman.

Unfortunately, the kitchen was empty when she entered. But more distressing to Hannah than the missing housekeeper was the absence of any suggestion that dinner might be in the oven.

She opened the door and scanned inside, just to be sure. Then she opened the fridge and surveyed the shelves.

"Looking for something?"

She started at the unexpected sound of the prince's voice behind her. When they'd returned to the house, she'd assumed that he would retreat to his office and stay there for the rest of the evening. That was, after all, his pattern.

"Caridad," Hannah said. "I haven't seen her all day."

"Well, I can assure you that you won't find her in either the oven or the refrigerator."

He smiled, to show that he was teasing, and she felt her cheeks flush. She hadn't yet figured out the prince or her feelings for him—aside from the jolt of lust she felt whenever he was in the same room. But as attracted as she was to Prince Michael, she was equally frustrated with the father in him. There were times he was so oblivious to his daughter and her needs that Hannah wanted to throttle him. And then there were other times, such as when he'd reached for his little girl's hand on the beach or when he'd slip into his daughter's room late at night just to watch over her while she slept—as she noticed he did almost every night—that his obvious love and affection for the princess made her heart melt. How could one man be both so distant and so devoted?

And how, she wondered, could one man have her so completely tied up in knots? Because there was no doubt that he did, and Hannah had absolutely no idea how to cope with her feelings.

She tried to ignore them, all too aware that Michael was completely out of her league, not just because he was her boss but because he was a prince. Her short-lived engagement to a British earl had forced her to accept that royals and commoners didn't mix, at least for the long term. Unfortunately, ignoring her feelings for the prince hadn't diminished them in the least.

"She and Estavan have weekends off," Michael continued

his response to her question about Caridad. "Unless I have formal plans for entertaining."

"Oh," Hannah replied inanely, thinking that was another check in the 'good prince' column. She also thought it was great for the housekeeper and her husband—and not so great for a woman whose kitchen expertise was limited to reheating frozen dinners.

"You don't cook, do you?" the prince guessed.

"Not very well," she admitted.

"Then it's a good thing I'm in charge of dinner tonight." She stared at him. "*You* cook?"

"Why do you sound so surprised?"

"I just can't picture you standing over the stove with a slotted spoon in one hand and your BlackBerry in the other. Your Highness."

Rather than taking offense, he smiled. "You do that a lot, you know."

"What's that?"

"Tack my title on to the end of a reply, as if that might take the sting out of the personal commentary."

"I don't mean to sound disrespectful, Your Highness."

"I'm sure you don't," he drawled. "But getting back to dinner, maybe you could try picturing the stove as a barbecue and the slotted spoon as a set of tongs."

"I should have realized that when you said you could cook what you really meant was that you could grill meat over fire."

"You forgot the 'Your Highness.'"

She smiled sweetly. "Your Highness."

"And at the risk of spoiling your illusions, I will confess that I also make an exquisite alfredo sauce, a delicious stuffed pork loin and a mouthwatering quiche Lorraine."

"But do you actually eat the quiche?" she teased.

"You can answer that question for yourself as it's on the menu for brunch tomorrow."

"And what's on the menu for dinner tonight?" she asked, as curious as she was hungry.

"Steak, baked potato and tossed green salad," he told her.

Her mouth was already watering. "Can I help with anything?"

"You just said that you don't cook."

"Can I help with anything that doesn't involve preparing food over a heat source?" she clarified.

He chuckled. "Do you know how to make a salad?"

"I think I can figure it out."

While Michael cooked potatoes and grilled steaks on the barbecue, Hannah found the necessary ingredients in the refrigerator for a salad. When Riley came downstairs, she gave her the napkins and cutlery and asked her to set them on the table.

The princess did so, though not happily. Obviously she wasn't accustomed to performing any kind of menial chores. And when her father came in with the steaks and potatoes, she looked at the food with obvious distaste.

"Can I have nuggets?"

"Not tonight." The prince had earlier uncorked a bottle of merlot and now poured the wine into two glasses.

"But I want nuggets," Riley said.

"You had nuggets for lunch," Hannah reminded her, and gave herself credit for not adding "almost every day this week."

The little girl folded her arms across her chest. "I want nuggets again."

"If she'd rather have nuggets, I can throw some in the oven," the prince relented.

"Yes, please, Daddy." Riley beamed at him.

Hannah opened her mouth, then closed it again without saying a word.

"Excuse us," he said to his daughter, then caught Hannah's arm and steered her into the kitchen.

"What's the problem with Riley having chicken nuggets?" he demanded.

"I didn't say anything, Your Highness."

"No, you stopped yourself from saying whatever was on your mind," he noted. "And since you didn't seem to have any qualms about speaking up earlier, why are you censoring your comments now?"

"Because I don't want to get fired after less than a week on the job."

"I won't fire you," he promised.

"Then I'll admit that I'm concerned about your willingness to give in to your daughter's demands," she told him. "She's not even four years old, and if you let her dictate what she's going to eat, she might never eat anything but chicken nuggets."

"It's just nuggets."

"No, it's not just nuggets. It's that you always give in to her demands."

"I don't always," he denied.

"And if you give in on all of the little things," she continued, "she'll expect you to give in on the not-so-little things and then, suddenly, you have no authority anymore."

She picked up the salad to carry it to the table, giving the prince a moment to think about what she'd said.

"Where are my nuggets?" Riley demanded when he followed Hannah into the dining room.

"It will take too long to make nuggets now," he said gently. "Why don't you just have what we're having tonight?"

Hannah cut a few pieces of meat from one of the steaks and slid them onto a plate along with half of a baked potato and a scoopful of salad. Although the prince didn't sound as firm as she hoped he would, she gave him credit for at least taking a stand.

The princess scowled at the food when it was set in front of her, then looked straight at Hannah as she picked the plate up and dropped it on the floor.

"Riley!" The prince was obviously shocked by his daughter's behavior.

The little girl, equally shocked by her father's harsh reprimand, burst into tears.

Hannah simply retrieved the broken plate from the floor and scooped up the discarded food to dump it into the garbage. Then she got another plate and prepared it the same way again.

"I want nuggets," Riley said, but her tone was more pleading than demanding now, and tears swam in her big brown eyes.

"Your daddy cooked steak and potatoes. You should at least try that before asking for something else."

Two fat tears tracked slowly down the child's cheeks. "You're mean."

"Because I won't let you have your own way?" Hannah asked.

"Because you told Daddy not to let me have nuggets."

She caught the prince's eye across the table. He looked helpless and confused, and though her heart instinctively went out to him, she felt confident that the situation was of his own making.

"You should sit down and eat your dinner," she suggested quietly.

He sat, but he continued to cast worried glances in his daughter's direction.

"If Riley's hungry, she'll eat," Hannah reassured him.

"I'm hungry for nuggets," the princess insisted.

"You're hungry for power." The retort slipped out before she could clamp her lips together.

Riley frowned at that.

"Don't you think that's a little unfair?" Michael asked.

"No, but I do think your daughter's demands are some-times unreasonable." Hannah finished making up Riley's second plate, but the mutinous look in the little girl's eyes as they zeroed in on the meal warned her that the food was likely destined for the floor again. So instead of setting it in front of her, she put it aside, out of Riley's reach.

Then Hannah deliberately cut into her own steak, slid a tender morsel into her mouth. Riley watched through nar-rowed eyes, her bottom lip quivering. Hannah ate a few more bites of her meal while the child watched, her gaze occasionally shifting to her own plate.

"I'm thirsty," Riley finally announced.

"There's milk in your cup," Hannah told her.

The princess folded her arms across her chest. "I don't want milk."

"Then you can't be very thirsty."

"I want juice," Riley said, and pushed the cup of milk away with such force that it hit Hannah's wineglass, knock-ing the crystal goblet against her plate so that it spilled all over her dinner and splashed down the front of Hannah's shirt.

She gasped and pushed away from the table, but the wine was already trickling down her chest, between her breasts. The prince grabbed his napkin and rounded the table, his gaze focused on the merlot spreading across her top. He squatted beside her chair and began dabbing at the stain.

Hannah went completely still. She couldn't move. She couldn't think. Heck, she couldn't even breathe, because when she tried, she inhaled his distinctly masculine scent and her hormones began to riot in her system. So she sat there, motionless and silent, as he stroked the napkin over the swell of her breasts.

Her blood was pulsing in her veins and her heart was pounding against her ribs, and he was all but oblivious to the effect he was having on her. Or so she thought, until his movements slowed, and his gaze lifted.

His eyes, dark and hot, held hers for a long minute. "I guess I should let you finish that," he said, tucking the linen into her hand.

She only nodded, unable to speak as his gaze dipped again, to where the aching peaks of her nipples pressed against the front of her shirt, as if begging for his attention.

"Or maybe you should change," he suggested, his eyes still riveted on her chest.

She nodded again.

"I want juice!"

Riley's demand broke through the tension that had woven around them. The prince moved away abruptly, and Hannah was finally able to draw a breath and rise to her feet.

"I'll be right back," she said, and retreated as quickly as her still-quivering legs would allow.

Michael sank back into his chair, then turned to face his daughter. He wasn't sure if he was angry or frustrated or grateful, and decided his feelings were probably a mixture of all those emotions—and several others he wasn't ready to acknowledge.

"Well, you've certainly made an impression today," he told Riley.

"I'm thirsty," she said again.

"Hannah gave you milk," he told her, trying to be patient. "And you spilled it all over the table and all over Hannah."

"I don't want milk, I want juice."

"You always have milk with dinner."

"I want juice," she insisted.

Though he had misgivings, he got up to get her drink. As he poured the juice into another cup, Hannah's words echoed in the back of his mind. *If you give in on all of the little things, she'll expect you to give in on the not-so-little things and then, suddenly, you have no authority anymore.*

He knew that she was right, and it irritated him that after less than a week with his daughter, Hannah had a better understanding of the child's needs than he did after almost four years. But the truth was, as much as he wanted to be a good father, he'd felt awkward and uncomfortable in the role from the very beginning. He'd constantly second-guessed everything he said and did around Riley, and whether it was a result of his ineptitude or not he knew Hannah was right: his daughter was turning into a pint-size dictator.

It was as if he was missing some kind of parenting gene—or maybe he'd deliberately suppressed it. When he and Sam got married, he knew that any pregnancy would be high-risk because of her diabetes and accepted that they might never have children. When she got pregnant, he'd been not only surprised but terrified. He knew what kind of risks she was facing, and he'd been so focused on her that he hadn't let himself think about the baby she carried.

Now that baby was almost four years old, the only care-givers she'd ever known were gone, and he'd hired a high school teacher to play nanny while he buried himself in his work, unwilling to even play at being a father. Was it any surprise that his daughter was acting out?

"Where's my juice?" she asked again when he returned to the table empty-handed.

"You can have juice with breakfast," he told her, trying to maintain a patient and reasonable tone.

"Now." She kicked her feet against the table.

"If you don't stop this right now, you'll have to go to bed without anything to eat or drink," Michael warned.

"You can't do that," Riley said, though there was a note of uncertainty in her voice now.

"I can and I will," he assured her.

His heart nearly broke when she started to cry again.

"It's Hannah's fault," she wailed. "She's making you be mean to me."

"Maybe, instead of always looking to blame someone else when you don't get your own way, you should start taking some responsibility for your own actions," he suggested.

She stared at him, completely baffled. He knew it wasn't because she didn't understand what he was saying but because the concept was completely foreign to her—because he had never before let there be consequences for her misbehavior. Instead, he'd made excuses—so many excuses, because she was a little girl without a mother.

While Riley considered what he'd said, Michael tried to tidy up the mess his daughter had made. He used another napkin to mop most of the spilled wine off of Hannah's plate, which made him recall the tantalizing image of the merlot spreading across her shirt, and the round fullness of the spectacular breasts beneath that shirt, and the blood in his head began to flow south.

He scowled as he righted her overturned goblet and refilled it. It had been a long time since he'd become aroused by nothing more than a mental image, and a lot longer since he'd been affected by a mental image of anyone other than Sam. He felt betrayed by his body's instinctive response to this woman, guilty that he could want a woman who wasn't his wife.

He knew that having sex with someone else wouldn't mean he was unfaithful. Sam was gone—he was no longer her husband but a widower. But he'd loved her for so long that even the thought of being with someone else felt like a betrayal of everything they'd shared and all the years they'd been together.

By the time Hannah returned to the table, the steaks and potatoes were cold. He offered to throw her plate in the microwave, but she insisted that it was fine. He didn't bother to heat his own dinner, either. He was too preoccupied won-

dering about the flavor of her lips to taste any of the food
that he put in his mouth.

He'd been so tempted to kiss her. When he'd been
crouched down beside her chair, his mouth only inches from
hers, he'd very nearly leaned forward to breach the meager
distance between them.

He didn't think she would have objected. It might have
been a lot of years since he'd sent or received any kind of
signals, but he was fairly certain that the attraction he felt
wasn't one-sided. He was also fairly certain that he'd never
experienced an attraction as sharp or intense as what he felt
for Hannah Castillo.

He and Sam had been friends for a long time before they'd
become lovers; their relationship had blossomed slowly and
rooted deep. What he felt for Hannah was simple lust, basic
yet undeniable.

It seemed disloyal to make any kind of comparison between the two women. Sam had been his partner in so many
ways and the woman he loved with his whole heart; Hannah
was a stranger on the periphery of his life, his daughter's
temporary nanny—and the woman with whom he was going
to be living in close quarters for the next two months. And
he was definitely tempted to take advantage of that proximity.

"Are you hungry now?"

Though she wasn't speaking to him, Hannah's question
interrupted his musings. Forcing his attention back to the
table, he noticed that Riley was eyeing the plate Hannah had
prepared for her, this time with more interest than irritation.

"If you dump it again, you won't have any dinner left,"
Hannah warned before she set the meal in front of the child.

His daughter immediately picked up a piece of potato
and put it in her mouth.

"Use your fork, Riley," Michael said.

She didn't look at him, but she did pick up the fork and

speared a wedge of tomato. It was obvious that she was still angry with him, but at least she was eating. Though he'd tried to sound firm when he'd threatened to send her to bed without any dinner, he wasn't entirely sure he would have been able to follow through on his threat.

When the meal was finally over, Riley had eaten most of her potato and picked at the salad, but she'd adamantly refused to touch the steak.

"Dinner was excellent," Hannah said, pushing her chair away from the table. "Thank you."

"You're welcome," he replied, just as formally.

"I'll clean up the kitchen after I get Riley ready for bed," she told him. "And then, if you've got some time, I'd like to talk to you about a few things."

Michael nodded, though he wasn't certain he wanted to hear what Hannah was going to say. He was even less certain that he should be alone with the nanny without the buffer of his daughter between them.

Chapter Six

Riley had made it clear to her new nanny that she was neither needed nor wanted, and as Hannah finished tidying up the kitchen after the princess was tucked in bed, she began to question her true purpose for being at Cielo del Norte. Maybe she was being paranoid, but when she finally cornered the prince in his office, the first question that sprang to her mind was "Did my uncle ask you to fabricate a job for me so that I wouldn't go to China?"

The prince steepled his fingers over the papers on his desk. "I didn't know anything about your plans to go to China," he assured her. "And this job is most definitely not a fabrication."

She had no reason to distrust his response, but she still felt as if he could have hired a local high school student to do what she was doing—and for a lot less money. "But Riley's instructors spend more time with her than I do," she pointed out to him, "which makes me wonder why I'm even here."

"You're here to ensure that the status quo is maintained."

"Your daughter needs more than a supervisor, Your Highness. And if you can't see that, then I'm wasting my time."

He leaned back in his chair, his brows lifted in silent challenge. "After less than a week, you think you're an expert on what my daughter needs?"

"I don't need to be an expert to know that a child needs love more than she needs lessons," she assured him.

"Riley isn't a typical four-year-old," the prince pointed out.

"Maybe she's not typical, but she is only four."

"She is also both gifted and royal, and she has a lot to learn in order to fulfill the duties and responsibilities that will be required of her in the future."

"In the future," she acknowledged. "But right now, knowing how to make friends is more important than speaking French."

"I disagree."

"I'm not surprised," she said, and couldn't resist adding, "but then, you probably speak impeccable French."

His gaze narrowed. "Is there a point to this conversation, Miss Castillo?"

His tone—undeniably royal-to-servant—gave her pause. She hadn't been sure how far she intended to push, but in light of his apparent refusal to give any consideration to her opinions, she felt that she had no choice but to make him face some hard truths. Even if those truths cost her this job.

"I took Riley into town yesterday afternoon," she said, then hastened to reassure him—though with an undisguised note of sarcasm in her tone—"Don't worry. We weren't gone any longer than the allotted two hours of free time."

"Did Rafe go with you?" he demanded.

She nodded, confirming the presence of the security guard whose job it was to protect the princess whenever she went out in public. Although Riley was young enough to be of little interest to the paparazzi, there was always the possibility of encountering overzealous royal watchers or, worse, a kidnapper.

"Where did you go?"

"To the bookstore."

The furrow between his brows eased. "Riley enjoys visiting the bookstore."

"Right inside the door was a display case for a new book she wanted, but the case was empty. Then Riley spotted another child at the cash register with a copy in her hands. When I told Riley it was probably the last one, she tried to snatch it out of the other girl's hands."

"She is used to getting what she wants when she wants it," he admitted a little sheepishly.

"Because you give her what she wants when she wants it," she pointed out. "And it's turning her into a spoiled brat."

"Miss Castillo!"

She ignored the reprimand, because as angry as he was with her, she was still angrier about Riley's behavior the previous afternoon.

"And when the child counted out her money and realized she was two dollars short, Riley actually smirked at her—until I gave the extra two dollars to the clerk so the other girl could take it home, and then the princess threw a tantrum like I've never seen before."

Michael scrubbed his hands over his face as he considered his response. "Riley's status as a royal combined with her exceptional talents make it difficult for her to relate to children her own age," he finally said.

"Her behavior has nothing to do with her blue blood or superior IQ and everything to do with her sense of entitlement."

"If this arrangement isn't working out for you, maybe we should consider terminating our agreement," he suggested in an icy tone.

She shook her head. "I'm not quitting, and I don't think you really want to fire me."

"I wouldn't bet on that," he warned.

"If you were sincere about wanting someone to help with Riley, then you need me," she told him. "You might not want to admit it, but you do."

His brows rose imperiously. "Do you really think so?"

"I doubt you'd have much difficulty replacing me," she acknowledged. "I'm sure you could find someone who is willing to step in and manage Riley's schedule and defer to her every command, and at the end of the summer, you and your daughter would be exactly where you are now."

"I'm not seeing the downside."

Hannah had never doubted that the princess came by her attitude honestly enough. She forced herself to draw in a deep breath, then let it out slowly. She was a commoner and he was a royal and her bluntness bordered on rudeness, but someone needed to shake up his comfortable little world to make him see the bigger picture—for his sake, and certainly his daughter's.

"The downside is that, if you let this continue, the princess's behavior will be that much more difficult to correct later on," she told him.

"Don't you think you're overreacting to one little incident?"

"If it was only one little incident, I might agree, Your Highness. But you saw how she was at dinner. And I suspect that her behavior has been escalating for a long time."

"Do you really think she knocked your wineglass over on purpose?" His tone was filled with skepticism.

"I believe that she was acting out of frustration, because she's so accustomed to getting her own way that she doesn't know how to cope when she doesn't."

He was silent for a moment, as if he was actually considering her words. And when he spoke, his question gave her hope that he had finally heard what she was saying. "So what am I supposed to do?"

"You need to make some changes." She spoke gently but firmly.

"What kind of changes?" he asked warily.

Before Hannah could respond, his BlackBerry buzzed.

"That's the first one," she said, as he automatically unclipped the device from his belt to check the display.

"It's my secretary. I have to—"

"You have to stop putting your business before your daughter."

"That statement is neither fair nor accurate," he told her, as the phone buzzed again. "There is nothing more important to me than my daughter."

"And yet, when I'm trying to talk to you about her, it's killing you not to take that call, isn't it?"

Even as he shook his head in denial, his gaze dropped to the instrument again.

"Answer the phone, Your Highness." She turned toward the door. "I'll set up an appointment to continue this discussion when it's more convenient for you."

Hannah's words were still echoing in the back of his mind while Michael gathered the files and documents that he needed for his meetings in Port Augustine. He didn't expect her to understand how important his business was, why he felt the need to keep such a close eye on all of the details.

He did it for himself—the business was a way to be self-supporting rather than living off of his title and inheritance, and it was something to keep him busy while his daughter was occupied with her numerous lessons and activities. He also did it for Sam—to ensure that the business they'd built together continued not just to survive but to thrive. And while it did, his sense of satisfaction was bittersweet because his wife wasn't around to celebrate with him.

Ironically, the company's success was one of the reasons that Sam had been anxious to start a family. The business didn't need her anymore, she'd claimed, but a baby would. Michael had assured her that he still needed her, and she'd smiled and promised to always be there for him. But she'd lied. She'd given birth to their daughter, and then she'd abandoned both of them.

He knew that she would never have chosen to leave them, that she would never have wanted Riley to grow up without a mother. But that knowledge had done little to ease his grief, and so he'd buried himself in his work, as if keeping his mind and his hands occupied could make his heart ache for her less.

Except that he rarely did any hands-on work himself anymore, aside from occasional projects for a few of the firm's original clients, his pro bono work for the National Diabetes Association and a few other charitable causes. For the most part, he supervised his employees and worked his connections to bring in new clients. And although he'd claimed that he was too busy to take a two-month vacation, the truth was, he could easily do so and know that his business was in good hands. The knowledge should have filled him with pride and satisfaction, but he only felt…empty.

Truthfully, his greatest pride was his daughter. She was also his biggest concern. After almost four years, he felt as if he was still trying to find his way with her. Their relationship would be different, he was certain, if Sam had been around. Everything would be different if Sam was still around.

Your daughter needs more than a nanny—she needs a mother.

He knew it was probably true. But he had no intention

of marrying again just to give Riley a mother. He had no intention of marrying again, period.

You are still young—you have many years to live, much love to give.

While he appreciated Caridad's faith in him, he wasn't sure that was true. He'd given his whole heart to Sam—and when he'd lost her, he'd been certain that there wasn't anything left to share with anyone else.

Of course, Riley had changed that. He'd never understood the all-encompassing love of a parent for a child until he'd held his baby girl in his arms. And as Riley had grown, so had the depth and breadth of his feelings for her. But knowing what to do with a baby didn't come as instinctively as the loving, and for the first year of her life, he'd relied on Marissa and Brigitte to tend to most of Riley's needs.

And then, just when he'd thought he was getting the hang of fatherhood, he'd realized that Riley needed so much more than he could give her. So he made sure that there were people around to meet her needs—tutors and caregivers—and he turned his focus back to his business.

When he told Hannah about his intended trip back to Port Augustine after lunch on Sunday, she just nodded, as if she wasn't at all surprised that he was leaving. Of course, she probably wasn't. She'd made it more than clear the previous night that she thought he valued RAM above all else. While that wasn't anywhere close to being the truth, he wasn't prepared to walk away from the company, either.

"I'm the president and CEO," the prince reminded her. "Fulfilling those positions requires a lot of work and extended hours at the office."

"I didn't ask, Your Highness," she said evenly.

"No, you'd rather disapprove than understand."

"Maybe because I can't understand why you don't want to spend any time with your daughter," she admitted.

"It's not a question of want."

"Isn't it?" she challenged.

He frowned. "Of course not."

"Because it seems to me that a man who is the president and CEO of his own company—not to mention a member of the royal family—would be able to delegate some of his responsibilities."

"I do delegate," he insisted. "But ultimately, I'm the one who's responsible."

"But it's your wife's name on the door, isn't it?"

"What does that have to do with anything?"

She shrugged. "Maybe nothing. Maybe everything."

"Could you be a little more indecisive?" he asked dryly.

"I just can't help wondering if your obsession with the business isn't really about holding on to the last part of the woman you loved."

"That's ridiculous," he said, startled as much by the bluntness of the statement as the accusation.

"I agree," she said evenly. "Because the business isn't the only part you have left of your wife. It's not even the best part—your daughter is."

"And my daughter is the reason you're here," he reminded her. "So you should focus on taking care of her and not lecturing me."

She snapped her mouth shut. "You're right."

"Especially when you couldn't be more off base."

"I apologized for speaking candidly, but I was only speaking the truth as I see it, Your Highness."

"Then your vision is skewed," he insisted.

"Maybe it is," she allowed.

"The potential client is only going to be in town a few days," he said, wanting to make her understand. "If the meeting goes well, it could turn into a big contract for RAM."

"What would happen if you skipped the meeting?" she challenged. "Or let one of your associates handle it instead?"

"The client specifically asked to deal with me."

"And if you said you were unavailable?"

"We would lose the account," he told her.

"And then what?" she pressed.

He frowned. "What do you mean?"

"Would you miss a mortgage payment? Would the bank foreclose on your home?"

"Of course not, but—"

"But somehow this meeting is more important than the vacation you're supposed to be sharing with your daughter?"

She was wrong, of course. But he could see how it appeared that way, from her perspective.

"The timing of the meeting is unfortunate and unchangeable," he told her, "which is why you're here to take care of Riley in my absence."

"Don't you think it would be better if Riley had more than a week to get to know me before you left?"

"I agree the circumstances aren't ideal," he acknowledged. "But I trust that you can manage for a few days."

That was apparently her job—to manage. While her lack of experience had given her some concern about taking a job as a nanny, Hannah had sincerely looked forward to spending time with the young princess. But the truth was, she spent less time with Riley than did any of the little girl's instructors.

And while she rarely saw the prince outside of mealtimes, their weekend beach outing aside, just knowing he had gone back to Port Augustine somehow made the house seem emptier, lonelier. Or maybe it was the weather that was responsible for her melancholy mood. The day was gray and rainy, Riley was busy with one of her countless lessons, leaving Hannah on her own.

After wandering the halls for a while—she'd spent hours just exploring and admiring the numerous rooms of Cielo del Norte—she decided to spend some time with Caridad.

Although she'd only been at the house for a week, she'd gotten to know the housekeeper quite well and enjoyed talking with her. But Caridad was up to her elbows in dough with flour all over the counters, so she shooed Hannah out of her way.

Hannah felt as if she should be doing something, but when she finally accepted that there was nothing she *had* to do and considered what she *wanted* to do instead, she headed for the library.

It was, admittedly, her absolute favorite space in the whole house. She had always been a voracious reader, and on her first visit to the room she'd been thrilled to find that the floor-to-ceiling bookcases were stocked with an eclectic assortment of materials. There were essays and biographies; textbooks and travel guides; volumes of short stories, poetry and plays; there were leather-bound classics, hardback copies of current bestsellers and dog-eared paperbacks. She spent several minutes just perusing the offerings, until a recent title by one of her favorite thriller writers caught her eye.

She settled into the antique camelback sofa with her feet tucked up under her and cracked open the cover. As always, the author's storytelling technique drew her right in, and her heart was already pounding in anticipation as the killer approached his next victim when a knock sounded on the door.

The knock was immediately followed by the entrance of a visitor and, with a startled gasp, Hannah jumped to her feet and dropped a quick—and probably awkward—curtsy.

"I beg your pardon, Your Highness, you caught me—"

"In the middle of a good book," the princess finished with a smile, as she offered her hand. "I'm Marissa Leandres, Michael's sister."

Of course, Hannah had recognized her immediately. Although the princess kept a rather low profile and wasn't a usual target of the paparazzi, she made frequent public appearances for her favorite charities and causes.

"I recently read that one myself and couldn't put it down," Marissa admitted. "So if I'm interrupting a good part, please tell me so, and I'll take my tea in the kitchen with Caridad."

"Of course not," Hannah lied, because after being banished by the housekeeper, the prospect of actual human company was even more enticing than the book still in her hand.

"Good," the princess said, settling into a balloon-back chair near the sofa. "Because I would love for you to join me, if you have a few minutes to spare."

"I have a lot more minutes to spare than I would have anticipated when I took this job," Hannah admitted.

The other woman's smile was wry. "I guess that means that my brother, once again, chose to ignore my advice."

"What was your advice?"

"To give Riley a break from her lessons, at least for the summer."

"So I'm not the only one who thinks that her schedule is a little over the top for a not-quite-four-year-old?" Even as the words spilled out of her mouth, Hannah winced, recognizing the inappropriateness of criticizing a member of the royal family—and to his sister, no less.

"Please don't censor your thoughts on my account," Marissa said. "And I absolutely agree with you about Riley's schedule. Although, in his defence, Michael believes he is doing what's best for Riley."

"I'm sure he does," she agreed, even if she still disagreed with his decision to leave Cielo del Norte—and his daughter. Thinking of that now, she apologized to the princess. "And I'm sure the prince must not have known of your plans to visit today because he went back to Port Augustine this morning."

Marissa waved a hand. "I didn't come to see him, anyway. I came to meet you. And I would have come sooner, but I've been tied up in meetings at the hospital, trying to get final approval for the expansion of the neonatal department at PACH."

"The Juno Project."

Marissa smiled. "Of course you would know about it—your uncle has been one of my staunchest allies on the board."

"He believes very strongly in what you're doing."

"Don't encourage me," the princess warned. "Because if I start talking about what we want to do, I won't be able to stop, and that really isn't why I'm here."

Another knock on the door preceded Caridad's entrance. She pushed a fancy cart set with a silver tea service, elegant gold-rimmed cups and saucers, and a plate of freshly baked scones with little pots of jam and clotted cream.

"Thank you," Marissa said to the housekeeper. "Those scones look marvelous."

Though she didn't actually smile, Caridad looked pleased by the compliment. "Would you like me to serve, Your Highness?"

"No, I think we can handle it."

"Very well then." She bobbed a curtsy and exited the room, closing the door again behind her.

"She makes that curtsying thing look so easy," Hannah mused. "I always feel like I'm going to tip over."

Marissa smiled as she poured the tea.

"It does take some practice," she agreed. "But I wouldn't worry about it. We don't stand on ceremony too much in my family—well, none of us but my mother. And it's not likely you'll have occasion to cross paths with her while you're here."

The statement piqued Hannah's curiosity, but she didn't feel it was her place to ask and, thankfully, the princess didn't seem to expect a response.

"So how are you getting along with my brother?" Marissa asked, passing a cup of tea to her.

"I don't really see a lot of the prince," Hannah admitted.

"Is he hiding out in his office all the time?"

"He's working in his office all of the time," she clarified.

"He does have the National Diabetes Awareness Campaign coming up in the fall," the princess acknowledged. "He always gives that a lot of time and attention—and pro bono, too."

Her surprise must have shown on her face, because Marissa said, "I know Michael sometimes acts like it's all about making money, but he does a lot of work for charities—Literacy, Alzheimer's, the Cancer Society—and never bills for it."

Hannah knew that his wife had been diabetic, so she should have expected that awareness of the disease was a cause close to his heart, but she hadn't expected to learn that he had such a kind and generous heart.

"I didn't know he did any of that," she admitted.

"Michael doesn't think it's a big deal," the princess confided. "But giving back is important to him. After Sam died…I don't know how much you know about his history, but he went through a really tough time then."

"I can't even begin to imagine," Hannah murmured.

"Neither can I," Marissa confided, "and I was there. I saw how losing her completely tore him apart—nearly decimated him. I tried to be understanding, but I don't think anyone really can understand the magnitude of that kind of grief without having experienced the kind of love that he and Sam shared.

"It took him a long time to see through the fog of that grief—to see Riley. But when he finally did, he put all of his efforts into being a good father to his little girl. He prepared her bottles, he changed her diapers, he played peekaboo."

As hard as Hannah tried, she couldn't imagine the prince

she'd only started to get to know over the past week doing any of those things. While it was obvious that he loved his daughter, it seemed just as obvious to Hannah that he was more comfortable with her at a distance.

"He made mistakes, as all new parents do, but he figured things out as he went along. Then he found out that Riley was gifted, and everything changed."

"Why?"

"Because Michael was just starting to find his way as a father when one of the specialists suggested that Riley would benefit from more structured activities, as if what he was doing wasn't enough. So he asked Brigitte to set up some interviews with music teachers and language instructors and academic tutors, and suddenly Riley's day became one lesson after another. Honestly, her schedule for the past six months has been more intense than mine."

While Hannah doubted that was true, she did think the princess's insight might explain Riley's bed-wetting episode. It wasn't that the little girl was regressing to her toddler habits, just that the signal of her body's need hadn't been able to overcome the absolute exhaustion of her mind.

"I think that's when he started spending longer hours at the office, because he felt like Riley didn't need him."

"I've tried to talk to the prince about his daughter's schedule," Hannah admitted now. "But he seems…resistant."

The princess's brows lifted. "Are you always so diplomatic?"

She flushed, recalling too many times when she'd freely spoken her mind, as if forgetting not just that he was a prince but also her boss. "I'm sure His Highness would say not."

Marissa laughed. "Then I will say that I'm very glad you're here. My brother needs someone in his life who isn't afraid to speak her mind."

"I'm only here for the summer," Hannah reminded her.

"That just might be long enough," Marissa said with a secretive smile.

Hannah didn't dare speculate about what the princess's cryptic comment could mean.

Chapter Seven

It was ten o'clock by the time Michael left the restaurant Tuesday night, but he did so with the knowledge that the prospective clients were going to sign a contract at nine o'clock the following morning. He didn't need to be there for that part of things—he'd done his job, gotten the client's verbal commitment; the rest was just paperwork. The documents had already been prepared by his secretary and the signing would be witnessed by the company vice president, so there was no reason that Michael couldn't head back to Cielo del Norte right now. True, it would be after midnight before he arrived, but he wasn't tired. In fact, the drive would give him a chance to let him unwind.

But for some reason, he found himself following the familiar route toward his home in Verde Colinas.

He unlocked the door but didn't bother turning on any lights as he walked through the quiet of the now-empty house toward his bedroom. It was the bedroom he'd shared with his wife during their twelve-year marriage. Even the bed was the same, and there were still nights that he'd roll over and reach for her—and wake with an ache in the heart that was as empty as his arms.

For months after she'd gone, he could still smell her perfume every time he walked into their bedroom. It was as if her very essence had permeated every item in the room. Each time, the scent had been like a kick to the gut—a constant reminder that while her fragrance might linger, his wife was gone.

He wasn't sure when that sense of her had finally faded, but now he was desperate for it, for some tangible reminder of the woman he'd loved. He drew in a deep breath, but all he could smell was fresh linen and lemon polish.

He stripped away his clothes and draped them over the chair beside the bed, then pulled back the covers and crawled between the cool sheets.

He deliberately shifted closer to Sam's side of the bed, and he was thinking of her as he drifted to sleep.

But he dreamed of Hannah.

The prince had told Hannah that he would probably be away overnight, but he was gone for three days.

At first, despite the nightly phone calls to his daughter, it didn't seem as if Riley was even aware of her father's absence. But then Hannah noticed the subtle changes in the little girl's behavior. She went about her daily routines, but she was unusually quiet and compliant at mealtimes, and she wet her bed both nights. The first morning that Hannah saw the damp sheets in a heap on the floor, she waited for Riley's tirade. But the little girl only asked if she had time to take a bath before breakfast.

By Wednesday, Hannah was desperate for something—anything—to cheer up the little girl. It was the only day of the week that Riley's lessons were finished by lunchtime, so in the morning, she dialed the familiar number of her best friend.

"I'm calling at a bad time," she guessed, when she registered the sound of crying in the background.

"Gabriel's teething," Karen replied wearily. "It's always a bad time."

"Maybe I can help," Hannah suggested.

"Unless you want to take the kid off of my hands for a few hours so I can catch up on my sleep, I doubt it."

"I was actually hoping to take Grace off of your hands for a few hours, but I might be able to handle the baby, too."

She must have sounded as uncertain as she felt, because Karen managed a laugh. "The new nanny gig must be a piece of cake if you want to add more kids to the mix."

"I wouldn't say it's been a piece of cake," Hannah confided. "But I really would appreciate it if Grace could come over and hang out with Riley for a while."

The only response was, aside from the background crying, complete and utter silence.

"Karen?" she prompted.

"I'm sorry. I'm just a little—a lot—surprised. I mean, Grace is a great kid, but she goes to public school."

Hannah laughed. "She is a great kid, and I think it would be great for Riley to play with someone closer to her own age." Although her friend's daughter had just turned six and the princess wasn't quite four, Hannah didn't have any concerns about Riley being able to keep up with Grace. "So—will you come?"

"I'm packing Gabe's diaper bag as we speak," Karen assured her.

"Could you bring some of Grace's toys and games, too?"

"Sure. What does the princess like to play with?"

"That's what I'm trying to figure out," Hannah admitted.

For the first time since Hannah arrived at Cielo del Norte, she felt as if she and Riley had a really good day. Of course, it was really Grace's visit that made the difference for the princess. After Riley got past her initial hesitation about meeting someone new, the two girls had a wonderful time together. They played some board games, made sculptures with modeling clay, built towers of blocks—which Gabe happily knocked down for them—and sang and danced in the music room. The adults observed without interference until Grace suggested playing hide-and-seek, then Karen insisted on limiting their game to only four rooms, to ensure that her daughter didn't wander off too far and get lost.

Hannah was amazed by the transformation of the princess into a normal little girl. And while Karen still looked like she would benefit from a good night of uninterrupted sleep, she thanked Hannah for the invite, insisting that the change of venue and adult conversation were just what she needed to feel human again. For her part, Hannah was happy to have the time with her friend—and thrilled to cuddle with ten-month-old Gabe.

"Did you have fun playing with Grace today?" Hannah asked when she tucked Riley into bed later that night.

The princess nodded. "Her mommy is very pretty."

The wistful tone in her voice made Hannah's heart ache for the little girl who didn't have any memories of her own mother. "Yes, she is," she agreed. "Her mommy is also one of my best friends."

"I don't have a best friend," Riley admitted. "I don't have any friends at all."

"Only because you haven't had a chance to make friends. That will change when you go to school in September."

Riley looked away. "I don't want to go to school."

"Why not?"

The little girl shrugged. "Because I won't know anyone there."

"It can be scary," Hannah admitted. "Going new places,

meeting new people. But it's going to be new for all of the other kids, too."

"Really?"

"Really," Hannah assured her.

"When did you meet your best friend?" Riley wanted to know.

"The first year that I came to Tesoro del Mar to live with my uncle Phillip."

"He's my doctor," Riley said, then her little brow furrowed. "But why did you live with your uncle? Where was your daddy?"

Hannah thought it was telling—and more than a little sad—that Riley didn't ask about her mother. Because, in her experience, it was more usual for little girls to live with their daddies than with both of their parents.

"My daddy lived far away."

"Why didn't you live with him there?"

"I used to," Hannah told her. "Before my mother died."

The princess's eyes went wide. "Your mommy died, too?"

Hannah nodded. "When I was a few years older than you."

"Do you miss her?"

She nodded again. "Even though it was a very long time ago, I still miss her very much."

"I don't remember my mommy," Riley admitted, almost guiltily.

Hannah brushed a lock of hair off of the little girl's forehead. "You couldn't," she said gently, hoping to reassure her. "You were only a baby when she died."

"But I have a present from her."

"What's that?"

The princess pointed to the beautifully dressed silken-haired doll on the top of her tallest dresser. Hannah had noticed it the first time she'd ever ventured into the room, partly because it was so exquisite and partly because it was the only doll the little girl seemed to own.

"I call her Sara."

After the little princess in the story by Frances Hodgson Burnett, Hannah guessed, having seen a copy of the book on Riley's shelf of favorites.

"That's a very pretty name," she said. "For a very pretty doll."

The child smiled shyly. "Daddy said she looks just like my mommy, when she was a little girl. And he put her up there so that she could always watch over me." Then she sighed.

"Why does that make you sad?" Hannah asked her.

"I just think that she must be lonely, because she has no one to play with."

"Are you lonely?"

Riley shook her head, though the denial seemed more automatic than sincere, and her gaze shifted toward the doll again. "There's always a teacher or someone with me."

"You are very busy with your lessons." Hannah took Sara off of the dresser, smoothed a hand over her springy blond curls. The princess watched her every move, seemingly torn between shock and pleasure that her beloved Sara had been moved from her very special place. Hannah straightened the velvet skirt, then adjusted the bow on one of her black boots, and finally offered the doll to Riley.

The child's eyes went wide, and for a moment Hannah thought she might shake her head, refusing the offer. But then her hand reached out and she tentatively touched a finger to the lace that peeked out from beneath the doll's full skirt.

"But maybe you could spend some time with Sara when you're not too busy?"

She nodded, not just an affirmation but a promise, and hugged the doll against her chest.

"And maybe Grace could come back to play another time," Hannah continued.

The last of the shadows lifted from the little girl's eyes. "Do you think she would?"

"I think she'd be happy to." She pulled the covers up to Riley's chin. "Good night."

"'Night," Riley echoed, her eyes already drifting shut.

Hannah switched off the lamp on the bedside table and started to tiptoe out of the room.

"Hannah?"

She paused at the door. "Did you need something?"

There was a slight hesitation, and then Riley finally said, "Daddy sometimes sits with me until I fall asleep."

And as Michael hadn't been home for the past two nights, his daughter was obviously missing him. "I'm not sure when your daddy's going to be home," she admitted, because he never spoke to her when he called except to ask for his daughter and she hadn't felt entitled to inquire about his agenda.

"Could you stay for a while?" Riley asked. "Please?"

"I would be happy to stay," Hannah told her.

The princess's lips curved, just a little. "You don't have to stay long. I'm very tired."

"I'll stay as long as you want," she promised.

Hannah wasn't very tired herself, but the night was so dark and quiet that she found her eyes beginning to drift shut. She thought about going across the hall to her own bed, but she didn't want to tiptoe away until she was certain that Riley wouldn't awaken. So she listened to the soft, even sounds of the little girl's breathing…

Michael had stayed away longer than he'd intended, and he was feeling more than a little guilty about his extended absence. And angry at himself when he finally recognized the real reason behind his absence—he'd been hiding.

His sister would probably say that he'd been hiding from life the past four years, and maybe that was true to a certain extent. But for the past three days, he'd been hiding from something else—or rather some*one* else: Hannah Castillo.

Since she'd moved into Cielo del Norte, she'd turned his entire life upside down. She made him question so many things he'd been certain of, and she made him feel too many things he didn't want to feel.

After two long, sleepless nights alone in his bed in Verde Colinas, he'd accepted that he couldn't keep hiding forever.

Besides, he missed his daughter, and hearing her voice on the phone couldn't compare to feeling the warmth of her arms around his neck.

Whether Hannah believed it or not, Riley was the center of his world. Maybe he spent more hours in his office than he did with his child, but it was the time he spent with her that made every day worthwhile. It was her smile that filled the dark places in his heart with light, and her laughter that lifted his spirits when nothing else could.

Even now, as he tiptoed toward her room, his step was lighter because he was finally home with her.

Of course, being home also meant being in close proximity to Hannah again, but he was confident that he would figure out a way to deal with the unwelcome feelings she stirred inside of him. And anyway, that wasn't something he was going to worry about before morning.

Or so he thought until he stepped into Riley's room and saw her in the chair beside his daughter's bed.

He stopped abruptly, and her eyelids flickered, then slowly lifted.

"What are you doing here?" Though he'd spoken in a whisper, the words came out more harshly than he'd intended.

Hannah blinked, obviously startled by the sharp demand. "Riley asked me to sit with her until she fell asleep."

"I would hope she's been asleep for a while," he told her. "It's after midnight."

"I guess I fell asleep, too."

"You should be in your own bed," he told her.

She nodded and eased out of the chair.

He moved closer, to adjust Riley's covers. As he pulled up the duvet, he noticed that there was something tucked beneath her arm. He felt a funny tug in his belly as he recognized the doll that Sam had bought when she learned that she was having a baby girl.

It was the only thing Riley had that was chosen specifically for her by her mother. Now its dress was rumpled and its hair was in disarray and one of its boots was falling off. He tried to ease the doll from Riley's grasp, but as soon as he tried to wriggle it free, her arm tightened around it. With a sigh of both regret and resignation, he left the doll with his daughter and caught up with Hannah outside of the room.

He grabbed her arm to turn her around to face him. "What were you thinking?" he demanded, the words ground out between clenched teeth.

The nanny blinked, startled by his evident fury, and yanked her arm away from him. "I don't know what you're talking about, Your Highness, but if you're going to yell at me, you might not want to do so right outside of your daughter's bedroom."

He acknowledged her suggestion with a curt nod. "Downstairs."

Her eyes narrowed, and for just a second he thought she would balk at the command. Maybe he wanted her to balk. Her defiance would give him a reason to hold on to his fury, because touching Hannah—even just his hand on her arm—had turned his thoughts in a whole other direction. But then she moved past him and started down the stairs.

She paused at the bottom, as if uncertain of where to go from there.

"My office," he told her.

She went through the door, then turned to face him, her arms folded over her chest. "Now could you please explain what's got you all twisted up in knots?"

"The doll in Riley's bed."

He saw the change in her eyes, the shift from confusion to understanding. Then her chin lifted. "What about it?"

"It's not a toy."

"Dolls are meant to be played with," she told him firmly.

"Not that one."

She shook her head. "You don't even realize what you're doing, do you?"

"What *I'm* doing?" he demanded incredulously, wondering how she could possibly turn this around so that it was his fault.

"Yes, what *you're* doing. You told Riley this wonderful story about how her mother picked out the doll just for her, then you put it on a shelf where she couldn't reach it, so that the only tangible symbol she has of her mother stayed beautiful but untouchable."

He scowled at her. "That's not what I did at all."

"Maybe it's not what you intended, Your Highness," she said in a more gentle tone, "but it's what happened."

He'd only wanted to preserve the gift for Riley so that she would have it forever. But he realized now that Hannah was right, that in doing so he'd ensured that she didn't really have it at all.

He shook his head, the last of his anger draining away, leaving only weariness and frustration. "Am I ever going to get anything right?"

He felt her touch on his arm. "You're doing a lot of things right."

He looked down at her hand, at the long, slender fingers that were so pale against his darker skin, and marveled that she would try to comfort him after the way he'd attacked her. She truly was a remarkable woman. Strong enough to stand up to him, yet soft enough to offer comfort.

"That's not the tune you were singing the last time we discussed my daughter," he reminded her.

Her hand dropped away as one side of her mouth tipped up in a half smile. "I'm not saying that you're doing *every-thing* right," she teased. "But I do think you have a lot of potential."

"If I'm willing to make some changes," he said, remembering.

She nodded.

"Do you want to talk about those changes now or should we just go up to bed?"

He didn't realize how much the words sounded like an invitation until she stepped back. He didn't realize how tempted he was by the idea himself until he'd spoken the words aloud.

"I meant to say that if you're tired, you can go upstairs to your own bed," he clarified.

"Oh. Of course," she said, though he could tell by the color in her cheeks that she had been thinking of something else entirely. Unfortunately, he couldn't tell if she was intrigued or troubled by the something else.

"I apologize for my poor word choice," he said. "I didn't mean to make you uncomfortable."

"You didn't."

He took a step closer to her, knowing that he was close to stepping over a line that he shouldn't but too tempted by this woman to care. "You didn't think I was propositioning you?"

"Of course not," she denied, though her blush suggested otherwise.

"Why 'of course not'?" he asked curiously.

She dropped her gaze. "Because a man like you—a prince—would never be interested in someone like me."

There was a time when he'd thought he would never be interested in anyone who wasn't Sam, but the past ten days had proven otherwise. Even when he wasn't near Hannah, he was thinking about her, wanting her. He knew that he shouldn't, but that knowledge did nothing to diminish his desire.

"You're an attractive woman, Hannah. It would be a mistake to assume that any man would not be interested."

"You're confusing me," she admitted. "In one breath, you say that you're not propositioning me, and in the next, you say that you find me attractive."

"Actually, my comment was more objective than subjective," he told her. "But while I do think you're a very attractive woman, I didn't hire you in order to pursue a personal relationship with you."

"Okay," she said, still sounding wary.

Not that he could blame her. Because even as he was saying one thing, he was thinking something else entirely.

"In fact, I wouldn't have invited you to spend the summer here if I thought there was any danger of an attraction leading to anything else."

"Okay," she said again.

"I just want you to understand that I didn't intend for this to happen at all," he said, and slid his arms around her.

"What is happening?" she asked, a little breathlessly.

"This," he said.

And then he kissed her.

Chapter Eight

She hadn't anticipated the touch of his lips to hers.

Maybe it was because her head was already spinning, trying to follow the thread of their conversation. Or maybe it was because she would never, in a million years, have anticipated that Prince Michael might kiss her. But whatever the reason, Hannah was caught completely off guard when the prince's mouth pressed against hers.

Maybe she should have protested. Maybe she should have pushed him away. But the fact was, with the prince's deliciously firm and undeniably skillful lips moving over hers, she was incapable of coherent thought or rational response. And instead of protesting, she yielded; instead of pushing him away, she pressed closer.

It was instinct that caused her to lift her arms and link them behind his head, and desire—pure and simple—that had her lips parting beneath the coaxing pressure of his. Then his tongue brushed against hers, and everything inside of her quivered.

Had she ever been kissed like this? Wanted like this? She didn't know; she couldn't think. Nothing in her limited experience had prepared her for the masterful seduction of his lips. And when his hands skimmed over her, boldly sweeping down her back and over her buttocks, pulling her closer, she nearly melted into a puddle at his feet.

She couldn't have said how long the kiss lasted.

Minutes? Hours? Days?

It seemed like forever—and not nearly long enough.

When he finally eased his lips from hers, she nearly whimpered with regret.

Then she opened her eyes, and clearly saw the regret in his.

It was like a knife to the heart that only moments before had been bubbling over with joy. Being kissed by Prince Michael was, for Hannah, a dream come true. But for Prince Michael, kissing her had obviously been a mistake, a momentary error in judgment.

Her hand moved to her mouth, her fingertips trembling as they pressed against her still-tingling lips. Everything inside her was trembling, aching, yearning, even as he was visibly withdrawing.

"I'm sorry." He took another step back. "I shouldn't have done that."

He was right. Of course, he was right. What had happened—even if it was just a kiss—should never have happened. He was Riley's father and her employer. But, even more importantly, he was a prince and she was *not* a princess. She was nobody.

That was a lesson she should have learned years ago, when Harrison Parker had taken back his ring because she didn't have a pedigree deemed suitable by his family. But all it had taken was one touch from the prince, and she'd forgotten everything but how much she wanted him.

How had it happened? One minute they'd been arguing

and in the next he'd claimed that he was attracted to her. Then he'd kissed her as if he really wanted to. And when he'd held her close, his arms wrapped around her, his body pressed against hers, she'd had no doubt about his desire. But then he'd pulled away, making it clear that he didn't want to want her.

Proving, once again, that she simply wasn't good enough.

"Hannah?"

She had to blink away the tears that stung her eyes before she could look at him.

"Are you okay?"

The evident concern in his voice helped her to steel her spine. "I'm fine, Your Highness. It wasn't a big deal."

He frowned, and she wondered—for just a moment—if he might dispute her statement. If maybe he, too, felt that it *had* been a big deal.

But in the end, he only said, "I was way out of line. And I promise that you won't be subjected to any more unwanted advances."

"I'm not worried about that, Your Highness," she said confidently.

And she wasn't.

What worried her was that his kiss hadn't been unwanted at all.

He dreamed of her again.

Of course, this time the dream was much more vivid and real. And when Michael finally awakened in the morning with the sheets twisted around him, he knew that it was his own fault.

He never should have kissed her.

Not just because he'd stepped over the line, but because one simple kiss had left him wanting so much more.

It wasn't a big deal.

Maybe it wasn't to Hannah, but to Michael—who hadn't

kissed anyone but Sam since their first date so many years before—it was.

He didn't feel guilty, not really. His wife had been gone for almost four years, and he knew she would never have expected him to live the rest of his life as a monk. But he did feel awkward. If he was going to make a move on anyone, he should have chosen a woman he would not have to interact with on a daily basis from now until the end of the summer, and especially not an employee.

He winced as he imagined the headlines that a sexual harassment suit would generate, then realized he was probably being paranoid. After all, to Hannah the kiss "wasn't a big deal."

He would just have to make sure that he kept his promise, that absolutely nothing like that ever happened again. And count down the days until the end of the summer.

After Hannah ensured that Riley was wherever she needed to be for her first lesson of the day, she usually returned to the kitchen to enjoy another cup of Caridad's fabulous coffee and conversation with the longtime housekeeper of Cielo del Norte.

But when she approached the kitchen Thursday morning, she could hear that the other woman already had company— and from the tone of her voice, she wasn't too pleased with her visitor.

"This isn't open for discussion," Caridad said firmly.

"But it isn't fair—"

"Whoever said life was supposed to be fair?"

"You never made Jocelyn go to summer school," the male voice argued.

"Because Jocelyn didn't struggle with English Lit."

"She would have if she'd had Mr. Gaffe as her teacher."

"You complained about the teacher you had last year, now you complain about this teacher—maybe the problem isn't the teachers but the student. And maybe you should have paid a little more attention to the lessons and a little less to Serik Jouharian last term."

Based on the dialogue and the tones of their voices, Hannah guessed that Caridad was talking to her son. She knew that the housekeeper and her husband had five children—four girls and, finally, a boy. Kevin was the only one still living at home and, according to Caridad, he was responsible for every single one of her gray hairs.

"The only reason I even passed that course was because Serik was my study partner," the boy told her now.

"Then you'd better pick your study partner as carefully this time."

Hannah peeked around the corner in time to see Caridad kiss her son's cheek, then hand him his backpack. "Now go, so you're not late."

"Serik," Hannah said, as Kevin exited the room. "That's a beautiful name."

"Serik was a beautiful girl. An exchange student from Armenia, and I thanked God when school was done and she went back to her own country." Caridad sighed. "He was so smitten. And so heartbroken when she said goodbye."

"I guess he's at that age."

"The age when hormones lead to stupid?"

Hannah laughed. "He seems like a good kid."

"He is," Caridad admitted. "And smart. He's always got good marks in school, except for English. I thought if he took the next course at summer school, when he only has to focus on one subject, he might do better, but he's done nothing but complain since the course started."

"He's a teenager and it's the summer," Hannah said. "Of course he's going to complain about being stuck in school."

"He says he'd rather be working, and if I let him get a job, he could help pay for his education. But I worry that a job would take time away from his studies, jeopardizing his chances of getting a scholarship."

"I could tutor him," she offered.

"No offense, but I can't imagine that a nanny knows too much about senior English."

"You might have noticed that I don't know too much about being a nanny," she said. "That's because I'm a teacher in my real life."

"Your real life?"

"Well, nothing about this seems real to me." She looked around at the kitchen that was bigger than her whole apartment in the city. "It's as if I've fallen through the rabbit hole."

"Should we call you Alice?"

She smiled. "No. Riley's already confused enough without giving a new name to the new hire."

"So how did an English teacher end up taking a summer job as a royal nanny?"

"Desperation."

"Prince Michael's desperation or your own?"

"Both, I guess. He needed someone who could step in right away while he continues to look for a full-time caregiver, and I needed a job and a place to stay for the summer because I sublet my apartment with the intention of spending the break teaching in China." She shook her head in response to the lift of Caridad's brows. "Don't ask."

"We can't afford a tutor," Caridad admitted. "Prince Michael offered to hire one when he heard that Kevin was struggling, but I couldn't let him do that when he already does so much for us."

"I'm already getting a paycheck, and I really do love to teach."

"I wouldn't feel right—taking something for nothing."

"We could exchange services," Hannah suggested. "Maybe you could teach me to cook?"

"Not likely," the housekeeper said.

Hannah couldn't help but feel disappointed by her response. Cooking lessons would at least give her something to do while Riley was busy with her tutors, but unlike her, Caridad probably had more than enough to keep her busy.

"You don't think you'd have the time?" she guessed.

"I don't think you could learn," the older woman admitted bluntly. "You don't know the difference between browning and burning."

Hannah couldn't deny it was true—not when the housekeeper had asked her to keep an eye on the garlic bread while she put a load of laundry in the wash. All Hannah had to do was take the tray out of the oven when the cheese started to brown. But then Riley had come into the kitchen to get a drink and she'd spilled her juice, and while Hannah was busy mopping up the floor, the cheese was turning from brown to black.

"Don't you think that's a little unfair?" she asked, because she had explained the extenuating circumstances behind the mishap.

"Maybe," Caridad agreed. "But not untrue."

Hannah had to laugh. "No, not untrue," she admitted as she poured herself a fresh cup of coffee. "But is that any reason to let your son struggle?"

The housekeeper hesitated. "It's only the first week. I want to see him at least make an effort before you bail him out."

Hannah and Riley spent the following Saturday afternoon on the beach again, but the prince made no effort to join them. And although the three of them had dinner together, as usual, the prince immediately retreated to his office after the meal was done.

It was Monday before Hannah worked up the nerve to knock on his office door.

She could hear him talking, and she pictured him pacing

in front of his desk with his BlackBerry in hand. It seemed as if it was *always* in hand. His voice rose, as if to emphasize a point, and she took a step back. Maybe she should come back later. Maybe she should forget trying to talk to him at all—or at least choose a different venue for their conversation. The last time she'd been in his office with him was when the prince had kissed her.

Okay, it probably wasn't a good idea to think about that kiss right now. Except that since Wednesday night, she'd barely been able to think about anything else.

She realized that she couldn't hear him talking anymore, and knocked again, louder this time.

"Come in."

She pushed open the door and stepped inside.

He looked up, as if surprised to see her. He probably was. They'd both been tiptoeing around each other for the past several days.

"We never did finish the conversation we started to have about Riley," she reminded him.

"I assumed if there was cause for concern I would hear about it."

"Well, actually, I do have some concerns. Primarily about her eating habits."

"I have lunch and dinner with my daughter almost every day," he said. "Other than her preference for chicken nuggets, I haven't observed any problem."

"I wouldn't say it's a problem," she hedged. "At least not yet."

His brows lifted. "You came in here to talk about something that isn't yet a problem?"

She felt her cheeks flush. "Riley seems to eat a lot for such a young child, and she has dessert after lunch and dinner—every day."

"So?"

"If she continues to eat the way she does now, it won't be

long before she's battling weight and possibly even health issues."

"She's not even four."

She didn't disagree with what he was saying, and it wasn't Riley's weight that worried her. It was the pattern that she could see. She knew there was an easy fix for the problem, but only if the prince agreed to cooperate.

"She eats too much and exercises too little," she said bluntly.

"Should I hire a personal trainer for her?"

"No, Your Highness, you should stop hiring people and start spending time with her."

His brows lifted in silent challenge.

"I know I haven't been here very long," Hannah said. "But I've noticed that you don't interact with Riley very much outside of mealtimes."

"Then maybe you've also noticed that I have a lot of work to do and Riley is busy with her own lessons."

"Yes, I have noticed that, too," she admitted. "And I think that's why Riley is overeating."

"I'm not following."

She hesitated, torn between reluctance to disturb the status quo that obviously mattered to him and determination to open his eyes to some harsh truths. In the end, she decided his relationship with Riley was more important than anything else—her job included.

"The only time Riley sees you throughout the day is at lunch and dinner, so she does everything that she can to extend those mealtimes," she explained. "As soon as her plate is cleared away, you disappear, and I think that she's asking for second helpings so that you stay at the table with her. It's not because she's hungry, but because she's starving for your attention, Your Highness."

His gaze narrowed dangerously. "How dare you—"

"I dare," she interrupted, "because you entrusted Riley

into my care and I'm looking out for her best interests, Your Highness."

"Well, I don't believe it's in my daughter's best interests to put her on a diet."

She was horrified by the very thought. "That isn't what I'm suggesting at all."

"Then what are you suggesting?"

"That you rearrange your schedule to spend a few hours every day with Riley, somewhere other than the dining room."

"You can't be serious," he said, his tone dismissive. "And even if you are, she doesn't have that much time to spare any more than I do."

"Which is the other thing I wanted to talk to you about," she forged ahead before she lost her nerve.

"Go on," he urged, albeit with a decided lack of enthusiasm.

"A four-year-old needs time to play, Your Highness."

"Riley has plenty of time to play."

She shook her head. "She plays the piano, but she doesn't do anything else that a typical four-year-old does—anything just for fun. She paints with watercolors but doesn't know what to do with sidewalk chalk. She doesn't know how to jump rope or hit a shuttlecock, and she's never even kicked a soccer ball around."

"Because she isn't interested in any of those things."

"How do you know?" Hannah asked softly.

He frowned. "Because she's never asked to participate in those kinds of activities."

"Did she ask for piano lessons?"

"No," he admitted. "Not in so many words. But when she sat down and began to play, it was patently obvious that she had a talent that needed to be nurtured."

"And how do you know she's not a potential all-star soccer player if you don't give her the opportunity to try?"

"If she wants to kick a ball around, I have no objections," he said dismissively. "Now, if that's all—"

"No, it's not all," she interrupted. "There's the issue of her French lessons—"

"If there's any issue with her French lessons, you should discuss it with Monsieur Larouche."

"And I suppose I should direct all inquires about her Italian lessons to Signora Ricci and about her German lessons to Herr Weichelt?"

"You're starting to catch on."

She bristled at the sarcasm in his tone. "I thought we were past this already. Why are you acting like you don't care when I know that you do?"

"You're right," he agreed. "I do care—enough that I've hired qualified people to ensure she has everything she needs."

"When we talked the other night—" she felt her cheeks flush and prayed that he wouldn't notice "—you said that you were willing to make some changes. All I'm asking for is a couple of hours of your time every day."

He drummed his fingers on his desk, as if considering. Or maybe he was just impatient for her to finish.

"You said you wanted to get it right," she reminded him. "The only way to do that is to spend time with your daughter. To get to know her and let her get to know you, and that's not going to happen if you insist on keeping nannies and business obligations between you."

"It's the business that allows me to pay your salary," he pointed out to her.

"I'll gladly take a cut in my pay if you promise to give Riley at least two hours."

Once again, Hannah had surprised him. "I don't usually let my employees set the conditions of their employment."

"But this isn't a usual situation, is it?" she countered. "And I know you want what's best for Riley."

How could he possibly argue with that? And truthfully, he didn't want to. Although it was against his better judgment to give in to a woman whom he was beginning to suspect would try to take a mile for every inch he gave her, he wasn't opposed to her suggestion. After all, his time at Cielo del Norte was supposed to be something of a vacation from the daily demands of his company.

It's hardly a vacation if you're working all the time.

He heard Sam's words, her gently chiding tone, clearly in his mind.

It had been a familiar argument, and one that he'd always let her win—because it hadn't been a sacrifice to spend time with the wife that he'd loved more than anything in the world. But Sam was gone now, and without her a vacation held no real appeal. And yet he'd continued to spend his summers at the beach house because he knew that she would be disappointed if he abandoned the tradition. Just as he knew she'd be disappointed if he didn't accede to Hannah's request.

During Sam's pregnancy, they'd had long conversations about their respective childhoods and what they wanted for their own child. Sam had been adamant that their daughter would grow up in a home where she felt secure and loved. She didn't want Riley to be raised by a series of nannies, as he had been raised. Michael had agreed. He had few fond memories of his own childhood—and none after the death of his father—and he couldn't deny that he wanted something more, something better, for Riley. Except that without Sam to guide him, he didn't know what that something more and better could be.

Now Hannah was here, demanding that he spend time with his daughter, demanding that he be the father that Sam would want him to be. And he couldn't—didn't want to—turn away from that challenge. But he had to ask, "How do you know that spending more time with me is what Riley wants or needs?"

"Because you're her father and the only parent she has left," she said simply.

It was a fact of which he was well aware and the origin of all his doubts. He knew he was all Riley had—and he worried that he wasn't nearly enough. And he resented the nanny's determination to make him confront those fears. "Why is this so important to you?" he countered. "I mean, at the end of the summer, you'll walk away from both of us. Why do you care about my relationship with my daughter?"

He saw a flicker of something—sadness or maybe regret—in the depths of her stormy eyes before she glanced away. "Because I want something better for her than to get an email from you twenty years in the future telling her that she has a new stepmother," she finally responded.

Dios. He scrubbed his hands over his face. He'd forgotten that Hannah wasn't just Phillip Marotta's niece but that she'd lived with the doctor since coming to Tesoro del Mar as a child. Obviously there were some unresolved father-daughter issues in her background, and while those issues weren't any of his business, he knew that his relationship with his own daughter *was* his concern. And if Hannah was right about Riley's behavior, he had reason to be concerned.

"Okay," he agreed.

"Okay?" She seemed surprised by his acquiescence.

He nodded and was rewarded with a quick grin that lit up her whole face.

"I'd like to start this afternoon," she told him.

He glanced at his schedule, because it was a habit to do so before making any kind of commitment with respect to his time, and because he needed a reason to tear his gaze away from her mesmerizing smile. She truly was a beautiful woman, and he worried that spending more time with her along with his daughter would be as much torment as pleasure.

"If that works for you," Hannah said, as if she was expecting him to say that it didn't.

"That works just fine," he assured her.

She started for the door, paused with her hand on the knob. "Just one more thing."

"What's that?"

"When you're with Riley, the BlackBerry stays out of sight."

Chapter Nine

When Caridad told her that Monsieur Larouche had called to cancel his morning lesson with Riley, Hannah took it as a positive sign. Not for Monsieur Larouche, of course, and she sincerely hoped that the family emergency wasn't anything too serious, but she was grateful for the opportunity to get Riley outside and gauge her interest in something a little more physical than her usual activities.

Whether by accident or design, Karen had left a few of Grace's toys behind after their visit the previous week, including the little girl's soccer ball. And when Riley's piano lesson was finished, Hannah lured her outside with the promise of a surprise.

The princess looked from her nanny to the pink ball and back again. "What's the surprise?"

"I'm going to teach you how to play soccer."

"Soccer?" Riley wrinkled her nose.

"It's fun," she promised. "And very simple. Basically you

run around the field kicking a ball and trying to put it in the goal."

"I know what soccer is," the child informed her. "I've seen it on TV."

"It's not just on television—it's the most popular sport in the world."

"I don't play sports."

Hannah dropped the ball and when it bounced, she kicked it up to her thigh, then juggled it over to the other thigh, then back down to one foot and over to the other, before catching it again. "Why not?"

"Because I'm a princess," she said.

But Hannah noticed that she was looking at the ball with more curiosity than aversion now. "Oh—I didn't realize that you weren't allowed—"

"I'm allowed," Riley interrupted. "But I have more important things to do."

"Okay," Hannah agreed easily, slipping her foot under the ball and tossing it into the air.

"What does that mean?" the child demanded.

"I'm simply agreeing with you," she said, continuing to juggle the ball between her feet. "Playing soccer isn't important—it's just fun."

"And it's time for my French lesson anyway," the princess informed her, the slightest hint of wistfulness in her voice.

"You're not having a French lesson today."

"But it's Monday. I always have French after piano on Monday."

"Monsieur Larouche can't make it today."

Riley worried her bottom lip, uncomfortable with last-minute changes to her schedule.

"But if you'd rather study than learn to play soccer, you can go back inside and pull out your French books," Hannah assured her.

"Can you teach me how to do that?" Riley asked, mesmerized by the quick movements of the ball.

"I can try." She looked at the girl's pretty white dress and patent shoes. "But first we'd better change your clothes."

As Hannah scanned the contents of the child's closet, then rifled through the drawers of her dressers, she realized that dressing Riley appropriately for outdoor play was easier said than done.

"Who does your shopping?" she muttered.

"My aunt Marissa."

"It's as if she was expecting you to have tea with the queen every day." She looked at the shoes neatly shelved in three rows on the bottom of the closet. There were at least fifteen pairs in every shade from white to black but not a single pair without tassels or bows or flowers.

"Tesoro del Mar doesn't have a queen," the princess informed her primly. "It's a principality."

Hannah continued to survey the child's wardrobe. "Do you even own a T-shirt or shorts? Or sneakers?"

Riley shrugged.

"Well, I think before we get started, we need to find a mall."

"There's a bookstore at the mall," the little girl said, brightening.

"Shorts and shoes first," Hannah insisted. "Then we'll see."

"Maybe we could find a book about soccer," Riley suggested.

Hannah had to laugh. "You're pretty clever, aren't you?"

"That's what my teachers say."

"We'll go shopping after lunch," Hannah promised.

Though Michael didn't believe that Riley was starved for his attention as Hannah had claimed, he did make a point of paying close attention to her behavior at lunch. And he was dismayed to realize that the nanny was right. As soon as he had finished eating and she thought he might leave the table, she asked if she could have some more pasta salad. And after she finished her second helping of pasta salad, she asked for dessert.

"What did you want to do after lunch?" he asked her, while she was finishing up her pudding.

"I have quiet time until four o'clock and then…" The words faded away, and Riley frowned when she saw him shaking his head.

"I didn't ask what was on your schedule but what you wanted to do."

The furrow in her brow deepened, confirming that Hannah hadn't been so far off base after all. His daughter truly didn't know what to do if it wasn't penciled into her schedule.

"Because I was thinking maybe we could spend some time together."

Riley's eyes grew wide. "Really?"

He forced a smile, while guilt sliced like a knife through his heart. Had he really been so preoccupied and neglectful that his daughter was surprised by such a casual invitation?

"Really," he promised her.

"Well, Hannah said we could go shopping after lunch."

He looked at the nanny, his narrowed gaze clearly telegraphing his thoughts: *I agreed to your plan but I most definitely did* not *agree to shopping*.

"Your daughter has an impressive wardrobe that is completely devoid of shorts and T-shirts and running shoes," she explained.

"So make a list of what she needs and I'll send—"

One look at his daughter's dejected expression had him changing his mind.

With an inward sigh, he said, "Make a list so that we don't forget anything."

* * *

After two hours at the mall, with Rafe and two other guards forming a protective circle around the trio of shoppers, Michael noted that Hannah was almost as weary of shopping as he. But they had one more stop before they could head back to Cielo del Norte—the bookstore. He bought her a latte at the little café inside the store and they sat, surrounded by shopping bags, and discreetly flanked by guards, in the children's section while Riley—shadowed by Rafe—browsed through the shelves.

"We got a lot more than what was on the list."

"You said she didn't have anything," he reminded her.

"But she didn't need three pairs of running shoes."

Except that Riley had insisted that she did, showing how the different colors coordinated with the various outfits she'd chosen.

"She gets her fashion sense from my sister," he told her. "One day when we were visiting, Marissa spilled a drop of coffee on her shirt, so she went to find a clean one. But she didn't just change the shirt, she changed her shoes and her jewelry, too."

Hannah laughed. "I probably would have put on a sweater to cover up the stain."

"Sam was more like that," he admitted. "She didn't worry too much about anything. Except official royal appearances—then she would stress about every little detail like you wouldn't believe."

He frowned as he lifted his cup to his lips. He didn't often talk about Sam, not to other people. It was as if his memories were too precious too share—as if by revealing even one, he'd be giving up a little piece of her. And he wondered what it meant—if anything—that he found it so easy to talk to Hannah about Sam now. Was it just that he knew he could trust her to listen and not pass judgment, or was it a sign that he was finally starting to let go of the past and look to the future?

"Well, I should have realized that Riley's closet wouldn't be filled with all those frills and ruffles if it wasn't what she liked," Hannah commented now.

"You weren't into frills and ruffles as a child?"

"Never. And when I was Riley's age…" She paused, as if trying to remember. "My parents were missionaries, so we traveled a lot, and to a lot of places I probably don't even remember. But I think we were in Tanzania then, or maybe it was Ghana. In either case, I was more likely running naked with the native children than wearing anything with bows."

He tried to imagine her as a child, running as wild as she'd described. But his mind had stuck on the word *naked* and insisted on trying to picture her naked now. After having seen the delectable curves outlined by her bathing suit, it didn't take much prompting for his imagination to peel down the skinny straps of sleek fabric to reveal the full-ness of creamy breasts tipped with rosy nipples that eagerly beaded in response to the brush of his fingertips. And when he dipped his head—

"Look, Daddy, I found a book about soccer."

Nothing like the presence of a man's almost-four-year-old daughter to effectively obliterate a sexual fantasy, Michael thought.

Then Riley climbed into his lap to show him the pictures, and he found that he didn't regret her interruption at all.

"That's an interesting book," he agreed.

"Can we buy it?"

He resisted the instinct to tell her yes, because he knew from experience that it wouldn't be the only book she wanted and he was trying to follow Hannah's advice to not give her everything she wanted.

"Let me think about it," he told her.

She considered that for a moment, and he braced himself

for the quivering lip and the shimmer of tears—or the hands on the hips and the angry scowl—but she just nodded. "Can you hold on to it while I keep looking?"

"I'll keep it right beside me," he promised.

Hannah watched the little girl skip back to the stacks. "She's so thrilled that you're here," she told him.

"I guess I didn't realize that it took so little to make her happy," he admitted.

"We've already been here longer than the two hours I asked for."

"I'm not counting the minutes," he assured her. "Besides, I'm enjoying this, too."

"Really?"

He chuckled at the obvious skepticism in her tone. "Let's just say, the shopping part wasn't as bad as I'd feared. And this part—" he lifted his cup "—is a definite pleasure."

"You better be careful," she warned. "Or you just might live up to that potential I was talking about."

He took another sip of his coffee before asking the question that had been hovering at the back of his mind. "Was your father so neglectful?"

"How did my father come into this?" she countered.

But the casual tone of her reply was too deliberate, and he knew that beneath the lightly spoken words was buried a world of hurt.

"I think he's always been there, I just didn't realize it before."

"It's true that my father and I aren't close," she admitted.

"Because he never had enough time for you," he guessed.

"He never had *any* time for me." She cupped her hands around her mug and stared into it, as if fascinated by the ring of foam inside. "I'm not even sure that he ever wanted to be a father," she finally continued, "but my mom wanted a baby and there was no doubt that he loved my mom, and I thought it was enough to know that my mom loved me."

"Until she died," he guessed.

"But then I had my uncle Phillip. He pretty much raised me after she was gone."

"I have to say, he did a pretty good job."

She smiled at that. "He was a wonderful example of what a father should be—of the kind of father I know *you* can be."

He hoped—for Riley's sake even more than his own—that he wouldn't disappoint her.

Despite the new outfit and the proper shoes, it didn't take Hannah long to realize that Riley was never going to be an all-star soccer player. It wasn't just that the child seemed to lack any kind of foot-eye coordination, but that she quickly grew discouraged by her own ineptitude. The more patient and understanding Hannah tried to be, the more discouraged Riley seemed to get.

So after a few days on the lawn with little progress and a lot of frustration, she took Riley into town again so that the little girl could decide what she wanted to try next. The sporting goods store had an extensive selection of everything, and Hannah and Riley—and Rafe—wandered up and down several aisles before they found the racquet sports section.

"I want to play tennis," Riley announced.

Since there was a court on the property, Hannah hoped it might be a better choice for the princess, who immediately gravitated toward a racquet with a pink handle and flowers painted on the frame.

Now she had a half-full bucket of tennis balls beside her with the other half scattered around the court. She'd been tossing them to Riley so that she could hit them with her racquet, with very little success. The child had connected once, and she'd been so startled when the ball made contact with the webbing that the racquet had slipped right out of her hand. But she'd scooped it up again and refocused, her big brown eyes narrowed with determination. Unfortunately, it seemed that the harder she tried, the wider she missed.

The prince would happily have paid for a professional instructor, but Hannah wanted to keep the lessons fun for Riley by teaching the little girl herself. But after only half an hour, neither of them was having very much fun. The more balls that Riley missed the more frustrated she got, and the more frustrated she got the less she was able to focus on the balls coming toward her.

"She needs to shorten her grip."

Hannah looked up to see a handsome teenager standing at the fence, watching them with an easy smile on his face.

"She needs a better teacher," she admitted.

"Kevin!" Riley beamed at him. "I'm going to learn to play tennis just like you."

The boy's brows lifted. "Just like me, huh?"

She nodded. "Hannah's teaching me."

"Trying to, anyway." She offered her hand. "Hannah Castillo."

"Kevin Fuentes," he said.

"Caridad and Estavan's son," she suddenly realized. "I've seen you helping out your dad around the yard." And she'd heard him in the kitchen, arguing with his mother, though she didn't share that information. "So you play tennis?" she queried.

"Every chance I get."

"Caridad says that Kevin's going to get a scholarship," Riley informed her. "But only if he pays attention in class and forgets the pretty girls."

Hannah couldn't help but laugh as the boy's cheeks flushed.

"You have an awfully big mouth for such a little kid," Kevin said, but the reprimand was tempered with a wry smile as he ruffled Riley's hair.

The little kid in question beamed up at him in obvious adoration.

"Do you want me to show her how to adjust her grip?" Kevin asked.

"I'd be extremely grateful," Hannah assured him.

The teenager dropped to his knees on the court beside her.

"I'm going to play just like you," the little girl said again.

"It took me a lot of years of practice." Even as he spoke, he adjusted the position of Riley's grip on the handle of her racquet.

"I'm a fast learner," she assured him.

"You need to learn to be patient," he told her, guiding her arm in a slow-motion demonstration of a ground stroke. "And to let the ball come to you."

He nodded toward Hannah, signaling her to toss a ball.

As soon as the ball left her hand, Riley was trying to reach for it, but Kevin held her back, waiting then guiding her arm to meet the ball.

The fuzzy yellow ball hit the center of the webbing with a soft *thwop,* and Hannah had to duck to avoid being hit by its return. Riley turned to Kevin, her eyes almost as wide as her smile. "I did it."

"You did," he agreed. "Now let's see if you can do it again."

After a few more easy tosses and careful returns, Riley said, "I want to hit it harder."

"You should work on accuracy before power," Kevin told her.

Riley pouted but continued to practice the slow, steady stroke he'd shown her.

"You're a lot better at this than I am," Hannah said, tossing another ball.

He gave a half shrug. "This comes easily to me. Trying

to figure out what Hamlet's actually saying in his infamous 'to be or not to be' speech doesn't."

"It's really not that complicated, although the language of the time can make it seem so," she said, not wanting to delve into the details of the tragic hero's contemplations about suicide in front of a four-year-old.

"And my teacher talks like he was born in Shakespeare's time."

"It can't be that bad," Hannah protested, tossing the last ball.

"It's worse," he insisted. "I have an essay due tomorrow in which I have to decide—in a thousand words—whether or not Hamlet really did love Ophelia."

She couldn't help but smile, thinking that—like most teenage boys—he'd much rather talk about the character's thirst for revenge than any of his more tender emotions. But all she said was, "*Hamlet* has always been one of my favorite plays."

He turned to look at her now, his expression a combination of surprise and disbelief. "Really?"

She shrugged, almost apologetically. "I like Shakespeare."

"Can we do some more?" Riley interrupted to demand.

"First lessons should be short," Kevin told her. "And the lesson's not over until you put all of the balls back in the bucket."

If Hannah had been the one to ask Riley to retrieve the scattered balls, she had no doubt the princess would have refused. But when Kevin spoke, the little girl happily trotted off to do his bidding.

"You're really good with her," Hannah noted.

"She's a good kid."

"Would you be willing to work with her on some other tennis basics some time?"

"Sure," he agreed readily. "It's not like I'm doing much of anything else these days, aside from summer school."

"Speaking of which," she said. "Why don't you bring your essay up to the main house tonight?"

His eyes lit up. "Are you going to fix it for me?"

She laughed. "You're assuming it needs fixing."

"It does," he assured her.

"Then we'll fix it together."

Friday morning after breakfast, Hannah and Riley were working on a jigsaw puzzle in the library when Caridad came in to water the plants. She looked from the little girl to the clock then back again and frowned.

"Signora Ricci is late today," she noted.

"Signora Ricci isn't coming today," Hannah told her.

The housekeeper held a towel beneath the spout of the watering can to ensure it didn't drip as she moved from one planter to the next. "Is she ill?"

"No, she's on vacation."

"She would not have gone on vacation without first arranging a replacement and certainly not without discussing the matter with the prince." The implication being that the prince would then have told her, which of course he would have—if he'd known.

"The vacation was my idea," Hannah admitted. "And more for the benefit of the princess than her teacher."

"You have talked to Prince Michael about this?" the housekeeper prompted.

"I tried, but the prince assured me that any concerns about his daughter's language instruction were best discussed with her instructor."

"I had my doubts," the housekeeper admitted, "when the prince first hired you. But now I think that maybe he knew what he was doing."

"Even if he would disagree?"

Caridad smiled. "Especially if he would disagree."

She finished watering the rest of the plants before she

spoke again. "Kevin said you're helping him with his Shakespeare essay."

"In exchange for him helping Riley learn to play tennis," Hannah explained, remembering their earlier conversation in which the housekeeper had expressed reluctance to accept help for her son without some kind of payment in return.

The housekeeper waved the towel in her hand, obviously satisfied by the exchange of services. "I have no objections," she said. "If you are half as good a teacher as you are a nanny, he will write a good paper."

Only a few weeks earlier, Hannah hadn't been certain that she even wanted to be a nanny, but in all of her years of teaching, she'd never received a compliment that meant as much to her as Caridad's.

Chapter Ten

There were still occasions when Michael had to return to Port Augustine for meetings with clients, but he rarely stayed away overnight. Unfortunately, today's meeting had stretched out longer than he'd anticipated because the client refused to be satisfied with any of the advertisement proposals presented to her.

Michael believed strongly in customer satisfaction, so he suggested that they continue their discussions over dinner. He'd learned that a less formal atmosphere often facilitated a more open exchange of information, but as they shared tapas and wine, he quickly realized that the client had chosen RAM less for the needs of her company and more for her personal interest in him.

He knew that he should be flattered, but truthfully he was growing tired of deflecting unwanted advances. Especially when he'd given her no indication that he was interested in anything more than a business relationship. But as he drove back to Cielo del Norte, he found himself wondering what

was wrong with him that he wasn't attracted to an obviously
attractive woman. A few weeks ago, he could have argued
that he just wasn't ready, that he couldn't imagine himself
with anyone who wasn't Sam.

Since Hannah had moved into Cielo del Norte, he'd realized that was no longer true. So why couldn't he be attracted to someone other than Hannah? What was it about
his daughter's temporary nanny that had got under his skin?

As a result of his unproductive dinner meeting, he returned to the beach house much later than he'd intended. Not
only had he missed hanging out with his daughter during the
day, but he was too late to tuck her into bed, as had become
their nightly ritual. When he went upstairs to check on her,
he found that she was sleeping peacefully with Sara tucked
under her arm. He brushed a light kiss on her forehead and
her lips curved, just a little, in response to the touch.

He went back downstairs, thinking that he would pour
a glass of his favorite cabernet and sit out under the stars
for a while. When he approached the kitchen, he heard the
sounds of conversation. The soft, smoky tone was definitely
Hannah's; the deeper, masculine voice wasn't as familiar.

It occurred to him then that she'd given up her whole
life to spend the summer at Cielo del Norte, and in the first
month that she'd been in residence, she hadn't asked for any
time off to go out. He knew that her friend Karen had visited a few times with her children, because Riley would tell
him all about her "best friend" Grace and describe in great
detail everything that they'd done together. But it was Hannah's visitor who was on his mind now.

Was the man in the kitchen an old friend? Maybe even
a boyfriend? He frowned at the thought. His frown deepened when it occurred to him that there had been no other
vehicles in the drive when he'd pulled in.

He paused in the doorway, shamelessly eavesdropping.

"Pay close attention to the characters of both Marlow and

Kurtz," Hannah was saying now. "And which one seems, to you, to be the real hero of the book."

It didn't sound like date conversation to him. On the other hand, he hadn't been on a date in more than sixteen years, so what did he know?

"But can't there be—"

Her guest looked up as he walked into the room, and the boy—Caridad's son, Michael realized with a sense of relief—pushed his chair away from the table to execute an awkward bow. "Your Highness."

He waved Kevin back to his seat. "I didn't realize you were...entertaining," he said to Hannah.

"I didn't realize you were home," she countered.

He noted the books that were open on the table, surrounded by scraps of paper with notes scribbled on them.

"We're working on the outline for Kevin's next assignment," she explained.

Michael surveyed the assortment of bottles in the wine rack, automatically reached for a familiar label. Maybe she did believe she was helping the boy study, but it was obvious to him that Hannah's student was more interested in her than in anything she was trying to explain to him.

"I thought school was out for the summer," he commented.

"For most people," Kevin said. "But my mom decided to torture me with summer school—as if spending ten months in the classroom wasn't already torture enough."

Hannah smiled as she gathered together the loose papers and inserted them into a folder. "Look on the bright side— if you get your credit this summer, you won't have to take another English course until college."

"That's still too soon for me," the boy grumbled.

"I want to see your draft outline by Wednesday," Hannah told him.

"I'll have it ready," he promised. Then he bowed again. "Good evening, Your Highness."

"Good evening, Kevin." He uncorked the bottle of wine. "So how long have you been tutoring my housekeeper's son?"

"It isn't a formal arrangement," she said. "And it doesn't interfere in any way with my taking care of Riley."

"I'm not worried—just curious as to how this arrangement came about, and whether Caridad knows that her son has a major crush on you."

"It came about because Kevin's been helping Riley with her ground stroke, and Caridad knows that his infatuation will be over before he signs his name to his final exam."

"How can she be so sure?"

"Teenage boys are notoriously fickle."

"That's probably true enough," he acknowledged, even as he mentally berated himself for being no less fascinated by the sexy curves outlined by her T-shirt than the teenage boy who had just left.

And no doubt he would have shown more interest in English Lit when he was in school if he'd had a teacher like Hannah Castillo. But all of the teachers at the exclusive prep school he'd attended had been male and seemingly as old as the institution itself.

She finished packing away her notes, then pushed away from the table. "I'm going to go check on Riley."

"I just did." He took two glasses out of the cupboard. "She's sleeping."

"Oh. Okay."

"Come on," he said, heading toward the sliding French doors that led out to the terrace. He bypassed the chairs to sit at the top of the steps, where he could see the moon reflecting on the water.

Hannah had paused just outside the doors, as if reluctant to come any closer. "It's late."

"It's not that late," he chided, pouring the wine. "And it's a beautiful night."

She ventured closer and accepted the glass he offered before lowering herself onto the step beside him. "How was your meeting?"

"I don't want to talk about the meeting." He tipped his glass to his lips, sipped. He didn't even want to think about the time he'd wasted, time he would much have preferred to spend with his daughter—and her nanny. "How did things go with Riley today?"

"I think we're making some real progress."

"I know she's enjoying the tennis lessons," he admitted.

Hannah smiled. "That's more because of Kevin than the game, I think."

He frowned. "Are you telling me that my daughter has a crush on the boy who has a crush on her nanny?"

"It's a distinct possibility," she told him. "At least the part about Riley's feelings for Kevin."

"I should have my brother talk to the Minister of the Environment about testing the water out here," he muttered.

She smiled again. "She's a little girl and he's a good-looking boy who pays her a lot of attention."

"You think he's good-looking?"

"That was hardly the most relevant part of my statement," she said dryly.

"Maybe not," he acknowledged. "But he's also seventeen years old."

"Relax, I don't think she's planning the wedding just yet," she teased.

"I was making the point of his age to you," Michael admitted.

"I know—oh!" She grabbed his arm and pointed. "Look."

Her eyes were wide with wonder as she stared up at the sky, but it was the press of her breast against his arm that snagged his attention.

"I've never seen a shooting star before," she told him.

She was still holding on to his arm, though he wasn't sure if she was conscious of that fact. And while he couldn't deny the quick jolt of lust that went through him, he realized that there was something deeper beneath the surface. A sense of happiness and contentment that came from just sitting here with Hannah. A sense of happiness and contentment that he hadn't felt in a very long time.

"It was right here on this terrace with my dad that I saw my first-ever shooting star," he told her.

She seemed surprised by the revelation, and he realized that she probably was. Over the past couple of weeks, they'd spent a lot of time together and engaged in numerous conversations, but either Riley was with them or was the center of those discussions. He certainly wasn't in the habit of sharing personal details of his own life.

"Did you spend a lot of time here as a kid?" she asked him now.

"Yeah. Although not as much after my dad passed away."

"It was probably hard for your mom, to return to a place with so many memories."

While he appreciated the sympathy in her tone, he knew that her compassion—in this instance—was misplaced. "It wasn't the memories she had trouble with, it was the lack of exclusive boutiques and five-star restaurants."

Hannah seemed puzzled by that.

"Do you know much about my family?" he asked.

"I know that your mother is the princess royal."

"And my father was a farmer."

"I didn't know that," she admitted.

"She claimed that she loved who he was, and then she spent the next fifteen years trying to change him into someone else. Someone better suited to her station."

She didn't prompt him for more information or pry for details, and maybe that was why he found it easy to talk to her. Why he found himself telling her things that he'd never told anyone else before.

"After my dad died, she changed her focus to my brother and I. She had such big plans and ambitions for us."

"I would think she'd be very proud of both of you."

His smile was wry. "She refers to RAM as my 'little company' and despairs that I will ever do anything worthwhile. And even Cameron's position in the prince regent's cabinet isn't good enough, because she wanted him sitting on the throne."

"What were her plans for Marissa?" she asked curiously.

"Lucky for her, my baby sister pretty much flies under Elena's radar."

"How does she manage that?"

"She's female."

Hannah's brows lifted.

"I'm not saying it's right—just that it is what it is. Even though the Tesorian laws were recently changed to ensure equal titles and property would be inherited regardless of gender, she's always believed that it's the men who hold the power.

"I remember how thrilled she was to find out that Sam was expecting—and how disappointed she was when she learned that we were having a daughter. She didn't even pretend otherwise."

"But Riley is such a wonderful little girl," she protested.

"And my mother barely knows her," he admitted. "She's the only grandparent my daughter has, and she doesn't even make an effort to spend time with her."

Not only did Elena not spend time with Riley, the princess royal had suggested sending his little girl away to boarding school, the mere idea of which still made Michael's blood boil.

"She's lucky, then, to have a father who's making such an effort to be part of her life," Hannah told him.

"I missed her today," he admitted, pushing all thoughts of his mother aside. "And I hated not being here to tuck her in."

"She was disappointed, but thrilled when you called from the restaurant to say good-night."

"She said you had a picnic on the beach at lunch."

"I thought it might take her mind off of the fact that you weren't here."

"She sounded as if she really enjoyed it," he said.

Hannah smiled. "She got a bit of a surprise when she threw the crusts of her sandwich away and the gulls swooped in to take them."

"Was she scared?"

"She did shriek at first, but then she was okay. She's already decided that she's keeping the crusts of her toast from breakfast tomorrow so that she can feed them again."

"Then we'll have to make sure we have toast for breakfast," he agreed.

And that was how they ended up on the dock the next morning. Except Hannah noticed that while she and Riley were tossing bread to the birds, the prince had wandered farther back on the dock. After the little girl had tossed the last few pieces to the hungry gulls, Hannah took Riley's hand and guided her back to where her father was standing, with his back to the water and his BlackBerry to his ear.

She put her hands on her hips. "What do you think you're doing?"

Michael stopped in midsentence. "I'm just—"

Before he could finish speaking, she'd grabbed the phone from his hand.

"We had a deal," she reminded him.

And he'd stuck to the deal, which had been a pleasant surprise to Hannah. At least until now. In fact, he'd been so diligent about following the rules that she was prepared to cut him some slack—after she'd made him feel just a little bit guilty.

"I know, but—"

"No phones, Daddy." It was Riley who interrupted his explanation this time, and before he could say anything further, she took the phone from Hannah and flung it over her shoulder.

Hannah gasped as Michael's head whipped around, his gaze following the instrument as it sailed through the air, seeming to tumble end over end in slow motion before it splashed into the ocean.

She knew that Riley had acted on impulse, without any thought about what she was doing or the potential consequences, and that the prince was going to be furious. The only possible way to do damage control was to get Riley to apologize immediately and sincerely. But when Hannah opened her mouth to speak to the little girl, the only sound that came out was a muffled laugh.

"I was in the middle of a conversation with the vice president of a major telecommunications company," the prince informed her.

"You'll have to tell him that your call—" she tried to muffle her chuckle with a cough "—got dropped."

He glowered at her.

"I'm sorry. I know it's not funny…" But she couldn't finish, because she was laughing.

"If you know it's not funny, why are you laughing?" he demanded.

Riley looked from one to the other, measuring her father's stern visage against her nanny's amusement, as if trying to figure out how much trouble she was in.

"I don't know," Hannah admitted. "But I can't seem to stop."

"She threw my BlackBerry into the ocean."

She was turning red from holding her breath, trying to hold in the chuckles.

His eyes narrowed. "You really *do* think it's funny, don't you?"

She shook her head, wanting to deny it. But her efforts were futile.

"Well, then," Michael said. "Let's see if you think this is funny."

She fell silent when he scooped her into his arms, suddenly unable to remember why she'd been laughing. The sensation of being held close in his arms blocked everything else out. Everything but the heat and hardness of his body—the strong arms holding on to her, one at her back and one under her knees; the firm muscles of his chest beneath her cheek. She was tempted to rub her cheek against him and purr like a kitten, inhaling the enticingly spicy scent of the furiously sexy man. Oh, if only he would hold her like this forever—

The thought had barely formed in her mind when she realized that he was no longer holding on to her at all. Instead, she was flying through the air.

The shock of that had barely registered before she hit the water.

She came up dripping and sputtering, obviously as surprised as he had been when Riley had tossed his phone in the water, then she resolutely began to swim back to the dock. Any sense of satisfaction Michael had felt when he sent her on the same journey was gone. In fact, looking at her now as she pulled herself up onto the ladder, he was feeling distinctly unsatisfied. And very aroused.

He stared. He knew it was impolite, but he couldn't help himself. She usually dressed conservatively, keeping her feminine attributes well hidden. But now, with her pale pink T-shirt and white shorts soaked through and plastered to her body, there was no disguising the delicious curves she had tried to hide—or the sexy lace bra that covered her pert, round breasts but couldn't conceal the tight buds of her nipples.

He swallowed, hard.

She was at the top of the ladder now, and he offered his hand to help her up the last step.

She eyed him warily for a moment before she accepted.

Her hand was cool, but the touch heated his blood, and he realized that he was in serious trouble with this woman. Because even now, when he should be angry and amazed, he couldn't deny the attraction between them. An attraction that continued to grow stronger with each passing day.

"All in all, I'd say you fared better than my phone," he noted, trying to maintain some equilibrium.

She shoved a handful of sopping hair over her shoulder and, with obvious skepticism, asked, "How do you figure?"

"Your circuits aren't fried." As his were—or at least in serious danger of doing so.

"Are you going to throw me in the water, too, Daddy?" Riley looked at him with an expression that was half hopeful and half fearful.

"I might," he said, scooping her off of her feet and into his arms.

Riley shrieked and wrapped her arms tight around his neck. "No, Daddy, no."

"But you did a bad thing, throwing my phone into the water," he reminded her. "So there should be some kind of punishment."

She nodded her head, still clinging to him.

"What do you think that punishment should be?"

His daughter wrinkled her nose, as if seriously contemplating an answer to his question, then offered her suggestion. "Maybe no broccoli for me for a month?"

It was all he could do not to laugh himself—because he

knew how much she hated broccoli. "Nice try, Princess, but I think the punishment needs to be a little more immediate than that and more directly linked to the crime."

"An apology?" she suggested. "Because I am very sorry, Daddy."

"That's a good start, but not very convincing."

"Very, very sorry," she said, framing his face in her hands and kissing first one cheek and then the other.

"Much more convincing," he said.

She smiled at him, and it was the kind of smile he hadn't seen on her face in a very long time—a smile full of such pure joy that it actually made his heart ache.

He glanced over her head at Hannah, hoping to telegraph his appreciation to her because he knew that she was responsible for so many changes he'd seen in his daughter in the past few weeks. She was watching them and smiling, too, and he saw that there were tears in her eyes.

Since her first day at Cielo del Norte, Hannah had witnessed more and more examples of the strengthening bond between father and daughter. They'd come a long way in a short while, she realized. From virtual strangers who shared polite conversation across the dinner table to a father and daughter who genuinely enjoyed spending time together.

Watching them together filled her heart with happiness—and more than a little envy. Because as much as she wanted to believe that she'd played a part in bringing them together, her role had been peripheral. She was the outsider, as she'd been the outsider through most of her life.

Even when her uncle Phillip had brought her back to Tesoro del Mar, she'd been conscious of the fact that she didn't really belong. All she'd ever wanted was a home and a family of her own, a place where she was truly wanted and needed. But she'd be a fool to think she could find it here—even for a short while.

But there were moments—rare and precious moments that she knew she would hold in her heart forever—when she truly felt as if she was part of their world. Like when Riley reached for her hand as they walked on the beach. Or when the little girl spontaneously reached up to hug Hannah as she tucked her into bed at night.

She'd known from the beginning that her time with Riley and the prince wouldn't ever be anything more than temporary, but that knowledge hadn't stopped her from falling for the princess. There was simply no way she could have resisted a child who needed so much and somehow gave back so much more.

No, it didn't surprise her at all that the little girl had completely taken hold of her heart. The bigger surprise—and much bigger worry—was that she was very close to falling in love with the princess's father, too.

Chapter Eleven

It was the sound of Riley's screams that had Michael bolting out of his office a few days later. The screams were coming from the tennis courts, and he raced in that direction. Caridad, also summoned by the sound of the little girl's calls, was right behind him.

"Help! Daddy! Help!"

He would have been the first to admit that his daughter had a tendency to melodrama and that she did everything at full volume. But he'd learned to tell from the tone of her cries whether she was sad or frustrated or hurt, and he'd learned to distinguish between playful and fearful shouts. But he'd never heard her scream like this, and the sound chilled him to the bone.

"Someone! Please! Quick!"

As soon as she saw him, her screams turned to sobs. "Daddy, Daddy, you have to help."

He dropped to his knees beside her. "What happened? Where are you hurt?" He ran his hands over her as he spoke,

BRENDA HARLEN 145

his heart in his throat as he tried to determine the nature of her injury. The way she'd been screaming, he'd sincerely feared that she'd lost a limb or at least broken a bone. But aside from the red face streaked with tears, she appeared to be unharmed, and relief flooded through him like a wave.

"It's n-not m-me," she sobbed. "It's H-han-nah."

By this time, the housekeeper had caught up to them, and he saw that she had gone directly to where Hannah was kneeling on the court. Though the nanny had a hand to her head, she didn't seem to be in any dire straits.

With Riley clinging to his side, he ventured closer.

"I'm fine," he heard her saying, trying to shake Caridad off as she helped her to her feet.

But the older woman was resolute, and as she steered Hannah toward one of the benches along the sidelines of the court, he finally noticed the blood.

He halted abruptly, his stomach clenching.

"I d-didn't m-mean to d-do it," Riley managed between sobs. "It w-was an accid-dent."

He squeezed her gently, trying to reassure her but unable to tear his own gaze away from the crimson blood dripping down the side of Hannah's face.

"You are not fine," Caridad said to Hannah. "And you need to sit down while I get a towel and the antiseptic cream."

He'd yet to meet anyone who could ignore a direct order from the housekeeper when she spoke in that tone, and Hannah was no exception. She sat where Caridad directed.

"Come on, Riley," the housekeeper said. "You can help me find what we need."

Michael knew that Caridad didn't really need Riley's assistance but was trying to distract her from the situation. And Riley was eager to help, obediently falling into step behind the housekeeper. Michael moved over to the bench to check on Hannah.

"I guess that will teach me to walk up behind a little girl with a tennis racquet," she said ruefully.

"Is that what happened?" He kept his tone light, not wanting her to know how badly his insides were shaking. He guessed that she'd been cut right above the eye, because that's where she seemed to be applying pressure, but he couldn't tell for sure.

Hannah managed a smile. "Your daughter has a good set of lungs on her."

"That she does," he agreed.

"I'm sorry about the panic. I was trying to calm her down, but she saw the blood and then just started screaming."

Riley raced over with a neatly folded towel. "This one's for your head," she said, handing one to Hannah. "You're supposed to put pressure on the cut to stop the bleeding. Caridad's bringing the rest of the stuff."

The rest of the stuff turned out to be a washcloth and a basin of warm water, which she used to clean the blood off of the area around the cut, and a first-aid kit, from which she took an antiseptic wipe to dab gently against the wound. Then she instructed Hannah to keep the pressure on and went back inside to finish getting dinner ready.

"There's a lot of blood, Daddy." Riley spoke in an awed whisper.

"Head wounds always bleed a lot," Hannah said, trying to reassure her. "I'll put a Band-Aid on in a few minutes and—"

The prince laid his hand over hers, forcing her to lift the towel so that he could take another look at the gash. The blood immediately began to flow again. "I'm pretty sure it needs more than a Band-Aid."

"I'm sure it doesn't," she insisted.

"You're not a doctor," he reminded her.

"No, but I grew up with one, and he—"

"And he would want you to have this checked out," the prince said firmly.

As it turned out, her uncle Phillip had been at a day conference in San Pedro, so he arrived at Cielo del Norte within an hour of the housekeeper's call. By that time, the bleeding had mostly stopped and Hannah was lying down on a sofa in the library, reading.

Riley was sitting with her, keeping her company while she waited for the doctor to arrive. Despite her repeated assurances that she was okay, the child insisted on staying by her side.

"You only had to call and I would have come to visit," her uncle chided from the doorway. "You didn't need to create all this drama to get me out here."

"I'm having second thoughts about it now," she told him, easing herself back up to sitting position.

"Hi, Doctor Phil," Riley said.

He smiled at the nickname and offered the little girl a lollipop that he took out of his bag. "For after dinner."

She nodded and tucked it into the pocket of her shorts.

Phillip sat down beside his niece. "So how did this happen?"

"I hit Hannah with my racquet," Riley confessed.

"Forehand or backhand?" the doctor asked.

Riley had to think for a minute before answering that one. "Backhand."

"You must have a pretty powerful swing."

"I've been practicing lots," she admitted, sounding torn between pride and regret.

"Okay, let's see what kind of damage you did," he said, moving to examine the wound.

Hannah winced when he tipped her head back.

"Headache?" he asked, all teasing forgotten.

She nodded slowly.

"I'll give you something for that after I stitch this up."

He offered to let Riley stay to watch while he fixed up the wound. The little girl had seemed enthused about the prospect, but as soon as the needle pierced through the skin the first time, she disappeared quickly enough.

"Are you enjoying your job here?" Phillip asked Hannah when Riley had gone.

"Other than today, you mean?"

"Other than today," he agreed with a smile.

"I am," she said. "There was a period of adjustment— for all of us—but I think we've come a long way in a few weeks."

"The young princess seems very taken with you."

"I think she's feeling guilty."

"That could be part of it," he admitted.

Hannah sat patiently while he tied off the sutures, thinking about the little girl.

"I still miss my mom sometimes," she finally admitted.

If her uncle thought it was a strange statement, or one that came from out of nowhere, he gave no indication of it. Instead, he said, "I do, too."

"But I have a lot of memories of the time we spent together. Good memories."

"And Riley has none of her mother," he noted, following her train of thought.

"Do you think that makes it harder for her—because she doesn't have any memories to hold on to?"

"I'm sure there are times when she's conscious of a void in her life, but she seems pretty well-adjusted to me."

"How long do you think someone usually grieves?"

He taped a square of gauze over the sutures. "I'm not sure there's an answer to that question. Each relationship is different, therefore each grieving process is different."

She thought about her father's latest email again—and her

own surprise and anger when she read his note. "I thought my dad would love my mom forever."

"I'm sure he will," her uncle said gently. "But that doesn't mean he couldn't—or shouldn't—fall in love again."

She nodded, but her thoughts were no longer on her parents' relationship or her father's remarriage. "Do you think Prince Michael could fall in love again?"

"I'm sure he could," he said with a slight furrow in his brow. "But I wouldn't want to speculate on when that might happen, and I don't want you to forget that this is only a summer job."

"Don't worry—I have no desire to give up teaching to be a full-time nanny," she assured him.

"That's not what I meant."

"What did you mean?"

"I know you had a crush on the prince when you were younger, and I'm worried that being here may have rekindled those feelings."

"I did have a crush," she admitted. "But it was a childhood infatuation. I didn't know him then, and I didn't even like him when I first came here—he was so distant and reserved."

"And now you've fallen in love with him," he guessed.

She shook her head. "No. I have feelings for him—" deeper feelings than she was ready to admit even to herself "—but I'm smart enough to know that falling in love with a prince could never lead to anything but heartache."

"You're not nearly as smart as you think if you honestly believe that you can control what is in your heart," he warned her.

As Phillip finished packing up his bag, Caridad came in to invite him to stay for dinner. He declined the offer politely, insisting that he wanted to get on his way.

Hannah was sorry to see him go—she had missed him over the past several weeks, but she was also relieved by his departure. Apparently he had shrewder observation skills than she would have guessed, and she was very much afraid he was right. And if she was falling in love with the prince, she didn't want her uncle to be a witness to her folly.

Because she knew that it would be foolish to give her heart to a man who could never love her back because he was still in love with his wife. And she feared that her uncle was right—that loving the prince might not be a matter of choice, and that she already did.

After dinner, Hannah joined the prince and his daughter in the media room to watch a movie. Riley insisted on sitting between them with the bowl of popcorn in her lap, and while the action on the screen kept her riveted for nearly ninety minutes, she did sneak periodic glances at the bandage on Hannah's head to ensure that it wasn't bleeding again.

"Bedtime," the prince told his daughter when the credits began to roll.

"I can't go to bed," she protested. "I have to stay up in case Hannah has a concuss."

"It's *concussion*," Hannah said. "And I don't."

"But what if you do?"

"Doctor Phil checked me over very thoroughly."

"But the medical book says you should be 'specially vigi—" She wrinkled her nose, trying to remember the word.

"Vigilant?" her father suggested.

She nodded. "You should be 'specially vigilant when someone gets hit in the head."

So that was what she'd been doing while Phillip stitched up Hannah's wound—reading up on head injuries.

"I appreciate your concern," she told the little girl. "But I'm really okay—I promise."

"You're not going to die?" The little girl's eyes were wide, her tone worried.

"Not today."

"Does it hurt very much?" The child didn't sound worried so much as curious now.

"Not very much," she said, and it was true now that the acetaminophen her uncle had given her was finally starting to take the edge off of the pain.

"Do you want me to kiss it better?"

Hannah was as surprised as she was touched by the offer. "I think that would make it much better."

Riley leaned forward and very carefully touched her lips to the square of white gauze that had been taped over the wound.

"Okay?"

She nodded.

"You have to kiss it, too, Daddy."

Hannah's panicked gaze met with the prince's amused one.

"It's really much better now," she said to Riley.

"But if one kiss helps, then two should help twice as much," the little girl said logically.

"You can't argue with that," Michael told her.

"I guess not," she agreed.

"Kiss her, Daddy."

So he did. He leaned down and touched his lips gently to her forehead, just above the bandage. It was nothing more than a fleeting touch, barely more than a brush against her skin, but it made everything inside of her melt. Oh yeah, she was definitely falling.

He pulled back, looking into her eyes again. All traces of amusement were gone from his expression now, replaced by an intense awareness that rocked her to her very soul.

"Is that twice as much better?" Riley wanted to know.

Hannah forced a smile. "Twice as much."

"Now that Hannah's boo-boo has been kissed all better, it's bedtime for you," Michael reminded his daughter.

"Will you take me up, Daddy?"

"You bet," he said, and swept her off of her feet and into his arms.

Hannah let out an unsteady breath as they disappeared through the doorway. She felt the tiniest twinge of guilt knowing that she'd lied to the little girl. Because the truth was that the prince's kiss hadn't made anything better, it had only made her desire for him that much harder to ignore.

When Riley was all snug under her covers, Michael kissed her good-night and went back downstairs to find Hannah. He wasn't happy when he found her in the kitchen.

"You're supposed to be resting," he admonished.

"I'm not on my hands and knees scrubbing the floor— I'm just putting a couple of glasses in the dishwasher."

"Nevertheless—" He took her arm and steered her out of the room. "I don't want your uncle mad at me because you weren't following his orders."

"I can't imagine he would hold you responsible."

"And Riley is very concerned about you, too," he reminded her.

She smiled at that. "If I'd known a little cut above my eye would change her attitude toward me, I'd have let her take a swing at me weeks ago."

"I'm not sure that's a strategy I would actually recommend to her next nanny."

He was only responding to her teasing, but his words were a reminder to both of them that the summer was almost halfway over. And when it was done, Hannah would go back to her own life, and he and his daughter would go on with theirs.

Not so very long ago he'd been thinking about the two months he'd planned to spend at Cielo del Norte as an interminable amount of time. Now that the first month had nearly passed, it didn't seem long enough.

Hannah returned to the media room and resumed her

place at one end of the oversize leather sofa. He'd been sitting at the other end earlier, with Riley as a buffer between them, but he sat in the middle now.

She looked at him warily. "Don't you have phone calls to make or projects to complete?"

"It's almost ten o'clock."

"That hasn't seemed to matter on any other night."

She was right. He was in the habit of disappearing back into his office again as soon as he'd said good-night to his daughter. But what Hannah didn't know was that he often just sat behind his desk, doing nothing much of anything except ensuring that he kept a safe and careful distance between himself and the far-too-tempting nanny. And if he was smart, he would have done the same thing tonight, except that he'd made his daughter a promise.

"Riley asked me to keep an eye on you."

"I'm fine," she insisted.

"She made me pinky-swear," he told her.

Her lips curved. "It's sweet of her to worry, but I'm not concussed and I don't need anyone watching over me."

"I know it," he acknowledged. "But Riley seems really concerned."

"A lot of kids are preoccupied by death and dying," she said. "I would guess it's even more usual for a child who's lost someone close."

Somehow he knew that she wasn't just talking about Riley anymore. "How old were you when your mom died?" he asked.

"Eight."

"What happened?"

"There was a malaria epidemic in the village where we were living at the time. I got sick first, and my mom didn't trust that the Swazi doctors knew what they were doing, so she called Phillip. By the time he arrived, I was on my way to recovery, but—" Her gaze shifted away, but not before he caught a glimpse of the moisture in her eyes. "But while she'd been taking care of me, she'd ignored her own symptoms. By the time the doctors realized that she'd been infected, too, the disease had progressed too far."

She tucked her feet up beneath her on the sofa. "I thought my dad blamed me," she confided. "And that's why he sent me away after she died."

"He sent you away?"

"No one admitted that's what happened. Uncle Phillip said that I would be better off in Tesoro del Mar, that traveling from village to village was no kind of life for a child, and my father agreed. But no one had seemed too concerned about that while my mom was alive, and no one seemed to think about the fact that they were sending me away to live with a man I barely even knew."

"I'm sorry, Hannah."

And he was. He couldn't imagine how traumatic it had been for a child who'd just lost her mother to be taken away from her only other parent.

"I'm not. At the time, I was devastated," she admitted. "But now I realize it was the best thing that could have happened. My uncle gave me not just a home, but a sense of stability and security I'd never had before. He was—and is—a constant presence in my life, the one person I know I can depend on above all others."

"Where's your father now?"

"Botswana, I think. At least, that's where his last email came from."

"The one that told you he was getting married again," he guessed.

"How did you know about that?"

"You once told me that you wanted me to work on my relationship with Riley so that she didn't get an email from me telling her that she had a new stepmother."

She winced. "I was upset. The message wasn't that he

was getting married but that he'd already gotten married. He didn't even think to tell me beforehand. And probably the only reason he thought to share the news at all is that they're coming to Tesoro del Mar in the fall and he hopes I'll get a chance to meet her."

"I can see how that would have pulled the proverbial rug out from under you," he admitted.

"But it shouldn't have," she said now. "Because the truth is, I don't know him well enough to be surprised by anything he does. In the past eighteen years, since Uncle Phillip brought me here, I've only seen my father half a dozen times.

"His work has always been more important to him than anything else. And I guess, when you trust that you've been called to a higher mission, it needs to be a priority," she acknowledged. "And I know he believes in what he's doing. He goes to the darkest corners of the world, he sees families living in poverty and he sees children struggling to learn, but he never saw me."

She sighed. "It hurt. For a long time. But I finally realized that he was doing what he needed to do, because the people he helps out need him more than I ever did."

He didn't think it was as simple as that, and he was furious with her father for turning a blind eye to the needs of his child and angry with himself because he'd been doing the same thing to Riley. And he was so very grateful to Hannah for making him see it and helping him to be a better father to his daughter.

"So will you go to meet her—your father's new wife?"

"Probably." Her lips curved just a little.

He lifted a brow, silently inquiring.

"My friend Karen suggested I show up with a husband in tow," she explained.

"Getting married just to make a point seems a little extreme, don't you think?"

---

156   *PRINCE DADDY & THE NANNY*

"More than a little, but I don't think she was suggesting an actual legal union."

"Have you ever been married?" he asked curiously.

"No."

"Engaged?"

"Haven't we covered enough of my family history for one night?"

He figured that was a *yes,* but decided to respect her wish not to talk about it. At least for now. "So what are we going to talk about for the rest of the night?"

"If you're really determined to hang out here babysitting me, that's your choice, Your Highness. But I'm going to watch some television."

"It's my choice," he agreed. "And it's my TV." And he snapped up the remote before she could.

She narrowed her gaze. "Don't make me wrestle you for it."

"Would you really?" He was certainly willing to let her tackle him. In fact, the more he thought about it, the more intrigued he was by the possibility.

"I would, but I'm supposed to be resting."

Another fantasy ruined, he handed her the remote.

Chapter Twelve

The rain was pouring down when Michael pulled into the drive at Cielo del Norte after a quick trip into town to meet with an old friend. It had been gray and drizzling for the better part of three days, but now the skies had completely opened up.

As he ran through the deluge to the front door, a flash of lightning split the sky, almost immediately followed by a crash of thunder. He winced, knowing how much Riley hated storms. If she was awakened by one in the night, he'd sometimes find her trying to crawl under the covers of his bed, her eyes squeezed tight and her hands pressed against her ears.

Inside, he shook the rain off of his coat and hung it in the closet. From the kitchen, he could smell the mouthwatering scents of roasted pork and sweet potatoes, but it was the music he heard in the distance that drew him down the hall.

Not surprisingly, it was coming from the music room. But

it certainly wasn't Riley practicing piano. In fact, it wasn't anything he had ever heard before. And when he pushed open the door, he saw something that he was certain he'd never seen before.

Riley was dancing—spinning and twirling, with her arms flying and her legs kicking. Hannah was right into the music with her, hips wriggling and body shimmying. And both of them were singing at the tops of their lungs about…he wasn't sure if he was unable to decipher the lyrics or if they just didn't make any sense, but both his daughter and her nanny seemed to know all the words.

He winced at the volume of the music, but he knew there was no way that Riley could hear the thunder over whatever it was that they were listening to—and no way they could have heard him enter the room. So he just leaned back against the wall and enjoyed the show for a few minutes.

One song led into the next, and they continued to sing and laugh and dance, and he continued to watch, marveling at the sheer happiness that radiated from his little girl. He couldn't remember ever seeing her like this—just being silly and having fun, and he realized that Hannah had been right about this, too. His daughter, despite all of her talents and gifts, needed a chance to simply be a child.

Impossible as it seemed, Riley's smile grew even wider when she finally spotted him.

"Look, Daddy! We're dancing!"

While Riley continued to move, Hannah's steps faltered when she realized that she and the child were no longer alone, and he would have bet that the flush in her cheeks was equal parts embarrassment and exertion.

"Don't let me interrupt," he said. "Please."

But she went to the boom box and lowered the volume, at least a little.

He picked up the CD case, looked at the cover, then lifted his brows.

"Grace let Riley borrow it," she told him, then grinned. "In exchange, Riley gave her a copy of Stravinsky's *Rite of Spring*."

He was suprised to learn that his little girl, who had a profound appreciation for the classics, could find such pleasure in jumping up and down and wiggling her hips to something called *Yo Gabba Gabba,* but he wasn't at all disappointed by the recent changes in her behavior.

"So what precipitated this dance-a-thon?"

"The precipitation," Hannah said, and smiled. "The rain made us give up on the idea of going outside, but Riley had a lot of energy to burn off."

"She's changed so much in only a few weeks," he noted.

"You say that in a way that I'm not sure if you approve or disapprove of the changes," she said uncertainly.

"I approve," he assured her. "I guess I'm still just getting used to it. I would never have said that she was unhappy before—but I've also never seen her as obviously happy as she is now. And to hear her laugh—the sound is so pure and full of joy."

"She's a wonderful little girl," Hannah assured him.

He had to smile, remembering that it hadn't been so long ago that she'd warned him that his daughter was turning into a spoiled brat. But then she'd taken Riley out of the familiar, structured world that she knew and changed all of the rules.

And while there had been a few growing pains in the beginning—and he was sure there would be more to come—he couldn't deny that he was impressed by the results.

"With a real passion for dance," the nanny continued.

Watching his daughter move, he couldn't deny that it was true. She might not have a natural talent, but she certainly had enthusiasm.

"My sister has a friend who—"

"No," Hannah interrupted quickly, then softened her refusal with a smile.

He frowned. "How do you even know what I was going to say?"

"Because I know how your mind works. And Riley doesn't need any more lessons. At least, not yet. Just let her have some fun for a while. And then, if she does want more formal training, enroll her in a class where she can learn along with other kids."

When the current song came to an end, Hannah snapped the music off.

"It's not done," Riley protested. "There's still three more songs."

"How many times has she listened to this CD?" Michael wondered.

"I've lost count," Hannah admitted. Then to Riley she said, "It's almost time for dinner, so you need to go wash up."

The little girl collapsed into a heap on the floor. "I'm too tired."

Michael had to smile. "If you're not too tired to keep dancing, you can't be too tired to twist the taps on a faucet," he said, picking her up off of the floor to set her on her feet. "Go on."

With a weary sigh, the princess headed off.

Hannah took the CD out of the machine and returned it to its case.

"Did you have any formal dance training?" he asked curiously.

She nodded, a smile tugging at the corners of her mouth. "Ballet, because my uncle Phillip was a lot like you in that he wanted to give me every possible opportunity. But after two years, my teacher told him that she couldn't in good conscience continue to take his money when it was obvious that I had less than zero talent."

"She did not say that," Michael protested.

"She did," Hannah insisted. "And truthfully, I was relieved."

"You looked pretty good to me when you were spinning around with Riley."

"We were just having fun."

"Will you dance with me?" he asked her.

She looked up, surprise and wariness in her eyes. "Wh-what?"

He moved to the CD player, pressed the button for the satellite radio—and jumped back when heavy metal screamed out at him. Hannah laughed while he adjusted the volume and scrolled through the preset channels until he found a familiar song.

"This one was at the top of the charts in my first year of college," he told her, and offered his hand.

"I don't recognize it," she admitted.

"Then I won't have to worry about you trying to lead," he teased.

Though she still looked hesitant, she finally put her hand in his.

"You really don't know this song?" he asked, after they'd been dancing for about half a minute.

She shook her head.

"Okay, now I have to ask—how old are you, Hannah?"

"Twenty-six."

Which meant that she was a dozen years younger than he, and while he'd been in college, she'd still been in grade school. But that was a long time ago, and there was no doubt that she was now all grown up. And soft and feminine and undeniably sexy.

He drew in a breath and the scent of her invaded his senses and clouded his mind.

"Hannah—"

She tipped her head back to meet his gaze, and whatever

words he'd intended to say flew out of his mind when he looked into those blue-gray eyes and saw the desire he felt reflected back at him.

He'd been fighting his feelings for her from the beginning, and to what effect? He still wanted her, now more than ever. And if she wanted him, too—and the look in her eyes made him believe that she did—then what was the harm in letting the attraction between them follow through to its natural conclusion?

They were, after all, both adults...but the little girl peeking around the corner was definitely not.

"Caridad said to tell you that it's dinnertime," Riley announced.

Hannah wanted to scream with frustration.

For just a minute, she'd been sure that the prince was going to kiss her again. And his gaze, when it flickered back to her now, was filled with sincere regret.

Regret that they'd been interrupted?

Or regret that he'd almost repeated the "mistake" of a few weeks earlier?

"Thank you for the dance, Hannah," he said formally.

"It was my pleasure, Your Highness."

He lifted her hand to kiss it.

She wanted a real kiss—not some lame fairy-tale facsimile. But then his lips brushed the back of her hand, and she felt the tingles all the way down to her toes.

It wasn't the passionate lip-lock with full frontal contact that she craved, but it wasn't exactly lame, either. And that made her wonder: if a casual touch could wield such an impact, what would happen if the man ever really touched her?

She was almost afraid to find out—and more afraid that she never would.

* * *

The next day, the sun shone clear and bright in the sky. After being cooped up for the better part of three days, Riley was thrilled to get outside and run around. In the morning, Hannah took her for a long walk on the beach. Michael watched from his office as they fed the gulls and wrote messages in the sand, and he wished he was with them.

He tore his attention from the window and back to his work. He was putting the final touches on a project for the upcoming National Diabetes Awareness Campaign, and if he finished it up this morning, then he could spend the whole afternoon with Riley and Hannah.

He wasn't sure when he'd started thinking of Hannah as Hannah and not "Miss Castillo" or his daughter's nanny—or when he'd started looking forward to spending time with her, too. In the beginning, when every step in his relationship with Riley seemed both awkward and tentative, he'd been grateful for her guidance. But somewhere along the line, he'd begun to enjoy her company and thought they might actually be friends. Except that he was still fighting against his body's desire to get her naked.

He pushed that idea from his mind and forced himself to get back to work.

He did finish the project by lunch, and afterward Riley invited him down to the beach to build castles in the sand. It was an offer he couldn't refuse, and he wasn't just surprised but disappointed when Hannah begged off. She claimed to want to catch up on some emails, but he knew that she was really trying to give him some one-on-one time with his daughter.

He appreciated her efforts. After all, she was only going to be with them until the end of the summer, at which time he and Riley were going to have to muddle through on their own—or muddle through the adjustment period with another new nanny. The thought made him uneasy, but he refused to delve too deeply into the reasons why. It was easier to believe that he was concerned about his daughter than to acknowledge that he might actually miss Hannah when she was gone.

After castle-building, they went swimming to wash the sand off, then Riley talked him into whacking some balls around the court with her. Hannah had told him that Riley was learning a lot from Kevin, and he was pleased to see that it was true. By the time they were finished on the court, he noticed that Hannah had come outside and was sitting on one of the lounge chairs on the terrace.

Riley spotted her at almost the same moment, and she went racing ahead. By the time Michael had reached the bottom step, his daughter was already at the top. Then she climbed right up into her nanny's lap and rested her head against her shoulder.

"It looks like you wore her out on the tennis court," Hannah said to him.

"She's had a busy day," he noted, dropping down onto the edge of the other chair.

Riley nodded her head, her eyes already starting to drift shut. "I'm ready for quiet time now."

Hannah smiled at his daughter's code word for "nap." "Quiet time's okay," she agreed. "But you can't fall asleep because it's going to be time for dinner soon."

The little girl yawned. "I'm not hungry."

"Caridad was making lasagna," Michael reminded her. "And that's one of your favorites."

"Is Hannah going to burn the garlic bread again?"

The nanny sighed. "I'm never going to live that down, am I?"

His daughter giggled.

"Well, in answer to your question, I can promise you that I am *not* going to burn the garlic bread because Caridad won't let me in the kitchen while she's cooking anymore."

"I'm glad," Riley said. "Because if you were helping her cook, you couldn't be here with me."

Hannah's lips curved as the little girl snuggled against her, but the smile faltered as she caught Michael's gaze.

"Is something wrong?" she asked quietly.

"What?" He realized he was scowling, shook his head. "No."

But he could tell that she was unconvinced, and he couldn't blame her. Because the truth was, *everything* about this situation was wrong.

She shouldn't be there. She shouldn't be on *that* chair on *this* deck cuddling with his daughter. That was *Sam's* chair—he'd painted it that particularly garish shade of lime green because Sam had thought it was a fun color. And this was *their* special place—where they used to come to escape the craziness of the world together. And Riley was *their* little girl—the child that his wife had given her life to bring into the world.

He felt a pang in his chest. Caridad was right—Riley needed more than a nanny, she needed her mother. But that was something he couldn't give her. Sam was gone. Forever.

He thought he'd accepted that fact. After almost four years, he should have accepted it. During that entire time, while he'd gone through the motions of living, he'd been confident that Riley was in good hands with Brigitte, and he'd been comfortable with his daughter's relationship with her nanny.

So why did it seem so different when that nanny was someone else? Why did seeing his daughter with Hannah seem so wrong? Or was the problem maybe that it seemed so right?

How was it possible that after only one month, Hannah had become such an integral part of his daughter's life—and his, too? It was hard to believe that it had been four weeks already, that it was already the beginning of August, almost...

The third of August.

The pain was like a dagger through his heart. The stab of accompanying guilt equally swift and strong. He reached for the railing, his fingers gripping so tight that his knuckles were white.

Dios—he'd almost forgotten.

How had he let that happen? How had the events of the past few weeks so thoroughly occupied his mind and his heart that the date had very nearly escaped him?

He drew in a deep breath, exhaled it slowly.

"I just remembered that there are some files I need from the office," he announced abruptly. "I'll have to go back to Port Augustine."

"Tonight?" Hannah asked incredulously.

"Can we go, too, Daddy?" Riley asked.

Not *I* but *we*, he realized, and felt another pang. Already she was so attached to Hannah, maybe too attached. Because at the end of the summer, Riley would have to say goodbye to someone else she cared about.

"Not this time," he told her, stroking a finger over the soft curve of her cheek. "It would be too far past your bedtime before we got into town."

"When are you coming back?" Riley asked.

"Tomorrow," he promised.

Riley nodded, her head still pillowed on Hannah's shoulder. "Okay."

"Are you sure everything's all right?" Hannah asked.

Concern was evident in her blue-gray gaze, and as Michael looked into her eyes, he suddenly couldn't even remember what color Sam's had been.

"I'm sure," he lied.

He'd loved his wife—he *still* loved his wife—but the memories were starting to fade. She'd been the center of his world for so many years, and it had taken him a long time to put his life back together after she was gone. Losing her had absolutely devastated him, and that was something he wouldn't ever let himself forget. And that was why he wouldn't ever risk loving someone else.

Chapter Thirteen

Michael didn't remember many of the details of Sam's funeral. He didn't even remember picking out the plot where she was buried, and he wasn't entirely sure that he had. It was probably Marissa, who had stepped in to take care of all of the details—and his baby girl—who made the decision.

Thinking back to that time now, he knew that Sam would have been disappointed in him. She would have expected him to be there for their daughter, and he hadn't been. Not for a long time.

But he was trying to be there for her now, trying to be the father his little girl needed, and he thought he'd been making some progress. There was no awkwardness with Riley anymore. Not that everything was always smooth sailing, but they were learning to navigate the stormy seas together.

Hannah was a big part of that, of course. There was no denying the role she'd played in bringing him and Riley together. And sitting here now, on the little wrought-iron bench by his wife's grave as he'd done so many times before, he knew that Sam would be okay with that.

He caught a flicker of movement in the corner of his eye and, glancing up, saw his sister climbing the hill. She laid the bouquet of flowers she carried in front of Sam's stone.

"Are you doing okay?" she asked gently.

"You know, I really think I am."

She nodded at that, then took a seat beside him.

They sat in silence for a few more minutes, before he asked, "Why did you come?"

"Did you want to be alone?"

"No, I just wondered why you were here. Why you always seem to be there when I need you—and even when I don't realize that I do."

"Because you're my big brother and I love you."

He slipped his arm across her shoulders. "I'm the luckiest brother in the world."

She tipped her head back and smiled.

"It would have been our sixteenth anniversary today," he said.

"I know."

"I thought we would have sixty years together." He swallowed around the lump in his throat. "She was more than my wife, she was my best friend—and the best part of my life. And then she was gone."

"But now you have Riley," his sister reminded him.

He nodded. "The best part of both of us."

Marissa smiled again. "I heard she's learning to play tennis."

"Dr. Marotta told you, I'll bet."

She nodded. "How's Hannah?"

"The stitches should come out in a couple of days, and she's learned to keep a distance from Riley's backhand." He waited a beat, then said, "She canceled almost all of Riley's lessons for the summer."

"Good for her."

He hadn't expected such unequivocal support of the decision. "You were the one who encouraged me to find a piano instructor for Riley," he reminded her.

"Because she has an obvious talent that should be nurtured. But you went from music lessons twice a week to five days a week, then added language instruction and art classes. And I know the deportment classes were Mother's idea, but you could have said no. Instead, the poor child barely had time to catch her breath."

Which was almost exactly what Hannah had said. And while Riley never complained about her schedule, he should have seen that it was too much. He should have seen a lot of things he'd been oblivious to until recently.

"So other than tennis, what is Riley doing with her spare time?" his sister wanted to know.

"She's...having fun."

"You sound surprised."

"I'd almost forgotten what it sounded like to hear her laugh," he admitted. "It's...magic."

Marissa smiled again. "Maybe I was wrong."

"About what?"

"To worry about you. Maybe you are beginning to heal."

He knew that he was. And yet, he had to admit, "I still miss her."

"Of course," she agreed. "But you've got to move on. You're too young to be alone for the rest of your life."

"I can't imagine being with anyone other than Sam," Michael told her, but even as he spoke the words, he knew that they weren't entirely true. The truth was, he'd never loved anyone but Sam, and it seemed disloyal to even think that he ever could.

But that didn't stop him from wanting Hannah.

* * *

Hannah had sensed that something was wrong when the prince suddenly insisted that he needed to go to Port Augustine the night before. It seemed apparent to her that what he really needed was to get away from Cielo del Norte, though she couldn't figure out why.

Over the past few weeks, as Michael and Riley had spent more time together and grown closer, she'd thought that she and the prince were growing closer, too. But his abrupt withdrawal suggested otherwise.

She wasn't surprised that he was gone overnight. It didn't make sense to make the drive back when he had a house in town. She was surprised when he stayed away through all of the next day. But Caridad seemed unconcerned about his whereabouts. In fact, the housekeeper didn't comment on his absence at all, leading Hannah to suspect that she might know where the prince was.

It was only Riley, because she'd been spending more and more time with him every day, who asked for her daddy. Hannah tried to reassure the child without admitting that she had no idea where the prince had gone—or when he would be back.

It was late—hours after Riley had finally settled down to sleep—before she heard the door open. She told herself that she wasn't waiting up for him, but she'd taken the draft of Kevin's latest essay into the library to read because she knew if she was there that she would hear the prince come in.

"I didn't know if you'd still be up," he said.

"I had some things to do."

He opened a glass cabinet and pulled out a crystal decanter of brandy. She wasn't in the habit of drinking anything stronger than wine, and never more than a single glass. But when the prince poured a generous splash of the dark amber liquid into each of two snifters and offered one to her, it seemed rude to refuse.

"You haven't asked where I've been all day," he noted, swirling the brandy in his glass.

"I figured if you wanted me to know, you'd tell me."

He sat down on the opposite end of the sofa, but with his back to the arm, so that he was facing her. But he continued to stare into his glass as he said, "It was Sam's and my anniversary today."

"You went to the cemetery," she guessed.

"Just like I do every year." He swallowed a mouthful of brandy before he continued. "Except that this is the first time I almost forgot."

Hannah eyed him warily, uncertain how to respond—or even if she should. She sipped her drink cautiously while she waited for him to continue.

"We celebrated twelve anniversaries together. This is only the fourth year that she's been gone, and the date almost slipped by me."

"You're feeling guilty," she guessed.

"Maybe," he acknowledged. He tipped the glass to his lips again. "And maybe I'm feeling relieved, too. Because in the first year that she was gone, I couldn't seem to not think, every single day, about how empty my life was without her, so the important dates—like her birthday and our anniversary—were unbearable."

He looked into his glass, and frowned when he found that it was nearly empty. "And then there was Mother's Day. She wanted nothing so much as she wanted to have a baby, and she never got to celebrate a single Mother's Day."

Beneath the bitter tone, she knew that he was still hurting deeply, still grieving for the wife he'd loved.

"I wasn't happy when Sam told me she was pregnant," he admitted.

Coming from a man who obviously doted on his little

girl, the revelation startled her more than anything else he'd said.

"I knew it was a risk for her," he explained, and rose to pour another splash of brandy into his glass. "Though she'd successfully managed her diabetes for years, the doctors warned that pregnancy and childbirth would take a toll on her body.

"After a lot of discussion and numerous medical consults, we decided not to take the risk. It was enough, I thought, that we had each other."

Obviously, Hannah realized, at some point that decision had changed.

"She didn't tell me that she'd stopped taking her birth control pills," Michael confided. "We'd always been partners—not just in the business but in our marriage. Neither one of us made any major decisions without consulting the other, so I wasn't just surprised when she told me that we were going to have a baby, I was furious."

Hannah didn't say anything, because she knew the prince wasn't trying to make conversation so much as he was trying to vent the emotions that were tearing him up inside. So she just sat and listened and quietly sipped her drink.

"I was furious with Sam," he continued, "for unilaterally making the decision that would cost her life, even if neither of us knew that at the time. And I was furious with my mother, for convincing Sam that I needed an heir—because I found out later that was the motivation behind Sam's deception."

And that, she thought, explained so much of the tension in his relationship with his mother.

"But in the end, I realized that I was most furious with myself—because I should have taken steps to ensure that Sam couldn't get pregnant. If I had done that, then I wouldn't have lost my wife."

He sank into the chair beside hers, as if all of the energy

and emotion had drained out of him so that he was no longer able to stand.

She touched his hand. "You might not have lost your wife," she agreed softly. "But then you wouldn't have your little girl."

He sighed. "You're right. And now, when I think about it, I know that even if I could go back in time, I wouldn't want to. I couldn't ever give up Riley, even if it meant I could have Sam back."

"They say there's nothing as strong as a parent's love for a child," she said softly, her throat tight.

"The first time I held her in my arms, I knew there wasn't anything I wouldn't do for her," he admitted. "For a few glorious hours, I let myself imagine the future we would have together—Sam and Riley and myself. And then Sam was gone."

The grief in his voice was still raw—even after almost four years. And listening to him talk about the wife he'd obviously loved with his whole heart, Hannah experienced a pang of envy. Would she ever know how it felt to love like that—and to be loved like that in return?

She'd thought she was in love with Harrison, but when their relationship ended, she was more angry than hurt. She most definitely had *not* been heartbroken.

"I'm sorry," he said. "I didn't come in here with the intention of dumping on you."

"Please don't apologize, Your Highness. And don't worry—I can handle a little dumping."

"Strong shoulders and a soft heart?"

She managed a smile. "Something like that."

"Can you handle one more confession?"

She would sit here with him forever if it was what he wanted, but she had no intention of admitting that to him, so she only said, "Sure."

"I met Sam when I was fifteen years old and while I

didn't realize it at the time, I started to fall for her that very same day. I was lucky enough that she fell in love with me, too, because from that first moment, there was never anyone else. Even after she died...I never wanted anyone else." His dark eyes lifted to hers, held. "Until now."

She swallowed.

"I know it's wrong," he continued. "Not that it's a betrayal of my vows, because I've finally accepted that Sam is gone, but wrong because you're Riley's nanny and—"

She lifted a hand to touch her fingers to his lips, cutting off his explanation. She didn't want to hear him say why it was wrong—she refused to believe that it was. If he wanted her even half as much as she wanted him, that was all that mattered.

Somewhere in the back of her mind it occurred to her that the prince was still grieving and that if she made the next move, she might be taking advantage of him in a vulnerable moment.

Then his fingers encircled her wrist, and his thumb stroked slowly over the pulse point there as if to gauge her response. As if he couldn't hear how hard and fast her heart was pounding. Then he lowered her hand and laid it against his chest, so that she could feel that his heart was pounding just as hard and fast, and the last of her reservations dissipated.

She knew there was no future for them, but if she could have even one night, she would gladly take it and cherish the memories forever.

"I want you, Hannah," he said again. "But the first time I kissed you, I promised that I wouldn't do it again."

"You promised that you wouldn't make any unwanted advances," she corrected softly.

"Isn't that the same thing?"

"Not if I want you to kiss me," she said.

"Do you?" he asked, his mouth hovering above hers so

that she only needed to tilt her chin a fraction to make the kiss happen.

"Yes." She whispered her response against his mouth.

It was the barest brush of her lips against his, yet she felt the jolt all the way down to her toes. She caught only a hint of his flavor, but she knew that it was rich and dark and more potent than the brandy she'd sipped.

"I want you to kiss me," she repeated, in case there was any doubt.

He responded by skimming his tongue over the bow of her upper lip, making her sigh with pleasure. With need.

"I want you," she said.

His tongue delved beneath her parted lips, tasting, teasing. She met him halfway, in a slow dance of seduction.

It was only their second kiss, and yet she felt as if she'd kissed him a thousand times before. She felt as if she belonged in his arms. With him. Forever.

No—she wasn't going to let herself pretend that this was some kind of fairy tale. She knew better than to think that the prince wanted to sweep her off of her feet and take her away to live out some elusive happily-ever-after.

But he did sweep her off of her feet—to carry her up the stairs to her bedroom. And the sheer romanticism of the gesture made her heart sigh.

"Say my name, Hannah."

It seemed an odd request, until she realized that she'd never spoken his name aloud. Maybe because she hoped that using his title would help her keep him at a distance. But she didn't want any distance between them now.

"Michael," she whispered, savoring the sound of his name on her lips.

He smiled as he laid her gently on the bed, then made quick work of the buttons that ran down the front of her blouse. She shivered when he parted the material, exposing her heated flesh to the cool air. And again when he pushed the silk off of her shoulders and dipped his head to skim his lips over the ridge of her collarbone.

"Are you cold?"

She shook her head.

How could she be cold when there was so much heat pulsing through her veins? When her desire for him was a burning need deep in the pit of her belly?

His mouth moved lower. He released the clasp at the front of her bra and pushed the lacy cups aside, exposing her breasts to the ministrations of his lips and teeth and tongue.

She wasn't a virgin, but no one had ever touched her the way he was touching her. The stroke of his hands was somehow both lazy and purposeful, as if he wanted nothing more than to show her how much he wanted her. And with every brush of his lips and every touch of his fingertips, she felt both desire and desired.

Her hands raced over him, eagerly, desperately. She tore at his clothes, tossed them aside. She wanted to explore his hard muscles, to savor the warmth of his skin, to know the intimacy of his body joined with hers.

Obviously he wanted the same thing, because he pulled away from her only long enough to strip away the last of his clothes and take a small square packet from his pocket.

"I didn't plan for this to happen tonight," he told her. "But lately…well, I began to hope it would happen eventually and I wanted to be prepared."

"I'm glad one of us was," she assured him.

His fingers weren't quite steady as he attempted to open the package, and he dropped it twice. The second time, he swore so fervently she couldn't hold back a giggle. But he finally managed to sheath himself and rejoined her on the bed, nudging her thighs apart so that he could lower himself between them.

"Will you do me a favor?" he asked.

"What's that?"

"When you remember this night, will you edit out that part?"

She smiled. "Absolutely."

But it was a lie. She had no intention of editing out any of the parts. She wanted to remember every little detail of every minute that she had with Michael. Because she didn't have any illusions. She knew this couldn't last. Maybe not even beyond this one night. But she wasn't going to think about that now. She wasn't going to ask for more than he could give. She was just going to enjoy the moment and know that it was enough.

His tongue swirled around her nipple, then he drew the aching peak into his mouth and suckled, and she gasped with shock and pleasure. He shifted his attention to her other breast, making her gasp again.

Oh yes, this was enough.

Then his mouth found hers again in a kiss that tasted of hunger and passion. His tongue slid deep into her mouth, then slowly withdrew. Advance and retreat. It was a sensual tease designed to drive her wild, and it was succeeding.

She whimpered as she instinctively shifted her hips, aching for the hard length of him between her thighs. Deep inside her.

She rocked against him, wordlessly pleading.

He entered her in one hard thrust, and her release was just as hard and fast. Wave after wave of pleasure crashed over her with an unexpected intensity that left her baffled and breathless.

While her body was riding out the last aftershocks of pleasure, he began to move inside of her. Slow, steady strokes that started the anticipation building all over again.

Had she honestly thought that this might not be enough?

It was so much more than she'd expected, more than she'd even dared hope for, more than enough. And still, he somehow managed to give her more, to demand more, until it wasn't just enough—it was too much.

His thrusts were harder and faster now, and so deep she felt as if he was reaching into the very center of her soul. Harder and faster and deeper, until everything seemed to shatter in an explosion of heat and light and unfathomable pleasure.

Michael didn't know if he could move. He did know that he didn't want to. His heart was still pounding like a jack-hammer and every muscle in his body ached, and yet he couldn't remember ever feeling so good. So perfectly content to be right where he was.

But his own contentment aside, he knew that Hannah probably couldn't breathe with his weight sprawled on top of her. So he summoned enough energy to roll off of her. But he kept one arm draped across her waist, holding her close to his side. After another minute, he managed to prop himself up on an elbow so that he could look at her.

Her hair was spread out over the pillow, her eyes were closed, her lips were slightly curved. She looked as if she'd been well and truly ravished, and he felt a surge of pure satisfaction that he'd had the pleasure of ravishing her. And he wanted to do so again.

He stroked a finger down her cheek. Her eyelids slowly lifted, her lips parted on a sigh.

"*Dios,* you're beautiful."

She smiled at that. "Postcoital rose-colored glasses."

He shook his head. "Maybe I've never told you that before, but it's true. Your skin is so soft and smooth, your lips are like pink rose petals and your eyes are all the shades of the stormy summer sky."

"I didn't realize you had such a romantic streak, Your Highness," she teased.

"Neither did I." His hand skimmed up her torso, from her

waist to her breast, his thumb stroking over the tight bud of her nipple. "I always thought everything was black or white—and for the past few years, there's been a lot more black than white. And then you came along and gave me a whole new perspective on a lot of things."

She arched into his palm, as if she wanted his touch as much as he wanted to touch her. She had incredible breasts. They were so full and round, and so delightfully responsive to his touch.

Sam's curves had been much more modest, and she'd often lamented her tomboy figure. Even when she'd been pregnant, her breasts had never—

He froze.

Her gaze lifted to his, confusion swirling in the depths of her blue-gray eyes.

"Michael?"

The unmistakable smoky tone of Hannah's voice snapped him back to the present and helped him push aside any lingering thoughts of Sam. As much as he'd loved his wife and still grieved for the tragedy of a life cut so short, she was his past and Hannah—

He wasn't entirely sure yet what Hannah would be to him, but he knew that even if she wasn't his future, she was at least his present.

He lowered his head to kiss her, softly, sweetly. And felt the tension slowly seep out of her body.

Yes, she was definitely his present—an incredible gift. The only woman he wanted right now. And so he used his hands and his lips and his body and all of the hours until the sun began to rise to convince her.

Chapter Fourteen

Hannah didn't expect that Michael would still be there when she woke up in the morning. She'd known he wouldn't stay through the night. There was no way he would risk his daughter finding him there. But it would have been nice to wake up in his arms. To make love with him again as the sun was streaming through the windows.

Making love with Michael had been the most incredible experience. He'd been attentive and eager and very thorough. She stretched her arms above her head, and felt her muscles protest. Very very thorough. But while her body was feeling all smug and sated, her mind was spinning.

She'd been fighting against her feelings for the prince since the beginning, and she knew that making love with him was hardly going to help her win that battle. But as she showered and got ready for the day, she knew she didn't regret it.

After breakfast, while Riley was in the music room practicing piano—simply because she wanted to—Hannah was in the kitchen sipping on her second cup of coffee while Caridad was making a grocery list.

"How many people are you planning to feed?" Hannah asked, when the housekeeper turned the page over to continue her list on the other side.

"Only the three of you," she admitted. "But I want to make several ready-to-heat meals that you can just take out of the freezer and pop in the microwave."

"Are you going somewhere?"

"Just for a few days, and I'm not sure when, but I want to be ready to go as soon as Loretta calls."

Loretta, Hannah remembered now, was Caridad and Estavan's second-oldest daughter who was expecting her first child—and their fourth grandchild. "When is she due?"

"The eighteenth of August."

"On Riley's birthday," Hannah noted.

"She mentioned that to you, did she?"

"Only about a thousand times," she admitted with a smile.

"A child's birthday is a big deal—or it should be." Caridad tapped her pen on the counter, her brow furrowed.

Hannah knew that there was more she wanted to say. She also knew that prompting and prodding wouldn't get any more information out of the housekeeper until she was ready. So she sipped her coffee while she waited.

"The princess is going to be four years old," Caridad finally said. "And she's never had a party."

Hannah was startled by this revelation, and then realized that she shouldn't be. Samantha had died within hours of giving birth, which meant that Riley's birthday was the same day that Michael had lost his wife.

"I don't mean to be critical—I know it's a difficult time for the prince. And it's not like her birthday passes without any kind of recognition.

"There's always a cake," Caridad continued. "Because I bake that myself. And presents. But she's never had a party."

"Why are you telling me?" Hannah asked warily.

"Because I think this year he might be ready, but he probably won't think of it on his own."

"You want me to drop some hints," she guessed.

The housekeeper nodded. "Yes, I think just a few hints would be enough."

"Okay, I'll try."

"But not too subtle," Caridad said. "Men sometimes don't understand subtle—they need to be hit over the head."

Hannah had to laugh. "I'll do my best."

Michael had thought that making love with Hannah once would be enough, but the first joining of their bodies had barely taken the edge off of his desire. After four years of celibacy, it probably wasn't surprising that his reawakened libido was in no hurry to hibernate again, but he knew that it wasn't as simple as that. He didn't just crave physical release, he craved Hannah.

Every time his path crossed with hers the following day, his hormones jolted to attention. Now that he knew what it was like to be with her—the sensual way she responded to the touch of his lips and his hands, the glorious sensation of sinking into her warm and welcoming body, the exquisite rhythm of their lovemaking—he wanted only to be with her again.

But what did *she* want?

He didn't have the slightest clue.

She'd been sleeping when he'd left her room, so he'd managed to avoid the awkward "What does this mean?" or "Where do we go from here?" conversations that purportedly followed first-time sex. Since Hannah was the first woman he'd been with since he'd started dating Sam almost eighteen years earlier, he had little firsthand experience with those morning-after moments. And now he didn't know what was the next step.

They had lunch and dinner together with Riley, as was customary, and the conversation flowed as easily as it usually did. There were no uncomfortable references to the previous night and no awkward silences. There was absolutely no indication at all that anything had changed between them.

Until later that night, when he left Riley's room after he was sure she was asleep, and he found Hannah in the hall.

It wasn't all that late, but she was obviously ready to turn in for the night. Her hair had been brushed so that it fell loose over her shoulders, and she was wearing a long blue silky robe that was cinched at her narrow waist. A hint of lace in the same color peeked through where the sides of the robe overlapped, piquing his curiosity about what she had on beneath the silky cover.

He'd intended to seek her out, to have the discussion they'd missed having the night before. But now that he'd found her, conversation was the last thing on his mind.

"Wow" was all he managed.

But apparently it was the right thing to say, because she smiled and reached for his hand. Silently, she drew him across the hall and into her room.

The robe was elegant but discreet, covering her from shoulders to ankles. But when he tugged on the belt and the silky garment fell open, he saw that what she wore beneath was a pure lace fantasy. A very little lace fantasy that barely covered her sexy curves, held into place by the skinniest of straps over her shoulders.

And while he took a moment to appreciate the contrast of her pale skin with the dark lace, he much preferred reality to fantasy. With one quick tug, he lifted the garment over her head and tossed it aside.

* * *

Afterward, he let her put the lace-and-silk fantasy back on, and they sat on her balcony with a bottle of wine, just watching the stars.

"Are you ever going to tell me about that engagement?" he asked her.

"It was a long time ago," she said dismissively.

Considering that she was only twenty-six, he didn't imagine that it could have been all that long ago, and he was too curious to drop the subject. "What happened?"

"It didn't work out."

He rolled his eyes.

"We met at university," she finally told him. "He was a member of the British aristocracy, I was not. As much as he claimed to love me, when his family made it clear that they disapproved of his relationship with a commoner, he ended it." There was no emotion in her voice, but he sensed that she wasn't as unaffected by the broken engagement as she tried to appear.

"How long were you together?"

"Almost four years." She lifted her glass to her lips. "They didn't seem concerned about my lack of pedigree so long as we were just dating—apparently even aristocrats are entitled to meaningless flings—but to marry me would have been a blight on the family tree."

Again, her recital was without emotion, but he saw the hurt in her eyes and silently cursed any man who could be so cruel and heartless to this incredible woman.

"I didn't imagine there was anyone living in the modern world—aside from my mother—" he acknowledged with a grimace "—who had such outdated views about maintaining the purity of bloodlines."

"And yet your mother married a farmer," Hannah mused.

"Elena is nothing if not illogical. Or maybe she believed that her royal genes would trump his." He smiled as an old memory nudged at his mind. "The first time I scraped my knee when I was a kid, I didn't know what the red stuff was, because I honestly believed that my blood was supposed to be blue."

She smiled, too, but there were clouds in her eyes, as if she was thinking of the lack of blue in her own veins.

"So did you at least get to keep the ring?" he asked, in an attempt to lighten the mood.

She shook her head. "It was a family heirloom," she explained dryly.

"He didn't actually ask for it back?"

"Before we even left the ancestral estate," she admitted.

"And you gave it to him?" He couldn't imagine that she would have just slid it off of her finger and handed it over. No, if she'd cared enough about the man to want to marry him, she wouldn't have been that cool about the end of their engagement.

"I threw it out the window."

He chuckled.

"It took him three hours on his hands and knees in the immaculately groomed gardens to find it."

"He must have been pissed."

"Harrison didn't have that depth of emotion," she informed him. "But he was 'most displeased' with my 'childish behavior.'"

"Sounds like you made a lucky escape." And he was glad, because if she'd married that pompous British twit, she wouldn't be here with him now.

"I know I did. I guess I just thought I'd be at a different place by this point in my life."

"You're only twenty-six," he reminded her. "And I don't think there are many places in the world better than this one."

"You know I didn't mean this place specifically." She

smiled as she tipped her head back to look up at the sky. "This place is…heaven."

"Cielo," he agreed. "And you are…*mi ángel.*"

After almost a week had passed and Hannah's apparently too-subtle hints about Riley's approaching birthday continued to go unnoticed, she decided that Michael needed to be hit over the head. Not as literally as she had been, she thought, rubbing the pink scar that was the only visible reminder of her clash with Riley's racquet now that her stitches had been removed. But just as effectively.

So on Thursday morning, after the little girl had gone to the tennis court with Kevin, she cornered the prince in his office.

"It's Riley's birthday next week," she said.

"I know when her birthday is," he assured her.

"Well, I was thinking that it might be fun to have a party."

"A party?" he echoed, as if unfamiliar with the concept.

"You know—with a cake, party hats, noisemakers."

He continued to scribble notes on the ad layout on his desk. "Okay."

She blinked. "Really?"

He glanced up, a smile teasing the corners of his mouth. "Did you want me to say no?"

"Of course I didn't want you to say no," she told him. "But I thought there would be some discussion first."

He finally set down his pen and leaned back in his chair. "Discussion about what?"

"I don't know. Maybe the when and where, the guest list, a budget."

"When—sometime on the weekend. Where—here. As for the guest list, I figure if it's Riley's party, she should get to decide, and I don't care what it costs so long as I don't have to do anything but show up."

Happiness bubbled up inside of her. She couldn't wait to race into the kitchen and tell Caridad the good news.

"If you let Riley decide what she wants, it could turn into a very big party," she warned.

"I think we're overdue for a big party." He slipped his arms around her waist, drew her close. "And this year, I feel like celebrating."

Her heart bumped against her ribs, but she forced herself to respond lightly. "Okay, then. I'll talk to the birthday girl when she comes in and get started making plans."

"Where is Riley?"

"On the tennis court with Kevin."

"You'll have to give me an updated schedule," he said, not entirely teasing. "I never know where to find her these days."

"We don't have a schedule—we're improvising."

"I can improvise," he said, brushing his mouth against hers.

Hannah sighed. "Mmm. You're good at that."

"How long is she going to be busy with Kevin?"

"Probably about an hour. Why?"

"Because I want to show you some of the other things I'm good at."

Her cheeks flushed. "It's nine o'clock in the morning."

"But you don't have a schedule to worry about—you're improvising," he reminded her.

"Yes, but—"

"I really want to make love with you in the daylight."

He was a very lucky man, Michael thought with a grin as Hannah took his hand led him up to her room. And about to get luckier.

When he followed her through the door, his gaze automatically shifted toward the bed upon which they'd made love every night for the past nine days—and caught on the enormous bouquet of flowers in the vase on her bedside table.

He picked up the card. "With sincere thanks for helping me survive summer school, Kevin."

She paused in the process of removing the decorative throw cushions from the bed when she saw him holding the card. "Isn't that sweet?"

"Sure," he agreed stiffly. "He's finished his course, then?"

She nodded. "He got an A-plus on his final essay to finish with first-class honors."

"Caridad must be thrilled."

"She promised to make baklava, just for me," Hannah told him.

She said it as if that was her favorite, and maybe it was. He didn't know too much about what she liked or didn't like.

"I didn't know you liked flowers," he said, as if that was an excuse for the fact that he'd never thought to give her any.

"Who doesn't like flowers?" she countered lightly.

There was no accusation in her words, no judgment in her tone. Of course not—Hannah had made it clear from the beginning that she didn't have any expectations of him. Not even something as insignificant as a bouquet of flowers. And though he couldn't have said why, the realization annoyed him.

Or maybe he was annoyed to realize that he'd never really made an effort where Hannah was concerned. He'd never even taken her out to dinner, and they only went as far as the media room to watch a movie. They came together after dark like clandestine lovers, without ever having had anything that resembled a traditional date.

He knew that was his fault. He wasn't ready to subject Hannah to the media scrutiny of being seen in public together. Going shopping with Riley didn't really count, because the press accepted that the prince would require the assistance of a nanny when he was out with his daughter.

But he knew it would be very different if he and Hannah ventured out together without Riley as a buffer between them.

It was difficult to date when you were a member of the royal family, even one not in direct line to the throne. There was no such thing as privacy, and rarely even the pretense of it. Every appearance, every touch and kiss, became a matter of public speculation.

Not that Michael thought she couldn't handle it. He had yet to see Hannah balk at any kind of challenge. No, it was simply that he wasn't ready to go public with a relationship that felt too new, or maybe it was his feelings that were too uncertain. And that he was unwilling to look too deep inside himself to figure them out.

"I don't know if I like the idea of a much younger man bringing you flowers," he said, only half joking.

"He didn't just bring flowers," she teased. "He kissed me, too."

His brows drew together; Hannah laughed.

"It was a perfectly chaste peck on the cheek," she assured him.

"Lucky for him, or I might have to call him out for making a move on my woman."

Her brows rose. "*Your* woman?"

The words had probably surprised Michael even more than they'd surprised Hannah, and were followed by a quick spurt of panic. He immediately backtracked. "Well, you're mine until the end of summer, anyway."

Hannah turned away on the pretext of rearranging the colored bottles on her dresser, but not before he saw the light in her eyes fade. When she faced him again, her smile was overly bright.

"And that's less than three weeks away, so why are we wasting time talking?" She reached for the buttons on his shirt.

"Hannah—" He caught her hands, not sure what to say, or even if there were any words to explain how he felt about her.

He cared about her—he couldn't be with her if he didn't. And he didn't want her to think it was just sex, but he didn't want to give her false hope, either. He didn't want her to think that he could ever fall in love with her. Because he couldn't—he loved Sam.

"I never asked you for any promises," she told him.

And he couldn't have given them to her if she had. But he could give her pleasure, and he knew that doing so would give him pleasure, too.

He stripped her clothes away and lowered her onto the mattress. Then he knelt between her legs, stroking his fingertips slowly over the sensitive skin of her inner thighs. He brushed the soft curls at the apex of her thighs, and she gasped. He repeated the motion, parting the curls so that his thumb stroked over the nub at her center, and she bit down on her lip to keep from crying out.

"It's okay," he told her. "I want to hear you. I want to know how it feels when I touch you."

"It feels good. So good."

As his thumb circled her nub, he teased her slick, wet opening with the tip of a finger. She whimpered.

"Michael, please."

"Tell me what you want, Hannah."

"I want you."

He wanted her, too. He wanted to spread her legs wide and bury himself in her. To thrust into the hot wetness between her thighs, again and again, harder and faster, until he felt her convulse around him, dragging him into blissful oblivion.

But first, he wanted to taste her.

He slid his hands beneath her, lifting her hips off of the mattress so that he could take her with his mouth.

She gasped again, the sound reflecting both shock and pleasure. His tongue slid deep inside, reaching for the core of her feminine essence. Her breath was coming in quick, shallow pants, and he knew that she was getting close to her edge. It wouldn't have taken much to push her over the edge, but he wanted to draw out the pleasure for her—and for himself.

With his lips and his tongue, he probed and suckled and licked. He heard her breath quicken, then catch, and finally... release.

He stroked and kissed his way up her body until she was trembling again. Her belly, her breasts, her throat. She reached for him then, her fingers wrapping around and then sliding up the hard, throbbing length of him. He sucked in a breath. She stroked downward again, slowly, teasingly, until his eyes nearly crossed.

She arched her hips as she guided him to her center, welcoming him into her slick, wet heat. The last threads of his self-control slipped out of his grasp. He yanked her hips up and buried himself deep inside her.

She gasped and arched, pulling him even deeper, her muscles clamping around him as she climaxed again. The pulsing waves threatened to drag him under their wake. He reached for her hands, linking their fingers together over her head, making her his anchor as he rode out the tide of her release.

He waited until the pulses started to slow, then he began to move. She met him, stroke for stroke. Slow and deep. Then fast and hard. Faster. Harder. This time, when her release came, he let go and went with her.

Chapter Fifteen

Once the prince had given his nod of approval to the birth-day party, Hannah was anxious to get started on the planning, so she turned to her best friend for advice. Karen outlined the five essential ingredients of a successful children's party: decorations, such as colorful streamers and balloons; games or crafts to keep the kids busy; cake to give the kids an unnecessary sugar high; presents for the guest of honor and loot bags for all of her friends—all of which should somehow coordinate with the party theme. And preferably, she added as an afterthought, outdoors so that the sugar-high kids weren't tearing through the house and destroying everything.

For Riley's first-ever birthday party, Hannah took her friend's list and gave it the royal treatment. She decided to go with a princess theme, since it was too obvious to resist.

The first glitch came when she asked Riley who she wanted to invite. The little girl mentioned her new friend, Grace, then added Kevin and Caridad and Estavan before rattling off the extensive list of all her aunts, uncles and cousins. She didn't mention her grandmother, and when Hannah asked about adding her to the list, the princess wrinkled her nose.

"Do I have to?"

"She is your grandmother, and you invited everyone else in the family," Hannah felt compelled to point out, even as she wondered if she was making a mistake.

But she couldn't help remembering Michael's comment about his mother barely knowing his daughter, and though she didn't think an invitation to one birthday party was likely to change that, she couldn't help hoping that it might be a start. And maybe, if the princess royal got to know Riley, she would give up on the idea of sending her away to boarding school.

"Everyone else in my family is nice," Riley said simply.

Hannah didn't quite know how to respond to that. She'd never actually met the princess royal and she didn't want to prejudge, but the princess's response made her wary.

"Would it be nice to invite everyone except her?" she prodded gently.

"No." Riley sighed, and considered her dilemma for another minute before she finally said, "Okay, you can put her on the list. But she doesn't get a loot bag."

After the guest list was finalized, Hannah turned her attention to other details. Taking her friend's advice to heart and unwilling to trust in the capriciousness of the weather, she rented a party tent to ensure that the celebration remained outside. Of course, when she called about the tent, she realized that she needed tables and chairs for inside the tent, and cloths to cover the tables and dress up the chairs. By the time she got off the phone, she was grateful the prince wasn't worried about budget.

"I just ordered a bouncy castle," she admitted to Caridad.

The housekeeper's brows lifted. "One of those big inflatable things?"

"It fits the princess theme," she explained.

"Riley will love it."

"And a cotton-candy cart and popcorn machine."

Caridad's lips twitched. "Apparently you know how to throw a party."

"You don't think it's too much?"

"Of course it's too much, but after waiting four years for a party, it should be a party worth waiting for."

"It will be," Hannah said confidently.

And it was. The tent was decorated with thousands of tiny white fairy lights and hundreds of pink streamers and dozens of enormous bouquets of white and pink helium-filled balloons.

The younger female guests got to make their own tiaras—decorating foam crowns with glittery "jewels" and sparkling flowers. Thankfully Hannah had realized that the crowns wouldn't be a big hit with Riley's male cousins, so they got to decorate foam swords. After the craft, they played party games: pin the tail on the noble steed, musical thrones and a variation of Hot Potato with a glass slipper in place of the potato. And, of course, they spent hours just jumping around in the inflatable bouncy castle that had been set up behind the tennis court.

For a minute, Hannah had actually worried that Michael's mother was going to have a coronary when she spotted it. The princess royal had gone red in the face and demanded that the "grotesque monstrosity" be removed from the grounds immediately. But Michael had been unconcerned and simply ignored her demand, for which the kids were unbelievably grateful.

Riley loved all of it. And she was completely in her element as the center of attention. Hannah was happy to remain in the background, making sure everything was proceeding as it should, but Michael made a point of introducing "Riley's nanny and party planner" to everyone she hadn't yet met. There was nothing incorrect in that designation, and it wasn't like she expected or even wanted him to announce that they were lovers. But she wished he'd at least given a hint that she meant something more to him than the roles she filled in his daughter's life.

That tiny disappointment aside, she really enjoyed meeting his family. She already knew his sister, of course, and was pleased when Marissa jumped right in to help keep things running smoothly. She was introduced to Prince Cameron, his very pregnant wife, Gabriella, and their daughter, Sierra. The teenage princess was stunningly beautiful and surprisingly unaffected by her recently newfound status as a royal, happily jumping in to help the kids at the craft table.

She also met Rowan, the prince regent, his wife, Lara, and their sons Matthew and William; Prince Eric and Princess Molly and their kids, Maggie and Josh; Prince Christian—next in line to the throne—his sister, Alexandria, and their younger brother, Damon. Even Prince Marcus, who divided his time between Tesoro del Mar and West Virginia, happened to be in the country with his wife, Jewel, and their two daughters, Isabella and Rosalina, so they were able to attend.

They were all warm and welcoming, but it was their interactions with one another that Hannah observed just a little enviously. It had nothing to do with them being royal and everything to do with the obvious closeness they shared. As an only child, she'd never known anything to compare to that kind of absolute acceptance and unquestioning loyalty, but she was glad that Riley did.

As for Riley's "Grandmama"—well, Hannah didn't get any warm and fuzzy feelings from her, so she just kept a careful distance between them. And she succeeded, until she went into the house to tell Caridad that they were getting low on punch. On her way back out, the princess royal cornered her in the hall.

"I'll bet this party was your idea," she said.

And so was adding your name to the guest list, Hannah wanted to tell her. But she bit her tongue. Elena Leandres might be insufferably rude, but she was the princess royal and, as such, was entitled to deference if not respect.

"Riley doesn't need to play at being a princess," the birthday girl's grandmama continued. "She *is* one. And this whole display is tacky and inappropriate."

"I'm sorry you're not enjoying yourself."

The older woman's eyes narrowed on her. "But you are, aren't you?"

"I can't deny that I like a good party, Your Highness," she said unapologetically.

"Is it the party or the fairy tale?" she challenged. "Do you have some kind of fantasy in your mind that you're going to ride off into the sunset with the prince?"

"I have no illusions," she assured the prince's mother.

"I'm pleased to hear that, because although my son might lack sense and discretion in his choice of lovers, he would never tarnish his beloved wife's memory or his daughter's future by marrying someone like you."

One side of Elena's mouth curled in a nasty smile as Hannah's cheeks filled with color. "Did you really think I wouldn't guess the nature of your relationship with my son? I know what a man's thinking when he looks at a woman the way Michael looks at you—and it's not about hearts and flowers, it's about sex, pure and simple."

She forced herself to shrug, as if the princess royal's words hadn't cut to the quick. "Sure," she agreed easily. "But at least it's really great sex. And while this has been a fascinating conversation, I have to get back outside."

"You have not been dismissed," Elena snapped at her.

"I beg your pardon, Your Highness," she said through

clenched teeth. "But the children will be getting hungry and I promised Caridad that I would help serve lunch."

"Well, go on then," the princess royal smirked. "I wouldn't want to keep you from your duties."

And with those words and a dismissive wave of her hand, she quickly and efficiently put the nanny in her place.

Hannah's feelings were in turmoil as she headed up the stairs to her own room. She was angry and frustrated, embarrassed that her own thoughts and feelings had been so transparent, and her heart was aching because she knew that what the princess royal had said was true.

Not that she believed her relationship with the prince was about nothing more than sex. They had fun together and they'd become friends. But she also knew that while Michael had chosen to be with her now, he'd made no mention of a future for them together. And she had to wonder if maybe one of the reasons he'd chosen to get involved with her—aside from the obvious convenience—was because he could be confident that their relationship already had a predetermined expiration date. At the end of the summer, she would be leaving. The time they'd spent together was an interlude, that was all, and she'd been a fool to ever let herself hope it might be more.

Marissa was coming down the stairs as she was going up, and the princess's quick smile faded when she got close enough to see the distress that Hannah knew was likely etched on her face.

"Riley asked me to find you," she said. "She said she's absolutely starving and wanted to know when it would be time to eat."

"Please tell her that I'll be out in just a minute, Your Highness." She was anxious now to move things along and get this party over with, but she needed a few minutes alone to regain her composure before she could face anyone. And especially before she could face Michael.

"Hannah." The princess touched her arm, halting her progress. "I just saw my mother walk out—did she say something to upset you?"

"Of course not."

But it was obvious that Marissa didn't believe her, and that she was disappointed by the obvious lie.

"I thought we were becoming friends," she said gently.

Hannah looked away so that the princess wouldn't see the tears that stung her eyes. "You've been very kind to me, Your Highness, but—"

"Will you stop 'Your Highnessing' me," Marissa demanded, "and tell me what she said to you."

"It wasn't anything that wasn't true," Hannah finally acknowledged.

The princess sighed. "I'm not going to make excuses for her. All I can say is that she's so unhappy, her only pleasure comes from making others feel the same way."

"I'm not unhappy," Hannah assured her. She was simply resigned to the realities of her relationship with the prince, but also determined. If they only had two more weeks together, then she was going to cherish every moment.

"Actually, there is one more thing I'd like to say," Marissa told her.

"What's that?"

"That you're the best thing that has happened to my brother in a long time, so please don't let my mother—or anyone else—make you question what you have together."

Despite Marissa's reassurances, the rest of the day was bittersweet for Hannah, her happiness tempered by the realization that she wouldn't be around to witness the celebration of Riley's fifth birthday. She was only going to be at Cielo del Norte with the prince and his daughter for another two weeks. After that, they would return to their home in Verde Colinas, and she would go back to her apartment in town and her job at the high school, and she knew that she was going to miss them both unbearably.

She tried not to dwell on that fact, and when everyone joined together to sing "Happy Birthday," it was a welcome diversion. Caridad had offered to make the cake, as she had for each of the princess's previous birthdays, and Riley was stunned by the three-dimensional fairy-tale castle confection that she'd created, complete with towers and spires and even a drawbridge.

After everyone had their fill of cake and ice cream, Riley opened her gifts. She enthused over all of them, showing as much appreciation for the Little Miss Tennis visor that Kevin gave her to the elaborate back-to-school wardrobe from her aunt Marissa. Of course, her absolute favorite gift was the *Yo Gabba Gabba* CD collection from Grace, and she insisted on putting on the music for the enjoyment of all her guests.

The prince had given his gift to his daughter at breakfast: a three-story dollhouse, which she had absolutely adored. Partly because it came with dozens of pieces of furniture, but mostly because it was from her beloved daddy.

Hannah had walked the mall in San Pedro three times looking for something special for the little girl. She didn't want it to be anything showy or expensive, just something that might remind Riley of the time they'd spent together after she was gone. She finally found it in a little boutique that sold an indescribable variety of items ranging from handmade lace and estate jewelry to the latest in kitchen gadgets and children's toys. At first, it caught her eye just because it was funky and fun: a three-foot-long stuffed caterpillar with a purple body and high-top running shoes on its dozens of feet. Then when she picked it up, she noted the name on the tag: EMME.

"It's a palindrome!" Riley exclaimed happily.

"It looks like a caterpillar to me," her father said.

Riley just rolled her eyes and shared a secret smile with Hannah.

Several hours later, after the guests had all gone home and the remnants of the party had been cleared away by the rental company, Riley's eyes were closed. Even when Michael touched his lips to her cheek, she didn't stir.

"She's sleeping," he confirmed.

"She had a busy day," Hannah noted.

"A fabulous day—thanks to you."

"I tried not to go too over the top," she said.

His brows rose. "You don't think it was over the top?"

"I nixed the suggested arrival of the birthday girl in the horse-drawn glass carriage," she told him.

"I'm in awe of your restraint," he said dryly. "But truthfully, whatever it costs, it was worth every penny. I've never seen her so happy."

"Now I'm regretting that I didn't get the carriage."

"Then what would we do next year?"

She knew he'd only meant to tease her with the suggestion that this party couldn't be topped, but the words were a reminder to both of them that there was no *we* and Hannah wouldn't be around for the princess's next birthday.

"Brigitte called today," he said, in what seemed to Hannah a deliberate attempt to shift the direction of the conversation. "To wish Riley a happy birthday."

"That was thoughtful," she said. "How is she adjusting to life in Iceland?"

"Not easily."

"Does she want to come back?"

He laughed. "No. As much as she's struggling with culture shock, she is very much in love with her new husband."

"Then what is it that you're not telling me?" Because she was sure that he was holding something back.

"She did ask if I'd found a full-time nanny," he admitted. "And when I said I had not, she suggested that I interview her friend Margaux for the position."

Hannah had to remind herself that this wasn't unexpected. She'd known all along that the prince would be hiring a new nanny because she was leaving at the end of August. "Why do you sound as if that's a problem?" she asked.

"Because I was hoping that I might convince you to stay beyond the summer."

Her heart pounded hard against her ribs. This was what she hadn't even realized she wanted—what she hadn't dared let herself hope for. "You want me to stay?"

"You've been so wonderful with Riley, and she's going to be devastated if you leave."

Disappointment washed the roots of barely blossomed hope from her heart. "She'll be fine," she said, confident that it was true. The child had already proven that she was both adaptable and resilient. It was her own heart that gave Hannah concern, because she knew that when she left Cielo del Norte, she would be leaving the largest part of it behind.

"Okay, maybe the truth is that I'm not yet ready to let you go," Michael acknowledged.

Not yet ready—but he would be. Neither of them had any expectations of anything permanent or even long-term. At least none that she was willing to admit to him now. "We still have two weeks before the end of the summer," she said lightly.

"What if I'm not ready then, either?"

She didn't know what to say, how to answer his question in a way that wouldn't give away the feelings in her own heart. Because the truth was, she didn't want him to ever let her go—she wanted him to love her as much as she loved him, and she knew that wasn't going to happen.

He was still in love with Riley's mother, and even if he wasn't, she knew he wouldn't ever love her. Not enough.

Her father hadn't loved her enough to keep her with him, and Harrison hadn't loved her enough to defy his parents. And if she wasn't good enough for the heir of some obscure earldom, there was no way anyone would ever consider her good enough for a Tesorian prince. The princess royal had made that more than clear.

"Let's not think about that right now," she said, leading the way across the hall.

So long as they had tonight, she wasn't going to think about tomorrow.

Afterward, Hannah would wonder how it happened, because she knew she didn't consciously speak the words aloud. She certainly hadn't intended to tell him of the feelings that filled her heart. But when he pulled her close, tucking her against the warmth of his body so that she felt secure and cherished in his embrace, her emotions overruled reason. And as she started to drift toward slumber, the words slipped from between her lips as if of their own accord.

"I love you, Michael."

His only response was silence. She wanted to believe that he was already asleep and that he probably hadn't heard her impulsive confession, but the sudden tension that filled his body proved otherwise. The muscles in the arm that was wrapped around her grew taut, and she felt the sting of tears in her eyes.

She hadn't intended to confide her feelings. She knew she would be leaving her heart at Cielo del Norte but she'd hoped to at least take her pride. But keeping the feelings to herself certainly hadn't diminished them, and she was through pretending.

She did love him—with her whole heart. And she loved Riley as if the little girl was her own child. But accepting the truth of her feelings forced her to accept the more painful truths that were equally evident: there was no place for her here, and no future for her with the prince and his daughter.

Once again, she was trying to fit in someplace where she could never belong.

Chapter Sixteen

The night after Hannah's whispered declaration of her feelings, Michael didn't go to her room. It was the first time since their first night together that he'd gone directly to his big, empty bed. He didn't sleep well. He wasn't even sure that he'd slept at all.

But he knew he was doing the right thing. To continue to be with Hannah when he didn't—couldn't—feel the same way she did wasn't fair to either of them.

It was on Tuesday, after two restless, sleepless nights, that she knocked on his office door.

"Excuse me for interrupting, Your Highness, but I was wondering if I could have a minute of your time."

He cringed at the formal tone of her voice, hating the distance between them. He wanted to hear her speak his name, not his title. He wanted to take her in his arms and hold her so close that he could feel her heart beating against his. He wanted to touch his mouth to hers, to feel her lips yield to his kiss. But he had no right to want anything from her anymore.

"Of course, Hannah," he responded to her request.

"I got a notice from St. Eugene's that I'll be teaching a new course in the fall, and I was hoping to go back to Port Augustine at the end of this week."

This wasn't at all what he'd expected. He wasn't ready for her to leave, and he had no intention of letting her go. She had agreed to stay until the end of summer, to take care of his daughter.

"What about Riley?" he demanded now. "How can you just abandon her?"

"I'm not going anywhere until you've found someone else to take care of her."

"And what if I don't find anyone else?" he challenged.

He wasn't sure why he was fighting her on this. It was only seven days, and even if he didn't have anyone else by then, he would be happy to spend more time with his daughter during that last week. He didn't need a nanny, but he needed Hannah.

He wasn't sure where that last thought had come from— or how it could simultaneously feel so right and make him break out in a cold sweat.

"Margaux has agreed to come for an interview tomorrow."

"You're so eager to get away from here that you called her to set this up?"

"No," she denied. "Margaux called here, on Brigitte's advice, to set a date and time to meet with you. I just took the message."

"You could have said that I would get in touch with her when I returned to Port Augustine," he countered.

She looked at him oddly, as if she heard the note of desperation he tried to keep out of his voice. But all she said was, "I thought you would want this settled before then—to make sure Riley will be in good hands when you go back."

He couldn't refute the logic in that. Instead, he asked, "Is there nothing I can say to make you stay?"

She hesitated for a moment, as if considering her response, then finally said, "You really don't need me anymore. You and Riley are going to be just fine."

"Have you told her that you're leaving?"

"She won't be surprised. She knows I have to go back to my real job."

Just as he'd known it was only a temporary assignment when he'd hired her, so why was he fighting it now?

"I'll let you know after I meet with Margaux tomorrow," he told her.

"Thank you," she said.

And then she was gone.

Hannah was transferring her clothing from the dresser to her suitcase when Riley came into her room.

"Who's that lady with Daddy?" she demanded. "Is it true that she's going to be my new nanny?"

"That's for your daddy to decide," Hannah told her.

The princess crawled up onto Hannah's bed and hugged her knees to her chest. "Why don't I get to decide?"

"Because you're four."

"That's not my fault."

Hannah tousled her hair and smiled gently. "It's not a question of fault, it's just the way it is."

Riley watched as she continued to fill the suitcase. Hannah forced herself to concentrate on carefully arranging each item, because she knew that if she looked at the little girl right now, she would fall apart.

After a few minutes, Riley spoke in a quiet voice, "I don't want you to go."

Hannah's throat was tight, her eyes burning with unshed

tears. She drew in a deep breath and settled onto the edge of the bed, trying to find the words that would make goodbye easier for both of them.

But as soon as she sat down, Riley scooted over to wrap her arms around her, squeezing her so tight that the dam that was holding back Hannah's tears began to crack.

"I don't want to go, either," she admitted. "But we both knew that I was only going to be here for the summer."

"The summer's not over yet," the princess pointed out.

She rested her chin on top of the little girl's head, so Riley wouldn't see the tears that slid down her cheeks. "No, but it's getting close."

After another few minutes, Riley asked, "Can I come visit you?"

Hannah knew it would be best to make a clean break, to walk away from Cielo del Norte and never look back, but there was no way she could deny the child's request. "That's up to your dad, but if he says yes, it's absolutely okay with me."

"When?" Riley demanded.

The characteristic impatience in her voice made Hannah smile through her tears. "Anytime."

Margaux was everything Brigitte promised she would be. She was compassionate and knowledgeable and professional, and though his daughter kept insisting that she didn't want a new nanny, Michael remembered that she'd been equally resistant to Hannah at first. So he offered her the job, and she accepted. And when she agreed that she could start right away, he released Hannah from her obligation to stay until the end of the month.

It seemed pointless to have Margaux move into the beach house only to have to move back to the city a week later, so he decided that he and Riley might as well return to Verde Colinas early. Maybe his excuses were just that—certainly

Caridad thought so—and maybe it was true that he didn't want anyone else in Hannah's room. Not yet, while the memories were still fresh. By next summer, he was confident that he would be able to think of it as simply the nanny's room again and not think about all the hours that he'd spent in there with Hannah, talking and laughing with her, and making love with her.

Back in the city, Riley seemed to settle into her new routines fairly easily. Since summer was almost over, he'd started some of her lessons again, but on a much more modest scale. His daughter was polite and attentive to her teachers, and she cooperated willingly enough with Margaux, but still, something didn't seem quite right.

It took him almost a week to realize why the house seemed so somber and silent. Because not once in that entire time, not once in the six days since Hannah had been gone, did he hear his daughter laugh.

When she unpacked at home, Riley put the doll that Sam had given her back in its special place on the shelf. The silly stuffed caterpillar that Hannah had given to her as a birthday gift went on the bed, and Riley slept with it hugged close to her chest every night.

He wished that he could comfort his daughter, but he missed Hannah as much as she did. Maybe he hadn't sent her away, but he knew that he was responsible for her leaving just the same. She'd told him that she loved him, and he hadn't dared speak of the feelings that were in his own heart. Because he hadn't been willing to admit them, even to himself.

Now that she was gone, he could no longer deny the truth. Hannah hadn't just shown him how to build a better relationship with his daughter, she'd helped him heal and gave him hope for the future—a future he now knew that he wanted to share with her.

* * *

During the first week after her return from Cielo del Norte, Hannah missed Riley so much that she actually felt a pain in her chest whenever she thought of the little girl. As for the prince—well, she didn't even dare let herself think of the man who had stolen her heart.

She kept herself busy. She washed curtains and scrubbed floors; she repainted the walls and bought new throw rugs and cushions. She knew what she was doing: trying to make a fresh start. She wasn't sure that her plan would actually succeed, but she'd realized that the only way she could sleep at night was to fall into bed completely physically exhausted.

After everything was cleaned and painted and rearranged, she carted all of her boxes out of storage and back into her apartment. As she unpacked her belongings, she was amazed to think that only two months had passed since she'd packed it all away. It really wasn't a lot of time, but so much in her life had changed during that period. She had changed.

But she was doing okay—until she got a letter from Caridad. The housekeeper just wanted to let her know that Loretta had finally had her baby—almost two weeks late— and that she and Estavan were the proud grandparents of another beautiful baby girl.

Hannah was genuinely thrilled for them, and she sent a card and a gift for the baby. She'd considered hand-delivering the items, but decided against it. The memories were still too fresh, her heartache still too raw. She did hope to keep in touch with Caridad, as the housekeeper had become a wonderful friend, but there was no reason for her to ever go back to Cielo del Norte.

No reason except that she'd left her heart with Prince Michael while she'd been there. It didn't seem to matter that he didn't want it; she knew that it would always belong to him.

So many times, she thought back to that last conversation

in his office, when he'd asked, "Is there nothing I can say to make you stay?" And she'd wondered if anything might have been different if she'd had the courage to speak the words that had immediately come to mind: *Tell me you love me.*

But she knew that even if he had actually said those words to her, she wouldn't believe them. Because actions spoke louder than words, and he'd already made his feelings clear. She'd told him that she loved him—and he didn't even give her the lame I-care-about-you-but-I'm-not-ready-for-a-serious-relationship speech. He'd said nothing at all.

Still, she knew the mistake wasn't in speaking of the feelings that were in her heart; the mistake was in letting herself fall in love with a man that she'd known all along could never love her back. But even that knowledge didn't stop her from missing the prince and his little girl.

She was grateful when school started up again in September. She was anxious to get back into the familiar routines, confident that a return to her normal life would help her forget about Michael and Riley and how much she missed both of them.

Still, she thought about contacting him. Every day, she experienced moments of such intense yearning that she was tempted to pick up the phone, not just to hear his voice but to check on Riley. If she did, maybe he would give her permission to visit the little girl, but in the end she decided that wouldn't be a good idea for either of them. Margaux was the princess's nanny now, and she deserved a chance to bond with the child without Hannah in the way.

She was confident that Riley would adjust to these new changes in her life without much difficulty. She truly was an amazing child, and Hannah just hoped that the prince didn't fill her schedule with so many lessons and classes again that she forgot to be a child.

Instead of contacting the prince, Hannah busied herself working on new lesson plans for the current term. She was rereading the first play for her freshman drama class when there was a knock at the door Saturday afternoon. She was feeling desperate enough for a distraction that she responded to the summons. If it was a vacuum cleaner salesman, she might even invite him in to do a demonstration in the hope that it would possibly give her a half-hour reprieve from her thoughts of Michael and Riley.

But when she opened the door, she realized that there wasn't going to be any reprieve—because the prince and his daughter were standing in her hall.

"Hello, Hannah."

She opened her mouth, but no sound came out. She didn't know what to say—whether to invite them inside or send them away. And she was afraid that whatever choice she made would only result in fresh heartache.

"You said I could come visit, remember?" Riley's smile was uncharacteristically tentative, as if she was unsure of her welcome.

Hannah managed a smile, though she felt as if her heart was splitting wide open inside of her chest. "Of course I remember."

"Can we come in?" the prince asked.

She wished she could say no. And if his daughter wasn't standing at his side, she would have refused. But there was no way she could close the door now.

She stepped back so that they could enter, while questions swirled through her mind. Why were they here? Why now? Subconsciously, she touched a hand to her brow. The scar above her eye had started to fade, but the wounds on her heart were still raw and bleeding.

"Hannah?" the princess prompted, her little brow furrowed with concern.

She dropped her hand away, forced a smile. "Can I get you anything?"

She wasn't sure what to offer—her mind had gone blank

when she'd seen them standing outside of her door and she honestly couldn't remember what was in her refrigerator.

"Not for me, thanks," the prince said.

Riley shook her head.

Hannah led them into the living room. As a result of all of the cleaning and painting and redecorating, she knew the apartment looked good. Hardly up to royal standards, but then again, she wasn't a royal.

"So—were you just in the neighborhood?" she asked, attempting a casualness she wasn't feeling.

"No, Riley wanted to see you." Michael tucked his hands into his pockets. "Actually, we both wanted to see you."

"We miss you," the little girl said.

"How is school?" she asked Riley, forcing a note of cheerfulness into her voice even as her heart cracked wide open.

"It's okay," the princess said.

"Have you made lots of new friends?"

"A few."

Hannah swallowed. "And everything's going well…with the new nanny?"

The little girl looked at her daddy, as if deferring the question to him.

"Margaux is…almost perfect," he said.

"That's great," she said, and hoped that she sounded sincere.

"Almost," Riley repeated.

"Is there a problem?" Hannah asked, genuinely concerned.

"The only problem," Michael said, "is that she isn't you."

"We want you to come back," Riley said.

"This isn't fair," Hannah said to the prince, glaring at him through the sheen of tears that filled her eyes. "You can't bring your daughter here to—"

"It was Riley's idea," he told her. "There was no way she was letting me come here without her."

"Please, Hannah." The princess looked at her, those big brown eyes beseeching.

Hannah could barely speak around the lump in her throat. "I'm not really a nanny," she reminded the little girl gently. "I'm a high school teacher."

"We both understand that," Michael assured her. "And the thing is, Riley and I had a long talk about it and agreed that, since she's in school now during the week anyway, she probably doesn't need a nanny."

"Then why are you here?"

"Because I do need a mom," Riley piped up.

"And I need a wife," Michael said. "So—" The prince looked at his daughter, she gave him a quick nod, then they spoke in unison: "Will you marry us, Hannah?"

She could only stare at them both, her eyes filling with tears all over again.

Michael nudged his daughter.

"Oh." The little girl reached into the pocket of her skirt and pulled out a small box. She tried to flip open the lid, but it snapped shut again—catching her finger.

"Ow." Riley shook her hand free, and the box went flying across the floor, disappearing under the sofa.

Hannah had to laugh through her tears.

"This isn't quite how I imagined the scene playing out," Michael admitted.

It was a scene she hadn't dared let herself imagine and still wasn't entirely sure was real.

"Can you trust that I have a ring or do I have to dig the box out from under the furniture before you'll answer the question?" he asked.

"I don't care about the ring," she assured him.

"It's a really pretty ring," Riley said, making Hannah smile.

"But you're not saying anything," he prompted.

"I've got it, Daddy." The princess held up the box she'd

retrieved from beneath the sofa. Then she came over and opened it carefully so that Hannah could see the gorgeous princess-cut diamond solitaire set in a platinum band. "Now you're supposed to say yes."

She wanted to say yes. More than anything, she wanted to say yes, and it had nothing to do with the ring. It had to do with the fact that the prince was offering her everything she'd ever wanted and more than she'd ever dreamed of, but she felt as if they were both forgetting a couple important issues. "I'm a commoner, Michael."

"Which only means you don't carry all of the baggage that goes along with a title," he assured her.

"I realize it's not a big deal to you, but maybe it should be. And your mother—"

"Has absolutely no say in any of this," he said firmly.

"Daddy told Grandmama that if she can't accept you, then she can't be part of our family," Riley told her.

"You talked to your mother…about me?"

"I wanted her to know that I won't tolerate any more interference in my life," he said.

"I don't want to be the cause of any dissension in your relationship," she said, both surprised and humbled that he would take such a stand for her.

"You're not," Michael assured her. "If anything, confronting my mother about her attitude toward you gave me the opportunity to clear the air about a lot of things. I'm not naïve enough to believe that we came to any kind of understanding, but I am confident that she won't cause any problems for us ever again."

He spoke with such certainty, she couldn't help but believe him. But she had other—and even bigger—concerns than the princess royal.

"Needing a wife—and a mother for Riley—aren't the best reasons to get married," she said softly.

He smiled as he took both of her hands in his. "Did I

gloss over the I-love-you-more-than-I-ever-thought-it-was-possible-to-love-somebody part?"

Her heart swelled so much in response to his words that her chest actually ached with the effort to contain it. "Actually, you skipped it altogether."

"It's true," he told her. "I didn't plan to ever fall in love again. Truthfully, I didn't want to ever fall in love again."

"Because you still love Sam," she guessed.

"Sam will always have a place in my heart," he admitted, "because she was the first woman I ever loved and Riley's mother. But the rest of my heart is yours, for now and forever. So now the question I need answered is: do you love me?"

"You know I do."

"Is that a yes?" Riley wanted to know.

Hannah laughed. "That is very definitely a yes."

The princess clapped her hands together. "Now you have to put the ring on her finger, Daddy."

So he did.

"And kiss her."

And he did that, too.

He kissed her very tenderly and very thoroughly, until all of the loneliness and anguish of the past few weeks was forgotten because her heart was too full of love to feel anything else.

And still he continued to kiss her—until Riley pushed her way in between them.

"Are we married now?" she asked.

"Not quite yet," the prince said.

Riley sighed. "Can Hannah come home with us tonight anyway?"

"What do you say?" he asked, drawing her to her feet. "Will you come home with us tonight?"

Home.

She looked around at the apartment that had been her

residence for almost three years and felt absolutely no regret about leaving. It was only a collection of rooms—cold and empty without the man and the little girl she loved.

"There is nowhere else I want to be," she said truthfully.

"Just one more thing," Michael said.

"What's that?"

"If you ever retell the story of my proposal, will you edit out the awkward parts?" he asked.

She shook her head. "Absolutely not. I'm going to remember each tiny detail forever, because this moment—with you and Riley—is my every dream come true."

Epilogue

ROYAL WEDDING BELLS TOLL AGAIN
by Alex Girard

Last summer, Prince Michael Leandres was looking for a nanny for his young daughter and hired a high school teacher instead. At the time, it might have seemed that he'd made an error in judgment, but the lucky guests in attendance when the prince married Hannah Castillo at the Cathedral of Christ the King on Friday night would definitely disagree.

The ceremony began with four-and-a-half-year-old Princess Riley tossing white rose petals as she made her way down the aisle and toward the front of the church where her father, immaculately attired in a classic Armani tuxedo, was waiting. Then came the bride, in a strapless silk crepe sheath by Vera Wang, carrying a bouquet of calla lilies and freesia, proudly escorted by her uncle, Doctor Phillip Marotta.

Despite the more than two hundred people in the church,

the bride and the groom seemed to have eyes only for each other as they spoke traditional vows and exchanged rings. The couple then veered from convention by each reaching a hand to Princess Riley and drawing her into their circle, and the bride made a public promise to the groom's daughter that she would always be there for her, too, to guide her through good times and bad. The little girl chimed in to assert that they would all be good times, now that they were finally a family.

And when the bride and groom and his daughter lit the unity candle together, there wasn't anyone in the church who doubted that the young princess's words were true.

* * * * *

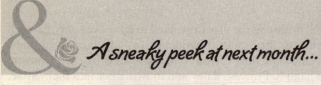

A sneaky peek at next month...

Cherish™

ROMANCE TO MELT THE HEART EVERY TIME

My wish list for next month's titles...

In stores from 20th July 2012:

☐ Once Upon a Matchmaker – Marie Ferrarella

& The Sheriff's Doorstep Baby – Teresa Carpenter

☐ The Sheikh's Jewel – Melissa James

& It Started with a Crush... – Melissa McClone

In stores from 3rd August 2012:

☐ Argentinian in the Outback – Margaret Way

& The Rebel Rancher – Donna Alward

☐ Fortune's Secret Baby – Christyne Butler

& Fortune Found – Victoria Pade

Available at WHSmith, Tesco, Asda, Eason, Amazon and Apple

Just can't wait?

0712/23